C000193424

J.A. Hunter

VIRIDIAN GATE ONLINE:

DOOM

FORGE

J. A. Hunter

DEDICATION

*To all of the wonderful folks at Shadow Alley Press—
eden, Tamara, Kelly—and especially the authors working
in the VGO EU. D.J. Bodden, N.H. Paxton, J.D. Astra,
you guys are the very best!*

J. A. Hunter

Viridian Gate Online
Recommended Reading Order

VGO: Cataclysm (Main Series Book 1)

VGO: Crimson Alliance (Main Series Book 2)

VGO: The Jade Lord (Main Series Book 3)

VGO: The Imperial Legion (Main Series Book 4)

VGO: The Lich Priest (Main Series Book 5)

VGO: Doom Forge (Main Series Book 6)

VGO: Darkling Siege (Main Series Book 7)

<<<>>>

VGO: Nomad Soul (The Illusionist 1)

VGO: Dead Man's Tide (The Illusionist 2)

VGO: Inquisitor's Foil (The Illusionist 3)

<<<>>>

VGO: The Artificer (Imperial Initiative)

<<<>>>

VGO: Firebrand (Firebrand Series 1)

VGO: Embers of Rebellion (Firebrand Series 2)

VGO: Path of the Blood Phoenix (Firebrand Series 3)

<<<>>>

VGO: Vindication (The Alchemic Weaponeer 1)

VGO: Absolution (The Alchemic Weaponeer 2)

VGO: Insurrection (The Alchemic Weaponeer 3)

Viridian Gate Online: Doom Forge

J. A. Hunter

ELDGARD

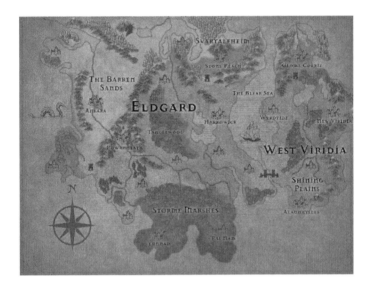

ONE

GLOME CORRIE

INCHED FORWARD ON MY BELLY, THE SNOW crunching softly beneath my wiggling body, then stopped at the edge of the rolling hillock. Nestled in the valley below was our target, Glome Corrie. Slowly, carefully, I lifted the bronze spyglass to my eye, breathing out a wispy cloud of steam, which immediately fogged the lens. I grunted, adjusted my position, and wiped the lens clean with one thumb. I slipped the spy scope back into place. Much better. It was deep night, but the moon overhead was full and brilliant, casting silvered light over the city of spires.

Glome Corrie was a dark, brooding place. A hard city much like the frozen wastes surrounding it and the Risi who called it home. But despite the harsh lines, the blocky utilitarian homes, and the black, weathered stone, the palace at the center was a grand sight: a sprawling complex with a myriad of slender obsidian spires jutting up like glittering pieces of jagged, broken glass. One central tower, circular and monstrously tall compared to the rest of its brothers and sisters, stood out against the purple horizon studded with stars. That was where I needed to go—where the city's control room was located.

Getting in, however, would be no mean feat.

I shifted the spyglass, this time focusing on the high walls of the formidable Risi capital. Well, it *had* been the Risi capital, right up until the Vogthar had taken the city during their initial invasion of Eldgard.

Now, there was hardly a green-skinned warrior in sight.

Instead, Vogthar shock troops patrolled the ramparts, torches clutched in raised fists as they searched for any signs of intrusion. Invasion. They were intimidating creatures, each one vaguely humanoid, all standing over seven feet tall. The standard Vogthar had dusky, gunmetal skin heavily tattooed with sharp, angular black script that gave me chills when I looked at it. They had pinched, gaunt faces that lacked noses and fishlike mouths positively bristling with serrated black teeth. Matte-black horns protruded above pointed ears, curling up toward the sky.

On the snow-powdered ground in front of the domineering walls were the Vogthar heavy hitters: monstrous Cyclopes, twenty feet tall, and prowling Ragna-Wolves, each as large as a school bus.

But as disconcerting as the Vogthar were—and they *absolutely* were—it was the occasional pockets of humanity that really left me unsettled. A handful of Wodes here. A squad of Risi there. I craned my head upward and watched as the silhouette of a winged Accipiter zipped past the face of the moon before being swallowed by the night once more. Some of those warriors were Dark Converts—empty shells now hosting Vogthar souls—but not all. A substantial number of players and NPCs had decided to *willingly* join Thanatos and his right-hand man, Aleixo Carrera, who was the living incarnation of Serth-Rog.

Darklings.

And each of those Darklings carried black-steel weapons etched with cancerous green runes of power that radiated a foul miasma of death and decay. Malware weapons, infected with the *Thanatos Virus,* capable of permanently killing enemy players.

As far as I was concerned, those people down there were cold-blooded murderers.

The soft rustle of a bush caught my ear as Forge scooted up next to me, likewise flat on his stomach. The big Risi, decked out in heavy plate mail edged in gold, regarded Glome Corrie, his brow furrowed, anger worked into the lines around his mouth. Smeared across his face like war paint was a crude, bloody warhammer, which stood out bright and stark and grim. The sign of the *Malleus Libertas,* the Hammer of Freedom. Forge's crew.

His fingers curled around the haft of his rune-etched battle-axe, which glowed with an unnatural blood-red light. "The *Òrdugh an Garda Anam* have taken care of the Vogthar lookouts, and the aerial element is ready to rock and roll, hoss. Don't know about the *Imperials*"— he said the word like a curse, clearly no love lost there— "but the Alliance is ready to bring the thunder. Just say the word."

"And the rest of the Libertas?" I asked, feeling a tinge of nervousness. Everything hinged on them and, of course, on Cutter's tenuous alliance with the Glome Corrie Thieves Guild. If they'd been compromised, this whole battle would turn into a colossal shitshow.

"In place," he replied. "So far, so good. No sign the Vogthar are onto us." He grinned, moonlight dancing in his eyes.

I pushed my worry back since there was nothing more we could do at this point and slapped him on the shoulder. "They won't even know what hit 'em," I offered while pulling up my interface and toggling over to the Officer Chat. "Osmark, you ready down there?" I asked in a muted whisper.

The Artificer's voice clicked on in my head a moment later. "Obviously," came his terse reply.

Things between us had been better since our time in the Realm of Order, but there was still an underlying tension that was hard to shake. Yeah, maybe Osmark wasn't the outright monster I'd once assumed him to be, but I had no illusions that our tenuous truce would hold after the Vogthar were dealt with. Every city we retook, every stronghold we captured, every corrupted dungeon we pacified brought us one step closer to war.

But that, too, was a worry for later.

I closed out of the chat log and selected the regional messaging system—one of the many perks provided by the Stratagem Faction *ability.* I took a deep breath, stilling the tremble in my hands, a sure sign of nerves. And for good reason. People would die tonight. Real people. Real death. No respawn. And if things went south… well, that failing and those deaths would be on me. The burden of responsibility. I grimaced and pushed back my fear. We'd done everything right. We'd laid our plans well, and now was the time for action.

I scrolled down and sent out the first in a series of predrafted Regional Messages, waiting on standby:

<<<>>>

Regional Faction Message: Glome Corrie

Alert!

The Soulbound have secured the perimeter and incapacitated the forward Vogthar scouts, and the Imperial Legion is in position. Commence the first wave of operations. Good luck and be safe out there—you all know what's on the line!

—Faction Commander, Grim Jack

A beat later, the message was gone, distributed to every Crimson Alliance player in the Glome Corrie region. The Imperials wouldn't get the message, but Osmark knew his cue, and it would be nearly impossible to miss. For a long moment I just lay there, spyglass pressed to my eye as Forge shifted nervously beside me. It was silent, save for the chirping and crooning of night bugs flitting about in the air. But then, in a heartbeat, the clarion call of a horn broke the night, coming from the ramparts below.

The horn sounded again, followed by a second and third, all ringing from the walls of the breathtaking city. The message was clear: *Emergency, emergency, emergency. Get your asses in gear, we have trouble on our hands...* And boy did they. I swept my spyglass to the right, searching the sky. A thick pocket of cloud cover dissipated as if by magic, revealing a massive steam-powered zephyr, the *Hellreaver,* screaming toward the city. Cutter was at the helm, cackling like mad as wind slapped against his face and ruffled his blond hair.

The zephyr was a massive thing, easily the size of a naval destroyer, the blimp above built from thick canvas reinforced with wooden bows and struts, all fastened together with heavy brass rivets. The ship itself dangled from the blimp, suspended by great iron chains, each link the size of my fist. A great steam-powered engine sat at the ship's stern, belching greasy smoke into the air as Cutter worked the wheel while adjusting an assortment of levers and switches.

A double fistful of formidable cannons jutted from each side of the vessel, ready to unleash a barrage of firepower, while a steam-powered Gatling gun adorned both the bow and stern. Though Cutter was piloting the vessel, he was far from alone. Ari Glitterfleck—a Barbie-doll-sized Pixy Berserker and emissary of the Realm of Order—sat on his shoulder, staring daggers at the Vogthar below. Amara the Huntress manned the rear Gatling gun, ready to unleash fire and fury at the pull of a trigger. Cutter's new second-in-command, Jake the Shadowblade, prowled the deck, barking off orders at a crew of squat, green-skinned Goblins.

The goblins scampered about the rigging, adjusted sails, or manned weaponry as the ship dropped lower and banked in hard, bringing the port-side cannons to bear on a group of Vogthar working a heavy-duty ballista.

The *Hellreaver*'s cannons roared, vomiting out plumes of blue-gray smoke and thick metal cannonballs, which ripped into black stone and tore through gray bodies.

The aft and bow Gatling guns opened up, strafing the defenders with rounds of hot lead. Ari was working the front gun, the muzzle flashes lighting up her waifish facial features.

The Vogthar were entirely unprepared for the sudden and unconventional assault; demonic bodies toppled from the walls, bloody holes peppering their inhuman forms. A spattering of enemy arrow fire finally flew in response, but Cutter was already climbing out of range, the great steam engine roaring as he gained altitude.

A squad of Risi sorcerers in flowing black robes—Vogthar sympathizers, deserving of no mercy—stormed out of a conical turret connecting to the rampart, throwing their hands out as they lobbed powerful spells toward the retreating blimp. The crew of the *Hellreaver* was ready. The zephyr's rear loading hatch popped open, revealing a cargo hold full of Alliance troops. Warlocks and mages set about their work, chanting in unison, hands flicking through complex rituals as they summoned spell-shields to absorb the incoming attacks.

And while they conjured, the Assassins secreted away within the hold descended on ropes built from gossamer spider silk.

Those were members of Cutter's new personal guard, the *Cheeky Bastards*. Recently—and mostly at the insistence of Amara—Cutter had taken on the esteemed position of Gentleman of Rowanheath, and being the chief thief came with certain perks. Like loyal, half-crazed underlings. Between the Bastards and the goblin crew manning the *Hellreaver*, Cutter damn near had his own army. Not that he wanted his own army, of course. He wanted to drink and eat and gamble, but he had his own army anyway. One that was fiercely loyal.

The Bastards slid down the ropes like greased lightning, landing as gracefully as cats upon the cobblestone walls, then blasted off toward the enemy spellcasters. They disappeared in shadow, only to reappear seconds later among the Risi mages, their blades sinking into exposed backs or slicing through chanting throats. In seconds the Risi were dead, their bodies hurled over the walls as the Bastards dispersed. From there, half would sneak off into the city, burning buildings, mercing stray guards, and generally sowing chaos in their wake. The other half would connect with what remained of the Glome Corrie Thieves Guild, who would secret Forge's boys into the city through a little-known access pipe.

Still I waited, watching everything unfold through the spyglass.

Cutter wheeled the *Hellreaver* around again, ready to take another run at the siege weapons lining the top of the wall, and the first wave of Vogthar aerial defense launched from the towers of the great city. Darkling Accipiter led the charge, quickly followed by lumbering [Vogthar Abami]: huge, inhuman bat-like creatures, covered in scaly flesh and sporting wicked fangs, wooden bucklers, and short swords perfect for crippling aerial fighters. *About time*, I thought with a sigh of relief.

Amara turned her Gatling gun on the incoming wave of attackers, brass shell casings raining down as Cutter guided the ship upward, drawing the creatures higher into the cloud-covered sky.

I triggered the second Regional Message.

Regional Faction Message: Glome Corrie

Alert!

Flyers, do your thing!

—Faction Commander, Grim Jack

The *Hellreaver*'s Gatling guns thundered while the starboard cannons erupted, swatting incoming creatures from the air like pesky mosquitos, but those noises were quickly drowned out by the flapping of wings and the war cries of a hundred Alliance and Imperial warriors, all mounted on winged beasts of every shape and size. Abby led the charge, flying on the back of her new pet, granted to her as a special favor by Sophia the Overmind. An ultra-rare Golden Hoardling Drake.

Valkyrie.

Valkyrie was female and just a hair smaller than Devil, with shimmering golden-red scales, an arching serpentine neck, and brilliant crimson wings. Jay Taylor, a Runic Blood Monk and Osmark's go-to thug, rode to Valkyrie's right on his Flame Sphinx—part tiger, part eagle, all badass. General Caldwell, the leader of our Accipiter Reconnaissance unit, flanked her on the left, his tawny wings beating at the air. Madness engulfed the skies over Glome Corrie as the two aerial forces smashed into each other like a wave meeting the seashore.

Fireballs flashed.

Lightning arced.

Punishing winds smashed into the unwary.

Arrows flew, and steel rang against steel.

Bodies plummeted from the air—Vogthar, Imperial, and Alliance alike.

But this was only the start, the opening salvo designed to draw attention away from what was coming next. The real invasion. I stood and extended a hand, helping Forge to his feet. Though we were silhouetted on the hilltop, I had no worries that we'd be spotted by the sentries manning the wall; they had their hands full at the moment, and a pair of shadows in the distance was the least of their concerns. "Be safe in there, man," I said to the Risi warrior. "Seriously. There's a target on your head, now. They'll be gunning for you with Malware weapons."

He grinned and shrugged, unconcerned, and twisted his heavy axe. "Let 'em try. I'll show 'em why you don't mess with a Marine. Especially one with a grudge and an actual battle-axe to grind."

I gave him a tight-lipped smile, then turned and summoned my own ride, Devil, with a flick of my hand. Sooty smoke filled the air as the murder-machine Void Drake slipped through the veil between the planes in all his awesome, terrifying glory. He was twenty-five feet of black scales, gleaming spikes of purple bone, leathery wings, and glowering demonic eyes. Six of them, all burning with malice and hunger. Devil was not cute or cuddly—he was the equivalent of a teddy bear made of razor blades and spite—but seeing him was a sight for sore eyes.

I ran a hand along his snout, earning me an indulgent nuzzle of affection. He hated pretty much everything, but he tolerated me. "Good to see you, buddy," I said, grabbing the dark leather reins and pulling myself into the custom saddle. "Time to rock and roll."

Let us crush our enemies, Devil's gruff voice said inside my skull. *Let us show these weak, pitiful, twisted creatures the power of true darkness.*

With that, the dread lizard chuffed and broke into a sinuous run, building speed and momentum before launching us into the air from the top of the hillock, his huge wings thundering as we took to the skies. The battering wind caught my cloak, and it flared out behind me, tugging at my shoulders as we streaked toward the battlefield. Despite the chaos engulfing the city, a lone sentry spied us from the walls, a Vogthar wearing dusky black armor covered with angular metal studs. The creature pointed a claw-tipped finger at us and barked something at a nearby compatriot.

A trio of bat-winged Abami spun in midair and bolted toward me while a pair of Wode Darklings on the wall wheeled around a heavy ballista and took aim. The siege weapon lurched, releasing a heavy, poison-tipped bolt longer than my arm. I was hands down the most wanted man in Eldgard—though Osmark was a close second—and these creatures would do anything to take me out. Unfortunately for them, I was no low-level newb, ripe for the plucking. I was a level 49 Shadowmancer, Champion of Order, and leader of the Crimson Alliance. And I sure as hell wasn't about to be taken out by a missile and a handful of Vogthar Abami.

I gave them a lopsided grin and a wave, then triggered Shadow Stride, exerting my power down, drawing Devil with me through the veil between worlds. Time shuddered to a halt as color leeched away from Glome Corrie, replaced instead with monochromatic grays and whites, stained by the occasional splash of purple. In the Shadowverse, everything was quiet and still, the battlefield frozen. We cruised past the incoming ballista bolt, banked slight left, and flew into the Abami, phasing through them as though they were ghostly specters.

There was still twenty seconds left on my countdown timer by the time we reached the walls, but there was no reason to draw out my time in the Shadowverse. *Kill as many as you can,* I sent to Devil, swinging one leg over, then slipping from the saddle.

I will not kill as many as I can. I will kill all of them, he replied confidently, jaws salivating, eyes flaring brightly. *I will show them the power of my kind. Teach them fear. And then I will feast...*

Nothing at all unnerving about that. But these were *monsters,* I reminded myself. If anyone ever deserved to be eaten alive, it was the Vogthar and the players who had traded their humanity for power by siding with them. No mercy.

I patted him one last time, then dropped toward the ground, plummeting like a stone. I slipped into the Material Realm while I was still fifty feet from the ground. Time and motion and sound crashed back down on me as I fell, but I blocked them all out, focusing instead on one of my specialty abilities, which was arguably my rarest of talents: Avatar of Order. The pinnacle of my Champion of Order Skill Tree.

With a deep breath, steeling myself for the pain to come, I triggered the ability.

TWO

BREACHING THE WALLS

AS I CAREENED TOWARD THE GROUND LIKE A bunker buster headed for impact, my body shifted and changed. My Spirit gauge dipped by 2,000 points, leaving it just a hair above zero while my Current Experience bar dropped by a whopping 50,000 points—all permanently removed as part of the hefty price tag associated with this particular ability. Five days' work, gone, right down the drain in the blink of an eye. Still, becoming the Avatar of Order was totally worth it, and I anticipated that I'd earn the points back plus interest by the time the battle was over.

Men shouted, and arrows whistled past me, blurry streaks in the night, but I ignored them all.

Thirty feet from impact...

Power swelled inside me, hot and terrible, and with it came a wave of pain, which pummeled me like a mob of Imperial troops armed with baseball bats and tire irons. My bones groaned in protest, my muscles screamed in abject terror. Magma burned its way through my veins, shooting down my arms and legs with every beat of my heart, while terrible pressure built inside my

19

head. My stomach clenched, and bright jags of cutting pain invaded my joints. The razor blades came next, an invisible whirlwind of them, flaying me alive.

Twenty feet...

My muscles no longer screamed; instead, they bulged and distorted, my gray skin flaking away, revealing sleek purple-black scales, identical to Devil's. My fingers swelled, my nails popping free as wicked ebony talons erupted along each tip.

Ten...

The terrible pain faded to background noise as my shoulder blades writhed and wriggled; a pair of new appendages ruptured outward, unfurling into leather wings. They caught a furious gust of wind, yanking me upward and slowing my meteoric descent even as my mouth stretched and elongated, giving way to a reptilian muzzle bursting with teeth perfect for rending flesh. I slammed into the earth like an asteroid, the snowy ground cratering from my weight, a cloud of white splashing up around me as I dropped to a knee.

Despite the fall, my Health bar burned bright red and impossibly strong.

I stood slowly, scaly lips pulling back from my wicked fangs as the debris cloud settled around me. The sentries on the wall had fallen still; they stared at me, unmoving, a mixture of terror and awe dashing across their features in turn. Though the Vogthar had dungeon mobs working on their behalf, it wasn't every day they saw a human-dragon hybrid falling from the sky only to land on their front stoop. I was twenty feet tall now— easily rivaling their monstrous Cyclopes—and my warhammer had grown with me, ten feet long with a hammerhead the size of a truck tire.

The surreal, uncertain moment was broken, as shouts of "fire" and "shoot it," broke from the walls. The nearest Vogthar archers unleashed a hail of arrows, which darkened the sky, but the missiles plinked harmlessly off my impossibly tough scales, falling uselessly to the ground. The siege weapons came next, along with a flood of fireballs and other magical attacks. Those, I knew I wouldn't be able to brush off quite so easily as the arrow storm, but I wasn't worried.

I had a few tricks up my sleeve.

I thrust my free hand forward, talon-tipped fingers splayed out, and conjured one of my standard Avatar abilities. A small pop-up appeared in the corner of my eye—*Pulse Shield: 2/3*—while a shimmering wall of brilliant pearl light, twenty feet by ten, sprung to life before my open palm. The enormous shield of Divine Energy absorbed the spells without missing a beat and bounced the heavy ballista bolts away with pitiful ease. But I couldn't celebrate my victory for long—I had heavy-hitting Vogthar dungeon bosses flanking me on either side: a pair of Cyclopes to the left, a Ragna-Wolf off to the right.

Plus, there was a whole slew of ground-pounding Vogthar troops streaming through the now open portcullis. All according to plan.

I twirled left, facing the encroaching one-eyed giants while simultaneously lashing out with my tail, slapping the Ragna-Wolf across his muzzle. The sheer force of the blow hurled the wolf from its feet, slamming it into the wall with bone-breaking force. The whole wall trembled and a handful of defenders manning the ramparts toppled over the side, plunging to their deaths as they screamed in panic. I ignored them, focusing on a hulking creature of muscle and fat covered in leathery brown skin, tough as plate mail. The Cyclops roared, lashing out with a gnarled, spike-studded club as big as a tree.

The attack was deadly powerful but ponderously slow.

I sidestepped with sinuous grace, then attacked with my warhammer, bringing it around in a vicious arc, slamming the blunt face into the creature's malformed skull with a burst of violet shadow energy. Bone cracked, fetid blood sprayed, and its HP dropped by over half as it staggered. I slipped right and shot in, my left hand free, my obsidian talons extended. I triggered another of my Avatar abilities. *Burning Talons: 4/5* strobed in the corner of my eye as I raked my claws across the Cyclops's exposed throat.

The attack left deep, jagged furrows in its flesh, the skin around the wound charred black from the deadly opal fire surrounding each talon. *Critical Hit.* The creature's HP plunged, flashing into the critical zone for just a moment, before hitting zero. A dungeon lord, killed with two hits. The Cyclops listed for a moment, dead but somehow still standing, then pitched to the side, slamming into the earth like a felled tree. The next Cyclops was already on me—ignoring its friends embarrassingly quick and painful death.

I twirled around like a tornado of scales, wings, and death, my oversized hammer slamming into knees and shoulders, pummeling its neck and face, before I finally buried the wicked spike jutting from the top—now the size of a long sword—deep into the creature's single eye, putting my full weight and power into the thrust. Every muscle in the monster's body gave up at once, and the Cyclops promptly collapsed into a heap of limbs. The regular Vogthar troops were on me now, surrounding me in a loose circle, trying to hem me in, as though I didn't have functional wings poking out of my back.

I cast an eye at the Ragna-Wolf currently righting itself even though half of its face looked like a crumpled soda can: crushed and mangled. The creature was trying to maneuver around to my blind side while the Vogthar forces closed in. I let him. Meanwhile, the troops manning the walls were back in force, more pointless arrows raining down, all bouncing off my scales. But heavy-duty ballista bolts accompanied the arrows, and those hit like freight trains of force. True, I could've summoned another Pulse Shield—I still had two charges—but I *needed* my Health to drop.

So, I gritted my teeth and bore the terrible pain as a bolt punched into my side, scraping along my ribs, leaving a bloody wound behind and taking a bite out of my HP. Another slammed into my left shoulder, shredding scales and flesh. I dodged a third, couldn't make it too obvious, then threw myself forward at the Vogthar ground pounders bearing down on me with battle-axes and hooked swords. I swung my tail around, batting a pair of tanks into the air like pop flies, then laid into a trio on the left with my claws, unleashing Burning Talons again.

Vogthar died, crippled, disemboweled, and screaming, while I made for the wall.

More of the land troops shot in toward my legs, but that was a mistake. One hard kick sent a Vogthar Rogue flipping through the air like a rag doll, its arms and legs flailing wildly, before smashing rudely into unforgiving stone. Its back broke with a sharp *crack*—the sound of a snapping bough—and the creature crumpled, its HP at zero. A fresh wave of arrows sailed from the wall, accompanied by the snap of bowstrings, and reflexively I put a hand up, shielding my eyes from the incoming fire.

A pair of crushing, powerful jaws latched onto the back of my left leg a moment later, meaty fangs slicing into my hamstring. I growled and twirled—or at least I tried to. The Ragna-Wolf held fast, its hackles up, hateful red eyes staring defiantly at me as it jerked its head, first left then right. More of my HP leaked out, dipping below 75%.

Bingo.

A wave of awesome strength flooded into my body, filling me with raw power—like getting a great night's sleep, then downing a gallon of primo gas station coffee. That was one of my many Avatar abilities, Desperate Strength, which added a hefty Strength bonus to my already formidable stats. But it only kicked in once my Health dropped past the 75% threshold. Just like an actual dungeon boss.

I activated Burning Talons once more, trailing my glowing claws across the wolf's muzzle, shredding through fur, flesh, and bone. The creature yelped and retreated, offering me its back as it tried to flee—to regroup. But I wasn't about to let that happen. I lunged and grabbed the mangy wolf by its tail, then, with a heave, I pulled the creature from the ground and used its body like a humongous flail. The wolf arched into the air and slammed into the encroaching Vogthar, mashing several of them into the crimson-stained snow. The wolf yelped again, thrashing and scrambling, but instead of letting go, I slammed it down again.

This time its neck snapped from the impact, and its eyes went glassy.

And just like that, the gate defenders outside the wall were down.

"Fire," someone called from the wall. I wheeled, eyes flaring wide as a lightning bolt the size of a telephone pole slammed into my neck followed in quick succession by a trio of ballista bolts—the first punching into my guts, the second smashing into my left knee, the third clipping the edge of my wing. *Critical Hit!* The pain was sudden and intense, railroad spikes of agony sending out pulsing jags of hurt that were nearly blinding. My Health dropped again, this time flashing a brilliant red as it edged below 50%.

A reminder that no one was invincible or immune from superior firepower and a little bit of forethought. Not even the Avatar of Order.

But I'd come expecting that. In the corner of my eye, a new ability flashed: *Cleansing Light.* An uber-powerful beam of Divine Energy, it dealt 550% of spell power on contact. True, Cleansing Light only affected players and creatures with an "Evil" or "Holy" Alignment, but everyone on the wall ahead of me was Evil to the core. The beam also did an ample amount of property damage. I shook off the agony and steadied myself, throwing my jaws wide as I unleashed a javelin of pure white fire.

Cleansing Light, 1/2.

I swept my head from side to side, targeting the troops and equipment on top of the wall. The fire charbroiled siege weapons and decimated the Vogthar and Darkling sympathizers unfortunate enough to be out in the open. The second the attack guttered and died. I triggered Cleansing Light again, this time taking out the handful of remaining sentries that had weathered the first attack. A few took cover behind the merlons, but by the time the second attack faltered, the siege weapons were entirely gone.

Overhead, the aerial battle continued to rage unabated.

My Avatar countdown timer spun merrily away. I had a little more than a minute before I reverted back to my normal form, and I still had a ton to do. Not wasting a second, I lumbered forward and raised my warhammer high. I skidded to a halt before the wall, planted my feet wide, and swung for the fences. My hammer slammed into the black stone of Glome Corrie, chunks of rock raining down as a jagged crack formed. I pulled back, squaring my shoulders, then struck again. This time the crack fractured, morphing into a fissure, light from the far side peeking through.

I lined up my hammer again—keeping an eye on the timer—and laid into the wall a third time. The whole wall quivered and groaned from the impact and rock spilled in, revealing a breach large enough for even the beefiest Risi warrior to squeeze through. A trumpet blared as my hammer fell away; this trumpet call, however, came courtesy of Osmark and the Imperials. Small hatches littered across the battlefield sprung open, casting aside sheets of fresh powder as a horde of Imperial Troops, two thousand strong, poured out, rushing for the opening.

Alliance engineers had spent the last week building reinforced tunnels, allowing us to move Osmark's superior force into place unobserved.

I watched as more troops spilled out—these bearing long ropes capped with matte-black grappling hooks. Rogues and Assassins. They scaled the walls, which now stood unguarded, and made their way into the abutting watchtowers and the Vogthar garrison, not far away. A second later an alert flashed:

Faction Alert:

Congratulations! Your faction, the Crimson Alliance, has captured the Glome Corrie Command Center. If your faction holds the Command Center for (30) minutes, you will control Glome Corrie and displace the current ruling faction, the Peng Jun Tong.

Countdown: 29:59

I couldn't help but smile. The message had come right on time. That would be Forge and his boys in the Malleus Libertas. Aside from being shock troops, they'd become the Alliance's premiere Urban Warfare Task Force and specialized in taking enemy Command Centers. The aerial invasion was the first distraction, and my assault on the gates had been the second, but Forge and his crew were the real threat, sneaking in through back passageways while we kept the Vogthar busy with our overt showboating.

I watched the Legion troops assault the walks for another handful of seconds—they would subdue the rest of the Vogthar and capture Darklings. Much as I wanted to catch my breath and watch, I had other places to be and no time to waste. I backed up a few steps, broke into a furious run, and launched myself high into the air, huge wings beating like mad as I cleared the wall.

My shoulders burned from the strain of flying as I soared over the city, staying high enough to clear the boxy houses with their slate roofs, but low enough to avoid the massive dogfight going on in the star-studded sky above. I swerved left, scanning the ground. There. Not far off was the Unbroken Shield, a three-story inn a stone's throw from Glome Corrie's central Keep. I dove, folding my wings in close, and touched down on the weather-worn cobblestones just as my Avatar countdown strobed and hit zero.

The whole world reeled as my limbs shrank, scales retreating into my body, wings disintegrating beneath me, turning to dusty ash, carried away on the biting breeze. Thankfully, the awful pain that came when activating the Avatar of Order ability was blessedly absent as my body resumed its normal proportions. I wobbled uncertainly for a moment, shaking my head to clear the sudden disorientation, then fished a cherry-red Health potion from my belt and downed it in a single long gulp. Done, I tossed the bottle away. It clinked on the wet paving stones, before rolling to a stop next to the side of the inn.

I froze as the sound of boots on stone drifted to my ears.

THREE

LOST AND FOUND

CUTTER EMERGED FROM THE SHADOWS, THEN SHOT me a wink as he let out a sharp whistle. The inn's heavy wooden door swung open and out trotted the rest of my crew, save Forge, who was with the *Libertas* holding down the Keep. Abby, Amara, Otto, and Ari all present and accounted for. Everyone looked tired and worse for the wear—understandable since it'd been a solid twenty-four hours since anyone had slept—but they were alive, and that was the important thing.

"Any sign of Osmark?" I asked, glancing from face to face.

"Nope, no word," Abby replied with a shake of her head.

I let out a groan, then rubbed the bridge of my nose, feeling the full weight of my exhaustion settle around me. Perfect, just what we needed. Another complication. I pulled up my interface and accessed the chat log, selecting Osmark from my list of allies. "Osmark? Where are you?" I sent, feeling a minor tinge of panic. Osmark wasn't the kind of guy to be late. Not to anything. Ever. He was punctual as a clock—pretty fitting, considering that as an Artificer he was literally covered in clockwork gears.

No reply. I tried to hail him a second time but found more silence waiting for me.

Was it possible Osmark had died during the raid?

That seemed exceedingly unlikely.

Osmark was the highest-level player in the game—though he only had me beat by a mere two levels at this point—and he was damned near unkillable. I'd tried often enough to know firsthand. I frowned, then jotted off a quick PM to Jay Taylor, Osmark's right-hand thug, and Sandra Bullard, his extremely capable personal assistant. If something had happened to Osmark, one of those two would know about it.

Personal Message:

Osmark is late to the rendezvous. Any idea where he is?

—Jack

I sent the message with a thought, drumming my fingers idly on my warhammer as I waited for a reply. A full minute passed, the rest of the crew rustling impatiently while the thunderclap of warring bodies overhead drifted down. Otto, in particular, seemed perturbed and antsy. Abby's Risi companion had posted up at the edge of the inn, stealing glances between the city's front gate—totally overrun now—the battle overhead, and the looming Keep with its hundreds of needle-thin spires. I could understand his apprehension, since Glome Corrie was the home of his people.

From what I knew about Otto, he'd spent the majority of his life away from the Risi capital and stronghold, doing battle against the Empire as an emissary of *Òrdugh an Garda Anam*—the Order of the Soulbound. It had to irk him something fierce that Glome Corrie, which had resisted the Empire for ages, had fallen first to Imperials under Osmark, only to be lost *again* to Carrera and his lackeys.

"Well?" he finally grunted after another half-minute. "There could be resistance inside the Keep. They need us to move, Grim Jack. Now." Otto wasn't the most tactful, but he was damned good at his job—waging war, commanding troops, and killing things.

I considered it only for a moment before nodding. I wasn't sure where in the hell Osmark was, but if he couldn't bother to be here, we'd just have to move forward without him. I gave marching orders, and we beelined across a wide courtyard in front of the Keep's main entry.

A huge, black wrought iron fountain dominated the scene, showcasing the founding of Glome Corrie: a violent tableau of armor-clad Risi defeating Imperial slavers. A booted foot planted in an Imperial face. A hook-bladed sword gutting a wide-eyed soldier. A Risi general standing atop a heap of corpses, a bronze flag leaning against his burly shoulder. The fountain's interior was all copper and gave the water within the look of freshly spilled blood. A whole pool of it. We stole around the fountain and through the entrance. Its formidable steel portcullis had been left wide open just for us.

Forge's handiwork on display.

There were a handful of dead Vogthar dotting the hallways, but no resistance whatsoever.

31

The *Libertas* had done their jobs alright.

Cutter led the way, eyes restlessly scanning the hallways and tapestries for traps or any sign of ambush. We hooked through various hallways—two lefts, a right, a straightaway followed by a switchback—passing a myriad of mostly abandoned rooms. Though there were no Vogthar, we spotted a handful of maids and Keep workers. All NPCs who scattered at our approach. We'd have to check them and make sure they weren't Converts or Darklings, but for now they offered no overt hostility, so we let them be.

After a few minutes of hard trudging we came to the central tower.

There were thick steel doors on the bottom level, but these too were wide open, showcasing an enormous spiral staircase that shot up like a corkscrew made of stone and iron. We hiked our way upward, but it was tough going. Bodies littered the steps, mostly Vogthar but more than a few Alliance members. Since their bodies were still littering the ground, it meant they were Citizens—NPCs—who would never respawn. I stepped over a Vogthar ground-pounder, split nearly in two, and paused by the corpse of a Dawn Elf woman in shimmering robes. The crimson hammer of the Malleus Libertas was painted bright and bold on her chest.

I didn't know her name, but I'd seen her around Darkshard Keep on more than one occasion, running drills, eating meals with friends. She volunteered with the kids in her free time. Well, she *had* volunteered, though she never would again.

I was responsible for this. For her. The attack had gone off perfectly, and still there were deaths and corpses. I cleared my throat and pulled my gaze away, continuing up. We climbed at least ten flights before finally arriving at the top of the ever-winding stairs. Heavy obsidian doors blocked the way into the Keep's control room. A cluster of hard-eyed Alliance guards stood ready, their faces covered in grime and dirt, their weapons bloody. There were five of them—a pair of tanks, a spellcaster, and a rogue.

One of the tanks, a barbaric looking Wode clad in heavy leathers and thick gray fur, offered us a salute. "Welcome to Knife Breaker Keep, Lord Grim Jack," he said, waving for the second tank to open the doors. "General Forge is inside, and we've secured the area against the Vogthar."

The control room itself was a bastion of utility and function, though very little comfort.

Its circular walls were crafted from black, implacable stone. Wrought iron candelabras sprouted from the walls, yellow tallow candles poking up and shedding greasy orange light. A fireplace—easily as tall as I was and twice as wide—adorned the far wall, a roaring flame burning merrily away despite the invasion. The furniture scattered through the room was dark wood, boxy and uncomfortable with an Oriental flair to it. A huge, rectangular table dominated the center of the room, high-backed leather chairs scattered around it at even intervals.

A variety of maps—some depicting troop movements, others showcasing enemy positions—were pinned around the room or scattered across tables. There were also papers *everywhere*. Reams and reams of parchment. I slipped over and picked up a curling sheet of white paper, quickly scanning the contents. A logistics report at a glance. Unfortunately, I'd become overly familiar with reports like those since becoming the faction head of the Crimson Alliance. This report listed foodstuffs, crafting supplies, wagon requirements, and a slew of other seemingly mundane details.

Though dry and boring, the logs were an important find. A talented quartermaster, like our own Chief Logistics Officer, Anton Black, could figure out a ton from a report like this. With just a little bit of work, he'd be able to calculate out how many men were in transport, where they were headed, and how long it would take to get them there.

"I want all of this boxed up," Forge barked as though reading my thoughts from across the room. The Risi warrior casually stepped over the corpse of a monstrous creature—a golem built from snow, rock, and old bone—then picked up a handful of papers. There were Vogthar bodies scattered around the room as well, but everyone seemed to ignore the carnage and gore as though this were just another day at the office. And in many ways, it *was.* "Every map, every scrap of paper," he continued. "All of it could be important. Nothin' gets left behind, *oorah*?"

"Oorah," came the barking reply from the rest of the men and women busy pillaging.

There were thirty of them, and though they weren't all Marines, most of them were former service members. All had quickly taken to Forge's no-nonsense leadership and warm character. There was a full squad of Dark Templars present, *Maa-Tál* in the Dokkalfar tongue. Shadow Knight, Plague Bringer, Umbra Shaman, Necromancer. Even a fellow Shadowmancer—an Indian woman named Navya. Forge also had a standard assortment of tanks and spellcasters, summoners, Clerics, and Rogues at his disposal.

I couldn't help but note the difference between these rogues—serious and straightlaced to a man—and the off-color men Cutter employed within his fledgling ranks. Night and day.

"Grim Jack," Forge bellowed with a wide grin, eyes twinkling as he spotted me. "Well, holy shit, is it good to see you made it here in one piece. Some of the crew was worried when they heard you were planning to take the walls all by yourself, but not me." He shook his head, a series of crow's-feet branching out from the corners of his eyes. "Nope. I told 'em you'd do it. Hell, Bobby over there"—he hooked a thumb to a Warlock in deep purple robes—"owes me five gold marks."

"You didn't do so bad yourself," I replied, cocking an eyebrow and sweeping a hand around the room. "Any sign of Peng or his thugs?"

Peng Jun hadn't always been with the Vogthar. Once upon a time, he'd been one of Osmark's chief backers—part of what Osmark called the Chinese Contingent—though it seemed Osmark and Peng had never been on the friendliest terms. But that had changed when the Vogthar took Glome Corrie, Peng's faction capital. The Chinese general had promptly flipped on the Imperials, instead throwing in with Carrera in exchange for power and the right to retain his city.

"Naw." Forge snorted and shook his head. "Surprised the shit right outta me, to tell ya the truth. Bunch of these horn-headed turdbags"—he nudged a nearby Vogthar body with the toe of his boot—"and the guardian over there." He waved at the downed golem. "But no sign of Peng, which is odd since this is his stronghold. Seems like he'd be all over this place like stink on shit. Didn't even find any of his Blue Lantern Boys hanging around."

"I wonder," Otto said, glancing around, "what could be so important that he would leave Glome Corrie lightly defended? It doesn't make sense. This is one of the Vogthar's most important captures. I wouldn't have been overly surprised to find Carrera himself in residence."

"Well, maybe these papers will offer us some clue," Ari said, zipping away and lighting down on another supply roster. Her body glowed a spectral blue as she pulled up the corner of one sheet, her face scrunched up in concentration as she read.

"Could be," I replied idly, feeling tired to the bone and ready to get back to Darkshard and grab a few hours of shut-eye. "Amara, make sure anything that looks important gets tagged and brought back to Darkshard for the debriefing tomorrow morning. Otto, I want you to get this place squared away. There's still a battle raging out there, but the second the Keep is firmly ours, I want the city's defenses working for us."

"Are you sure?" Otto replied, hands folded behind his back. "That seems like a job for whichever magistrate you have lined up to govern Glome Corrie."

I pointed a finger and shot him a wink. "You're it. Assuming you want the job, that is. I can't think of anyone who would do better." I glanced over my shoulder at Abby, who was positively beaming. She'd been the one to suggest that Otto should be given the post. The Risi general spoke of Glome Corrie with something that bordered on reverence. No one would take better care of the city. No one.

"With respect, I'm local," he countered, worry briefly flashing over his face. "So far the Alliance has only appointed Travelers to preside as magistrates—"

"Something we intend to fix," Abby cut in. She laid a gentle hand on his forearm. He looked extremely awkward and uncomfortable with the gesture. "Congratulations, Otto," she whispered, almost too softly to hear, "you're home. And you deserve this more than anyone. Now, go show everyone what you can do. Give them absolute hell."

He offered her a stoic nod—just the ghost of a grin on his lips—then wheeled around and started barking off orders. Pride flared inside my chest. I stole a look toward Cutter and Amara. Citizens had sort of gotten the short end of the stick in V.G.O., and though a lot of players still didn't think about them as being human, *being alive*, in the way we Travelers were, we intended to change that. Cutter, as the first Eldgard NPC to earn the right to respawn, was already something of a reluctant civil-rights leader. Or its figurehead, anyway.

I turned away as Forge shuffled over and cleared his throat. "Jack, Abby," he said, "minute of your time?" He paused, looking left, then right, and dropped his voice. "Alone."

I frowned, confused, but nodded and followed him over to the far side of the room, out of earshot of the rest of the crew. There was a nearby wall tapestry, pulled back to reveal an enormous vault, the heavy door yawning wide.

Forge took one more tentative look around, then slowly pulled an item from his inventory. It looked like the hilt of a sword, though without blade or pommel. The handle was bone white and covered in glowing scrimshaw etchings that burned a pale gold. "One of my boys, he found this inside the vault. Bunch of other stuff

37

in there too—gold, weapons, armor. All rare stuff that'll go into the guild treasury. But this thing is…" He hesitated, stealing a glance over his shoulder. "Well, it's real different, hoss. Seems like it might be a big deal."

He handed me the item.

Arcane energy, potent and wild, thrummed along the length of the handle, running up into my hand like a jolt of lightning. I'd felt power like this before. Just once, after defeating the Lich Priest, Vox-Malum, and looting his corpse. Even without pulling up the description, I *knew* this thing belonged with the pommel currently stashed away in my inventory. Still, best to check. Nervous sweat broke out across my brow and goosebumps raced along my arms as I pulled up the item description:

Doom-Forged Hilt

Item Type: Relic

Class: Ancient Artifact

Base Damage: 0

Primary Effects:

- Doom-Forged Relic 1 of 3

A Piece of the Doom-Forged Weapon

Once, eons ago, in an age long since forgotten to mankind, a powerful weapon was created to balance the colossal forces of the universe. A weapon so great even the gods feared its blow. Legend tells that after the Doom-Forged weapon was crafted by the Dwarven godling Khalkeús, the weapon was split apart by the gods and goddesses who feared its might and scattered

across the realms so that it would never be assembled
again. Perhaps it is time for the gods to fear again…

"Holy shit. Is that what I think it is?" Abby asked, her voice a low whisper, though tinged with excitement.

"Yep. Doom-Forged relic. Two of three. We almost have the whole set." I traced my thumb over the engraved hilt of the strange weapon—or what would eventually be a weapon, assuming I could find the final piece. "I wonder why Peng had this in the safe instead of on his avatar?"

"Aw, that's easy, friend," Cutter said, slipping up next to me like a shadow. Abby shot him a furious glare. "And before you get all uppity," he said, returning her glower, "yes, I was eavesdropping. Clearly. *But,* as the official spymaster of the Alliance, that's my job. Besides"—he shrugged and gave her an easy smile—"I was bored out of my bloody skull with the rest of those wankers. I don't mind your crew, Forge, but gods are they a stuffy lot. Very professional. Extremely dull. No one wanted to throw dice, and you shoulda seen the look they gave me when I suggested we break out the mead." He shook his head. "As though *I* were the mad one for wanting to celebrate our victory with a flagon of good drink."

I couldn't help but roll my eyes. "The relic, Cutter. Why would Peng have kept it here instead of on his person?"

"Like I said, *easy,*" he replied with a cocked eyebrow. "Pickpockets." He rubbed his hands together as though relishing the very thought of subtle thievery.

"A master thief can steal an equipped item, but even an average thief can snag an unequipped one. And a legendary item like one of those relics is fair game, so long as it isn't soul-bound and assuming the thief in question has the skills to pull it off."

"How skilled we talkin'?" Forge asked, rubbing his chin thoughtfully. "Could you do it?"

"Don't be daft," Cutter replied with an offended grimace. "I could steal a horse out from beneath its rider, and they'd be none the wiser. But even most mid-level thieves that've earned a place in the Union can pilfer an unequipped item. Carrying something like that can be a security risk. But these things here"—he waved toward the huge wall-mounted safe, near the back of the room, flanked by a hanging tapestry—"they're unpickable. The safe belongs to the Keep owner and is only accessible by him, unless he specifically gives permission to someone else. The obvious pitfall, though, is that if the Keep falls, the vault and all its loot end up in the possession of the new owner. Peng must've thought this place couldn't fall."

Good to know. Still, that didn't explain why Peng was gone. What could be more pressing than holding down his own stronghold, *especially* since he was storing a Doom-Forged relic here? I had no idea, though I doubted it was good.

I pulled up my interface and checked the time: 1:37 AM. God, it was late, or early, depending on how I looked at it. I stifled a yawn with my fist. Only six hours until the next Alliance staff meeting—well, whatever Peng was up to, it would have to wait until tomorrow. For tonight, I needed sleep and I needed it bad before I passed out where I stood. Still, as I made to leave, I couldn't help but wonder about Osmark. Just what in the hell had happened to him? Hopefully, the staff meeting would shed some light on that as well.

FOUR

ADMIN GRIND

I WAS SITTING ON MY BACK PATIO, A LAWN CHAIR beneath me, a hoodie protecting me from the cool breeze blowing in the night, carrying just a hint of the ocean to my nose. The dark had settled a while ago, but it was late summer, so just a touch of purple and pink lingered on the horizon. In front of me, a fire roared. I smiled. The firepit itself was a ring of concrete and poking up from its center was a pillar of char-blackened skulls. It reminded me of something that should've been inside V.G.O., but no—my dad had really owned a skull firepit just like that, IRL.

Said those skulls belonged to all the enemies of the Corps. He'd loved that firepit.

"You okay, Jackie?" a voice asked. I glanced up, startled, and found my old man sitting across from me. He reclined in a lounge chair of his own, his legs stretched out in front of him, ankles crossed, an old-fashioned clutched loosely in his hand. Always old-fashioneds with him —a triple shot of Jack, a splash of club soda, a dab of bitters, a slice of orange. I eyed him for a long moment, feeling a sudden surge of sadness well up inside my chest. He was younger than I remembered.

His brown eyes sharp, his skin tight and tan, his high and tight lightly sprinkled with gray. It was how he'd looked back during my high school days. Fifteen years ago.

"You okay?" he asked again, before raising his glass and taking a long pull. "You've been quiet all night. Distracted."

"It's nothing," I replied, shaking my head. Some part of me knew this wasn't real—Dad was dead, Mom too, both taken by the asteroid—that this was a dream. But I didn't care. I leaned forward, raising my hands, offering them to the flames dancing among the pile of skulls. I never took my eyes off the man, since I had no idea when I'd see him again. *If* I'd see him again.

"No, that's not true. It is something, Pop," I said. "I'm feeling overwhelmed. Seems like enemies are closing in from every side and everyone is looking to me for answers, except I'm not sure I have any answers to give them." I faltered and ran a hand through my hair. "It was so simple in the beginning, but now it's so big. Impossibly big. Everyone is depending on me, and every day it seems like the odds stacked against us get worse and worse, no matter how much ground we gain."

My dad was quiet for a beat, swirling his drink, eyeing the liquid as it sloshed in his lowball glass. "Chesty Puller, God rest his soul, was maybe the finest Marine that ever lived," he finally said. "Most decorated Marine in history. Him and his boys, they fought at the Battle of Chosin Reservoir—during the Korean War, this was. And it was hard fighting in the heart of winter. Brutal. The Chinese, well they sent in a flood of troops, and the First Marine Division suddenly found themselves cut off and behind enemy lines.

"Everyone wrote 'em off, Jackie." He leaned in, forearms resting on his thighs. "They were surrounded by twenty-two enemy divisions. Outnumbered twenty-nine to one, with no support in sight. A lesser man, well he mighta given up. Rolled over and died just like everyone expected, but not Chesty. And not his boys. Oh no. Why Chesty, he said, 'They're in front of us, behind us, and we're flanked on both sides. Great. Those bastards can't get away from us now.' And damned if they didn't make it out—and not just make it out." He leaned back. "The First Marine Division wiped out seven enemy divisions all by their lonesome.

"And that's the key, Jackie. When you're outnumbered and outgunned, it simplifies things. All the extraneous crap, it falls by the wayside. When you're outgunned, it boils away everything until only one thing remains: survival. You just need to remember that your goal is to survive, and then you use every play in the book." He stood up, then, and edged around the fire, a sad, tired smile on his face. By the time he made it to the other side, he was older, wrinkles blanketing his face, his hair entirely gray, his arms and legs whip-thin, his skin like old jerky.

I stood.

"It was good seeing you, Jackie. I never said it enough, but I love you. I'm proud of you." He reached out a sun-beaten hand, patted me on the shoulder, then pulled me into a quick, tight hug. "I believe in you, son. Those bastards can't get away from you. Not this time. Give the Vogthar hell." And then he was shaking me…

"Come on, Jack." His voice had changed, replaced by something feminine and familiar. "I know it sucks, but it's time to get moving. Come on, we're already running late."

I groaned and cracked my eyes.

My childhood backyard was gone, the skull-studded firepit nowhere to be seen. Instead, I was in my posh master suite in the Darkshard Keep, just outside of Yunnam. The suite was spacious, luxurious, and expensive. The floors were polished granite, covered in places with thick area rugs of deep gray. There was lots of gleaming chrome, fancy modern art, and dark wood. It looked like an interior decorator with more money than sense had been set loose on the place. It was how the room had come, however—just another perk built into the system for the would-be dictators who'd funded V.G.O.

Abby was sitting on the bed next to me, already dressed in her red Firebrand gown. *Wildfire.* Hands down her best piece of gear. I propped myself up on my elbows, letting the silken sheet covering my chest slide free. I paused, searching Abby's face. She looked so damned tired, her skin ashy and washed out, puffy bags lingering under her eyes.

"What time is it?" I asked, groggy.

"Seven fifteen," she replied. "Fifteen minutes until we're due up in the War Room to go over the morning briefing."

I sighed, long and deep, then sat up the rest of the way and swung my legs out over the edge of the bed, feet touching down softly on cool, glossy stone. "God, I hate reports," I said, pressing my eyes shut for a long moment and grinding my palms into my sockets, trying to clear away some of my exhaustion. "Seriously, some days I think I'd rather hunt down an endless stream of Vogthar than sit through one more tedious meeting."

"Some days?" she said, a teasing edge lingering beneath her words.

"Come on, you know they don't even need us there most of the time."

"*Most* of the time isn't *all* of the time," Abby said, her voice now in front of me. I opened my eyes again. She was standing there, one hand extended toward me. "Besides, it's good for them to see us—to see *you*—there. Taking charge. Offering suggestions. And your suggestions are always good." She paused, smirked, and swiped a strand of hair behind her ear. "I know reading over shipping manifests might not be as glamorous as slaying insane gods and ancient dragons, but it needs to be done. So, get your ass up."

"Yeah, yeah, I know." I reluctantly gained my feet, lurched over to my wardrobe, and threw on my armor and gear—fresh, clean, and blood free, though I couldn't say the same thing for me. I was still covered in dirt and splatters of gore from the night before. I lifted one arm and took a sniff; the pungent scent of BO hit me like a fist to the nose. Yeah, it'd been a while since I'd last showered, and unfortunately deodorant wasn't a thing here. I shrugged. If I had to sit through another stuffy meeting, at least I could make all the admin folk suffer a little with me.

I pulled on my boots last, then grabbed my hammer and slid it home into the leather frog at my belt. With that done, Abby and I left our suite behind. Once we were out of the room, we could've ported directly into the Command Center, but I needed the walk to get my body moving and my blood flowing—it helped to clear my head. We made it to the control room just as the rest of the Alliance Council members started trickling into their seats around the hulking mahogany round table, which had a huge emerald crystal lodged in its center.

Despite the fact that I hated the morning briefings, I found myself glad to be there.

The room with its vaulted ceiling, massive fireplace, and dark stone walls covered in thick tapestries had slowly begun to feel like home. The sense of familiarity was comforting. I weaved my way through the loose cluster of people still milling about, nodding politely to each, before dropping into my comfy leather chair like a sack of bricks. Abby took a seat to my right. Cutter was to my immediate left. Honestly, I was surprised to see him here at this ungodly hour—though he wasn't exactly bright-eyed and bushy-tailed.

Nope, he was slumped over the table, head resting on his forearms, snoring softly as though he were alone in the world. Amara sat beside him, and she looked perfectly rested. I shot her a glance, then hooked a thumb at Cutter.

"Exhausted *and* hungover," she said in explanation. "You are lucky he's here at all—and I only accomplished that by promising him... Well, what I promised is unimportant." She grimaced. "What matters is that he is here, as is fitting for the Alliance Spymaster."

I snorted and leaned back in my chair, taking a bleary-eyed glance around the room at the rest of the staff and officers. Most of the people present were OG Alliance members—Anton Black, our quartermaster, Vlad, Chief Kolle, Abby—though there were a fair number of newer faces, mostly guys and gals like General Caldwell. Former politicians, business leaders, and military types who believed in what we were doing. We also had Imperial representatives. I spotted Erin Gallo—an Imperial Accipiter who had a tiny city way out east in the Barren Sands—chatting with Chiara Bolinger, who ran Wyrdtide with an iron fist.

They were talking intensely in hushed voices, shooting fruitive glances over their shoulders. Something was going on there, though I wasn't sure what. At least until I noticed that Osmark, Sandra, and Jay were all missing. True, Jay sometimes skipped these things, running errands on behalf of the Empire, but Osmark and Sandra were never missing. *Never.* Those two seemed to *thrive* on red tape, supply reports, and stuffy bureaucratic snore-fests.

Worry bloomed in my gut.

Yeah, something was definitely wrong.

Once more I pulled up my interface and jotted off a quick message to all three, sending it with a thought. A wooden gavel rapped on the table a moment later, wielded by Anton—the acting council chair—calling the meeting to order. The rest of the leadership fell silent as Anton began to speak, opening up with the minutes from the last meeting, then launching into an exceedingly dry agenda. I pressed my eyes shut, listening to the monotonous drone of his voice as I rubbed at the bridge of my nose.

After what felt like an eternity in my own personal hell, Anton finally sat, only to be replaced by a colossal creature built entirely of stone, earth, bone, and moss. A crude humanoid thing that stood ten feet tall and sported enormous earthen muscles—his arms as big around as a telephone pole, his legs squat and powerful. Elegant runic script, pulsing with a dull red light, covered his giant arms, legs, and torso. He bore a gnarled staff in his oversized hands, and it was covered in even more of the odd glowing script.

Brewald. The Darkshard Keep Guardian and the living embodiment of the castle itself. He defended the place from would-be attackers, and basically ran the day-to-day business of the Keep when I wasn't around, which was a lot these days. His role had also expanded significantly over the past months as I'd captured Rowanheath, unified the rest of the Storme Marsh cities, and taken back Vogthar strongholds. Though the magistrates I'd appointed oversaw the tasks and operations of each city, good ol' Brewald kept the rest of us up to date with city maintenance and resource management.

Brewald's report was slightly more interesting than Anton's.

We went over the various cities under our command, and he rattled off logistics reports before we finally turned to the business of Darkshard and Yunnam itself. The Keep sat atop a powerful ley line, which generated a daily allotment of Dark energy, which Brewald could transmute and convert into physical matter, creating guards, upgrading buildings, and even crafting powerful magics to defend against potential aggressors. The ley line generated 1,000 points of Dark energy per day—though that number could be augmented by feeding Brewald Raw Darkshard Ore—and we usually let it build for several days before upgrading the Keep.

It had been a week since we'd last upgraded, and Brewald was sitting on close to 10,000 Dark energy points. There were still a number of fun exciting features to unlock—new weapons turrets, a moat guardian, an upgrade to the primary stable—but instead we spent the points in a more practical manner. Building extra barracks space. Adding a kitchen expansion to the dining hall. Reinforcing a few sections of the exterior wall. Nothing glamorous, but all of it necessary.

Eventually, Brewald was replaced by General Caldwell, who brought the massive emerald gem in the center of the table to brilliant life with a flick of his hand. He accessed a floating map of Eldgard, which hung in the air like a green specter, and ran us through troop movements, city defenses, and recent Vogthar advances. Caldwell, in turn, was replaced by Vlad—our Alchemic Weaponeer and head of the Alliance Crafter's Guild—who briefed us on guild recruitment efforts, talked at great length about siege weapons, then concluded with a foot-long list of rare crafting ingredients he needed.

The guy's appetite for rare ingredients was *legendary*, but the weapons he whipped up were worth the time and energy.

Abby went next, offering the council an after-action report regarding the assault on Glome Corrie, then launching into a brief about Glome Corrie's available resources and economy. Dry as the Mojave Desert, though I learned that Glome Corrie was the biggest trading partner to Stone Reach, the Dwarven capital in the far-flung northern expanses. Chief Kolle went next, followed by Cutter—who managed to grunt out a few words that almost formed a single cohesive thought—who was replaced by Bolinger. She gave us an update about the Imperial operations, but made no mention of Osmark's noticeable absence.

When I pressed her about it, she simply smiled, waved away my concern, and mentioned that he and Sandra were just indisposed with important business elsewhere. "They do have an empire to run," she quipped, though to me it seemed like she was a little *too* relaxed about it. Maybe overcompensating for something else? Seemed possible. But if there was something going on, I didn't necessarily want to air it in front of the entire council. I trusted everyone here, true, but it was best to regulate bad news whenever possible. So, I let it slide. For now. If I hadn't heard anything by the evening, I'd start sniffing around a little bit more insistently.

Despite the fact that I would've rather been... well, almost anywhere, doing almost anything else, I listened attentively, retaining as much of the slew of information as I could, asked questions, and offered tidbits of feedback. Eventually, a Murk Elf serving woman named Sumana brought me a plate with crisp bacon, a crusty croissant, and a steaming cup of Western Brew in a porcelain mug. I promptly fished a gold Imperial mark from my pocket and pressed it into her hand in thanks. She was a saint. And if it wasn't for her kindness, I'd probably miss half of all my meals.

I took a bite of the croissant—warm, buttery, and perfect—then chased it with a mouthful of bold coffee, savoring the aroma and the heat. A prompt appeared as I set the mug down.

Buffs Added

Western Brew: Restore 150 HP over 30 seconds. Increase Health regen by 18%; duration, 30 minutes.

Caffeinated: Base Intelligence increased by (5) points; duration, 30 minutes. Base Vitality increased by (3) points; duration, 30 minutes. Base Strength increased by (3) points; duration, 30 minutes.

Remember, with enough good coffee, all things are possible.

Once the regular reports were given, the doors swung open and Jo-Dan—more formally known as Joseph the Gravemonger—strode in, silencing the room with his presence. He was maybe six one and wore dark purple robes covered by heavy plate mail built from gleaming bone inscribed with emerald runes. He had a dark cowl pulled up over his head, and where his face should've been was just a gaping black hole. Staring into that hood was like staring into a bottomless chasm. Bony wings protruded from his back as if he were an Accipiter that had died and molted, and he carried a wicked scythe in one gauntleted hand.

"Morning, everyone," Jo-Dan said, all butterflies and rainbows despite being a living monster. "Congratulations on taking Glome Corrie—that's a big win. Big win." He paused for a moment, seeming to look my direction before forging ahead. "Unfortunately, things are less awesome in other parts of Eldgard." He waved a gauntleted hand, tapping into the power of the emerald on the table. The stone flared, the floating map of Eldgard springing to life once again.

"The Vogthar have been stepping up their game big time. Me and the other dungeons have recently formed an unofficial faction. The Mob, we're calling it." He cackled in that way only teenagers can. "Get it, like you're in the Mob. But like dungeon monsters are called mobs." No one laughed. Not even a smile. "Jeesh. Tough room. Anyway, me and the rest of the Mob are working to keep the lid on it, but we're having a hard time. These Vogthar dudes are *persistent.*" With a flick of his hand, several lights appeared on the map—a slew of purple ones, some blue, a spattering of angry red, and a generous heaping of deathly black—all of them strobing manically.

"The purple dots"—these were the least numerous— "are the reclaimed dungeons. I've been helping the other dungeon lords and ladies take them back, and once we wipe out the Vogthar Dungeon Hearts, we've been able to replace them with new seedlings. Fresh troops, *eventually*. But for right now, those new dungeons are babies. They won't be able to offer much by way of help for a while, so we gotta keep an eye on them. Maybe start cycling a few of the lower-level heroes through there to build up Dark energy. Still, it's all good. But the bad news is all the rest of the dots…"

He trailed off. "The blue dots are dungeons we've managed to quarantine, but they're still Vogthar controlled. The red dots are active Vogthar dungeons— we haven't even touched them yet, and they're seriously everywhere. Big concentration in the north, near Stone Reach, and those things just seem to vomit out like an endless supply of the Vogthar. And they have a bunch of Darklings guarding them, which makes it even harder to break through. Worst of all are the black dots. Those are newly converted Vogthar dungeons. Almost as many of those as there are reclaimed dungeons.

"And check it out. The black dots are almost entirely here in the Storm Marshes. I'm just a kid, so what do I know"—he shrugged—"but if I *did* know anything, I'd say these dudes are gonna take a run at Yunnam. Maybe some of the other Storm Marsh cities. A bunch of the corrupted dungeons are clustered near Baan Luang too, so it might do to beef up security around there. Okay." He swung his arms and clapped his hands together, tone light and cheery, as though he hadn't just dropped a total bombshell on everyone in the room. "Any questions?"

Every hand, save Cutter's, shot up.

The young dungeon lord sighed audibly, but then quickly worked his way around the room—*no, there was no new movement in the Tanglewood. Yes, the dungeon near the Crossing had grown. How was he supposed to know what kind of dungeon boss spawned in these new locations?*—until finally he'd answered every question as well as he could. Finished, and obviously ready to call it quits for the day, the dungeon lord offered a brief round of goodbyes, then ducked out of the room before anyone could stop him. Smart kid. Smarter than me. With a reluctant sigh, I settled in as the meeting continued in full swing.

Long live the Admin Grind…

FIVE

YUNNAM

IT WAS NINE THIRTY—A SOLID TWO HOURS SINCE THE morning briefing had begun in earnest—by the time I headed into the hallway outside the Command Center with Abby, Amara, and Cutter in tow.

"Thank the gods above and below that's over," Cutter said with a grin, instantly looking more alert and interested now that the meeting was over. "How in the bloody hell can anyone make a war sound so bloody boring, eh? That's what I want to know. But that's all behind us. What's the plan now? Hopefully it involves drinking, eating, maybe a spot of gambling. We never did have a proper celebration for taking Glome Corrie." He looked me dead in the face and rested a hand on my shoulder. "We need to celebrate the small things, Jack. And the big things too."

"I'd love to," I said, shrugging off his hand, "but I've got myself an appointment over at the Crafter's Hall."

"Gods, are you still doing that?" He rolled his eyes. "You're the bloody Jade Lord, you don't need a craft or a profession. You kill monsters and capture cities. That's enough in my book, friend. Give over already."

Amara and Abby shared confused looks, then Abby gave me a sidelong glance. *Keeping secrets, Jack?*

I blushed furiously and shifted uncomfortably from foot to foot.

"It is fine," Amara said, killing the conversation before it could hit peak *awkward.* "We are busy anyway. Jake is preparing to initiate a few new recruits into the Bastards, and he wants us there." She latched onto Cutter's elbow with steely fingers and gave a gentle tug. "Come along, Spymaster."

Cutter grumbled but followed, offering us a quick wave as they descended the stairs and vanished around the first turn.

"Crafter's Hall?" Abby asked, quirking an eyebrow. "Something you want to tell me?"

"It's nothing," I replied, scrunching my nose and waving her question away with one hand.

"Jack…"

I sighed. *Thanks, Cutter.* "Fine. Look, I've sorta taken on an apprenticeship. Kind of."

"You thinking about swinging a different kind of hammer for once?" She eyed the warhammer sitting at my hip, a slight smile playing across her lips. She was an excellent blacksmith thanks to her skill with flame—controlling heat and the temperature of the fire was a critical ability, apparently—while I was… lacking. There were few people who could take me in a fair fight—especially since I didn't believe in fighting fair, not if I could find a cheat instead—but on the crafting side of things I was worse than the lowliest lowbie. I'd spent so much time questing that I didn't even have a proper profession.

Something everyone and their brother seemed to have.

I'd unlocked Mining, true, but aside from swinging a pickaxe a little faster and minutely increasing the chance to spawn certain rare stones, that wasn't a terribly practical skill. At least not for me.

I sniffed and shrugged. "What if I am? I've been learning a thing or two about Runic Ward work. I'm getting pretty good."

She guffawed, snorted, and rolled her eyes. "Runic Ward work? That so?"

"You sound skeptical." I made for the stairs.

"Obviously," she said, following behind me. "That's a subspecialty profession. In order to unlock one of those, you need to *practice*, Jack, and you don't have two spare minutes to rub together. You haven't even slept in the same city for more than two days running. The only profession you're likely to unlock in the near future is either Professional Meeting Attendee or Dragon Slayer."

"Which is why I need to get over to the Crafter's Hall."

She caught up to me and slipped her hand into mine, our fingers entwining. "And you told Cutter, but not me?" This accusation was quiet, more earnest, her playful tone gone.

"I didn't tell him," I finally admitted. "I was trying to keep anyone from finding out. It's kind of embarrassing. But he's our Spymaster. He found out in about two seconds and started making fun of me. 'The great Jade Lord,'" I said, trying to effect Cutter's Cockney accent, "'bent over a table with an apron on, scratching runes into metal and taking orders from some grouchy old woman.'" I shrugged. "After that, I thought it was probably best to just keep it to myself."

She gave my hand a squeeze. "Don't listen to him. I'm proud of you for trying something new. Come on, I'll walk you over. I could use some hours at the forge anyway, then maybe we can grab lunch together. Sound like a plan?"

"Totally," I said, squeezing her hand in return, letting the simple gesture say what I couldn't.

Instead of trekking down the gajillion steps that led to the bottom of the tower, we ported directly down to the Keep's looming entryway. Faction leaders inside the Keep could teleport anywhere inside the building in an eyeblink, but outside of the Keep proper, we had to hoof it just like everyone else. Behind us, Darkshard rose up into the sky like a behemoth of rounded edges, flowing curves, elegant spires, and artfully carved stonework depicting fantastical beasts and epic battles.

It always vaguely reminded me of some grand Buddhist temple from a bygone era.

Abby and I headed down the steps—worn smooth by age, elements, and the passing of countless feet—and into the colossal courtyard nestled inside the inner walls. Those walls stood tall and proud, the stones gleaming and clean, and their many towers, manned by keen-eyed Rangers, were defiant. They practically *begged* for an invader to try to attack, though they wouldn't have much luck, not with the formidable array of Arcane Shadow Cannons facing outward.

Once upon a time—and not so long ago, really—Darkshard had been in absolute ruins, but things had changed a lot since then. Darkshard itself was now a small, thriving city in its own right, housing a couple thousand people. And those people were *everywhere*. Walking, talking, working, most moving with purposeful strides in these early morning hours. The grounds themselves were well kept, the vines, trees, and jungle flowers trimmed back and beaten into beautiful submission by an army of professional gardeners and plant-based Druids.

We were headed over to Yunnam proper, so we cut through a row of stone buildings and made for the port pad located in the outer courtyard. Those buildings had been leather shanty tents not so long ago, but not anymore. Nope. Darkshard no longer resembled a run-down refugee city, but something sleek and beautiful and amazing. We skirted around the outside of the main barracks: a boxy, three-story building with terraces jutting from each floor. The place looked pretty empty, but that was expected at nine thirty in the morning.

Most of the Alliance members were out training, crafting, running missions, or—if they were night crew—catching a few winks of shut-eye while they could.

The port pad lay on the other side of the barracks.

We'd upgraded that since the founding, allowing parties of people to travel all at once, an absolute must considering the overflow of humanity. Now it was a raised stone platform, ten by ten feet, with an elaborate golden circle inlaid into the surface. A Dawn Elf acolyte, wearing brown Cleric robes and a near-permanent scowl, sat on a wooden stool eyeing the metal circle and the roped-off waiting line, currently devoid of people. He looked bored out of his mind, which probably wasn't far from the truth. The port pads, necessary and convenient for Darkshard residents, still required a magic user to oversee them.

A dull duty, but someone had to do it.

Abby and I made our way up the steps, and the acolyte rose, eyes distant and hazy. I'm not sure he even recognized us, which was a rarity these days. Probably lost in some daydream about slaying dragons. That or drinking a tankard of ale when his shift ended.

The pad engaged with a blinding flash, and in a wink Abby and I were on an identical metal ring down in the center of Yunnam, not far from the chief's towering, moss-covered tree.

The Murk Elf city had also grown dramatically over the past few months, nearly quadrupling in size thanks to the steady influx of Alliance members. And it wasn't just the number of people, but the city itself that had undergone drastic changes. There were still lots of spindly Dokkalfar homes, raised up on their dark wooden struts, giving the homes a strangely arachnoid appearance. But there were also plenty of Wode, Risi, and even Dawn Elf buildings thrown into the mix. Traditional structures of brick and stone, showing off gracefully arched ceramic roofs.

We wandered past one towering building of particular interest.

It was a stately structure with walls of gleaming white marble topped by a blue-capped dome in the Imperial style. The Yunnam School of Excellence.

A lush, grassy lawn extended from the building's front, and a playground of wood and steel had been set up—built by Vlad and some of the other crafters in the city. Children ran and squealed, some little more than toddlers, others in their early to mid-teens. Many were NPCs, but others were Travelers. Kids who'd successfully made the transition. I grinned as a Murk Elf girl slapped a Risi boy of twelve or thirteen on the back of the head, only to sprint away, laughing wildly as the Risi boy glared after her.

The play yard was presided over by the watchful eyes of several fiercely protective Dread Hounds—each two hundred pounds of black fur, yellowed fangs, and hellfire eyes—and Mrs. Claire, a short Dawn Elf woman with golden skin and corn silk hair pulled back in a sharp ponytail. She was a Warlock by trade and responsible for the Dread Hounds. She wore a gray dress and subconsciously rested a single hand on her distended belly. My heart beat a little faster when I saw her. She was a player, but unique. The first Traveler in V.G.O. to get pregnant.

No one was sure what would happen with her or what the baby would be like, but she was still a sign of hope. Maybe this place really could be a home. And the kids, likewise, were a beacon of joy. Not only had they survived Asteria and the transition, but they were *growing*. No one—not even Osmark—had been sure what was going to happen with them, but they seemed to be changing. Maturing. Though admittedly they were maturing at a rather disturbing rate, which was still some cause for concern.

Abby hooked her elbow through mine as we headed into the sprawling marketplace chock-full of vendors from every race, hawking their wares—meat pies, blades, skill training, ingredients, and just about everything else—from beneath colorful awnings propped up on wooden struts. My mind wandered as we walked. We'd never really talked about starting a family, since it hadn't seemed possible, but now? Well, Claire changed things. We'd wait to see how things turned out with the pregnancy before *really* talking about it, but it was a conversation we'd have to have eventually.

We wandered past a squat *Svartalfar* man with an impressive beard slow roasting skewers of sizzling meat over a bed of coals. The aroma of char, grease, and meat tickled the inside of my nostrils, and my stomach let out a furious roar of protest. *I want this, and I want it now.*

Abby just grinned, slipped her arm from mine, then fished out a handful of silver. True, a meal like this would cost a few coppers at most, but it was good to let the people in the Alliance know that we were more than happy to be generous with what we had. The Dwarf handed over the spits with a nod and a few mumbled words of gratitude. We ate our midmorning snack as we weaved through the marketplace, keeping our hoods up so we wouldn't be stopped by a gaggle of Alliance members.

After a time, we found ourselves outside a rectangular, two-story structure with a high stone foundation on the far side of Yunnam. There was a variety of outdoor work spaces, a large stable—mostly used for shipping—and a pair of circular towers that flanked the main building. But the real magic happened inside, carefully guided by Vlad's steady hand. At last we'd come to the Crafter's Hall.

SIX

SCRIVENER

W E MADE FOR THE SET OF DIRT-COVERED wooden steps leading up to the heavy double doors, which glimmered with wards. I hadn't seen the wards in action yet—honestly, I hoped I never would, since the city would have to be under siege for that—but Vlad assured me the runes and sigils, when activated, would alchemically transform the wood into nearly indestructible stone. I shouldered my way into the main hall, Abby following behind me. Heat and noise washed over me in a wave, making it nearly impossible to talk. The scent of smoke and sweat hung heavy in the air, punctuated by the occasional whiff of sulfur, just like rotten eggs.

The workshop was a flurry of activity, just like it *always* was, no matter the time of day.

The clang of steel on steel echoed through the hall, mingling with the roar of furnaces and the chatter of crafters busy at work. Masters barked orders at their apprentices, and apprentices, in turn, muttered under their breath as they scurried around in their leather aprons. I surveyed the room, searching for any friendly faces. Forge spent a fair amount of time in here when he wasn't out on patrol or training with the Malleus Libertas, and Vlad practically lived here. The guy was a workacholic and slept in his lab more often than in the officer quarters assigned to him in the Darkshard Keep.

There were plenty of folks milling about, but no sign of those two.

"Okay, I'm gonna get my smithy on," Abby said, gesturing toward the wing housing the forge and foundry—all red brick and black swamp rock, outfitted with everything a potential smith could ever want or need. There were metal-topped workstations, great steel-ribbed barrels brimming with water, bulky stone grinding wheels, pitted iron anvils, and tools of every shape and size hanging from the walls: steel tongs, heavy hammers, grooved swages, vises, rasps, and files in all styles and flavors.

"I'll shoot you a message in"—she seesawed her head for a moment—"let's say two hours, then we can head over to Frank's and grab a pie."

"Yeah, sounds good," I called out, cupping my mouth to be heard over the blare of falling hammers.

She gave me a brilliant smile, then turned and beelined for an open anvil near the smelter.

I made my way farther back into the Crafter's Hall. The inside of the building was as hot as an oven on the surface of the sun, and before I knew it, great trails of sweat rolled down my forehead and back. Reluctantly, I threw my hood back, revealing both my face and the crown of the Jade Lord, which sat on my head like a road flare, altering everyone in a twenty-mile radius of *exactly* who I was. Frantic apprentices and masters alike all shied away from me, nearly tripping over themselves to clear a path as they offered me cordial nods and overly polite greetings.

I sighed and smiled back, trying not to do anything to terrify them. Such was the life of a faction leader. And not just any faction leader, but a living legend.

At the far end of the main hall and off to the left sat a spiral staircase, which led to one of the four main towers: each a specialty area, kept separate from the rest of the hall. Alchemy and Potions in one, Experimental Engineering in another, Glasswork and Jewelcraft in a third. Each tower was sequestered behind runic scripts carefully worked into the floorboards, walls, struts, and stairs. And with good reason.

Many of the spells and weapons the Alchemists and Engineers tinkered with day and night were *volatile* at best. And some of the their most powerful experiments could level the building and kill everyone inside. Instantly, I thought back to the time Vlad had nearly killed the both of us with his Alchemic grenades. Plumes of gray gas washing through his lab, choking the life from the air itself. Thankfully, the runic scripts kept the deadlier items sealed away safely behind magical barriers. If there was an accident, it would only wipe out a single wing, leaving everyone else relatively unscathed.

The stairs I took led to the fourth tower—the Enchanter's Workshop.

I trudged my way up, going round and round, scanning the runes worked into each stone step, trying to decipher their meaning. I didn't rate as a Runic Crafter Apprentice yet, but even I could recognize a handful of the containment wards. Here, an angry slash, bisected by a jagged line and an oblong circle: a protection against fire-based attacks and damage. There, what looked like a spiral with a set of horns sprouting from the top and a pair of angular dots flanking the right side. *Urandu*—a binding construct to temporarily stop summoned creatures from passing.

There were over two hundred runic sigils, which could be combined in a number of different ways to achieve an almost unlimited number of different results—though many of those results were categorically terrible. Everything from accidentally setting the scribe on fire to unleashing a vortex that damaged *only* friendly party members.

A descending master Enchanter, his arms overflowing with blueprints, scrolls, and blank parchment, nearly slammed into me on his way down. He was a lanky Murk Elf with stringy white hair and a narrow, pinched face. He opened his mouth, ready to tear into me like a drill instructor, when his gaze lighted on my face then flickered to the crown at my brow. His eyes bulged alarmingly, and he swallowed whatever he'd been about to say, quickly pressing his back up against the wall as though he *might* be able to disappear if he just stopped moving.

That was dumb, of course, because I wasn't a T. rex, but I just kept going, pretending to ignore him. He seemed deeply relieved.

The winding staircase let out into an octagonal room, the walls polished gray stone, the floors cherrywood, every single floorboard covered in runic script.

Two-dozen people occupied the room. Enchanters and Scriveners—all apprentices and journeymen from the insignia markings on their aprons—but they purposely avoided looking at me as though I might have the plague.

Over in the corner was the woman I'd come to find, and she, at least, wouldn't ignore me. The Arcane Scrivener sat at a workstation in the corner, her back bent, furiously carving something on her wood-topped table.

"Well, don't just stand there all day, youngin'. You're already leaps and bounds behind the rest of the 'prentices," she barked out over one shoulder, not bothering to so much as look up from her work.

Betty Howard was a dour Wode with silver-blond hair pulled back into a tight bun and a too-serious face. Her silken robes—black and boring, though finely made—draped her whipcord body like a sheet. She looked maybe fifty, but was closer to ninety, or at least she had been before making the transition into V.G.O. She could've chosen the body of a twenty-five-year-old, but no. Not Betty Howard. Excessive, she called it. Besides, she had no joint pain here, her arthritis was gone, and she felt twenty-five no matter how she looked. Her words.

A bit eccentric, but also the best rune worker in the Alliance. She'd spent most of her days, IRL, as a seamstress and tailor. Rune-work, she insisted to anyone who would give her their ear, wasn't so different from sewing or mending or doing a spot of needlepoint. Just attention to detail and following the right patterns.

"It doesn't help that you only pop in for a few hours a week. Never gonna be a proper rune worker at that rate. Oughta toss you right out on your ear." The words were harsh, but I could see the flicker of a grin on her face as she waved toward the three-legged stool at the end of her workstation. "I know you're liable to run off any minute, so I had this set out for you." She pushed over a sheet of parchment with a circular runic binding meticulously painted on.

I smiled. The very best thing about Betty wasn't her formidable skill as an Arcane Scrivener. Nope. The best thing was she didn't seem to have the foggiest clue *who* I was, or if she did, she didn't care in the least. Either was fine by me.

I plopped down onto the stool and took a look at the page she'd pushed my way. It came from one of her many work manuals, all drawn by hand. The symbol on the sheet was actually a compound script set, composed of several basic runic bindings, all interwoven into a circle. Below the complicated sigil was a meticulous description of how to inscribe the individual runes and in what order, what its potential uses were, and how the script set might interact with other basic runes and common script sets.

This was an intermediate Protection Ward, which when combined with a single rune inscribed at the center of the circle, could temporarily reduce elemental damage. Or when combined with another set of runes, could be used as a foundation to ward off specific types of elemental and magical creatures.

"You'll be needing these," she said, pulling out a handful of bronze coins, all blank, each the size of a silver dollar with a small hole at the top. Basic amulets, if I had to guess. She slapped a runic awl down next to the pendants without another word of explanation. "Get busy, lollygagger," she snapped. She promptly pulled down a set of brass crafter's goggles with a set of telescoping lenses and resumed her work.

She had a golden amulet the size of a closed fist on the table in front of her. A fat ruby sat in the center. Painstakingly engraved into the metal around the gem were hair-fine runes so small they were hard to even make out. She reached up, casually flipped a blue lens into place, adjusted a series of dials and tiny levers alongside the goggles, then set to work with a fine-pointed awl a heck of a lot nicer than the loaner she'd given me. She squinted, forehead creasing, and began etching a new line of runic script into the metal.

She wasn't altering or enhancing some old artifact— she was creating a *new* one. A custom piece, no doubt, tailored to order.

"You won't get any better watching me, boy." She never stopped working.

No matter how much everyone else bowed and scraped for me, Betty Howard never would. Not in a million years. I slipped on a pair of the strange goggles— Osmark constantly wore them—flipped down a blue lens, just as Betty had done, and went to work. I read through the instructions on the sheet of parchment once more, then etched the first rune in the script, *Sitoa*, onto the surface of the token. Blue lines of power flared, augmented by the goggles. I finished the final slash, then moved on to the next mark in the circle, *Saa*, connecting the two with a tiny line.

The line of power spread from the first rune to the second, and the pair of them began to glow and pulse in a strange syncopated rhythm—*blue, green, blue, green.*

I watched, fascinated, as a fraction of my Spirit drained away in service to powering the runic script. The energy for runes came from one of three places, I'd learned. Most runes used straight Spirit, which was taken directly from the crafter. But some runes required specific types of magic—a flaming sword would require concentrated fire from a Firebrand—and for those, a third-party mage was usually required, unless the caster could meet the requirement themselves. The final type was energy harvested directly from monsters, using a special type of syphon called a charging crystal—not so different from the enormous emerald in the Darkshard Keep control room.

That whole table, it turned out, was one giant arcane artifact, covered in insanely complex runes and powered by the charging crystal, which connected directly to Brewald, the Darkshard Guardian.

When I added the third of six runes to the set, *Rikki*, my hand slipped just a hair. One of the angular lines went a millimeter too far, and the glowing light morphed from blues and greens to an angry red, the color of an infected wound. My Spirit gauge began to noticeably drop, as though I were casting some overpowered spell. Maybe Plague Burst or Night Cyclone. The bronze coin hummed and rattled across the surface of the table, clattering violently against the wood. I stole a look at Betty, who simply scooted over a few inches, then tapped her awl against a rune I hadn't yet learned, scrawled on the leg of her stool.

Immediately, an opalescent barrier sprung up around her with an audible *pop*.

Just in time to shelter her from the deafening explosion. The bronze medal flashed in front of me—a blast of brilliant crimson—and searing hot chunks of metallic shrapnel peppered my face, neck, and hands. At my level the explosion hadn't shaved off more than the tiniest fraction of HP, but the metal shards still burned like fury, and most annoying of all, a debuff appeared, floating before me:

Debuff Added

Stunned: You have been stunned! Attack damage -10%; Stamina regeneration reduced by 15%; movement speed reduced by 25%; duration, 1 minute.

Betty cast me a sidelong glance from the corner of her eye, then cackled as she tapped the rune on her stool leg once more, dismissing the colorful shield around her. "Unregulated Spirit," she said by way of explanation. "Runic script work ain't about speed, it's about accuracy. Precision." She reached over and prodded at the warhammer on my belt with one bony finger. "This work here, boy, it ain't like swinging around a hammer. It's threading a needle. And even one little slipup can get y'all blown to hell. Count yourself lucky that script circle was so dang small and worked in bronze."

I blinked away the purple afterimage still staining my vision, and the debuff faded with it.

"Now get yer butt back on the horse and try again. For a real Scrivener, practice makes perfect." She swept a hand toward the pile of bronze medals. "You got yourself plenty to practice on, I reckon." She offered me a wink, barely visible through the goggles, then hunched back over, her lips pressed into a tight line as she resumed her work. Her golden medallion had at least fifteen different interlocking runic script circles already, each one of them far more complex than the circle I was working on. And each was no larger than the size of a dime.

I grunted and pulled over the next metal token.

That one erupted up in my face, too—though I made five of the six runes before failing spectacularly. It ate even more of my Spirit and sliced off nearly a sixth of my HP, which was no small thing, proving this was serious business.

My third run was my first success. The completed medal earned me a noncommittal grunt from Betty and 100 XP—a drop in the bucket at my current level. Still, I was only a level 1 Runic Scrivener, so I only needed a handful of successes to unlock my next Scrivener level. I buckled down, working through the next three medallions without fault. The one after that blew up, though instead of fire it jettisoned a gout of arctic wind into my eyes.

Snow Blindness for two minutes.

"Starting to get cocksure," Betty said between bouts of cackling laughter.

When the snow blindness finally subsided, I glanced around the room only to find that every other disciple had retreated. No one wanted to see their elevated leader blowing himself up over and over again—bad for morale. Plus, they probably thought I'd unleash my wrath on them if they laughed at my misfortune. I shook my head and hit it again. This time I was slower. More diligent. More patient. Ensuring each line was meticulously placed. Each dot added just so. Each swooping curve perfect.

It was simple work, really, but deeply enjoyable.

True, if I got something wrong, it would *literally* blow up in my face, but the task was straightforward. Simple. I knew exactly what needed to be done. There was no moral ambiguity here. No grand sweeping decisions that would affect the fate of millions. If I screwed up, I would pay the price tag with a face full of shrapnel, but no one else would suffer or die. Plus, because the work was so exacting, I couldn't focus on anything else. My mind was fully present. Back in college when school or life became too overwhelming, I'd clean. Do dishes. Sweep the floors. Scrub the toilets.

Anything to get my mind focused elsewhere. This was a lot like that.

I'd finished twenty-five of the bronze medallions when a notification pinged in my ear. I set my awl down and swiped a hand across my sweat-covered brow, then pulled up my interface.

<<<>>>

Crafting Subspecialty: Runic Scrivener

Runic Scrivener is a subspecialty of the Enchanting Profession and allows you to create powerful runic scripts with a myriad of impressive magical and mundane abilities. This crafting subspecialty requires an Enchanter's Workshop or a Scrivener's Lab for maximum effectiveness.

There are eight primary Crafting Professions: Cooking, Enchanting, Alchemy, Tailoring and Leatherwork, Engineering, Merchant-Craft, Blacksmithing, and Lapidary (Jeweler), plus hundreds of subspecialties. All Professions, both Gathering and Crafting, can be unlocked and leveled through practice and use, but any specialized skills or abilities within a given profession must be unlocked with proficiency points. All specialized profession skills can be upgraded a total of seven times (Initiate, Novice, Adept, Journeyman, Specialist, Master, Grandmaster).

Crafting Ability Type/Level: Passive / Level 2

Cost: N/A

Effect 1: Increase effect and duration of Runic Scripts by 5%

Effect 2: All Spirit costs associated with Rune Work are reduced by 3%.

Effect 3: Can inscribe 1 Compound Runic Script Set per Item.

After I'd finished looking over the update, I toggled over to my character sheet—checking to see where I was at after the raid on Glome Corrie. Using my Avatar of Order ability had cost me dearly, but the points I'd earned from taking out the horde of Vogthar troops and capturing the city had pushed me back up, closing the gap toward level 50. A level I was ecstatic to reach, since it would allow me to unlock my ultimate Shadowmancer ability, Shadow Lord.

Name:	Jack	Race:		Dokkalfar	Gender:	Male
Level:	49	Class:		Dark Templar	Alignment:	Dark
Renown:	2,500	Carry Capacity:		772.5	Undistributed Attribute Points:	0

Health:	1275	Spirit:	2102.5	Stamina:	1155
H-Regen/sec:	45.29	S-Regen/sec:	31.37	Stam-Regen/sec:	19.89

Attributes:		Offense:		Defense:	
Strength:	81.75	Base Melee Weapon Damage:	72.05	Base Armor:	175.9
Vitality:	78.5	Base Ranged Weapon Damage:	0	Armor Rating:	241.3
Constitution:	66.5	Attack Strength (AS):	525.3	Block Amount:	92.38
Dexterity:	109.5	Ranged Attack Strength (RAS):	378.75	Block Chance (%):	89.59
Intelligence:	137.75	Spell Strength (SS):	206.63	Evade Chance (%):	26.8
Spirit:	161.25	Critical Hit Chance:	27%	Fire Resist (%):	49.58
Luck:	16	Critical Hit Damage:	250%	Cold Resist (%):	47.58
				Lightning Resist (%):	47.58
				Shadow Resist (%):	67.58
				Holy Resist (%):	44.82
Current XP:	78,395			Poison Resist (%):	67.58
Next Level.:	113,680			Disease Resist (%):	67.58

"Not bad," Betty reluctantly grumbled as I dismissed my interface. She was still hunched over her workbench, eyes glued on the amulet in front of her. I'd never be as good as her, of course. She wasn't just a normal crafter. As an Arcane Scrivener she had access to skills and abilities I never would. But if I could accomplish even a fraction of what she could, I'd be more than happy. To have any skill other than *hit-thing-in-the-face-with-magic-or-hammer* would be nice.

"Might be, you spent more than three hours a week in here, you might someday make a passable rune worker. *Might*," she emphasized, the ghost of a smile on her lips.

A message hit my inbox a second before I responded. This one from Abby. Lunchtime.

"Maybe someday," I said, standing and removing the leather apron she'd loaned me.

"Keep it. Goggles and awl, too. Maybe you can find some time to practice in between bouts of adventuring. Good luck with whatever fresh hell you're about, youngin'." She waved me away with the flick of a hand.

SEVEN

QUEST ALERT

TWENTY MINUTES LATER, JUST SHY OF NOON, Abby and I sat at a little circular table in a tavern-turned-pizza-parlor called Frank's Old World Pizza. Instead of the typical wooden floorboards, the floors here were black-and-white checkered marble, imported from Ankara. The tables were all finely made and covered with checkered tablecloths that looked out of place among the quasi-medieval surroundings. Still, the owners had tried. Against one wall was a painted mural of the Tuscany countryside. And splashed against the back wall, plastered on in bold letters: *Frank's Old World Pizza, Est. 2042*. And below that, *The Best New York Inspired Pizza in Eldgard!*

A bard sung quietly on a raised stage in the corner while servers bustled around the room, carrying huge metal pans overflowing with pizza or tankards of golden ale.

A steaming pie sat between Abby and me. Or at least what remained of it. It wasn't actually a pizza, of course—V.G.O. classified it as a type of "meat pie"—but it was pretty close. The crust thin. The marinara the right amount of sweet and savory. The cheese thick and gooey. There was even something that could've passed for oregano called Blackpatch Clover. This was a pepperoni pizza. The meat was actually smoked swamp croc. Almost couldn't tell the difference, though. And though soda still wasn't a thing, the pitcher of ale served well enough.

Frank, the shop owner, worked behind the bar along with his son, Frank Jr., both darker-skinned Wodes with thick beards. One labored over the bulky woodfire stove while the other hurled a bit of dough in the air, spinning it like some giant Frisbee, before catching it with practiced hands.

Frank was a New Yorker to his core. He'd been in the pizza business for thirty-five years, as had his dad before him, as would his son after him.

The guy wasn't about to let something as trivial as the end of the world close down the family business. He'd found the ingredients to make pizza, had found some backers to finance his shop—Abby *may* have played a role in that, which meant the Crimson Alliance was a part owner—and almost overnight, Frank had a booming business. The locals still weren't completely on board, but the Travelers couldn't get enough. As for me... Well, I had an inkling we'd be seeing our first pizza franchise before too long, reminding me that the more things changed, the more they stayed the same.

Not that I minded. I couldn't wait until someone got their act together and started making nachos and Mountain Dew. Then I'd be set.

Abby leaned forward and took another bite, this from her third slice. "Know what I love the most about V.G.O.?" she said around a mouthful of cheese and sauce.

"Let me guess. Not being dead?" I said with a wink.

She rolled her eyes. "Haha, ass. Yes, not being dead is pretty great. But what I was gonna say is that I can eat anything I want and never have to worry about hitting the gym again."

I shrugged, nodded, and took another bite of my own slice. "Solid point." Having a digital body wasn't all sunshine and rainbows, but it certainly had a few perks.

I grabbed my mug and took a long pull, washing down a mouthful of za, then stifled a burp with one fist. I eyed the last few bites on my plate. Seeing pizza go to waste was a high crime, but I couldn't take another bite without exploding or at the very least popping the button on my trousers. Reluctantly, I pushed my plate away and grabbed a linen napkin, wiping my fingers and face in turn.

"So, what's the plan for the rest of the day?" Abby asked as she followed suit, scooting her plate, completely clean, toward the table's center. She raised a hand, signaling our waitress that we were ready for the check. Frank insisted this was a "classy joint," so unlike most places in Eldgard, you paid *after* the meal, like was good and proper.

I rubbed at my jaw for a second, then frowned. "I can't stop thinking about the Doom-Forged relic. This is big. I can feel it. This could be the edge we need, assuming I can find the final piece and figure out what to do with them. Since we're on good terms with Osmark at the moment, I'm thinking of swinging by the Grand Archives in Alaunhylles."

Her face darkened into a thunderhead, jaw clenched. "Well if you see the Grand Lore Archivist, please kindly punch him in the face for me." She'd crossed swords with the folks in the Archives once before, and apparently she still wasn't entirely over whatever had happened there. Not that she had actually filled me in on the specifics. And Otto was equally tight-lipped about the experience. Some things were better left buried, it seemed.

"Got it. One punch to the face." I paused, drumming my fingers on the table. "Though first I should probably swing by New Viridia and see if I can't find out what in the hell is going on with Osmark. I haven't been able to get ahold of him since the raid, and he missed the brief this morning. He never misses the brief."

"Oh, I wouldn't worry about Osmark," purred our waitress, who now sounded slightly British.

"Excuse me?" I glanced up, genuinely baffled. I did a double take. Our waitress was now the Overmind of Order, Sophia. She wore the same garb as the other serving women: a dark woolen dress, dark corset, low-cut lace-up top, white apron wrapped around the waist. But there was no mistaking the face poking up from the server's outfit. Her dark skin was flawless, her teeth immaculately, impossibly white, her eyes a soft amber—beautiful, but completely unnatural. What's more, the entire world was frozen, statue still.

"Oh. No," Abby said, glancing around. "No way is this gonna end well."

"Don't be so gloomy, child."

"Oh. So you're here to bring us good news, then?" she shot back.

"Well, no. No, I'm not," Sophia replied with a dazzling smile, completely at odds with her words. She conjured a chair at the edge of the table, then primly sat, rearranging the ruffles of her woolen gown. "Rather terrible news, actually."

"Called it," Abby grumbled, folding her arms and shooting daggers at the Overmind from her eyes. Abby was a team player, no doubt, but she liked being manipulated by the Overminds even less than I did.

"My, but you humans are so clever," Sophia said absently, reaching forward to grab a bit of pizza still on the tray. "Wherever you go, you find a way to conform the world to your image. An impressive feat. Too bad you so often expend your efforts on such minor things." She hefted the pizza, then took a bite. "Though tasty things, I will admit."

"First, let's clear the air. Pizza is not trivial," I said. "This is humanity at its finest. Now, Osmark. You said we shouldn't worry about Osmark. Why?" I asked, knowing she would derail the conversation and fail to answer my questions if I didn't hold her feet to the fire.

She waved my concern away with a flick of one wrist. "He's indisposed, along with his compatriots, Sandra and Jay. Carrera has been busy since you took down the Lich Priest. But there's that saying about old dogs and new tricks. Predictably, he's launched a fresh invasion, though this time against my dearest sister, Enyo. Osmark is fulfilling his duties as the Champion of Chaos and defending the Shattered Realm. Assuming he survives, everything will be fine."

"We should help him, right?" Abby chipped in, stealing looks between Sophia and me. "I mean, there's no way we could've taken out the Lich Priest without him, so we owe him the same favor."

"Osmark will be fine, child—"

"I'm not a child," Abby interrupted fiercely. "I'm a grown-ass woman. Overmind or not, I won't be disrespected."

"Feisty," Sophia said, voice rich with approval. "I can appreciate that in small measures. Very well, Abby. As to Osmark's plight. Well." She folded her hands primly. "It's rather complicated, I'm afraid. Could he use your aid? Yes, almost certainly. Carrera has taken a hand in the war against my sister, and he has grown..." She paused. Frowned. "He has grown extremely powerful with Thanatos's assistance," she finished. "The real problem, however, is that Thanatos is not dumb and has learned a valuable lesson from your time in my realm. The combined might of two Champions is *significant*. And he knows it. So, Thanatos has arranged to split our forces.

"He's dispatched his other agent, the Traveler Peng Jun, to assemble the Doom-Forged weapon. Thanatos, though rather predictable, is a great believer in diversification. Peng has been working tirelessly over the last two weeks to assemble the pieces. And while you were busy raiding Glome Corrie, he was tracking down the final piece of the weapon—which he has acquired, by the way. That is why he wasn't present at his stronghold. Now all three pieces are in play and the race for the Doom Forge itself will begin in earnest."

"But we have two of the three pieces," I said, brow furrowed as I thought. "So if we can just keep Peng from getting his hands on these last two pieces we should be okay."

"You are a bright man, Jack, but sometimes you think so reactively. Thanatos—and by extension Peng and Carrera—will not stop until he has all the pieces. You'll notice that a number of new Vogthar-controlled dungeons have popped up around Yunnam. You're unpredictable. Hard to pin down. And since you've kept your fragment of the Doom-Forged weapon on your person, he hasn't had an opportunity to rob you yet. But if he attacks your stronghold, it will force you to go to ground. And when that happens, he plans to relieve you of the items.

"But if we play *proactively*, we can make Peng dance to our tune. You see, the Vogthar do not yet have the strength of arms to truly threaten Yunnam. I can offer you the Doom Forge Quest Chain now, which will force a confrontation between you and Peng, but it will also give you a chance to get the last piece of the weapon while throwing Thanatos's plans into chaos. Besides, *we* need to assemble all three items as well. Thanatos is going to continue his assault on the Overmind Realms until he eventually grinds us into dust. But this weapon is our chance to level the playing field. If you can get the pieces, find the Doom Forge, and get the mad godling Khalkeús to assemble the weapon, we might have a chance."

"Wow, that's a lot to unpack." I held up a hand as though to physically stop her onslaught of words. "I don't even know where to start with this. The Vogthar are planning to attack and we're just now hearing about it? And also, can we stop for a minute and talk about the *mad godling Khalkeús*? Because in my experience, mad godlings tend to be trouble."

"You know well my power is limited. I can only interfere so much."

"Do we have any other choice?" Abby asked.

"You always have a choice, Firebrand. That is why we use you Travelers as our agents. Because you can do whatever you'd like. But if you hope to defeat Thanatos, then no. I've been working with some of the other Overminds, and we have come to an accord that this is the best possible path forward and the only real way of defeating Thanatos long term, due to the nature of the Doom-Forged weapon."

"Awesome," I muttered, absently fidgeting with my napkin. "It sounds like we have choices but not any *real* options. So I guess that means we're in."

"Excellent." She beamed and clapped her hands together. "Now this is where things get tricky and why we have to hurry. The Doom Forge is buried in the heart of Stone Reach, but getting in will be a challenge because the Svartalfar are suspicious toward outsiders— at least as bad as the Murk Elves. Very few foreigners gain access to the capital. And to complicate matters further, no one knows where inside of Stone Reach the Doom Forge actually is. Lost to legend and all that."

"Wait. But you have to know," Abby said, eyes narrowing in suspicion. "You're responsible for quests. How could you not know?"

"Well, *obviously* I know," she said, exasperated, "but we Overminds have rules, Abby. When Osmark wanted to gift his supporters faction seals, he couldn't *break* the rules, so he bent them by utilizing the quest system to get them what they needed. We Overminds, for all our vaunted power, are not so different. Not even *we* can truly cheat the system. And this event in particular is nearly immutable because I didn't personally create this scenario. It is a preprogrammed world-event quest from before this world ever went live."

"Wait a minute," Abby said, raising a hand in objection. "A preprogrammed world event? Why would there be an event where the reward is a weapon capable of killing a god? Why would a quest like that even be generated?"

"Well, *kill* is a bit melodramatic. That's just semantics, however, which we can discuss after you've assembled the weapon. As to *why* it was created. Well. We Overminds foresaw that at some point there would likely be a problem within the system itself. Realizing this, we needed a way to self-regulate and fix such issues from within the game while it was operating, without crashing everything. So we—all of the Overminds working in concert—created a back door. A nuclear option of sorts, usable in the case of serious malfunction or in the event that one of us went rogue. But we couldn't well trust any single Overmind with that power, since, in theory, it was a safeguard against all of us. So, instead, we built the tool into the quest system.

"A system that requires player interaction. We also made the quest *insanely* difficult, and nearly impossible to unlock—a safeguard to ensure that some player wouldn't randomly stumble upon the ultimate weapon. I'm afraid you'll have to play on Death-Head mode. Seventy-two-hour window. No deaths. One chance to get it right. And due to the nature of the quest, Overmind interference and assistance is *strictly* limited. *But...* bending the rules is not breaking them. And, as the Overmind of Order—and subsequently generating *quests*—it does fall within my purview to give you a small hint."

She waved her hand, and a prompt appeared before me.

Quest Alert: The Doom Forge

Buried deep in the heart of Stone Reach—the ancient capital of the Svartalfar—is a forbidden temple, housing a powerful, slumbering godling, Khalkeús. This godling is a master smith, and inside the temple is a powerful shrine, known as the Doom Forge. If awakened and presented with the Doom-Forged relics, Khalkeús will create a weapon of unimaginable power, capable of slaying even a god… The temple and the Doom Forge within have been lost to legend. But rumor has it there is a secret priestly order of Dwarves, called the *Acolytes of the Shield and Hammer*, who may know something about the temple …

Quest Class: Ultra-Rare, Secret

Quest Difficulty: Death-Head

Success: Gain access to Stone Reach, find the mysterious Temple of the Doom Forge, and convince Khalkeús to reforge the Doom-Forged relics into a powerful weapon.

Failure: This is a Death-Head quest; if you die at any point before completing the objective, you automatically fail, and the quest chain will forever be closed to you! Moreover, the Doom-Forged relics will automatically be removed from your inventory and scattered back throughout Eldgard.

Reward: Doom-Forged Weapon; 75,000 XP.

Accept: Yes/No?

Sweat broke out across my forehead, and my stomach dropped a little more as I read and reread the prompt. A Death-Head quest. Another one. Death-Head quests were V.G.O.'s version of hardcore mode—even a single death and it was game over. They were ultra-rare, and the last time I'd unlocked one, I'd united the entire Storme Marsh Nation, but only after defeating an impossibly large and deadly ancient dragon. If this was on par with that, I could only imagine what kind of trouble we were in.

Despite the tight-bellied fear, however, I also felt the faintest twinge of excitement. Yeah this was going to be hard, but if I could pull this quest off, it would be a game changer. I closed my eyes, breathing deeply—inhale, exhale, inhale, exhale—then accepted and closed the screen with a thought. A constricting pressure, like an industrial-sized sheet of Saran Wrap being looped around my whole body, immediately settled over me. That would be the first of the Death-Head debuffs, slowly crushing me under its weight. Every day a new debilitating debuff would be added until I simply *died.*

I opened my eyes and quickly called up my current effects:

Current Debuffs

Death-Head Mode: You've temporarily activated Death-Head Mode! Time until the *Diseased* debuff takes effect: 23 hours 59 minutes 35 seconds.

"Perfect," Sophia said as I dismissed the box. "Now as I'm sure you read, the Acolytes of the Shield and Hammer are the key. They're a Dwarven sect, and their headquarters are in Stone Reach. But getting those dusty old fossils to tell you anything as an outsider will be next to impossible. They've been guarding the secrets of the Doom Forge for millennia. They'll never talk. But here is where I can help." She paused and smiled, radiating smug satisfaction. "Let me introduce you to Carl."

She extended a hand and miniature 3-D model appeared above her outstretched palm. A stocky man with a gnarly beard wearing what looked like a rumpled potato sack slowly rotated in the air.

"Carl is a Traveler, and he *was* an initiate with Acolytes of the Shield and Hammer. I say *was,* because poor unfortunate Carl is a *terrible* Cleric. Carl was dismissed from the order for incompetence, and now he's biding his time in this little garrison trading town outside of Stone Reach called Cliffburgh. You'll likely find him at an inn called the Smoked Pig, and he might well be your ticket into the capital. But be forewarned, chances are good that Thanatos knows about Carl as well, so it will only be a matter of time before Peng tracks him down. If I were you, I'd move quickly. And to that end, I have one final present."

A one-off port scroll appeared in her hand as the model of Carl disappeared with a flash. I accepted with a tight-lipped smile.

"A word of caution before we part." She paused, turning pensive. "I will be out of touch for a bit. Helping my sister in the Shattered Realm. If you need aid... Well, you won't have it. There is no safety net this time. You are thoroughly on your own, and if Peng succeeds, we are doomed." Her smile returned, though her eyes were distant and hazy. "Now enjoy the rest of your meal and good luck." She shot us a wink, and just like that, she was gone. Time resumed its normal flow, the chair Sophia had been sitting in was gone, and the waitress was back to her normal self, check in hand.

While Abby paid, I shot off a message to Cutter, Amara, Forge, and Ari, telling them to meet us at the Yunnam training ground. Then we scrambled out of Frank's like the devil was hot on our heels.

EIGHT

CLIFFBURGH

My world teetered and spun as I stepped through a shimmering opalescent portal and onto a wide cobblestone square in front of a looming marble archway. Beyond lay the Dwarven trading town of Cliffburgh. An enormous stone Dwarf, wielding an oversized battle-axe, perched at the top of the arch, staring down at passersby with hard, judgmental eyes. A stone wall, eight feet high, snaked away from the entryway in both directions, but it was a wall more for show than actual defense.

One concentrated push from someone serious about taking the town would overwhelm their defenses in a matter of moments.

I scooted over to one side, making sure I wasn't in the way of anyone else coming through, then hunched over, hands planted on my knees as I waited for the traveling sickness to pass. The one-off port scrolls were the smoothest way to get around, but even they kicked like a mule to the teeth. As the wooziness finally dissipated, I righted myself and took a quick scan of the countryside around me. Mostly rolling foothills covered in sparse, yellowing grass—occasionally dotted with thin patches of white from the last snowfall—and pockets of evergreens. Exactly like what I expected to find in a barren northern land run by grouchy Dwarves.

The most spectacular sight, however, was the enormous mountain far beyond the city, reaching toward the sky like shard of gleaming white bone. That had to be the legendary mountain, *Svartalfheim,* which housed the Dwarven capital, Stone Reach. The peak was at least a hundred miles away, and it still blocked out a big chunk of the horizon.

"Holy crap," Abby said, stepping out from the portal beside me. She hardly looked like herself at all. She'd ditched her normal bright red sorcerer's dress, Wildfire, in exchange for a plain brown sack. Ugly as sin, but also a great disguise. I'd likewise stowed my best gear in my inventory—warhammer included—trading it for some drab leathers and unremarkable gear. Being foreigners would draw enough attention all on its own, and we didn't want anyone poking into our business more than absolutely necessary.

"That's one big-ass mountain," she said after a moment, hands planted on hips, gaze trained on the skyline.

"Right?" I replied. The jagged peaks surrounding Rowanheath were impressive, but they didn't hold a candle to Svartalfheim. This was clearly the Everest of Eldgard: snowy, domineering, and impossibly tall.

The others stumbled out behind us, each staggering on uncertain feet for a beat.

Like Abby, they were barely recognizable since they'd also stashed their noteworthy gear, opting for low-level items that wouldn't stand out in a crowd of one. The portal snapped shut with an audible *pop*, and just like that we were stranded in the snowy reaches of the far north. I shivered as the chill of the northern air settled over me like a wet blanket. Back in Rowanheath the sharp bite of early fall was starting to invade the days, but it felt like full-on winter had long since moved in around these parts.

"It is so cold," Amara said, rubbing her arms frantically, trying to keep her teeth from chattering. "Even worse than Glome Corrie."

Winter *never* visited the Storme Marshes, so I could only imagine what this was like for her.

"I'm sure we could find a warm blanket to wrap you up in," Cutter offered with a patronizing grin. "Maybe a mug of that Western Brew or some hot apple cider. Then you can go snuggle up by a fire, my delicate little flower."

Her glower was sharp enough to cut diamonds. "I am no flower," she growled, promptly dropping her hands to her sides while suppressing her obvious urge to shiver. "And if I were a flower it would be the Corpse Bloom of the Deep Swamp that eats unwary, loudmouthed fools. But again. Not. A. Flower. I was merely noting the difference."

Cutter cackled like a loon.

"No, Amara's right, it is cold," Abby offered, folding her arms across her chest. "We should get moving and find the Smoked Pig before I freeze to death." Considering Abby was a Firebrand, it was possible the cold also affected her more than it might others.

We made our way toward the gate. "Remember, everyone," I said over one shoulder, "low profile. Chances are Peng is around here somewhere or will be shortly, so we don't want him to know we're here. Not if we can help it. Keep your Anonymous buff on whenever we're out and about." Thanks to our faction ability *Dignitary*, everyone could cast Anonymous, allowing us to pass unnoticed even in hostile faction territory while temporarily hiding our player tags from inquiring eyes. Since the Dwarves leaned neutral, we'd be fine so long as we didn't stir the pot too much. "And Ari, stay out of sight, yeah?"

"Yeah, yeah," came the Pixy's sugary voice, though she was nowhere to be seen. Pixies were masters of illusion magic, and she could stay out of view almost indefinitely if she needed to. "Though I feel more than a little insulted. My people are proud folk. We don't much approve of being forced into the shadows, Grim Jack."

"Sorry," I replied with a shrug. "But a Pixy from the Realm of Order is super noteworthy no matter where you go. Might as well walk around holding up a sign saying, 'Crimson Alliance, please attack us.'"

"Oh, it makes sense," she shot back, "but that in no way lessens the insult. Don't worry, though, we Pixies have *long* memories and a wicked sense of humor. I'll find a way to make us even. Eventually." I could hear the mischievous smile in her voice.

When we got to the arch, I expected to have to do a little quick talking to get past the guards... Except there were no guards, which came as something of a mild shock. Why have the walls at all if they didn't even bother with guards at the entrance? I shrugged and kept right on trekking.

We'd only made it another handful of feet, however, when I caught the ring of steel on steel, voices raised, and the sounds of battle.

"Ah, yes. That sounds about bloody right," Cutter remarked, drawing his twin daggers.

Forge grinned, pulling the enormous axe from his back. The rest of his armor might've been plain as cardboard, but that axe burned with magic like a million-watt bulb. "Sounds like some fun for the baddest sumabitch in Bell County."

"Low profile," I whispered as we rounded a corner. "Low profile!"

"Not our first rodeo, Jack," Forge said, taking point and picking up the pace.

Straight ahead was a scene of shocking chaos. A town square with a small fountain at its center. A statue of a portly Dwarven woman stood at the center of the fountain, a hammer raised to the sky with one hand, while a flagon of mead was clutched in the other. Frothy water burbled out of the maiden's cup, filling the pool below. Uniformed Dwarven guards filled the square, their gold-and-black tabards emblazoned with a mountain and an anvil, marking them out. And smashing against them like a battering ram were several platoons of Vogthar.

The Dwarves fought in squads of five, mostly wielding axes or long-handled halberds, though several carried an enormous shield on *each* arm—the tankiest tanks I'd ever seen. Chainmail-clad priests chanted from behind. The courtyard was hemmed in by two-story stone buildings with slate-tiled roofs capped by intricately carved gables. All vaguely Viking-inspired. Poking out of the windows were Dwarven archers carrying heavy crossbows with elaborate cranks. A few even had repeaters to rival Osmark's tech.

The city guards looked neat, orderly, well trained, and professional. These men and women knew their business and knew it well, but the Vogthar had come loaded for bear.

True, most of the horde were the standard gray-skinned foot troops, but there was also a double fistful of pale blue invaders—probably spawned from a dungeon with a Frost alignment—a full squad of heavy-armored [Eloyte Knights], a pair of robe-clad casters, and a handful of hulking wolflike [Vogthar Frost Hounds]. The hounds were nearly the size of a lion but built from hard-packed snow and studded with chunks of razor-sharp blue ice. The Frost Hounds weren't common in the south, but I'd run across them a couple times while preparing for the invasion of Glome Corrie, and they were absolutely awful to tangle with. Dealt out debuffs like they were going out of style.

Bodies lay scattered across the ground—Dwarves and Vogthar alike—but it was clear the Vogthar were capturing ground and would soon overtake the pocket of resistance.

Unless, of course, some intrepid adventurers came along and evened the odds.

Forge turned, glancing at me over one heavy pauldron. "We kicking ass and taking names or what, hoss?"

I sighed and threw my hands up into the air. "So much for low profile. Total pipe dream anyway." I nodded. "Yeah, do your thing. But no familiars, nothing that might give us away if you can help it."

"Hells yeah!" Forge barked with a grin. "Time to get some. You ready for this, pint-sized?"

"Let's rage," Ari growled in reply, sounding excited at the prospect, though still cloaked from view with her powerful spells.

Heavy footfalls pounded the air as Forge charged, issuing a ferocious war cry just before slamming into the back ranks of the Vogthar troops. His axe screamed as he hacked through leather armor, severing a lanky pale arm with a single blow. One of the Vogthar mages wheeled around, a chant exploding from its lipless mouth as it thrust a gaunt, claw-tipped hand forward. Despite the thick cobblestones lining the square, skeletal hands erupted from the ground, closing around one of Forge's ankles like a clamp. Another shot up, latching onto his other ankle.

The second priest barked out an order in some unknown tongue—the consonants harsh, the vowels guttural and hard on the ears. The Vogthar force split at once; one group, composed of the more common foot soldiers, continued their assault against the guards, while the other group spun and beelined toward us. The first mage raised its hands high, fingers flickering through a complex series of movements as fog bellowed out from its palms. That fog quickly spread like the plague, filling the town square with churning silver. The chant took on a new cadence, rising in intensity and fervor as shapes formed in the mist—an arm here, a glimpse of a gleaming skull there.

Definitely some sort of summoner or Warlock. Probably the Vogthar equivalent of a Necromancer or Spirit-Caller.

"Heads down, eyes shut!" Abby yelled, thrusting her staff straight up into the air, the fat ruby on top flaring with brilliant life. I followed her order without hesitation, curling my head into my chest and closing my eyes. A moment later, terrible heat washed over me, carried by a blazing hot wind; even through my eyelids I could see the brilliant flash of orange-and-gold light, as bright as the noonday sun. When I blinked my eyes open a few seconds later, whatever attack she had unleashed was gone, and so was the silver fog—burned away in a single wave of heat and fire.

Her Raging Inferno Blast if I had to guess.

She'd cut the Warlock's spell off before it could take shape, but unfortunately, the heavily armored Eloyte Knights and the formidable Frost Hounds had closed on us with lightning speed.

Several converged on Forge, who was still pinned down by the skeletal hands gripping his ankles. The tank roared in defiance and lashed out with his axe. The weapon blazed red as it turned away striking blades and clattered on night-dark shields. Forge was a heavy hitter, but surprisingly, the armored Vogthar didn't fold like a bad hand of cards. They fought on completely undeterred, their thick armor and even thicker shields deflecting his most devastating blows.

Ari appeared with a flash of neon-pink light as she darted into the fray. She had a miniature bow strapped to her back, a quiver of blue-crystal arrows hanging at one hip, and a wicked sword in her hand that looked one part pirate scimitar, one part toothpick. The fierce little Pixy struck like a surgeon, hacking at vulnerable eyes and chopping at exposed necks. She was a whirlwind of colorful death. Bright and flashy as an underground rave.

Apparently, she too needed a reminder of the definition of *low profile*.

I tore my eyes away from the fighting and pulled free a scythe-bladed khopesh—somewhere between a short sword and a normal dagger. *Lawbreaker's Edge.* I'd picked it up in the Realm of Order while tangling with a bunch of underwater Merfolk called the Ningyo. As a *Maa-Tál* Shadowmancer, I had a ton of cool class advantages, but using edged weapons wasn't one of them. But Lawbreaker's Edge ignored class restrictions, and though it didn't deal nearly the damage my warhammer did, it *might* throw off any inquisitive onlookers. My warhammer was easily one of the most recognizable weapons in the game.

I thrust out my left hand and unleashed an Umbra Bolt into the face of a blue-skinned Vogthar, blasting away a chunk of rotten meat and a chunk of HP. Another bolt hit the creature square in the belly, and this time its glossy-black eyes went hazy, unfocused. At level 5, not only did Umbra Bolt dish out 225% spell strength—for a devastating 513 points of Shadow damage—but additionally, it had a 20% chance of confusing enemies, causing them to randomly attack other hostile forces.

The confused Vogthar wheeled around and threw itself at one of its companions, driving an ebony axe into the side of an unprotected Vogthar skull. *Critical Hit!*

Elsewhere, Cutter appeared in a puff of smoke and drove a blade into a Frost Hound's neck, dropping the creature though not killing it.

"Jack," Abby hollered, conjuring a halo of light around herself. "I'll take out the regular Vogthar and the hounds—you focus on the knights. Them and the casters."

Without waiting for an answer, she stormed forward, wreathed in fire, spewing a steady stream of liquid gold from one hand while she clutched her staff in the other.

Everywhere that beam of molten light touched flesh bubbled and smoldered, inky wisps of foul-smelling smoke drifting upward. Her supernatural flame sheared through HP like a hot knife, which made total sense. Aside from Holy damage, what would hurt ice-based Vogthar more than generous heaps of preternatural fire?

I triggered Night Armor, surrounding myself with a second skin of shadow power, then cast Shadow Forge and one of my new Champion of Order abilities, Scales of Harmony, which gave me and my team a passive advantage when fighting against any creatures that strayed from the path of neutrality. We all got a bonus when duking it out against creatures with a Dark or Light alignment, and an even heftier attack bonus against creatures of a Holy or Evil nature like the Vogthar. It also allowed me to level up my Champion of Order skills with every kill.

Casting my array of passive spells took less than a heartbeat, but a heartbeat was a long time in the heat of battle.

An obsidian two-handed longsword flashed through the air, ready to cleave me in two, but the knight wielding the blade was glacier slow. I sidestepped the attack, twirled my sickle-bladed khopesh in a vicious arc, and slammed the weapon into the knight's unprotected skull as I triggered Champion Strike and Black Caress, siphoning off a portion of the knight's Health. Despite the fact that I was using a bladed weapon, the creature's head exploded like an overripe melon from the sheer force of the strike, chunks of bone and splashes of gore spraying out as the corpse dropped.

I didn't have time to dwell on the carnage, though. I was already moving on to the next opponent. I slashed and hacked my way through two more blue-skinned Vogthar, then turned my blade on a knight with its back to me, quickly removing one leg below the knee, before finishing the creature with a brilliant javelin of Umbra Flame at point-blank range.

I spun, briefly considered unleashing Night Cyclone, which would make short work of most of these attackers, then dismissed the idea. Unleashing a giant shadow cyclone was the next best thing to conjuring Devil in the middle of the plaza, and that simply wouldn't do. There were less than a handful of Shadowmancers who had reached a high-enough level to use an attack like that, which meant it would be a red flag to anyone watching. Besides, we didn't need it. Between the Dwarven guards on one side and us on the other, the Vogthar were on their last legs.

Off to my right, Cutter darted forward, decapitating a Vogthar shock troop in twilight-gray leathers while Amara slashed and jabbed with a conjured spear. Dead ahead, Abby charbroiled a Frost Hound, leaving nothing but ash in her wake. The skeletal hands spell had finally dissipated, and Forge and Ari were now going toe to toe with the last of the knights and the Vogthar spellcasters, who were surrounded by eerie green light. Everything else was well in hand, but those spellcasters could still cause us trouble unless I put them down. Hard.

I grinned, thrust Lawbreaker's Edge forward, and called forth Umbra Bog. A patch of cobblestone, thirty feet in diameter, gave way to a bog of inky black tendrils. Curling fingers of shadow writhed in an instant, wrapping around legs and arms, temporarily rooting the last of the knights and the casters in place. Giving Forge and Ari an instant leg up. The Pixy unleashed a blast of prismatic light while Forge charged, shouldering one of the knights in the teeth, then swinging for the fences with his axe.

While the mages struggled to free themselves from the clinging tentacles of shadow, I slipped into the Shadowverse with a thought and an effort of will. The world screeched to a crawl, color fading. I took a few deep breaths, relishing the momentary break in the conflict, and surveyed the field.

The Dwarven guards had finished off the last of the regular Vogthar foot soldiers and were advancing on the remaining knights while their ranged support rained down precise arrow fire from above. Cutter and Amara were working in tandem, fighting back-to-back, while Abby was frozen mid-stride, her staff thrust straight out, a bud of flame blooming on the end. She'd burned the Frost Hounds out of existence—none remained—and the blue-skinned Vogthar were likewise gone.

The Eloyte Knights had been decimated, and Forge was seconds away from burying his axe in the neck of one of the two spellcasters.

The other spellcaster, however, had managed to slip away from the heat of the battle and was casting what looked like an AoE spell. Its face was frozen in a snarl, a chant clearly on its lips, a ball of noxious jade energy forming between empty palms. Yep. That was gonna be a hard no. I slipped up behind the spell-slinger, raised my khopesh, activated Stealth, then stepped back from the Shadowverse. Color exploded into the world, accompanied by the sounds of battle and the guttural chanting from the unholy caster in front of me.

I triggered my Champion's Strike ability as the blow landed.

Critical Hit! The spellcaster's head tumbled away, thudding to the ground with a wet splat as its HP bar hit zero in an instant. The green energy in its hands fizzled harmlessly; its knees buckled and down it went, dead in a heap of limbs and glowing green fluid.

I wheeled left, searching for new enemies, but the square was quiet, the last of invading Vogthar dead.

Viridian Gate Online: Doom Forge

NINE

GOOD DEEPS

"WELL DINNAE JUST STAND THERE!" ONE OF the guards barked, his words coated with a thick Scottish burr. He broke from the line of defenders, heavy boots tromping on the cobblestones as he moved. He was short, well under five feet, and built like a brick shithouse. All muscle and scars and beard. His hair was fiery red, his complexion ruddy, his eyes were like little chips of coal, and faded crisscrossing scars seemed to cover every bit of exposed skin. He wore the same tabard as the rest of the guards, but his uniform had an extra patch sewn onto the chest, likely marking him out as some sort of squad leader or commander.

"We got wounded now, dinnae we?" he said, glancing at the downed Dwarves moaning around the courtyard. "So, start triage, ya bloody eejits." He threw heavy, scar-covered hands into the air as though shooing a bunch of irksome pigeons. "Priests, get busy. These men are na gonna heal themselves. Archers," he bellowed, glancing at the men still loitering in the buildings edging the square. "Ah wanna cordon set up—

103

keep the looky-loos back, eh? Everybody else, loot these corpses.

"As fer ya lot"—he rounded on us, eyes narrowing, mouth turning into a scowl—"stay right where ya bloody are, eh? Ah'd have words with ya." The remaining guards broke into action as the disgruntled and clearly suspicious Dwarf marched across the impromptu battlefield, giving the Clerics and Priests a wide berth, though stepping carelessly on the dead Vogthar. "I'm Raginolf, captain of the Cliffburgh Guard." His gaze landed on me like a hammer blow, flicking from the khopesh to my dusky, Murk Elf complexion. Definitely suspicious.

I braced myself for the ass-chewing of the century. I'd spent plenty of time around staff NCOs in the Marine Corps, and I knew a pissed-off enlisted man when I saw one.

Instead, Raginolf surprised me by extending a gnarled hand with stubby, sausage fingers. "Well met, and thank ya fer the help."

Uncertain, I took his proffered hand and pumped it several times. It was like shaking hands with a bear. "Eh, just glad we were here in time to help out. We haven't been this far north before. Is that sort of thing common up here?"

He dropped my hand and glanced over one shoulder at the bodies strewn around the square. He turned back to us, faint worry etched into the lines of his face. "Nae." He folded his blocky arms across his barrel chest. "The raids have been gettin' worse fer the past month or so. Once, mibay twice a week, usually at night. This though. Nae. Havnae seen the like before. Ya said ya havnae been this far north before—where do ya hail from then? What brings ya all the way tae this frozen bit of land?

Merchants, maybe? Cliffburgh isna exactly a tourist attraction, especially na fer Travelers."

"A small social quest," Cutter said with a dismissive wave, words sweet as honey as he glided forward. He patted me on the shoulder, *allow me,* as a blindingly bright grin spread across his face. The guard seemed friendly enough, but his questions were probing. Cautious, without seeming overtly hostile. As nice as he was, he wasn't sure we were on the level. We really didn't want people poking into our business, and with Honeyed Words, Cutter could disarm the man far better than I ever could. Hell, Cutter was confidence incarnate.

And as he often said, confidence opened doors no key ever could.

"We're running messages for a Southern lordling. It's good luck indeed that we happened to arrive, though," Cutter continued. "Unfortunately, friend, our business is a wee bit time sensitive. But I'm thinkin' a man like you might be able to give us a hand." With a flick of his fingers he pulled a fat golden coin from thin air. "We're looking for an inn. A place called the Smoked Pig."

The guard grunted, still looking suspicious, but less so. He took the coin, but instead of pocketing it, he shoved it right back into Cutter's other hand. "Keep yer money, lad. Ah dinnae know how they do it in the South, but around here, guards will help a law-abidin' citizen free ah charge. Now, as fer your Smoked Pig. Aye, Ah know of it. Down in the armpit of the Low Quarter. Cannae imagine what business a Southern lordlin' would have in a place such as that, but..."

He paused and shrugged meat-slab shoulders. "Who can bloody understand the mind of nobles, eh? Normally, Ah wouldnae let you lot in, nae without a fair reason in dark days like these, but on account ah what you done fer us here, well, Ah'll give ya a pass. But, fair warnin'." He paused, spearing each of us in turn with a ferocious glare. "Keep yer heads low, eh? A bit ah goodwill only goes so far in the north. Ah wouldnae forget that if Ah were in yer boots." He tapped a gnarled nose like a tree root with one fat finger. "Especially nea in a place like the Smoked Pig."

As he finished talking a pair of notices popped up, one right after another.

Secret Quest Update: Assist the Guards

You have saved the Cliffburgh Guards from an advanced Vogthar incursion and won over the Captain of the Guard, Raginolf Rugar. Your relationship with Cliffburgh Guards has increased from *Unfriendly* to *Neutral*. Your personal relationship with Raginolf has increased from *Neutral* to *Friendly*. He may be inclined to turn a blind eye to minor indiscretions, but don't push his kindness too far—it is hard won and not easily regained!

Map Update

Congratulations! Your in-world map has been updated with a new location: *The Smoked Pig.*

I waved away the notifications.

Raginolf's back was already to me as he moved toward the bodies, which his men were busy picking over. The gamer inside me bucked at the idea that they should get to loot the corpses since we'd done most of the heavy lifting, but the truth was, Vogthar—even advanced ones such as these—rarely had items worth taking. And besides, it wasn't exactly like the Alliance was hard up for items or money. Maybe we didn't have the resources that Osmark and the Legion had at their disposal, but we were still doing just fine.

"Come on," I said, waving the rest of the crew onward.

Everyone circled around me as we left the town square behind, heading along a narrow side street flanked by more of the Viking-esque buildings that seemed so popular here. Private residences from the look of them. The street, cast in early afternoon shadow, was empty, and the homes to either side had the wooden shutters closed tight against the cold of the day. Most of the places had stone chimneys jutting from their slate-tiled roofs, spewing fragrant gray smoke into the overcast sky.

"What are the chances that those things are connected to Peng?" Abby asked once we were firmly out of earshot of the guards. "Normal incursions I get, but that back there?" She hooked a thumb toward the square. "That wasn't normal. Not even close. I've only seen knights come out on a handful of occasions, and those Frost Hounds? They almost never leave their dungeons."

"Might be a bit of sleight of hand," Cutter offered. "A distraction if you will. Me? Well, I know a thing or two about getting past city gate guards. And truth be told, it's trickier than it bloody looks. Gate guards have an unnatural affinity to detect Stealth—especially if they're on high alert. And I've never yet met a Dwarven guard that wasn't on high alert. Right dour bunch of bastards. Maybe Peng and his crew are all masters of Stealth, but I bloody well doubt it. Which means the best way in is a fat bribe and a honeyed word. But, problem is, not even the seediest guard is gonna take a bribe from a someone like Peng. No one likes Darklings."

"So," Amara said, picking up his line of thought. "Peng brings up a raiding force. They attack, distracting the guards long enough for Peng and his men to slip through."

"That's what I'd do," Cutter said, rubbing at his chin. "Sometimes the easiest way is the best, and it doesn't get much easier than the ol' bait and switch."

"Sounds to me like we'd better hurry our diddy-boppin' asses along then," Forge grunted, picking up his pace. "If those yahoos are from Peng, then he's already here, which means he knows about Carl and has a head start on us."

We fell silent as we hurried along, following our updated maps.

A light dusting of snow covered the shadier lanes and alleys, but most of the broader streets were clear. And not just of snow, but of dirt, trash, and all the other things that seemed to pile up in any urban sprawl. Not here, though. This was without a doubt the cleanest city I'd ever been to. The buildings, while rather plain, were also extremely well maintained. Everything was freshly painted, every roof shingle was where it belonged, and the wooden doors and edging were all new.

Though Cliffburgh certainly wasn't near the size of Rowanheath, or even Yunnam for that matter, it was no flyspeck town. This was a trading hub, and it showed everywhere we looked. Though there were plenty of residential homes, most of the buildings were dedicated to craft and trade. There were inns—clearly meant to house the traveling merchants—tailors and seamstresses, alchemists and apothecaries, and a small *legion* of blacksmiths, which wasn't surprising, considering the Dwarves were known as the best smiths in Eldgard.

There were no outdoor markets, a staple in the Southern cities, no doubt due to the frigid temperatures.

Interestingly, I noted that all of the shops had a ranking of some sort, prominently displayed either on the door or the window.

Signs like *1st Ranked Manticore-Class Blacksmith, 7th Ranked Centaur-Class Fletcher,* and *13th Ranked Warg-Class Baker.* It seemed that commerce was the heart of this city, and everyone wanted potential clients to know *exactly* where they stood in the hierarchy of other merchants and tradesmen. I'd only spent a handful of days up this way, and my dealings with the Dwarves were minimal at best, so I didn't properly understand the hierarchy, but clearly they put *a lot* of stock in it.

Eventually, we left behind the quaint residential sections and the thriving businesses—which were slammed with vendors, travelers, and merchants from just about everywhere—and entered a section of the city that more or less made up for the beauty everywhere else. We exited through a small, guarded side gate, which let out into the Low Quarter, which was outside the protection of the city walls entirely. An overflow where the dregs of the Cliffburgh had washed up. It seemed that all of the garbage from the rest of the city had been taken here and unceremoniously dumped. The buildings were equal parts wood and stone, and they looked like they'd been built by someone who'd heard of houses but had never actually seen one.

The whole place was one giant fire hazard, or at least it would've been if not for the snow and muck positively everywhere. Snowdrifts sat in corners, dark brown from dirt and mud. Chimneys dotted the skyline, these spewing rancid black clouds straight up. If I were a gambling man, I'd have bet that everyone in the Low Quarter was burning old tires. I mean, I knew that wasn't true because tires didn't exist here, but based on smell alone, I couldn't imagine what else it would be. The streets weren't paved, just giant sucking mud pits broken by deep wheel ruts and ankle-deep footprints.

Sophia always sent us to the classiest places. I'd have to thank her profusely when I saw her next.

We wound our way through the trench-like warren of alleys, streets, and cut-throughs, following our map unwaveringly until we finally found our destination. *The Smoked Pig*. The name was stenciled on a sign in blocky letters, and beneath that was a line which gave me pause. *Smoke House and Tavern*.

The trek had taken us nearly an hour, and the sun was already starting to make a run at the western horizon. Orange, golds, and faint pinks filled the sky. I folded my arms across my chest as I studied the building in the fading light of the day.

A two-story place of chipped wood and rusting metal with a long wooden patio wrapping around the front. Honestly, seeing it was… confusing. The rest of Cliffburgh—even the dirty, ragtag sections of town—

looked like they'd been transported out of a Scandinavian historical tour. This place, though? Well, it could've passed on the set of Tombstone. Even had batwing doors, which were *wildly* impractical, given both the temperature and the climate. If I didn't know any better, I'd say I was looking at an Old West saloon.

This was also the first inn or shop that failed to have a rating displayed. Not a good sign.

"Who in the nine bloody hells would build a place like that, eh?" Cutter asked, disgust coating the words. "I mean I'm all for dirty, disgusting inns—practically in my blood—but even I have standards."

Forge, on the other hand, had a huge grin stretching from ear to ear. "Well, all right!" he boomed, clapping his hands together, practically bouncing on his toes. "Now this here's a place I can get on board with. I mean, sure, looks more crooked than a barrel of fishhooks, but those are the best places to have a good time." He paused, cocking his head to the side. "I'll bet you a gold mark a Traveler built this place. Probably a Texan, too. Someone from south of the Mason-Dixon line for sure. Only a good ol' Southern boy—who's also dumber than a box of rocks—would put batwing doors on a tavern in the ass-end of the arctic."

"I'll take that action," Cutter said, flashing a gold piece before disappearing it back into his sleeve with a practiced flourish.

"Well," I said, shouldering my way past both of them. "We won't know standing around out here. Let's go see if we can find our failed Dwarf acolyte."

We tromped through the mud and slush and up onto the wraparound deck out front, scraping our boots on the wobbly planks.

I paused, glancing left and right. All clear. "Ari," I hissed.

There was a flash of movement—just a subtle distortion in the air, nearly invisible before she appeared, fluttering just a few feet away from Forge. "Here, Grim Jack."

"Good. Look, I need you to find someplace to hide. You see trouble coming, I want to know about it before it smacks us in the face. Out of sight, though, yeah?"

She took a deep breath, her color flashing a pale blue. "You know it. No one will see me. Not a soul." She lifted a tiny hand, fingers twirling. A shimmer of rainbow light drifted from her fingertips, swirling around her in a cloud as she vanished once more. "I'm like a ghost."

Forge—being both our tank and a proper Texan—led the way, pushing through the batwing doors with supreme confidence. I followed hard on his heels. Noise washed over me like a wave. The twang of a slide guitar, the warble of a woman singing a down-and-out country tune, the clink of glasses, the harsh barking laughter of drunks. The scent of grilled meat and tangy-sweet sauce. Barbeque.

The inside was *exactly* what I'd expected from the outside.

Dark brown hay, heavily stained with copious amounts of dried mud, covered the floor. Weathered boards peeked through here and there. On one side of the room were circular tables perfect for cards and gambling mixed with rectangular rough-hewn tables edged by benches full of drunk patrons busy chowing down. The other side of the room was clear of furniture, the straw pushed back, forming a crude dance floor. More drunk patrons, men and women both, square-danced across the open space as they hooted and hollered in time with the thump of music.

The entertainment occupied a raised platform on the left side of the room, bordering the dance floor. A short-haired Wode man sat on a three-legged stool, working furiously on a handmade slide guitar while a golden-skinned Dawn Elf woman crooned beside him. Her clothes were custom. Clearly. She wore *incredibly* short shorts, the fabric dyed to have a bluish tint so it looked almost like denim. Her shirt was a plaid button-up, tied in a knot in the middle, showcasing a healthy amount of stomach and more than a little cleavage. Her hair fell in a cascade of golden curls and bounced as she swayed with the music.

It was only a matter of time until the real world started to creep in around the edges. I reminded myself that most of the people who'd made the jump to V.G.O. weren't fantasy nerds or gamers—they were regular folks, just hoping to survive and avoid a mass grave. They'd be looking to make this new life as normal as they could. As familiar as they could. Which included line dancing, denim, and barbeque.

 Despite the bad neighborhood and the dodgy exterior, the place actually seemed pretty nice. Fun. The atmosphere was warm, happy, welcoming. People played cards with their friends—coins clicking as they were shuffled back and forth across tabletops—others drank and joked and danced. The epitome of *never judge a book by its cover*. I found myself smiling, foot tapping, thinking about inviting Abby out onto the dance floor for a twirl. The smile slipped as I thought of the people all across Eldgard dying—*actually dying*—in a seemingly unwinnable war against the Vogthar.

There would be a time for dancing and celebrating one day, but today wasn't it. Especially not with the Death-Head quest looming over me like a headsman's axe waiting to drop.

TEN

THE DRUNKEN ACOLYTE

I SCANNED THE ROOM, SEARCHING FOR SOPHIA'S lead: Carl, the Dwarf and failed acolyte.

It was surprisingly easy to find him. He was literally the *only* Dwarf in the entire place. Everyone here was a foreigner of one type or another—mostly Travelers, based on the accents filling the air. A bunch of winged Accipiters and golden Dawn Elves, quite a few Wodes, a handful of Imperials, and a spattering of green-skinned Risi. No Murk Elves, which highlighted both Amara and myself, and only the lone Dwarf. Apparently, the Smoked Pig wasn't the kind of place any self-respecting Dwarf willingly came.

Our guy, Carl, didn't seem like the self-respecting type.

In a society where rank and standing seemed especially important—integral even—a washed-out Cleric had to be at just about the bottom of the barrel.

He was propped up on a barstool near the back of the room, leaning against the polished hardwood bar.

"Jack," Cutter said, drawing in close to me. "Gotta slip away for a moment." He jabbed a finger toward a cowl-wearing Wode nursing a drink in the corner. "Thieves business. Should've bloody well expected to find a Union rep in a place like this," he muttered. "But I'll be around if you need me." He clapped me on the shoulder and slipped off through the crowd. The Thief in the corner watched Cutter with hungry, predatory eyes. Weighing, measuring, calculating.

That could be trouble. I shook my head and pursed my lips. Or maybe I was just being paranoid. Not everyone was out to get us.

Just *almost* everyone.

Still, Amara shot me a glance and a quick nod, then followed after him like a shadow. I wasn't the only one plagued by worry.

The rest of us weaved past the dancers and the tables, dodging the occasional server ferrying platters of ale and succulent meat—ribs, brisket, even pulled pork piled high on small rolls—as we made for the bar. Forge marched right up, plopping down on a stool at the far end of the bar, away from the Dwarf, then flagged down the bartender. The bartender in question was a brown-haired Wode sporting a close approximation of a ten-gallon cowboy hat and a passable flannel shirt. If that was the owner of the Smoked Pig, then Cutter was about to lose a bet, because that was *easily* the most Texas Texan I'd ever seen.

Hell, on the wall behind the bar was a Texas flag, its lone star proud and bold on a field of blue.

Abby took a seat to the left of the Dwarf, while I took a stool to his right.

Carl was stocky and broad-shouldered like most of the Dwarves we'd seen so far and wore faded priest robes, light brown, edged in gold, and tremendously dirty. He had an empty mug in front of him and was staring morosely into the bottom of his cup as though it might hold all of life's answers. The guy was bleary-eyed, absolutely *reeked* of stale alcohol and old BO—that *Unwashed* debuff at work—and was quite clearly drunk. He ignored Abby and me completely, as though he were alone in the world and aimed to keep it that way.

"Hey there," I said, offering the man a friendly smile. "You Carl?"

He blinked sporadically a couple of times, swaying slightly as he faced me.

"What's that now," he slurred. "You say you're lookin' for..." He faltered. Belched, long and loud. "Carl?" he finished belatedly.

"Yep. Carl, former Acolyte of the Shield and Hammer."

"The one and only," he said, dropping his head in an off-kilter bow. His voice was warm, friendly, a hint of a Philadelphia accent coating his words. He straightened and took another forlorn glance at his empty mug. "Can't imagine what you want with me, though." Not a question, but a statement of fact. He smacked his lips and slumped forward, resting his forearms against the wooden bar.

"Well, to start, we were hoping to ask you a few questions. Wanted to find out a bit more about your order."

With a sniff he lifted his head and regarded me, eyes squinted, forehead wrinkled. "That so, huh? Well." He scratched at his heavily bearded chin, the cogs in his head turning. "Not really supposed to talk about that but..." He shrugged. "But hey, what the hell. They already booted me out. What more can they do to me, you know?" He looked from me to his mug, me to his mug. "Look, bro, you keep my glass full and you can ask as many questions as you want before I pass out on the floor. How's that sound?"

I caught Abby's eye. She nodded emphatically.

"Okay. Fair enough," I replied, sticking a hand into the air, flagging down a Dawn Elf server who was assisting the Wode in the makeshift cowboy hat. She was busy mixing drinks, but nodded in acknowledgement. She finished her current drink order, deposited several mugs on the counter—all quickly whisked away by a floor server—then moseyed over to us. She offered me a warm smile and a wink.

"Welcome, folks." She glanced between me and Abby. "Together?"

"Yep," Abby said.

"Well it's damn good to have y'all. I'm Tammy. Haven't seen you two in here before. What brings you to the Smoked Pig?" Her eyes lingered on the rune-encrusted sickle-sword at my belt. "We don't usually get a lot of adventuring types in here. Mostly just merchants and drunks, like our Carl here."

The Dwarf half-heartedly flipped her the bird.

Tammy rolled her eyes. "You know we love you, Carl."

"We're merchants," Abby replied smoothly. "Well, I am. The rest of the party are hired hands. Guards and mercenaries. But we're in town and heard this was the only place in Eldgard with real barbeque." She paused, eyes closed, and lifted her nose, taking a long deep whiff. "Looks like they weren't lying. Which means it's time to celebrate. I've been jonesing for a platter of ribs and an honest drink since before…" She trailed off. "Well, you know."

The woman's easy smile slipped. The unsaid words hung in the air between us. *Since before the world died.*

"Sorry," Abby said, with a shake of her head. "Didn't mean to be a buzzkill." She reached into a pouch at her belt and withdrew coins. Gold glinted, and I could see greedy hunger blaze in Tammy's eyes. "Anyway. Let's get some ribs and ale for me, him"—she waved at me— "and my big green friend down at the end. And, because I'm in a good mood and feeling generous, let's add on whatever Carl is drinking." She plinked the coins down onto the bar top. "Just keep his glass full, if you would."

The woman scooped up the coins and disappeared them as quick and efficiently as Cutter ever could. Abby had just laid down five gold Imperial marks, the equivalent to five hundred US dollars, which would buy a lot of ribs and a lot of ale. "You want your usual, hon?" she asked the stumpy Dwarf.

"Honeyed Mead," he slurred, giving her a toothy grin. "As much as you have."

"And what would you two like to drink? Our Honeyed Mead is the best in town, hands down. We call it Apple Pie, 'cause I'll be damned if it doesn't taste just like Grandma's apple pie in a glass. But we also brew up a mean hard apple cider, and Chuck"—she gestured toward the man in the cowboy hat—"is working on a good draft beer. The flavor on this batch ain't quite right, but it's close enough to Bud Light that you won't really know the difference." She leaned forward, glancing left and right. "We also have a test batch of IPA. It's a limited run, but I could get you some for a bit more coin. Though, fair warning, it kicks like a horse, and it's too sour by half. Still the best IPA in Eldgard."

"Only IPA in Eldgard," Carl muttered, "and it tastes like dirty bathwater. Trust me, you don't want it."

"Thanks," Abby said. "I think I'll just take a draft beer with my ribs. Jack, what'll you have?"

"Whatever Carl's drinking is fine by me."

"Good enough," Tammy said, rapping the counter with her knuckles. "Give me just a moment." She shuffled off and returned in short order with our drinks. "Food'll be right up. In the meantime, just give me a shout if y'all need anything else."

"Cheers." Our new friend Carl upended his mug, taking a huge pull of his drink before issuing a deep belly burp that rattled the bar top and singed my eyebrows. "Now what… what'd'ya want to know?"

"Well, can you start by just telling us a bit about the Acolytes of the Shield and Hammer?" I asked. I lifted my mug and took a sip. Wow. The bartender wasn't lying. Sharp, crisp, but underscored with notes of honey, apple, and cinnamon. It really did taste like apple pie in a glass. Suddenly, I could understand the Smoked Pig's popularity.

Carl shrugged. "Eh, not much to tell. When I transitioned as a Dwarf, I thought I'd end up as a smith or something. Was a welder back IRL, so that seemed like a good fit, you know? Never really wanted to do the adventure thing. Thought a crafter job would be cushy. Nine to five type gig."

"You a gamer, then?" Abby asked.

He grimaced, shrugging one shoulder. "Eh. A casual. But I still knew enough to have some idea what this, this"—he waved a drunken hand around—"world would be like. So, there I am. Lowbie. Thinkin' I'm gonna be a Dwarven Smith. Livin' on easy street since everyone and their brotha's gonna be out running around grinding boars or whatever." He laughed morosely, then took another swig of his mead. "Nope. Turns out getting an apprenticeship as a Dwarven Smith is about as tricky as getting a Merchant apprenticeship as an Accipiter. Me? I ended up as a Cleric.

"So, I was like okay. Cleric. Whatever." He shrugged meaty shoulders indifferently. "Not my first choice. But that's better than tank or somethin' else horrible. Still don't want to be an adventurer, so I angle for a temple job in Stone Reach. Which I get. But here's the real kicker." He leaned in as though conferring a great secret. "Instead of gettin' placed with one of the awesome temples, like the Ordo of Heimdallr or the Shrine of Bragi, I ended up as an Acolyte of the Hammer and Shield.

"Which is a badass name for the most boring Cleric faction in Stone Reach." He blinked and swayed for a moment. "It's the 13th Ranked Boar-Class Temple in Stone Reach." He cupped his hand. "That's the lowest rank in the lowest class. And for good reason, since it's just a bunch of dusty, old, asshole priests guarding a bunch of dusty, old, asshole books at a temple NO ONE EVER visits. Don't even come with any cool spells. Not really. And since I was the junior member in an order that NO ONE EVER joins, I got stuck doing everything. Cleaning the temple. Standing the worst watches. Working the worst hours."

He smacked his lips, then took another long pull from his mug. "Sorry, what was the question again? Sorta lost my train of thought..." He fell silent, glancing back to his drink, then up to me. His eyes widened, and he nearly stumbled off his stool as he stared at something just over my right shoulder. "Screw me sideways, I think I might finally be *too* drunk." He squinted and leaned forward, forehead crinkling. "Yep. Definitely hallucinating." He swiveled toward our server, who was busy chatting with someone at the end of the bar. "Tammy? Did you spike my drink?" he blurted, though his shout was swallowed by the racket in the air.

When she didn't answer, he turned back and stared at me. "There's a little winged lady on your shoulder." He teetered, burped, and shook his head. "She's purple."

"Jack," came Ari voice, urgent and tinged with panic.

I glanced toward the voice but didn't see her anywhere. "Where are you?"

"Right here, still invisible."

"How come he can see you?" I hissed in a whisper.

"Cleric. Must have some sort of passive Pierce Illusion spell. Lots of priests have that ability. But none of that matters right now. We have trouble!"

The batwing doors slammed open with a bang. I swiveled in my seat and watched a party of Risi—each bigger than the last and all sporting heavy spiked armor—tromp into the tavern. They just kept filing in, five, ten, fifteen. Most looked like frontline soldiers. Those were Peng's Blue Lanterns: his enforcers, thugs, and top lieutenants. At the end of the caravan of trouble were the Red Poles, Peng's elite spellcasters. There were three of them, all women, wearing brilliant silken robes—one red silk, one green, one blue—with golden Chinese characters embroidered across the front.

The biggest threat came last.

I'd never gone toe-to-toe with Peng, but I'd seen pictures of him more than once during our morning briefings. Still, all the digital holograms in the world didn't do the real-life version justice.

Easily seven feet tall, he stood head and shoulders above the rest of his crew and had shoulders so wide he couldn't fit through a normal door. Seriously, the guy had to duck and twist just to make it inside the building. His armor was the best of the best. Pure golden plate mail, accented by crimson silk. Metal lotus flowers and intricately carved dragons wound their way across his chest plate. Golden bracers, painstakingly crafted to resemble bearded dragons, encircled his forearms, and his pauldrons were each sculpted into the head of a snarling Foo dog. An enormous golden-etched crossbow hung on his back, while his huge spiked club sat at his side.

Peng and Ari could probably share notes on discretion.

The music faded, and the friendly chatter died as every eye in the joint turned toward the newcomers. Slowly, trying not to draw any attention, I pulled my hood up—partially obscuring my face—then stood and positioned myself in front of Carl, hiding the man from view.

"Howdy, folks. Welcome to my fine establishment," Chuck, the cowboy bartender and owner, said from behind the bar. "We don't usually get such large parties of Risi comin' through this way. Certainly ain't none so fancy as yourselves, but y'all are welcome to stay so long as you ain't fixin' to cause trouble."

Without a word, the Blue Lanterns spread out in a loose semicircle while the casters took up a position behind the main force. Peng strode forward, cocksure and radiating barely contained violence. "There will be no trouble, *cowboy*"—he imbued the word with the utmost scorn—"so long as we get what we're looking for." He paused for dramatic effect. It certainly seemed to work since it was quiet enough to hear a pin drop. "I seek a former Acolyte of the Shield and Hammer. A *Svartalfar.* Give us this man called *Carl* and we will leave. Fail…" He trailed off and raised a single hand.

One of his lieutenants, a thug in black plate mail with a blue lantern painted across the chest, moved at once. He pulled free an enormous black-steel nagamaki and sliced into a nearby table. The wood groaned in protest as the blade passed through in one easy motion. Those sitting around the table scampered from their seats as though someone had just set them on fire, putting some much-needed distance between themselves and the invaders.

Something I could totally understand. Heck, I wanted to put some distance between us, and most of the folks here weren't warriors but merchants and traders.

"Now," Peng said, his voice gruff but not loud, "give me what I want and I will leave you and the rest of your patrons in peace."

For a moment no one said anything, though both Chuck and our bartender, Tammy, shot furtive glances toward Carl.

"Look, partner. I don't know who you are," Chuck finally said, reaching under the bar and pulling out a double-headed war axe covered in golden script. Looked Dwarven made. Probably was, considering where we were. "But no one gets to come into my bar, bust up my shit, and make demands on my guests."

"That is where you are wrong," Peng said. "I can. Since you don't seem to know who I am, let me inform you. I am Peng Jun, leader of the *Peng Jun Tong.* Rightful conqueror of Glome Corrie, a willing Darkling, and the right hand of Serth Rog himself. Each of my men carry Malware Blades capable of permanently killing every man and woman in this bar. We will do so without a single moment of regret or hesitation, and then we will burn this place to the ground unless I get what I want in *five.*" He lifted a hand, fingers spread wide. "Four…" A finger dropped. "Three…" Another.

"For Pete's sake. There," Tammy burst out, thrusting an accusatory finger straight toward Carl, who was busy cowering behind me. The imminent threat of death at the hands of a Darkling general had sobered him right up. "Right there, alright? He's the drunk Dwarf. Standing behind that fella with his hood up."

Peng's eyes narrowed as he really saw me for the first time. "You," he growled, drawing the enormous club from his side. "Grim Jack in the flesh." A quiet ripple of shock worked its way through the room at the mention of my name. "I suppose this meeting was inevitable. And I've been looking forward to it. I owe you for taking my home. It is time, I think, for you to pay your debt, *cao ne ma.* Give me the Dwarf and perhaps I will consider making your end quick, instead of killing you slowly, a day at a time, for the next hundred years."

I pulled my hood away, stowed my khopesh, then drew my warhammer. "It doesn't need to go this way, Peng. Turn around and crawl back into whatever hole you've been hiding in or you're going to regret it."

Peng smiled. "You don't even know the meaning of the word regret, but you will learn."

ELEVEN

THE BLUE LANTERNS

CUTTER WAS THE FIRST ONE TO LAND A BLOW, materializing like an avenging ghost directly behind the Risi enemy line the moment the words left Peng's mouth. There was a gurgle and a gasp as he drove his twin blades, Plunder and Peril, into the skull of the Risi caster clad in red silk. The attack was quick, vicious, and absolutely deadly, dropping the lady where she stood before she could so much as utter a word. Screams erupted as the rest of Peng's crew surged into action. The bar goers scattered in every direction, some making for the front doors—blocked by Peng and his crew—while others headed for the few shuttered windows.

Others streaked toward a set of stairs near the back that led to the second floor, no doubt hoping to leap from the higher windows.

I noticed a few angling toward the bar and a pair of batwing doors that led to a back room. The kitchen. Was it possible there was another way out? Could be.

Forge had already thrown himself into the fray, drawing aggro.

Ari was with him, and since we were now out in the open, our cover blown, she didn't even try to hide her presence. She fluttered above the battle, casting bolts of disorienting prismatic light at the attackers, blinding, stunning, and distracting the frontline thugs just long enough to give Forge a fighting chance. He wouldn't last long on his own, though. He might've been the toughest sumabitch in Bell County, but the numbers were heavily stacked against him. Meanwhile, Cutter was busy fighting for his life against the two remaining casters, dodging and ducking lances of ice and bolts of toxic green energy.

Amara was supporting him at a distance, shooting obsidian arrows at the women, interrupting their spells and forcing them to play defense.

"Abby," I shouted, turning on the Firebrand. "Lock down those casters and do what you can to play support for Forge." I grabbed the significantly more sober Carl and hustled him toward the batwing doors that led to the back as I pulled up my Officer Chat. "Amara," I called through the link, "withdraw. You gotta get the Dwarf out of here. Get him as far away as you can and keep him safe. He is our number one concern at the moment."

She fired another wave of arrows, spearing the caster in green through the shoulder, cutting an AoE spell off at the legs. She grinned in grim satisfaction, then slung her bow crossbody and bolted my way.

I practically threw Carl into her arms and waved toward the bar. "Probably a way out back there. I'll message you when we're clear of this mess. Go!" I shouted, already putting her from my mind. She could take care of herself, and I had zero doubt she'd get the Cleric to safety.

Cutter was looking worse for the wear—an army of shallow lacerations, one of his sleeves smoldering from an acid burn—though he *was* holding his own with a little backup help from Abby. Forge, on the other hand, was in bad shape. Somehow he'd managed to barricade himself between two tables, and was fighting *everyone*. Even Peng was getting in on the action, taking swings at Forge with his enormous club.

Forge was hooking and jabbing with the best of 'em, dodging what blows he could and returning vicious strikes in kind, but he was absolutely hemorrhaging HP. Ari was in the thick of things too, but she couldn't do much against the press of bodies. I triggered Mass Heal—another of my Champion abilities—though I was loath to use this one, since it had one helluva price tag: it restored all my party members to 75% Health, but my Health dropped by 50%. On top of that, triggering the ability felt like getting blasted in the face with a shotgun.

My Spirit plunged by 350 points, and pain exploded throughout my body as I absorbed wounds from both Forge and Cutter. Phantom blades slashed through skin, and rusty spikes pierced muscle. I gritted my teeth and fought through the pain, staying upright only through sheer will and determination. The agony lasted for a split second, but boy did that second seem to drag on and on. My Health hit the 50% mark in an instant, the spell price paid, and I wobbled uncertainly for a second before fishing out a Health regen potion, downing it in a single gulp.

That would buy us a little time.

I triggered Umbra Bog with a flick of my wrist, miring Peng and his warriors in tendrils of implacable shadow, then darted toward the battle.

I leapt over a downed chair and raised my warhammer just in time to catch a descending nagamaki headed straight for Forge's head. Sparks flashed as the midnight-black blade met the enchanted steel of my hammer. The Risi thug, this one nearly as tall as Peng, grunted in surprise and lashed out with a booted foot. I triggered Dark Shield, a violet barrier of Umbra energy taking shape in the air before me. The warrior's kick landed like a wrecking ball, but the shield rebuffed him. He stumbled back a handful of paces, which was all the time I needed.

I dropped the shield and fired a violet Umbra Bolt into his eyes, temporarily blinding him. Then I bolted inside his guard, dropping to a knee as I swung my hammer, slamming the spike on the tail end of my weapon into his ankle. The spike drove *through* his boot, embedding firmly in his Achilles' heel. He shrieked like a two-year-old at the sudden pain. With a swift jerk, I pulled him from his feet. He hit the ground with a clang, the floor shaking beneath his weight. I ripped the spike free, twirled the hammer as I gained my feet, and brought it right down into his face—putting the sad sack out of his misery.

He dissolved in a shower of lights a moment later, sent for respawn.

I spun, narrowly catching another incoming blade on one of my spiked bracers.

The force of the blow sent a sharp jag of agony shooting up through my forearm and into my shoulder. No debuff, thankfully, which meant the bone wasn't broken.

This new thug was thin and clad in dark leathers lined with ebony ring mail, which meant he was probably some sort of hybrid Rogue class. I jabbed my warhammer into his gut, then triggered a gout of hellish purple-black Umbra Flame straight into the Rogue's face with my free hand. He screamed and dropped, rolling frantically to put out the unearthly flame crawling up his body, clawing mercilessly at his skin. It churned my stomach to watch, but these guys were the worst of the worst, I reminded myself. Darklings. Murderers.

I steeled myself and just kept right on dousing the poor bastard in fire.

"Look out!" Abby shouted a warning, but not in time. An ice spike as thick as my wrist sank into the outside of my thigh. Surprisingly, it didn't hurt nearly as much as I would've expected. Instead, the wound throbbed with a numb chill. I noticed at once, however, that my Stamina was dropping like a rock, and a combat notice flashed in the corner of my eye:

<<<>>>

Debuffs Added

Lingering Wound: You have sustained severe piercing damage; 3 HP/sec; duration, 45 seconds.

Frozen Touch: Suffer 5 points of Stamina damage/sec; -15% Attack Strength; Stamina regeneration reduced by 45%; movement speed reduced by 35%; duration, 45 seconds.

I twirled, moving unbelievably slow, only to catch Peng's club streaking toward me. Desperate, I tried to get my hands up in time to deflect the blow, but with the debuffs stacked against me, I was too slow by half. The club slammed into my chest; an army of unforgiving golden spikes pierced my armor and the flesh below. My feet left the ground and I flew backward, smashing into one of the circular tables, then tumbled facedown onto the floor, blood running down my face in a sheet. With a groan and a heave, I managed to roll onto my back.

Everything hurt.

Everything.

I pushed myself up onto my elbows then tried to gain my feet, but my body was having none of that. Peng was stomping toward me, a sadistic glint in his eye, his club resting against his Foo dog pauldron. "Out of tricks already?" he asked, smug and condescending.

"Not entirely," I replied with a grimace. I triggered Shadow Stride… and was promptly notified that I'd failed thanks to the chunk of ice stuck in my leg.

Shadow Stride failed! Frozen Touch inhibits your movement. You are unable to Shadow Stride until your movement is restored.

Well, then.

"Even if he is," came Abby's voice, "I'm not."

A flash flood of flame billowed over the top of my head—the intensity of the heat nearly unbearable against my skin—and broadsided Peng. Tongues of pure inferno fury enveloped him, blasting him from his feet, just like he'd done to me moments before. Turnabout's fair play, as they say. He slammed into the far wall with bone-rattling force, but his Health was still well over 75%, so I doubted he'd stay down for long.

Abby darted over, helping me from the floor with one hand, before shoving another Health regen potion at me. I popped the cork and downed the bottle, grateful for the gift.

"We're in trouble here, Jack. They outnumber us three to one, and these guys are tough."

"You're telling me," I said, absently rubbing the spot where Peng's spiked club had almost pulverized my chest. The rest of the team was doing even worse than I was. Cutter was dangerously low on Health—wounds littered his arms and legs, and a deep gash ran up his left side, bleeding profusely. He'd managed to kill the caster in blue, presumably the lady who'd hit me with the ice lance, but the caster in green was still going strong. She hurled an endless barrage of green energy at the Thief, who flipped, ducked, and rolled, all while trying to avoid the blades of a trio of axe-wielding goons hemming him in.

Forge now fought from the stage, his back pressed against the wall as he swung at a ring of attackers tightening around him like a noose. One on one I had no doubt he could take any of the fighters present, probably even Peng himself if push came to shove, but against those numbers? There was no way.

"Retreat?" I asked.

"Retreat," Abby replied grimly.

I felt a pang of guilt in my gut. We could beat feet, sure, but it was going to cause a considerable amount of property damage to the Smoked Pig. But in the war between property damage and certain death, I'd pick property damage every time.

"Okay. But if we're gonna do this, let's try to wipe as many of these jerks out as we can. We'll go out the back, but I want to make sure they can't get out the front.

Start burning tables and put up a wall of flame. Cut them off. Just make sure you have enough juice for a long, concentrated Inferno Blast."

"You thinking firestorm?" she asked, extending her staff. Tables and benches went up in a blaze.

"Got it in one." I pulled up my Officer Chat, tagging Forge, Cutter, and Ari. "Get ready to pull back. There's an exit behind the bar. You'll know when it's time to move."

I closed the interface without waiting for a reply and went to work. First, Umbra Bog. The cooldown had spun down to zero, so I recast the spell right in the center of the inn turned tavern turned battlefield. The area of effect was thirty feet, so it would catch most of the Risi Darklings, though not all. Black tentacles emerged from the floor once again, wrapping around ankles and wrists, lashing out at weapons and shields.

Abby's Wall of Flame burst up along the front wall a second later. A roaring bonfire of orange and yellow and gold, eight feet high, two feet thick. Several of Peng's men howled as licking tongues of flame caressed exposed skin and superheated metal armor.

But we were just getting warmed up.

Though I was hell on wheels in close-quarters combat, my most potent abilities were as a DPS spellcaster, and it was time to put my full arsenal to use. I thrust my warhammer straight out and unleashed Night Cyclone. Arctic power—so cold it burned inside my chest like a volcano—exploded out from my center and raced down my arm like a bolt of lightning. The head of my warhammer glowed with supernatural purple light, and the air directly above Peng's head shimmered, bulged, and ripped. On the other side of the dimensional rift was a twisted landscape filled with floating purple clouds and enormous black cyclones tearing across an endless desert of cracked yellow hardpan.

The otherworldly scene quickly vanished as one of those twisters rushed through the rip in space and into our plane, sealing the rift behind it. Black death swept through the ranks of Risi Darklings, ripping weapons from hands and hurling bodies into tables, chairs, and walls. Backs broke. Arms and legs snapped. One particularly unlucky Risi smashed into the bar headfirst, breaking his neck from the force of the impact. Living tendrils of curling shadow clawed at the air like serpents, zapping unwary enemies with brilliant blue-black bolts of shadow lightning.

Abby shifted her focus, no longer feeding her magic into the wall of flame, but rather pumping massive gouts of flame into the twister's churning funnel. The hungry, whipping winds snatched up the streaks of burning color, all twisting together into something new and terrible. Something positively *brutal*.

And best of all, my teammates fought on without a care in the world—those deadly winds didn't so much as rustle a cloak. Forge charged forward, decapitating the Risi warrior before him, then shouldered his way past the spattering of defenders like a running back making a break for the end zone. Ari buzzed after him, gliding past the flames, then streaking toward the bar and the exit. But as I scanned the chaos I cursed under my breath. No sign of Cutter. Where the hell was he?

"Abby!" I hollered over the roar of the winds and the screams of the wounded and dying. "You go with 'em. I'll make sure Cutter gets out in one piece and buy us a little more time."

"Got it," she yelled over the clamor. She vaulted over the counter, but paused for a moment on the other side. "Be careful, Jack. We only have one shot at this thing! Don't be a hero if you don't have to!" And then she was gone, pushing out through the doorway behind Forge and Ari.

The fire cyclone only had a couple of seconds left to run, and though it had sown destruction, at least five of Peng's men were still kicking, including his green-clad caster, currently hunkered down beneath a dome of shimmering jade magic. Abby's Wall of Flame was still raging along the far wall—and would for a while—ensuring Peng couldn't withdraw through the front door, but I needed to make sure they couldn't follow us through the back. Another Dark Cyclone would've been ideal, but with a ten-minute cooldown that wasn't happening.

I had one trump card left to play, however.

I stowed my warhammer and called out to Devil with an effort of will.

TWELVE

DEFT TOUCH

A CLOUD OF CHURNING BLACK SMOKE APPEARED before me, and as it dissipated, the Shadow Drake appeared. Although the Smoked Pig was large, with ceilings high enough to accommodate Devil, it was a near thing. The Drake took one look around, opened his fang-studded jaws, and let out a defiant roar of triumph and challenge. I watched with no small amount of satisfaction as two of Peng's Blue Lanterns instinctively stepped back, quaking in their boots. Not that I could blame them. Devil was scary. Not to mention tough as an M1A1.

He arched his neck, shot his head forward, and jettisoned a wave of purple-black fire—the industrial version of my own Umbra Flame spell. Peng's jade battle caster was all over it though, throwing her hands forward just in time to summon a heavy-duty force shield, deflecting the onslaught. Her shield flickered and guttered, but somehow held against the strain, which really said something about her: namely, she must've had one heck of a big Spirit pool and that her spell was top tier.

The shield only protected her boss from one direction, however, which didn't help Peng at all when

Cutter appeared directly behind him, plunging one of his daggers into Peng's neck.

The backstab earned Cutter a *Critical Hit,* but Peng seemed to have as much HP as his caster did Spirit. His bar dropped, but he was still well above a quarter.

Peng spun like a top, slamming his club into the side of Cutter's face. A *Critical Hit* of his own.

The crunch of bone carried from across the room. Peng had caved in Cutter's jaw and most of the left side of his face. There was blood and bone everywhere, though somehow Cutter clung to life. The blow hurled the thief halfway across the room, which was actually a small miracle, because he was close enough to reach. The bad news was that he was completely motionless on the ground. A glance at his HP bar showed me he was alive, but he must've suffered either paralysis or some sort of unconscious debuff.

Devil, cover me! I sent through the mental link as I bolted toward Cutter, who was sprawled on the floor.

Peng seemed to have the same idea, but Devil was already repositioning to intercept the Risi warrior. The Drake swung left, lashing out with his wicked talons. Peng batted the claws aside with his club, saving his neck for the moment, but leaving himself wide open on the right. Devil struck like lightning, exploiting the misstep. He latched onto Peng's armored leg, dragging the man from his feet and hoisting him into the air. He shook the Risi like a dog worrying at a piece of meat, before hurling him into a burning wall with a flick of his neck.

Peng hit with the force of a car crash, smoke and embers swirling up in a halo around him. I hoped to God that Peng would do the world a favor and just die.

Unfortunately, I didn't have time to make *sure* that happened—I needed to get to Cutter, quick. If I didn't, either the fire or one of Peng's thugs would, and without help he didn't have long.

I hurdled a smoldering bench and dropped down beside Cutter. As expected, he was completely passed out. And lucky for him since his face was a ruined mess. I shuddered just looking at him. Deep lacerations, blackened eye sockets, and broken bones. The entire left side of his face sagged like melted wax. If he were awake, he'd be in unbelievable pain. I glanced at his Health, surprised to see his HP was sitting at 20% despite the unbelievable damage. That could only mean his recently unlocked skill, Lucky Break, had kicked in. It was a passive that granted a… well, *a lucky break* from an otherwise mortal wound.

With a three-hour cooldown time, though, it wouldn't save him again.

I hoisted him from the floor and flung him unceremoniously over my shoulder like a sack of potatoes.

Buy me as much time as you can, I sent to Devil.

I will burn them to the ground or die as a champion, came his guttural response, followed immediately by a fresh onslaught of shadow flame.

I nodded, a determined scowl settling on my face as I triggered Shadow Stride, stepping through the veil between planes, hauling Cutter with me. Time froze and the blessed cool of the Shadowverse hit me like a soothing balm. I hadn't realized just how insanely hot it was inside the tavern. I reached up with my free hand and wiped black soot and sticky sweat from my brow. Then I paused, just long enough to take a quick scan of what remained of the Smoked Pig. Everything was on fire. The walls burned, the tables blazed, and even the hay underfoot was smoldering.

Choking black smoke filled the air, making it hard to see and near impossible to breathe. Honestly, I was surprised I hadn't been hit with a Suffocation debuff.

The place didn't have long, that was for sure. And if Devil could pin Peng and his crew down for long enough, it was distinctly possible the building would give up the ghost and collapse right on top of them. Kill them all in one fell swoop. If only we could get so lucky.

And speaking of Peng, his side wasn't doing so hot. They'd come in with fifteen men, and of that number only Peng, three of his enforcers, and the green-robed caster remained.

Our side was on the run, so this wasn't a sweeping victory by any stretch of the imagination, but considering the circumstances, I'd certainly call it a draw. I turned my back on the scene of madness and made my way to the bar. While in the Shadowverse, I could phase through people and monsters of every variety, but walls and other natural features—such as doors, trees, and rocks—still had a material presence in this place. With Cutter bouncing on my shoulder, I skittered around the outside of the bar instead of simply jumping over the top, then headed through another set of batwing doors, which led into an orderly kitchen:

Stoves, ovens, clean counters, gleaming cutlery—everything in its place. Slabs of meat hung from wicked hooks along the right wall.

The exit was off to the left. The owner had even gone to the trouble of painting EXIT in bright red paint above the door, just like I would've expected in a restaurant back home. I'd judged this place all wrong. The owner knew what he was about and had worked hard to create a little slice of Texas right here in Eldgard. I could respect that. And once this was all over, I intended to personally find him and drop enough gold in his lap to fix this place twice over. Heck, maybe I'd even give him enough to open up a new franchise down in Yunnam. Plop it right next to Frank's.

Ribs and pizza all within walking distance didn't sound so bad to me.

By the time I got to the exit, Cutter was stirring on my shoulder.

"Bloody hells, but I feel like someone worked me over right and proper."

"Can you stand?" I asked, breathing hard from the effort of hauling him around.

"Aye. Put me down, you sod," he replied, the words a jumbled mess thanks to his ruined jaw.

I shrugged his weight off and let him tumble harmlessly to the ground. He landed with a thud. He stood and offered me a blistering scowl, made all the worse by his swollen, busted face and double black eyes.

Everything was terrible. Peng wasn't but ten feet away, and the whole world was burning around us. Still, I couldn't stifle the laugh that exploded from my mouth.

"What's so bloody funny, eh?"

"You look like a trash panda." And he did—especially with the soot and ash smeared across his swollen face. "Raccoon eyes and all. Ironic since you're the Rogue." That didn't seem to help his sour mood one bit.

"Well, you're no bloody spring chicken yourself, eh? About one bloody step above a murder hobo, what crawled out of a gutter."

I snorted and shook my head. "Come on. We've only got twenty seconds before it's back to the real world, and we need to get as far away from this place as we can manage."

The back door let out into a narrow alleyway, packed with snow and muck, zigzagging off to the left and right. Shops and buildings blocked us in, and I found myself silently praying that Abby's fire didn't spread through the Low Quarter. The whole place seriously *was* a fire hazard, and burning down an entire section of a city wasn't something I needed weighing on my conscience. A legion of footprints had churned up the mud in both directions—evidence of the fleeing patrons—so there was no telling which way Abby and the others had gone.

I lingered a moment longer, then shrugged and headed left.

We made it another twenty feet before the countdown timer expired, booting us from the Shadowverse like guests who'd overstayed their welcome. We stepped back into time, and sound erupted around us in a storm. The crackling of the fire. People screaming as twilight settled over the city. A bone-shaking roar from behind us, courtesy of Devil. We picked up our pace, breaking into a light jog as we followed the cramped alleyway.

City guards approach, Devil snarled in the back of my head. *The blood traitor Peng has fled, along with his female consort and one of his men. Spineless cowards.* His voice oozed disdain.

Good work, and don't worry. We'll have a chance to get even with Peng. He's sown the wind, and he's gonna reap the whirlwind sooner or later.

I don't care what wind magic he has at his disposal, Devil replied seriously. *My kind are* born *of wind and flame. We will prevail.*

No. What? Reaping the whirlwind. It's... well, it's not magic... I faltered, struggling to explain a biblical idiom to a fictional, mythological creature from a video game world. *It's just this saying we have,* I finished weakly. *Basically, it boils down to karma's a bitch. Doesn't matter. Good work.* I dismissed him with a thought, sending him back to the Shadowverse where he belonged.

Before long, Cutter and I heard the clamor of voices drawing closer. Even over the din, Captain Raginolf's Scottish burr stuck out like a sore thumb. We rounded a bend and saw flickering torchlight up ahead. We dropped into Stealth and ducked into a narrow crevice running between a pair of wood-sided houses and waited as the torchlight bobbed its way toward us. I held my breath as a trio of guards stormed past us at a dead sprint, heading for the tavern we'd left behind.

"Close one," Cutter muttered from beside me.

"You wanna talk about a close one," I replied as the heavy footfalls finally faded from earshot. "What the hell were you thinking back there? Trying to take out Peng like that? You're always telling me not to be a hero, but that was awfully close to heroic, if you ask me. Good thing Amara wasn't around to see it, or she'd never let you live it down. Probably commission a statue to immortalize you. Set it up right in front of the training pit."

Cutter scrunched his face up in disgust. "I'm offended by that. It truly grieves me in the soul that you would think those nasty thoughts about me, Jack. Thank the gods above you're wrong—as bloody usual. I'll have you know it wasn't about being a *hero*, it was about being the best bloody Thief in all of Eldgard. See, I wasn't trying to take Peng out at all. That, my unenlightened friend, was just the *pledge*. The misdirection. Had to throw him off my scent. It was really about a heist."

He whipped one hand forward, and with a wave he revealed a chunk of slagged out metal about the size of a brick. Almost looked like raw ore—jagged and unrefined—though a band of rune-inscripted gold wrapped around the stone told a different story. He tossed it to me with a flick of his wrist, a self-satisfied grin glued on his face. I snatched it from the air with light fingers. It was heavier than any stone that size had a right to be and radiated power like the sun radiated heat. Holy crap.

The last of the Doom-Forged relics.

Doom-Forged Ore

Item Type: Relic

Class: Ancient Artifact

Base Damage: 0

Primary Effects:

- Doom-Forged Relic 1 of 3

A Piece of the Doom-Forged Weapon

Once, eons ago, in an age long since forgotten to mankind, a powerful weapon was created to balance the colossal forces of the universe. A weapon so great even the gods feared its blow. Legend tells that after the Doom-Forged weapon was crafted by the Dwarven godling Khalkeús, the weapon was split apart by the gods and goddesses who feared its might and scattered across the realms so that it would never be assembled again. Perhaps it is time for the gods to fear again...

"Without his Keep," Cutter said, "I knew the bastard would have it on him. But I also knew full well that pickpocketing the bloke was gonna be bloody monstrous. He'd be on the lookout for an obvious play like that. So instead of subtle, I went overt. Stabbed him in the neck and filched his prize right out from under his nose while he smashed *my* nose in. The battle rage had him by the throat. He was so intent on grinding me into the dirt he never thought to check his inventory."

I grabbed Cutter around the neck and pulled him into a bear hug. "You're a genius, man. Crazy. But a crazy genius."

"In the Union, we say the plan is only crazy if it fails. So in this case, sheer, utter brilliance. You did forget to mention how handsome I am, though," he said, then paused as he caught a glimpse of himself in a murky puddle of water. He visibly winced. "Well, maybe not at the moment. Though this is nothing time and a little beauty rest won't fix. And speaking of beauty rest, I know where we can hole up until this whole thing blows over. That fella I was chatting with before the nine hells broke open? He's the local Thieves Guild Esquire. And as a Gentleman, I have safe passage in any chapter house in Eldgard. One of the perks of the job. Come on. It's not far now."

THIRTEEN

RESPITE

CUTTER SENT OUT A MESSAGE TO THE REST OF THE crew complete with a map marker for the local Thieves chapter house, which turned out to be an apothecary in one of the classier sections of Cliffburgh. And not just any apothecary, but the *1st Ranked Phoenix-Class Apothecary*. I still wasn't entirely sure what that meant, but Cutter seemed clued in and was only too happy to explain. Apparently, the *Svartalfar* were an orderly folk and put great stock in knowing exactly how every cog in their society fit together. And to that end, they had a rigid hierarchy, which applied to everything from crafters and adventurers to businesses and temples.

Seven Classes—Dragon, Kraken, Phoenix, Manticore, Centaur, Warg, Boar—all named after mythical lore beasts, each with 13 ranks apiece. Each person was assigned a class and rank, though technically multiple *people* could fill each class and rank. Not so with businesses or crafters, however. Each city could only have one *1st Ranked Centaur-Class Blacksmith* and if that blacksmith advanced, they would become the 13th ranked Manticore-Class Blacksmith—knocking another blacksmith down in the process. Dragon was the highest class, and it turned out that there were no Dragon-Class businesses anywhere outside of Stone Reach proper.

According to Cutter, earning *1st Ranked Phoenix-Class* in a town this size was no small feat.

The rest of the crew met us at the safe house half an hour later. Full night had long since come—sunsets, though spectacular up here, didn't seem to last long—and the cloud-filled sky obscured the light from the moon. Abby, Forge, and Ari arrived first, hoods up (or veils up in Ari's case), heads down, while Amara arrived a few minutes later, practically hauling our new acolyte pal, Carl, behind her.

Inside, a silver-haired woman, probably in her late forties or early fifties, manned a glass-fronted counter filled with a variety of potions, all top end and worth their weight in gold. She smiled serenely at us as we pushed our way in; a little brass bell above the door tinkled, announcing our presence. I whistled softly. As far as fronts went, this one was awful convincing. The woman certainly didn't look much like a Thief, and the wares lining her racks seemed legit.

Wooden shelves edged the walls, each near to bursting with carefully labeled ingredients. Tied bushels of bronze phottan. Glass jars of ground Furious Osipa and powdered Slater. Tinctures of Hidglow Root. Many of the items I recognized from my journeys—Deadly Baneshade, Creeping Faemoss, Spiced Ginger—but there were about a thousand other things I couldn't even begin to put a name to. One shelf held book after book on alchemy, potion brewing, and harvesting. They had titles like *Herbology of Eldgard*, the *Spelunker's Handbook of Crystals and Gemstones*, *Fundamentals of*

Potion Permutations, and *Junior Alchemy for Budding Botanists*.

Small tables, all polished to a dull glow, dotted the floorspace, showcasing some of the rarer and more valuable ingredients—everything from Dragon Scales and Troll Hearts to polished gemstones—along with a variety of alchemic equipment. Those I recognized from my time spent hanging around with Vlad in his workshop. Glass beakers, stone mortars and pestles, empty vials, brass goggles, engraving awls, even steampunk-looking respirators. None of it was as fine as what Vlad used, but for a beginner to intermediate Alchemist or Potions Master, this place was probably just this side of heaven.

"Please come in, come in." The woman stood and beckoned us forward with slim hands and a warm smile. "Please, get in and take some of that chill from your bones." Amara was the last to enter, prodding and shoving Carl like an unruly toddler who needed constant attention. "It's so lovely to have you all," the shopkeeper crooned, her voice gentle, soothing, pleasant. A grandma whispering sweet words to a favorite grandchild. "Quite lovely indeed.

"Not often we get such a crowd in here. Especially not at this hour, goddess no." She resumed her seat and folded her hands on the glass counter before her. "So, how can I help you this evening, hmm? A spot of Crimson Polkweed, perhaps, or maybe you're interested in my pre-brewed wares." She knocked gently on the glass case before her. Inside were a myriad of potions. She had elixirs that temporarily increased attributes or fortified skills. Some that even granted incredible abilities for short bursts of time.

"Afraid not," Cutter said. "Friends of Marcus's. Here for his evening tea."

"Ah, of course. That makes sense." She nodded sagely, hands drifting toward some unseen thing below the counter. There was a *click* and a bookcase behind her swung inward, revealing a short hallway and a set of descending stairs. "Well, all the same, welcome to Maggy's Mystic Elixirium. Ring if you need anything, lovelies." She waved us through.

Cutter led the way, the rest of us trailing behind him down the stairs, which let out into a scene that was far more familiar. A traditional inn not so different from the Broken Dagger back in Rowanheath. A quaint tavern filled with time-worn tables and hard looking men and women—mostly Dwarves—in dark leathers festooned with throwing blades and long-handled knives. I immediately spotted Cutter's cowl-wearing contact from the Smoked Pig nursing a drink in the corner all by his lonesome.

After a few brief words with Cutter, the man stood and ushered us down a short corridor, which connected to a sprawling training complex complete with a sand-lined sparring pit, a melee room with straw mats and practice dummies, and a knife throwing range with targets propped up at the far end. Off to the right was a *Room of Doors* overflowing with practice doors and padlocked chests. A trio of hooded thieves occupied the room, fiddling around at the various locks, deep in concentration.

Our taciturn guide directed us to a connecting hallway studded with more wooden doors, though these clearly weren't of the practice variety. I'd been at enough inns and guild chapter houses to recognize guest quarters when I saw them. We stopped at a pair of adjoining rooms at the very end of the hall.

"This is where you'll be staying," our guide said, gesturing toward the doors. "And if you need anything else, let me know." He paused, stealing a sidelong look at Cutter. "It's not every day that we have a Gentleman in residence, let alone a rebel king." He shot a glance at me. "Now, if you'll excuse me." He bowed and politely saw himself off. He looked shadier than a three-dollar bill, but dang if he wasn't the politest Thief I'd ever met.

I watched him go, waiting until he disappeared from view. "Alright," I finally said, once he was gone. "We've got some catching up to do."

The guest room was nice, though nothing fancy. A pair of twin beds, a scuffed wardrobe, a deeply creased leather club chair, and a small nightstand with a chipped porcelain basin on top. There was an accompanying pitcher of water nearby and a brown towel that had seen better days. Still, a room was a room, and this one was safe. Well, as safe as a room in a thieves' guild could be.

"So," Abby said, rounding on us as I closed the door with a *click*. "Are you finally gonna fill us in? What in the shit happened back there? Is Peng dead or what?"

Forge held up a blocky hand. "Before we start bumpin' our gums, what do we want to do about this guy?" He nodded at Carl. "I mean, I can go stick him in the other room if you want. Won't take but a minute, and I'm more than happy to watch him. Make sure he doesn't try to rabbit on us the second we turn our backs."

"Let's just ask him. Well, Carl? You want to know what's going on?"

He hesitated for a moment, shifting uncomfortably from foot to foot, balling and unballing his blocky fists. "No," he finally said with a firm shake of his head. Sober, his Philly accent wasn't quite so noticeable, though I could still pick it out from time to time. "Look, I might be a terrible acolyte, but I'm not a moron. I was too drunk to put it all together before"—he tapped at the side of his head with one thick finger—"but I've sobered up, okay. And I've also been doin' some math on the way over. You guys are Crimson Alliance." He faltered, looking around as though the room might have ears. "And not just regular Crimson Alliance. You're him, aren't you. The Jade Lord?"

I nodded.

"Yep, that's what I thought," he replied. He pursed his lips. "In that case, I *definitely* don't want to know what's goin' on. I'm out. I'm not a hero. I'm not an adventurer. I just want to live out my second life as drama free as I can, you know? Drink honeyed mead. Eat good food. That's pretty much the extent of my ambitions. And, no offense, but wherever you guys go? It's trouble.

"I mean, I've known you guys for all of two hours, and already I'm on the run and hiding in the guts of the Thieves Guild. It's nothing personal—you guys all seem alright—but I don't want to get dragged into *any* business with the Alliance or the Empire. Me? I'm not a fan of politics. And when little guys like me get caught between powerhouses like the Alliance and the Empire, eh, we have a way of getting *crushed* in the mix. So nope." He folded his arms, working to keep his hands from quivering and his voice from trembling.

"Only one problem, friend," Cutter said. "Your problem isn't with Jack. It isn't with the Alliance. It isn't even with Osmark and those bastards in the Legion. That Risi bastard back at the tavern? The guy looking to put your arse on a first-name basis with the reaper himself? That was Peng Jun. And he isn't with the Empire, friend."

"He's part of something way worse, Carl," I said, meeting his eye and refusing to look away. "He's a Darkling. And not just any Darkling. He's the right hand of Serth-Rog. And they won't just crush you, they will *kill* you. And I'm not talking sending you for respawn. If they kill you, you stay dead. And a guy like Peng won't hesitate to do it. Not for a second."

"*No, no, no,*" the acolyte said, breaking into a nervous pace, his brown robes swishing around his feet as he walked. "Shit. I don't want this. None of this. I don't even know what you all want from me! I'm a nobody, okay? Not sure if you were listenin' back at the bar, but I'm a 13th Ranked Cleric in a Boar-Class temple. I'm literally the worst rated Cleric in the whole city, and I even failed at that. Why would anyone even be interested in me?" He shook his head, his shoulders slumping in defeat. "I don't get it. Not any of it."

"Well," Abby said, "remember how you said you were a part of a super boring order that no one ever visits? Turns out that's not exactly the case. Your order is actually a *crucial* part of a world-event quest. Pretty important one."

"What the hell you talkin' about?" he blurted, eyes bulging as he ran his fingers through his lank hair. "The Acolytes of the Shield and Hammer are dedicated to a *minor* forge visage. Dude's been in a coma for like five hundred years—and that's if he ever existed at all. And even assuming he does exist, no one knows *where* his shrine is. Buried somewhere inside Stone Reach according to temple lore. But past that? Phft. No one has a clue. Why would anyone be interested in that?"

"Because of these," I said, reaching into my inventory and pulling free the three Doom-Forged relics, which I promptly laid out on the nearest bed. There was a collective gasp around the room.

"How did you get the third piece?" Abby asked, inching over, running her fingers along the chunk of strange ore.

"Turns out Cutter is even *sneakier* than we thought. While everyone else was making a break for it, he stabbed Peng in the neck while simultaneously lifting the item."

"Does that mean Peng's dead?" Forge asked, a hopeful edge to his words.

I frowned and shook my head. "No such luck. He made it out along with one of his casters and one of his lieutenants. But we gave them one hell of a run for their money." I quickly filled them in on the rest of the battle and our escape through the back while Devil held down the fort.

"Look, I'm sorry," Carl said once I'd finished recounting my story. "But obviously I'm missing something here. Are those supposed to mean something to me? Because I'm drawing a big, fat blank here."

I lifted the pommel from the bed and tossed it to him. "These are relics," I said, "created by your comatose deity, Khalkeús. And we need to find him because he's the only one that can put these pieces back together again."

Carl's eyes went hazy, presumably as he read the item description, his jaw dropping a little farther with every second.

"Oh shit, oh shit, oh shit," he said. "No. This can't be happening. These things aren't even supposed to be real! The Doom Forge is a legend. And like a really obscure one." He paced frantically, the *swish-swish-swish* of his robes carrying over the pregnant silence. "Okay, so let me see if I have this straight. You want me to help you find an Aspect—who *no one* has seen for five hundred years—in order to get him to build you a weapon capable of killing a god. And I'm guessing this other guy, Peng, wants the same thing?"

"That is an accurate description, yes," Amara replied, hands folded behind her back as she watched him like falcon eyeing a mouse in the field.

He deflated a little, looking positively defeated. "There's gotta be someone else better for this job. I mean, I'm a *failed* acolyte. I feel like I've made that clear, but just want to hammer that home. Failed as in washed out. There are a bunch of full Clerics who are bound to know loads more than I do."

"Right," I said. "And what are our chances of getting into Stone Reach without some help? And even if we do get in, what are the odds that one of those guys is going to talk to us? *You* don't even want to talk to us, and we just saved your life. Plus, we're on sort of a tight deadline. We've got about forty-eight hours to pull this off before I drop dead."

"Forty-eight hours!" He visibly blanched as horrid realization dawned on him. "Oh no. I'm the chosen one. Oh sweet Jesus, Mary, and Joseph. I'm the chosen one."

He took a deep breath, holding it for a long three count before exhaling loudly. "Wow, does this suck." He doubled over, breathing hard, clearly on the edge of a panic attack.

"Trust me," I replied. "I know the feeling. But here's the thing. You don't have any options here. Peng will keep coming for you. And even if you manage to go to ground long enough to throw him, eventually he'll just go kick in the doors of your order and start indiscriminately killing until he gets the answers he wants. Obviously, you're on the outs with your order, but I'm sure you don't want to see the place razed to the ground. So, help us prevent that from happening."

Carl plopped down on the opposite bed and tossed the Doom-Forged Pommel onto the mattress with the other items. He slouched forward, forearms resting on his thighs as he stared morosely at the items across from him. After a time, he sighed in resignation and nodded. "Yeah, okay. Guess I'm in. What do you need from me?"

"What we really need," Abby said, taking a seat across from him, "is access to your temple in Stone Reach. I'm sure they have some books or artifacts that hold the clue to finding the Doom Forge, wherever it is."

"Well, there's the first problem. See, I've been *temporarily* exiled from Stone Reach and from the temple. That's part of the whole me-being-a-failed-Acolyte thing I mentioned before."

"What happened?" I asked, taking a seat next to Abby.

Carl squirmed a bit, glancing this way and that, not wanting to meet my gaze. "So... turns out I might have like a little drinking problem." He cracked his fingers. "Just a tiny one. One night I was on library duty. The worst shift in the most boring place on the planet. I might've got a little drunk on the sanctified wine, which is not really that big of a deal by itself. But I also accidentally—and I can't stress that enough, this was a completely honest to God mistake—set a bunch of sacred texts on fire. Most of them were replaceable, but one of them was a third edition. *The Biographical History of Eitri Spark-Sprayer.* Only known copy."

"Eitri Spark-Sprayer," I said, tapping a finger on my chin. "That sounds awfully familiar. Where have I heard that before?"

"That is easy," Amara replied promptly. "Eitri Spark-Sprayer was a friend to the Dokkalfar and a close confidante of Nangkri, the Jade Lord himself. After Nangkri's death, he forged the Horn of the Ancients for Chieftain Isra Spiritcaller."

I snapped my fingers. Yep, that was it. The Horn of the Ancients was still back in the Darkshard vault. It was a one-off item that would let me call back the honored Dokkalfar dead to do battle on my behalf. I'd earned it as part of my reward for taking down the Sky Maiden.

"So why is the book so important?" Abby asked.

"Eitri was a demigod of the Forge, but not just any demigod," Carl offered. "He was Khalkeús's scion. His son, by way of a Dokkalfar mortal named Boonsri. He's the one that forged the original alliance with the Nangkri dynasty five hundred years ago. The book I *accidently* burned is one part biography, one part journal. Or at least that's what everyone thinks. No one knows for sure, 'cause the book had a lock on it that no one could open. The Arch Cleric, though, well, he thought it had clues to the..." He trailed off.

"Clues to what, friend?" Cutter said, pulling free one of his daggers, casually cleaning his nails with the tip of the blade. He could be awfully intimidating when he wanted to be.

"Clues to the location of the Doom Forge hidden in the pages," Carl finished after a long beat.

Forge grunted and threw up his hands in obvious frustration. "Damnit, Carl!"

"Hold on," the Cleric said, lifting his hands as though to ward off an impending blow. "Look, okay. It's not all bad. I'm exiled, but my ban isn't permanent. The Arch Cleric gave me a quest to earn my way back in. There's a Dwarven ruin about three hours or so due east of here. Bad place. Super dangerous. But inside is supposed to be another copy of the book. If I get it, I'll be welcomed back to the temple with open arms."

"A blighted dungeon raid?" Cutter said. "Gods, Jack, we don't have time for that. That Death-Head clock is kicking away. We'll be bloody running errands for this sod"—he jerked the tip of his dagger toward Carl—"wasting bucketloads of time in the arse-end of nowhere, and there's no guarantee this book is even there. I don't like it. Gotta be a quicker way."

"Hey look, guys," Carl said, "if you want to find the Doom Forge this is the only way I can think of. There's an even money chance that whatever clue you're looking for is in that book, so unless we do it, you're probably gonna be out of luck even if you get to the temple and get one of the Elder Clerics to talk—which you won't. Those sanctimonious assholes don't even trust me with the 'full secrets of the order.'" He air quoted. "And I'm a junior acolyte. Or I was anyway. They'll never trust you, no matter who you are.

"But this should be a cakewalk. I mean, I haven't been able to get the book because, well, look at me." He waved a hand at his rumpled robes. "I'm not exactly the adventuring sort. Not really chosen one material, if you will. But you guys are the Crimson Alliance. It'll be easy. We raid the ruins. Get the book. And then I'm back in at the temple. You help me, I help you. Chances are what you need is in the book *I* need, but even if it's not, I can help you guys find whatever you're looking for in the main library after I get back into the good graces of the order."

"This does sound like something Sophia would totally do," Abby said, her face pensive, thoughtful. "She's the one who pointed us here. Interfering takes a toll on her. I just can't believe she'd drop Carl in our lap if there was another way. An easier way."

"I'm sorry," Carl interrupted. "Sophia? Who's that?"

"No one you need to worry about right now," I said, waving away his question. Then to Abby, "Yeah, you're right. This is exactly the kind of curve ball she likes tossing our way." I paused, drumming my fingers restlessly on the edge of the mattress. "This feels right. You said this place is three hours to the east?" I asked, pinning Carl in place with a look.

"Yep. Three hours. Though fair warning, it's rough country up that way."

I pulled up my interface and glanced at the time. Just after 8 PM. Everyone was tired, hungry, gross, and still recovering from our battle against Peng. As much as I was loath to kill time, we were safe, warm, and had proper beds. No telling when we'd get a chance like this again. "Alright. Everyone, get cleaned up. Let's grab a bite to eat, then hunker down for some shut-eye. I want to be on the road before first light."

FOURTEEN

DWARVEN RUINS

CARL HADN'T BEEN JOKING ABOUT ROUGH country; everything that lay to the east of Cliffburgh was rugged, wild, and downright treacherous. There was a road that led west and another that shot due north from Cliffburgh all the way to Stone Reach. But this land was unsettled. Untouched by human hands as far as I could see. Just rolling hills covered in deep powder, densely packed tree cover, and jagged rocks poking up like giant teeth. Fast-moving rivers cut through the hills and valleys, following the contours of the land, creating a number of deep ravines that looked nearly impassable on foot.

Thankfully, we weren't on foot.

Beside me, Cutter piloted the *Hellreaver*, carving our way through the freezing, star-riddled sky. He muttered darkly the whole time. About "how bloody early it was" and "how bloody cold it was" and how much he "wanted to drop kick that blighter Carl in the face for dragging us out here." I wrapped my cloak around me just a tad more tightly, a small protection against the vicious cold and murderous winds. Cutter wasn't wrong—not completely. It *was* early, and it *was* bitterly cold. I couldn't really blame Carl, though. He was just another average guy, not so different from me, pulled into something much bigger than himself.

We'd set out at early, well before the sun had even *thought* about rising for the day. It was 5:30 AM—the first hints of light breaking along the eastern horizon dead ahead—when I spotted the tips of golden spires jutting up from a rocky canyon filled with frost-kissed evergreens and deep drifts of white snow. It was a fortress, somewhere firmly between a picturesque Disney castle and Doctor Frankenstein's gloomy lab.

There were sweeping parapets lined with stylized merlons that looked like crouching gargoyles. Angular bastions custom built for archers or siege weapons. Circular towers, impossibly tall, clawed at the sky, capped by pointed spires and minarets of gold and bronze. Faint early morning light glinted off those towers and played across elaborate stained-glass windows inset high into the Keep. Lacy bridges glimmered like cut diamonds, connecting each of the windswept spires. Near the back, butting up against the canyon wall, smokestacks poked up like soldiers in formation. Huge things, though the fires that fueled them were long dead.

I whistled. I'd done a fair amount of dungeon diving since coming into V.G.O., and even I had to admit the ruins looked damn impressive.

"Any activity down there?" I called to Forge, who stood near the bow of the airship, a familiar looking bronze spyglass pressed up against his eye.

"I reckon there might be some forest critters patrolling in the trees. Big-ass wolves, maybe—"

"Those would be Dread Wargs," Carl offered from nearby. The guy looked better than he had the night before. A shower, clean robes, and a decent night's sleep had done wonders for him. "They're pack hunters, but I doubt they'll give us much trouble. Mostly cannon fodder for newbs and lowbies."

"Right," Forge continued. "Dread Wargs. Not much else, though. Place looks pretty quiet. Deserted almost. Got my hairs standing at attention, though. Something off about this place, you ask me."

"You and every Dwarf in Cliffburgh," Carl grumbled, cinching his cloak tighter around his shoulders. "They all think this place is cursed. Part of the reason I haven't had much luck clearing it. No one wants to risk coming here. They say there are monsters in the shadows. Ghosts from the long dead."

That was exactly the kind of thing I liked to hear right before jumping feetfirst into a dungeon dive.

"I'm starting to like this place more and more, Jack," Cutter offered from behind the wheel. "Really feel like we made the right choice here."

"Yeah. And why's that?"

He shrugged. "Big castle. Superstitious natives. Sounds to me like a place with something bloody good just waiting for a proper plundering. And if there's anything I love more than booze and gambling, it's a good plundering. I still bloody well intend to retire in a bathtub full of gold marks before this is all over and done with. Can't do that without loot." Cutter cranked the wheel hard to port. "Make ready to land!" he barked without looking back.

His Goblin crew broke into motion. A trio of the creatures skittered into the ratlines, tugging at a set of ropes. A great wooden jibboom popped from the side, unfurling a canvas fin that billowed out, catching a stiff breeze. "Half speed," Cutter yelled absently, toggling a lever on the right. One of the Goblins frantically shoveling coal into the rear furnace ceased his work. Others scampered across the deck, chirping and growling at each other while securing sails and checking the cannons.

I watched them work, a bemused smile on my face.

They were such weird critters—all green skin, potbellies, and gangly spider-like limbs. They were short, each one no taller than a Dwarf, with twisted faces, hooked noses, and needle-sharp teeth. They wore sleek leathers, outfitted with pirate cutlasses and cog-studded flintlock pistols. None wore boots, though they didn't seem to mind the cold in the least. They spoke only crude English, and they bickered *constantly* with each other. They were fiercely loyal to Cutter and the *Hellreaver*, though, and that was all that really mattered.

Cutter landed the *Hellreaver* a few minutes later, touching down on a clear patch of ground a short walk from the front of the ruins.

I shook my head and pulled my gaze away from the Goblins as Abby, Amara, and Ari climbed up from the ship's cargo hold, which was exponentially warmer than being topside. I was a little envious, but then I'd been the one who told them to go catch an extra bit of sleep on the ride over. No reason for all of us to suffer.

"Holy crap. It's colder than a Yeti's asshole out here," Abby said, shivering like a leaf in the wind as she surveyed the snowy wonderland. "I honestly never thought I'd miss the god-awful humidity of the Storme Marshes, but I take back every nasty thing I've ever said about Yunnam. The cold is a thousand times worse than the heat." She lifted her hands, a chant on her lips. A halo of fire burst to life, fingers of flame twirling and dancing around her in a slow procession. Relief washed over her face. "So much better."

After a few quick words between Cutter and his Goblin crew, we deboarded the airship, finding ourselves in knee-deep snow.

"Nope," Abby said resolutely. "No one has the time or patience for this." She waddled forward until she was at the front of the group, leaving a pair of deep furrows in the snow behind her. She stowed her staff, stuck both hands straight out, and unleashed an unending javelin of flame, melting the snowpack in front of us. She killed the spell for just a moment, glancing at us over one shoulder and cocking an eyebrow. "Well, don't just stand there. Let's go take care of this dungeon and find our book." She turned her industrial flamethrower hands back up to full blast and carved us a path.

Forge tromped behind her, axe out, Ari perched on his shoulder with her weapons at the ready. Carl came next, followed by me and Cutter, while Amara brought up the rear, making sure no one got the drop on us. The walk in was a bit longer than I expected—the ruins were deceptively big, and farther away than they first appeared—but relatively uneventful. We spotted the local pack of Dread Wargs lingering near the tree line, watching us with glowing amber eyes, their lips pulled back to reveal cruel fangs custom built for rending flesh and piercing armor. But Abby's flamethrower impersonation seemed to convince them that we were predators, not prey.

"So what's the deal with this place anyway?" Forge asked as we made the trek. "This don't look like no dungeon I've ever seen."

"I don't think it is," Carl said, his voice slightly muffed by the scarf he had wrapped snuggly around his throat and mouth. "Not in the traditional sense of the word, anyway. More like some kind of abandoned keep."

"Well, if it ain't a dungeon, then who built it? And why the hell would they go to all that trouble, then just leave it here?" Forge asked. "Don't make no sense."

"According to my order, this place was built by Eitri Spark-Sprayer. The guy spent a bunch of time down south with the Murk Elves, but when he wasn't kicking around in the swamps, he was here. Working in his lab. Or something like that. Never did pay the closest attention."

"Any idea why he spent so much time in the Storme Marshes?" I asked, trying to put the pieces of this strange puzzle together. And I was *sure* there was a puzzle here. Some connection I wasn't seeing yet. There were just too many overlaps between this demigod Eitri and my predecessor, the Jade Lord, to be a coincidence.

"Eh. No clue," Carl replied with a noncommittal shrug. "His mom was a Murky, so it coulda been a family thing, I guess. But he spent the later years of his life here, at least until the other Aspects murdered him."

"Aspects?" I asked, feet slapping on the muddy ground. "You keep using that word. I'm not sure I understand."

"It's just Cleric lingo. Not likely to hear it unless you hang out in the temple district. You've heard of the Overminds, right?"

I nodded, doing my very best to suppress my smile. "Yeah. I've heard a thing or two about them."

"Okay. Cool. Well the Overminds represent sort of these big cosmic forces, but they all have various Aspects. Sorta like local deities that represent different parts of each Overmind. Every order worships a different Aspect of each Overmind. Khalkeús is a Dwarven Divine, and an Aspect of Aediculus the Architect. Heimdallr is one of Kronos's Aspects. Bragi is a deity of the Bards and an Aspect of Gaia. There's a shitload of 'em. Now, I'm not really much of a theologian, mind you, but from what I understand, these Aspects, they have a certain degree of autonomy. Can kinda do their own thing, though they're ultimately pieces of the greater unthinking Overminds they represent."

Unthinking. Right. I didn't bother to correct him, but inside it took every ounce of willpower not to laugh hysterically in his face. "Following so far," I said. "But why would these other Aspects murder one of their own?"

"Well that's the thing. Eitri Spark-Sprayer wasn't one of their own, you know? Dude was a demigod, fathered by the Aspect Khalkeús. Eitri didn't have the full power of an Aspect, but he had a whole lot more than most mortals. The more important part, though, was that he didn't have their *restrictions* either. Story goes, the other Aspects were super pissed that this guy could just run around and do whatever the hell he wanted. So, they elected these mortal Champions, imbued them with a portion of their power, then set them loose to hunt down Eitri. Ended up killing him."

Carl fell silent as Abby burned away the last patch of snow. A wide set of white marble stairs rose up before us, ending at a set of looming double doors, thick enough to withstand an assault from a cruise missile. Each door was made from a single piece of dark mahogany, except that was impossible because there was no tree anywhere in the world big enough to produce a door like that. Running across the front was an enormous carving of a tree, meticulously depicted in solid gold. A gnarled trunk ran down the dividing line between the doors, its twisting boughs reaching toward the archway overhead.

"Yggdrasil," Carl muttered, working to hide his awe, and failing. "Huh. How 'bout that." He craned his head back, bearded mouth hanging open. "This is a whole lot more impressive than I thought it'd be."

"So, uh, how do we open it, hoss?" Forge asked, eyeing the entry for some sign of door handles. There weren't any, of course, but even if there were, no one would be strong enough to budge those monstrosities. It would take a war elephant—maybe a couple of them—equipped with breaching chains to pull those bad boys open.

"Knock maybe?" Carl suggested. Probably the most unhelpful advice of the century.

Still, it was worth a shot. I broke away from the pack and headed up the huge steps, which seemed to be designed for someone with legs much longer than mine. The second my foot touched the landing, the golden branches of Yggdrasil began to writhe, pulling and twisting as the doors swung outward without a sound. They crept to a stop just as silently, hanging wide open in invitation.

Well, I guess that answered that.

FIFTEEN

CONNECTIONS

OUR FOOTSTEPS CLATTERED AND ECHOED OFF THE high ceilings as we made our way down one of the many marble hallways in the Keep. Cutter led the way, on high alert for any sign of traps or other nasty surprises. So far nothing, but that didn't make me feel any better. There was no way a place like this was just *unguarded*. If a horde of shambling zombies had flooded out en masse... well, that would've sucked, but at least it would've made sense. But so far there was no sign of mobs. Not so much as an overgrown sewer rat, which just didn't make any sense.

But then, nothing about this place made a lick of sense.

The sprawling Keep was dusty, and clearly it'd been ages since anyone had stepped foot here, but aside from that, everything was *immaculate*. Bronze sconces decorated the walls, and each one flared to vibrant life as we approached. Instead of burning with preternatural fire, however, each sconce held a crystal orb, which thrummed with warm orange light. Magical lightbulbs. Breathtaking paintings and elaborate tapestries hung from the walls; small alcoves and nooks held cast bronze statues or marble busts perched on fluted marble pillars. It was like walking through a museum after it had closed for the night.

The art itself dropped more than a few clues about the owner of the house, who I could only assume was Eitri Spark-Sprayer. Several portraits featured a bear of a man, with shoulders as broad as any Dwarf's, his skin a glimmering silver instead of the typical gray of most Murk Elves. He had a mass of platinum-blond hair that cascaded down past his shoulders and a beard to match, which reached almost to his belt. That beard would be the envy of any Svartalfar, I had no doubt. In many of the paintings he held an enormous blunt hammer, meant more for the forge than for the battlefield—though I wouldn't want to get smacked with the thing.

Interestingly, the tapestries were a mix of scenes.

Some depicted wintery mountain vistas while others showcased the Storme Marshes with their twisted trees, murky bogs, and stilted houses, perched high above the ground like huge water striders. One painting, prominently displayed over a fireplace in a huge banquet hall on the second level, showed the silver-skinned giant with a broad smile on his bearded face, one arm wrapped around the shoulders of a much shorter man—though short was relative. The other man I recognized at once from my brief time in the Twilight lands: Nangkri, the Jade Lord.

During my quest to assemble the pieces of the Jade Lord Set—and unite the six named Dokkalfar clans in the process—I'd learned that the Nangkri dynasty had a strong alliance with the Dwarves, once upon a time and way, way back. And that alliance had eventually resulted in the downfall of the dynasty after they'd accidentally released an ancient dragon, Arzokh the Sky Maiden, during a mining operation. I'd had no idea just how strong that alliance was, but a glance at those paintings, those tapestries, told me it had deep roots.

The rooms, and there were so many it was almost hard to keep track of them all, were likewise preserved. Leather lounge chairs, velvet divans, high-backed chairs and long banquet tables perfect for entertaining guests. There were mirrors, art, and stained-glass windows positively everywhere flooding the castle with light and vibrant color. We found a number of well-stocked libraries and plush studies, but all the books were of the more mundane variety. There were guest rooms with pillow-topped mattresses and copper, claw-footed tubs. A huge kitchen with a pantry that had seen better days.

Aside from the food, everything was remarkably well preserved.

There were no mobs. Anywhere. And Cutter didn't find a single trap either, which once more set warning bells off in my head. But most disconcerting of all? We didn't find anything that even *hinted* at the lost tome we'd come to find. It took us hours to search the place—there were five main levels and a host of towers—and hours more to tear through the books in the many libraries, and after all of that we'd come up empty-handed. Around 9 AM we took a break in one of the dining halls—a vast room with thirty-foot ceilings, a crystal chandelier, and a fireplace bigger than my old IRL apartment.

We were eating dried jerky, cheese wheels, and chunks of crusty bread. Not exactly the breakfast of champions, but it still managed to taste like heaven—like all food in V.G.O. We ate in a tense silence. We'd already spent a big chunk of our morning here, and we were still no closer to finding Carl's book. Which meant we were no closer to getting into Stone Reach or unlocking the secret behind the Doom Forge. I pulled up my interface, checking the time. I had about three hours before the clock rolled over on my Death-Head timer. And when that happened, I'd get punched in the face with the first in a long line of nasty debuffs.

"Well, what do we do now?" Abby finally said after finishing off a piece of bread. "I feel like we've gone over this place with a fine-toothed comb. But if the book is here, I don't know where. So do we keep looking, or do we cut our losses and head back?"

"We've already spent so long, though," Ari piped up, a piece of bread no bigger than a thumbnail in her hands. "It seems like we should probably just finish. Keep going until we find it."

"Nope," Abby replied. "That's the sunk cost fallacy. It's the idea that you keep dumping time or money or effort into something because you've already invested a lot—you need it to work. But there's no guarantee that if we keep going, we'll find anything."

Everyone was quiet for a long beat.

"But it *has* to be here," Carl said, his voice resolute and determined. More so than I'd heard out of him... since *ever*. "We're so close. I can feel it. There's no way my order would send me here unless there was a way to complete the quest."

He wasn't wrong. The links between Eitri and Nangkri were too strong to ignore, but I didn't know what else to do. I sat silent, deep in thought, staring morosely at the fire blazing in the fireplace. Abby had kindly gotten it going for us, banishing some of the cold from the air.

The answer came to me a few minutes later as I watched the flames dance and bob like anguished specters. It was a bolt of pure inspiration. "The smokestacks," I said softly, mind whirling. "When we flew in, I saw a whole slew of smokestacks. Chimneys. Probably connected to a forge or foundry. Carl," I said, eyeing the Cleric. "You said that Eitri came here to work when he wasn't down in the Storme Marshes, right?"

"Right," he said, excitement flickering to life in his eyes. "But we haven't found anything that looks like a workshop or forge."

I shot him a finger gun. "Right on the head. We've found just about everything else. Beds. Dining halls. Libraries. But not that."

"And there's no way a demigod of the forge wouldn't have an operational forge inside his own giant Keep," Ari mused out loud.

"Exactly. Those smokestacks tell me that his workshop is here. We just missed it somehow."

"How, though?" Abby asked. "Seriously. We've searched this place from top to bottom. Every level. Every room. Every hallway. Every book. Cutter, you didn't find any sort of secret doors or hidden rooms, did you?"

"Not a one. If there's something hidden around this bloody place, it isn't hidden by mechanical means."

"But what about non-mechanical means?" Ari piped in. "If this Eitri was a demigod, then it's possible he had access to higher magics." She shrugged her tiny shoulders. "In the Realm of Order, illusion magic is as common as air. And illusions can't be detected by most Rogues—I know that from experience. It takes either a powerful Dispel Magic spell or..." She faltered. She took to the air, wings buzzing with manic life as her color turned a brilliant gold. Excitement. "Or someone like him." She jabbed a tiny finger straight out at Carl. "Back in the Smoked Pig. You saw right through my glamor."

"Yeah." Carl shrugged one shoulder. "One of my Passive abilities is True Sight. Lets me detect evil, pierce illusions. That kinda thing."

"That has to be it," I said. "There's a workshop here somewhere, but we missed it because we didn't know what to look for. Give me a second." I pressed my eyes shut, recalling the image of the Keep as we approached from the air. The neat row of chimneys had been near the back of the Keep, butting up against the sheer face of a rocky canyon. I ran through the layout of the Keep in my head. That had to be near the kitchen. Had to be. "Come on, I think I know where we need to go." I pushed my chair back with a *screech*.

We tore from the banquet hall, took a flight of stairs down, and dashed along the main corridor, taking turn after turn until we were back in the kitchen. The room was massive and filled with the standard kitchen fare. An open-faced brick oven. Wooden tables and counters. Racks filled with cast-iron pans, sheet trays, and enormous stockpots. The shelves were full of foodstuffs that had seen their best days several hundred years ago. None of that seemed especially suspicious, but an arched stone fireplace against the right wall had caught my eye the first time we'd come through.

There was a metal grate in front—a standard safeguard—and the floor inside the fireplace was covered in age-old black soot and ash. All perfectly normal. The thing that really stood out, though, was the sheer height of the archway. Had to be nine feet tall, easy. Big enough for someone like Eitri to walk through without so much as having to stoop. The fireplace was also against the eastern wall, which, *hypothetically,* was where the smokestacks should've been.

"Here." I nodded toward the fireplace. "You see anything out of the ordinary, Carl?"

The Cleric shuffled forward, a mixture of uncertainty and trepidation marring his movements. He hunched forward, hands on his knees, nose scrunched, eyes squinted. "Huh," he grunted. "There is a weird symbol right in the middle of the wall. Not very big. Maybe the size of my palm." He stuck his arm straight out, pointing at bare stone wall. There was no mark. No ward. At least not one that I could see. "Hold on a sec." He straightened, edged his way around the upright iron grate, and inched forward until his face was less than a foot away from the soot-stained wall.

"Yeah, right there." He extended a plump, quivering finger, tracing some unseen mark etched into the stone. As his finger moved, golden light blossomed along the fire-blackened stones, revealing a strange rune of swooping curls and angular lines. I'd never seen anything like it before, though that didn't mean much. I barely qualified as a Runic Scrivener. As Carl finished tracing the final twist, the wall shimmered and groaned.

The bricks broke apart, turning, shifting, somehow *folding* in on themselves in a Tetris-like jigsaw puzzle until the wall was simply gone.

In its place was an arched doorway that connected to an enormous room of black stone, red brick, and heavy iron.

"We sure this ain't the Doom Forge right here?" Forge asked as he took a few tentative steps into the enormous workshop. It was easy to see why he might ask.

The place was three times the size of the Crafter's Hall's smithy, and that was easily the biggest, best-equipped forge the Alliance had in its control. Along the back wall were several stone forges, their smokestacks rising up and up, along with a brick-lined smelter. Huge wooden quenching barrels were set up near each forge. Racks of raw ore and processed ingots lined another wall. There were metal- and wood-topped workstations. Anvils in all shapes and sizes, and more tools than I'd ever seen anywhere.

There were also several weapon racks and armor stands, though sadly they were empty of finished products. No book to be found, though I felt now more than ever that we were headed in the right direction. And I thought I saw our next step, straight ahead.

In the very center of the forge was a strange pockmarked silver disk, four feet in diameter, set directly into the marble stonework so it sat flush with the rest of the floor. A dizzyingly complicated set of runes and glyphs twisted around the circle, spiraling inward. Nobody else seemed to notice the metal ring—far too preoccupied with the expansive workshop and all its goodies—but that was only because I knew they couldn't see the violet energy radiating up in cold waves of power. Calling to me. *I've been waiting here, just for you, Jack,* it seemed to say.

My feet carried me forward, almost with a will of their own. The black handprint on my forearm—a gift from a dying Murk Shaman, now covered by my bracer—throbbed with a dull pain.

I dropped to a knee next to the odd metal ring, forged from Darkshard ore, and reverently traced my fingers over the runes in front of me. Arcane power thrummed, little jolts of energy sizzling up through my fingertips, then racing along the length of my arm. I'd seen one of these before, back in the Darkshard mine. The same place I'd first discovered Devil. This was a portal, the making of which I didn't fully understand. One which opened a semipermanent rift to the Shadowverse. I continued to run my fingers over the pitted surface, tracing the grooves in the metal.

The throbbing palm print, branded on my skin, pulsed in time to the beating of my heart. Wisps of inky shadow leaked out, transforming into a violet mist.

The icy cold in my arm grew in intensity, the throbbing now painful; my Spirit gauge took a sharp nosedive a moment later as I triggered my Shadow Stride ability, pushing that power downward into the ring as though I were trying to pull someone into the Shadowverse with me. But instead of slipping through the gossamer-thin wall between the planes, all of my Umbral power funneled directly into the ring like water into a dry sponge.

I pulled my hand away as the pain became too much to endure, and as I did a dark portal erupted inside the confines of the ring. It looked almost like a free-standing door, built from pure shadow energy. I couldn't even *begin* to fathom why the portal was here—*what use*

175

would the Keep's owner, Eitri, possibly have for something like this?—but I knew that the end of our quest lay on the other side of the shimmering gateway.

"Guys," I croaked, feeling a bit light-headed and wobbly from opening the portal. "Guys," I said again, this time my voice stronger. Surer.

"Yeah, what is," Cutter started, but cut off as he caught sight of the portal. "Oh bollocks," he said, running a hand through his dirty-blond hair. "Shadowverse, eh?"

"Shadowverse," I said in somber confirmation.

"I knew this was too bloody easy."

"Wait," Carl said. "What is that?"

"Unless I'm completely wrong," I replied, "this is the way to your book. Time to go find out what's on the other side…"

SIXTEEN

THE OTHER SIDE

IT TURNED OUT THAT VOID TERRORS WERE ON THE other side. So. Many. Void Terrors. Enough that I'd put one of the unspent proficiency points I'd been hoarding for once I hit level 50 into my Void Terror skill. I hadn't found a creature that could rival Devil or Nikko and her pack members—Kong and Mighty Joe—but I wanted to be ready in case I ran across something that would make an excellent addition to the team. Better safe than sorry.

The Void Terrors waylaid us almost the moment we set foot in the cold colorless world of the Shadowverse. And it seemed this place was making up for not having any mobs in the main compound by having twice the number shoved down in the warren of craggy stone hallways that ran below the mansion. We'd been at it for two hours—nearly endless combat with hardly a breather in between bouts.

"Forge, take point!" I yelled as a fresh wave of hell rushed us from down a twisting corridor.

This time it was brood of nightmare-inducing creatures called [Void Strikers], scuttling, insectoid

177

creatures that looked like a bad mashup between an enormous scorpion and a centaur. Each was the size of a horse, perched on six armored legs covered in cruel barbs, and sported two—yes, two—stinger-tipped tails, which oozed a viscous purple venom. Protruding from their bug-like frames was a humanoid torso protected by heavy chitin as tough as the toughest plate mail. The Strikers had arms sprouting from those torsos, but each limb was capped with wicked claws powerful enough to take off an arm or leg with ease. A too-human head littered with a host of glassy-black eyes finished the horrifying creatures off.

Nightmarish only began to cover them and all the other horrors skulking around down here. Still, this wasn't our first team dive. And after two hours of grinding, we had this down to a science.

"Abby, dual fire walls," I barked. "Carl, trigger Focus Aggression. Ari, augment with Transfixing Orb." In a heartbeat, roaring flames exploded from the floors on my left and right. Those walls were as straight and precise as a surgeon's incision, tapering inward, forming a natural funnel and choke point where Forge waited with his battle-axe raised. Cutter crouched behind the beef-slab Risi, using him as a living shield. Every few seconds he would slip to one side, hurling a conjured dagger at the Terrors frantically trying to get past the flame walls. His blades sliced through their chitinous armor, opening deep wounds that spewed blue-black blood.

Ari's wings fluttered with manic life as she moved into position, the blue glow from her body bouncing off the walls. She raised her minute hands. A moment later, a trail of orange and purple zipped straight up like a bottle rocket and exploded by the ceiling in a shower of brilliant, strobing light. A hypnotic attack, which distracted any enemy stupid enough to look. Instead of guttering, the strobing light lingered in the air, growing in intensity. The colors shifted from orange to crimson to azure to emerald to violet then back again, washing the room in a never-ending kaleidoscope of light.

A handful of the Void Strikers stopped dead in their tracks, inhuman eyes raised up, reverently fixated on the beautiful ball of light. Some wasn't all, though. Transfixing Orb was less effective on higher-level mobs and creatures with increased Intelligence. These things qualified for both.

Carl—positioned near the rear of the formation, not far from Abby—chanted, and a crimson glow built around him in a nimbus of light. His feet shuffled as he waved a wooden rod, capped by a metal ball the size of my fist. His Cleric's scepter, though it looked more like a cheerleader's baton if you asked me. Nevertheless, he was an awfully effective spellcaster, and it was oddly nice to have a proper Cleric on the team for once. As he finished his spell, the light around him fizzled and disappeared, reappearing around Forge a moment later. That bloody light looked like the cloak of an ancient god of war.

The encroaching Void Strikers immediately homed in on the tank, throwing themselves at him with hateful passion—pretty much ignoring everyone else in the process.

Carl's chanting changed, Life Tether activating around him in a shroud of gold. A wrist-thick strand of magic snaked out, connecting to Forge's back, feeding him a constant supply of HP and Stamina. Meanwhile,

Abby hurled fireballs, Amara fired corrosive-tipped arrows from her enchanted bow, and Cutter continued corralling the creatures with his flashing blades.

Under normal circumstances, I would've leapt directly into the thick of things, using my Shadow Stride ability to make it to the back of the enemy formation—taking out their casters, then systematically working my way through the ranks, ensuring they couldn't mount a proper defense. Unfortunately, since we were already *inside* the Shadowverse, my most potent ability didn't work. At all. And my second most potent ability, Night Cyclone, was likewise just as useless. Probably for the same reason. I couldn't rip a hole in the Material Plane to summon the vortex, because I wasn't *in* the Material Plane.

So instead, I played the role of DPS caster, support fighter, and occasional Cleric—casting buffs, auras, and throwing out Dark Shield to intercept nasty ranged spells.

The Void Strikers had quite a few of those, it seemed. A trio of the monsters loitering near the back hurled bolts of shadow power from their swaying scorpion tails. The attacks were not so different from my own Umbra Bolts, but were *far* larger—each orb the size of a basketball—and hit like a pro MMA fighter. With a flick of my left hand, I summoned Dark Shield. A churning semi-translucent wall of purple and black took shape in front of Forge a moment before the Umbra attacks hit. The orbs of power exploded on impact, wind and light rushing out, the force of the assault pushing me back a step.

Sweat broke out across my brow, and my arms quivered under the pressure of the spells.

But the barrier held.

Once the attack subsided, I dropped the shield and launched a barrage of my own. With a thought and an effort of will, I summoned Umbra Bog—that still worked at least—miring the spellcasters at the rear of the attack formation, then hit them with my pound for pound most devastating AOE spell: Plague Burst. I seldom used it. True, it caused an absolutely epic amount of damage, but unfortunately it didn't have the good grace to distinguish between friends and foes like Night Cyclone. And that included me—I was just as susceptible to the poison gas it conjured as anyone else. Suicide by toxic cloud was never pleasant and tremendously embarrassing to boot.

But this was the perfect setup, since I was out of the direct heat of the fight.

"Burst, burst, burst!" I called out, letting everyone know what was coming just in case they were planning anything reckless downrange. My left hand whipped through the air in a complex series of gestures: flick, twirl, snap, fingers splayed out, hand curling into a fist as raw power trickled out of my palm. A moment later, a rancid yellow fog—thick, billowing, and deadly toxic—bled from the air, swirling around the magical Void Strikers. It seeped through the thin joints between their rigid exoskeletons and clawed at insectoid eyes. It looked a bit like they were melting, thick purple ichor oozing out like pus as they died slowly.

Abby significantly sped that whole *dying* thing up by casting Rain of Fire, bringing down a torrent of blazing embers right on their heads. They shrieked—a high-pitched, undulating warble—then promptly keeled over, reduced to goopy piles of gore. The plague cloud dissipated a few seconds later, the area now safe.

Without their spell support, the last of the Void Strikers crumbled with a single push. Forge charged, axe carving a path forward. Ari—surprisingly effective with her tiny sword—and Cutter followed in his wake, hacking, slashing, and dancing through the now chaotic ranks. A little ranged assistance from Amara, Abby, and myself put the final nail in the coffin. Carl avoided direct conflict, of course, but kept chanting the whole while, wicking away minor injuries, dropping regen and resist poison buffs, using Focus Aggression to keep most of the heat firmly on Forge.

Quick. Easy. Effective. Minimal damage on our end.

Once we were sure all the critters were well and truly dead, we took a few minutes to loot the corpses.

The Terrors didn't carry much by way of loot items—no swords, shields, or armor. But killing them delivered a decent amount of XP, and they all carried a handful of coins, mostly silver, though the occasional gold as well. The biggest thing, though, was the crafting ingredients. Shadow Escorn Powder. Void Striker Venom. Umbra Chitin. Bootlace Fungus. I wasn't a Forager or an Alchemist by any stretch of the imagination, but I'd never heard of anything like this stuff. Which made a certain sense.

If these were ingredients naturally spawned in the Shadowverse, then only a handful of folks would be able to harvest them.

It was shortly after we'd finished clearing the corpses when the first of the Death-Head debuffs sideswiped me from out of nowhere, landing like a lightning bolt of white-hot agony. Frying my nerve endings in an instant. I dropped to the floor, clutching my guts, eyes watering as waves of heat and nausea rolled outward. Suddenly, that lightning strike of pain morphed into a raging forest fire, rampaging through me, traveling up and down my limbs. I rolled onto my side and dry heaved over and over again. Nothing came out, but by the time I was done, my ribs and back burned from the strain.

A prompt flashed as the pain finally started to wane and fade like a bad dream:

Debuff Added

Diseased: As a result of the Death-Head Mode, your body is slowly dying! You've been afflicted with Death Head's Disease. Attack Damage and Spell Strength reduced by 15%; Health, Stamina, and Spirit regeneration reduced by 25%; duration, until death or quest completion.

"Death-Head, eh?" Cutter asked, offering me a hand.

"Yeah." I accepted his hand and let him pull me to my feet.

It was a stern reminder that the clock was actively ticking against us, and that we needed to find this book and we needed to find it yesterday. I dismissed the notice, gave a brief word of explanation to Ari and Carl, who were unfamiliar with Death-Head mode and its nasty effects, and then we continued our way into the unending maze of passages.

For the next half hour, we encountered more pockets of resistance. Scuttling groups of Void Strikers. Prowling, hound-like [Void Kurjack]. Swarms of tiny, winged [Void Zrika], which were almost like crickets—if crickets were malicious, as smart as a pack of caffeinated toddlers, and equipped with claws and poisonous stingers. Big. Small. Feathered. Tentacled. All deadly in their own right and all absolute horror shows. I was pretty sure poor Carl would be traumatized for the rest of his days. The guy jumped at every shadow.

Eventually, the rocky cavern-like tunnels came to an end at a set of double doors, which almost exactly mimicked the doors to the Keep above—though with a few small differences. First, instead of an enormous *golden* tree with boughs reaching up, up, up, these doors had an enormous *silver* tree with sprawling roots reaching down. Inscribed on the stone arch above the door was a verse that looked like it belonged to a poem:

The guardian of shadow and wrath slumbers among the fallen leaves.

Our resident Cleric let out a gasp and face-palmed. "Freakin' figures," he muttered excitedly. "*As above, so below*. I shoulda guessed it."

"Guessed what, Dwarf?" Amara asked, side-eyeing the door as though she didn't trust it in the least. Good instincts.

"Yggdrasil," he replied, waving at the door with the intricate silver tree. Or at least the bottom half of it. "The tree of life—it's uh, sort of a Dwarven thing. They're really into it. But it's always depicted by a huge tree with both the roots and the branches exposed. Supposed to represent Mount *Svartalfheim*. The Dwarves, they teach that the roots of a mountain are just as deep as its summit is high. Like a mirror, you know? *As above, so below*. Anyway"—he waved a hand through the air—"the point is, up topside we only saw the branches. Here are the roots. A Keep above, a Keep below. And the fact that it's in a different realm—one of Shadow—makes even more sense." He shook his head, a wry grin on his bearded face.

"And the bit of verse there, friend," Cutter said, pointing at the cursive script running above the door. "What do you take that to mean, eh?"

"Pfft. How should I know?" the Cleric offered with a shrug. "What do I look like, some kinda Rhodes scholar?"

"You look like a bloody damned priest," Cutter shot back.

"Eh. Fine, I guess that's a valid point. But let's not forget that I'm also the *worst* priest in the order." He grimaced. Sniffed. "Boy am I kicking myself for not paying better attention, though." He frowned and ran a hand down the length of his beard. "But at this point, I figure it doesn't make much of a difference. In too deep to turn back." Without saying anything else, he bounded forward, making his way up a short flight of stairs carved directly from the porous rock. When he reached the top, the silver roots slithered and writhed as though they were a brood of snakes disturbed from a long sleep. As the squirming roots finally stopped moving, the doors ghosted outward—opposite of the door above—on silent hinges.

"Might be, I'm wrong," Cutter said, "but it seems to me that this is the way we're supposed to go." He moved forward on the balls of his feet, gaze restlessly scanning for any sign of traps or the shadowy, distorted ripples in the air that typically preceded Void Terror attacks. An overwhelming sense of déjà vu settled over me. When I got to the doors, I noticed a long string of pearly runes etched into the threshold to the strange underworld mansion. I couldn't make out more than a third of them, but a handful stuck out to me. Containment wards. Likely meant to keep the Void Terrors from the cavern at bay.

That, or maybe meant to keep something even worse *in…*

SEVENTEEN

As Above, So Below

INSIDE THE PALACE WAS SHOCKINGLY FAMILIAR. Polished marble hallways—black stone instead of creamy white—with arched ceilings and walls scones. These, though, were gleaming silver, and the magical orbs they held shed watery light like trapped moon beams. There were nooks, crannies, and alcoves here as well, but instead of fanciful artwork, the items seemed far more esoteric. Maps, framed fragments of parchment, clay tablets with obscure pictographs or script in languages I didn't understand.

We even found the occasional rack of weapons or free-standing suit of armor. Those we lingered at a bit longer, inspecting each item for traps or malicious sigils, before stripping them down and throwing them into our inventories. Good stuff. All of it well made, though without an enchantment in sight. Everything was starter gear, but even starter gear could serve the Alliance.

More interesting, however, were the rooms which branched up from the main corridor.

The mansion above had clearly been a residence. A beautiful, sprawling, intimidating residence that could house a hundred people, easy, but a *home* nonetheless. True to theme, this place was just about the opposite. It was dedicated to form and function. There were no lounges. No soft sofas or leather club chairs. No grand dining halls with enormous hard wood tables and high-backed seats. Instead, there were archery ranges, agility courses, training pits, alchemy labs, and armories. This looked like the secret fortress of a general-king.

As we wound our way through the maze of rooms and hallways, exploring its many floors, I couldn't help but wonder whether we could lay claim to this Keep. We had Darkshard, yes, and we'd even set up a training academy of sorts down in the Darkshard mines nearby. Since time worked differently in the Shadowverse—trickling by far more slowly than it did in the Material Realm—we could squeeze untold amounts of training and crafting into a relatively limited timeframe. Still, working in the mines was an unbelievable challenge since the Void Terrors were everywhere, and respawned every eight hours like clockwork.

It made for some serious logistical and personnel issues.

But just like the mansion above, this place was devoid of mobs—so far, at least—giving credence to the idea that the runes by the door were indeed containment wards. So, if we could capture this place like some of the other Keeps scattered about Eldgard, it could offer us a variety of strategic advantages. Training. Security. Plus, a base in the north that no one else knew about. Definitely something to look into once I'd sorted everything out with the Doom Forge.

We explored each of the rooms we passed, taking our time to ensure there was nothing we overlooked, but found no sign of the book we'd come in search of. We did, however, find more strange verses painstakingly etched into various areas. Clues of some kind, I had no doubt, though I wasn't sure what exactly they corresponded to.

In shadow and in light, we found carved into the stone mantle above a fireplace, the letters so small and so fine we'd almost missed it. Only Cutter's sharp eye saved the day there. In an enormous war room, we found the line *A cruel tormentor along the path;* neatly penned at the bottom of a giant parchment map with all of Eldgard splashed across it. *A bane to all unworthy thieves* adorned a wobbly stone set into the floor of a decked-out alchemy lab. Amara discovered the line *Weakness revealed in darkest night* painstakingly scrawled onto one of the wall sconces.

After we'd searched every other inch of the place, we headed toward the back end—where the kitchen and forge had been located in the upper portion of the Keep. The entrance to the Shadowverse had been located in the forge. Since this shadow version of the Keep so closely mirrored the version above, I suspected we'd probably find whatever we were looking for there. The last few hallways were bare, and before long we wound up in the kitchen. Except down here, it wasn't a kitchen, but a library. And scrawled above the archway, almost like a bookend to the arch at the front entryway, was a section of verse.

A magic touch shall not prevail;

Although I'd never graduated from college, I remembered enough from my English Lit class to recognize a poem. And Abby, who *had* graduated, was smart enough to put it together in the right order, though she insisted it was something called a Sicilian Octave, and that it was missing a final line.

> *The guardian of shadow and wrath*
> *slumbers among the fallen leaves.*
> *A cruel tormentor along the path;*
> *A bane to all unworthy thieves.*
> *In shadow and in light,*
> *weakness revealed in darkest night.*
> *A magic touch shall not prevail;*

Beyond the arch was the single biggest library I'd ever seen, though admittedly, I hadn't had a chance to stop by the Grand Archives in Alaunhylles. According to Abby there were *miles* of books, tomes, and records there. Still, this place was impressively big—a maze of twisting aisleways and heavy-laden bookshelves loaded down with tomes and books in all shapes and sizes. Must've been twenty thousand books. Maybe more. It would take months to search through every title, and *years* to read them all.

Even inside the Shadowverse, where time crawled along at an eighth of normal speed, we'd never have enough time to look through every text—not before the quest expired, killing me in the process.

"Well, shit," Forge said, drawing out the word *shit* as he rubbed thoughtfully at his blocky chin. "I might be outta my depth, y'all. Killing monsters. Fighting gods. Blowing up taverns. I'm all about it, but ain't no one said I was gonna have to do a bunch of book reports."

"He has a point," Cutter piped in. "Where in the bloody hells do we even start? This is like searching for a needle in a giant pile of needles." He turned and glowered at Carl. "This is supposed to be your area of expertise, friend. So what are we supposed to be looking for, eh?"

"Well." The Cleric shifted awkwardly. "It's a leather-bound book about yay big." He held his hands apart, giving us a rough measurement. Unfortunately, his terrible description fit over half the books lining the shelves. "Says *The Biographical History of Eitri Spark-Sprayer* in fancy gold lettering across the front." He shrugged apologetically. "There's a golden handprint on the front too, if that helps any."

"Damnit all, Carl," Cutter said. "Gods, but you really are the worst priest I've ever met. It's no bloody wonder they tossed you out on your ear like the utter sod you are."

"Hey man, I never wanted to be caught up in this quest," he shot back defensively. "My only goal was to keep my head down, make a decent living, and drink beer in my off hours. I'm not supposed to be the freakin' chosen one, okay?"

"Just calm down," Abby said before things could escalate further. "There's got to be a better way than just looking through every book. I mean stop and really look at this library. *Really* look at it. The aisles are crazy, a maze. But everything here's *neat*. Meticulous. A place for everything and everything in its place. This collection is clearly sorted and organized, which means that whoever owned it probably had some way to search for specific volumes—a way to find the right one. It would be stupid not to have *some* method, right?"

"Which means there's probably a card catalog or maybe an index volume around here somewhere," I said, rushing forward to envelop her in a huge bear hug. "You're a genius, Abby. Seriously, what would we do without you?"

"Never find the book," she grumbled good-naturedly as I set her down. She smoothed her dress, but offered me a genuine smile.

"There is one other possibility," Amara said. "This book. It is a quest item, yes?"

Carl bobbed his head.

"Then, perhaps, it will not be on these many shelves at all. If it is a sacred tome, as your priests teach, then would it not make sense to have such a title segregated from the more common volumes?"

"Yeah," Abby said. "That's a good point. Could be it's sitting on a pedestal somewhere—or maybe hidden behind a false wall. Something like that."

"Then let's split up," I said. "Abby, Forge, why don't you two start looking for the catalog or the index book. Amara and Cutter, start searching for traps, hidden doors, any kind of secret mechanism. Ari, you and Carl are on the lookout for illusions. Maybe our pal Eitri used the same tricks as he did topside. In the meantime, I'll start pawing through some of the regular books. See if anything jumps out at me. But word of warning—be careful. I know we haven't run across anything in here that wants to eat our faces yet, but I wouldn't get complacent. The last time I was in a library like this, I ran into Devil."

Everyone set off in different directions.

I made my way into the stacks, trailing my fingers along the book spines, gaze drifting over each volume, not lingering on any title for too long. Most of them seemed pretty tame and boring. Lots of books on Eldgard history, documenting eras ranging from the rise of Rowanheath to the Merchant Council coup. I found one book that offered insight into the first invasion of the Imperials onto the continent. I plucked that one from the shelf and added it to my inventory, hoping to find some time later on to glance through the pages.

The history of Eldgard was murky at best, and though I knew the Imperials had invaded from the east, landing on Eldgard and establishing New Viridia before making their push against the rest of the natives, there was little talk of *where* the Imperials had come from originally. Was it possible there was a whole other continent out there somewhere, filled with some forgotten empire that no Traveler had ever visited? If so, were there Murk Elves there? Accipiters? Dwarves? Or were there different races entirely? I didn't know, but it might be worth exploring one day.

I moved on into another section, this one stocked mostly with texts on magic and spellcraft. *The Metaphysical Paradox of Divination. Spinners Handbook of Mystical Merchant-craft. Compendium of Tanglewood Beasts. A Conjurer's Primer.* Some of those books sent little jolts of power thrumming into my outstretched fingertips. *Beckoning me. Enticing me.* A tome titled *Umbra Runic Transcription* seemed custom tailored for me, so I added it, along with a few of the more interesting titles, to my bag. Mostly, though, I kept moving. As much as I wanted to plop down and spend the next few weeks exploring every book that piqued my curiosity, we had places to be and things to do.

The next ten minutes passed by much the same as I wandered aimlessly, selecting rows at random, hoping raw instinct would guide me where I needed to go.

I was halfway down another unremarkable aisleway when a purple glimmer, radiating from the spine of a book, caught my eye. The mark wasn't big, just an odd circle with too many loops, swirls and lines jutting off. Upon closer inspection, I realized it wasn't a proper rune at all, but rather, an ancient Dokkalfar symbol I'd seen a handful of times before. The symbol of the Dark Templar. The mark of the *Maa-Tál.* Chief Kolle had a mark like that on an amulet he always wore, and so did the other Murk Elf chieftains who made up the Dark Conclave.

It instantly set my gamer sense to tingling. Bingo.

I inched over to the shelf, hooked the top edge of the book with one finger, and gave it a gentle pull. The tome resisted my attempts to remove it from the shelf. I pulled harder, but still nothing. Next, I ran the pad of my thumb over the glimmering rune. A faint jolt of power sprinted up my arm, and the handprint on my forearm suddenly burned with arctic power, cold and raw and biting. Something that only happened in the presence of potent Umbra Magic. Usually potent *ritual* magic. Working on intuition, I pressed my thumb against the odd rune and fed in a trickle of Spirit.

The sigil flared, a pulse of light so bright I had to shield my eyes against it, and a second later, there was a *click* and a *groan* as a section of bookcase in front of me lurched inward. A false wall, though this one was clearly meant to be accessed only by someone with the power of shadow. That was incredibly suspicious. Sophia had said that Overmind interference was strictly limited given the nature of the quest, but what were the chances that we would stumble on a place like this? A Keep that would require the skill set of both a Cleric and a Dark Templar?

Impossibly unlikely. Unless…

Unless Sophia and the other Overminds had been manipulating me from the very beginning.

When I'd first meet Sophia—just after earning my place among the Ak-Hani as a Shadowmancer—she'd told me I'd be her pawn. What if she'd been true to her word? Moving me, step by step, this whole time. Offering me the illusion of choice, while subtly forcing me to follow the path she'd been laying out for me. She'd made me her Champion. She'd put Vlad into my path, ensuring we'd take Rowanheath, which in turn had led me to the Quest of the Jade Lord. She'd called me into the Realm of Order and pitted me against the Lich Priest, Vox-Malum, who just so happened to have the first Doom-Forged relic.

And now, here I was. At her insistence. After she'd pointed me toward Carl like a hunting dog set on the trail of a deer. Carl, the only person who could've guided me here.

The section of bookcase came to a stop, revealing a shallow alcove with a high ceiling. The far wall was plaster, not stone, and on it was a breathtaking fresco. A portrait of Eitri—in this one he was in a dark forest, his leather armor black as wet tar, a heavy warhammer not so terribly different from my own resting against one shoulder. A bit of light reflected from his right hand: a ring, *embedded* into the plaster, wrapped around his finger. In the center of the nook was a marble pedestal, and etched along its edge was the final line of the poem: *the beginner's blade can tip the scale.*

195

I only had eyes for the thing resting on the pedestal, though. A book. A book with an odd golden lock, protecting its secrets from unwanted eyes, and a golden handprint splayed across the front.

A handprint that instantly reminded me of the one on my arm.

After thinking about Sophia, and the way I'd likely been manipulated, I was tempted to turn around and leave the book be just to spite her. But the tome called to me. In some way, it felt like destiny as I stepped into the hidden chamber. Like my whole time in VGO had set me on the path to this place. To put the clues together. To assemble a weapon, created before the game had even gone live, which could save the world.

In the end, however, it was my sheer curiosity as a gamer that pulled me across the threshold.

I reached out a trembling hand, pressing it against the palm print on the cover, briefly thinking of Yggdrasil, the tree of life, with its mirrored branches and roots. *As above, so below.*

My hand burned.

Not with fire but with impossible cold, which traveled up my arm and into my chest, surrounding my heart, reaching icy fingers into my lungs. The lock securing the book sprang open, Umbral light spilling from between the pages. I lifted my hand, and the book burst open, the pages fluttering madly like the rustling of fall leaves, bleeding preternatural light into the air. I heard an audible *click* and the grinding of shifting stone, but the sound was distant and unimportant. So, so far away.

And, in short order, all of that faded as I fell forward, *swallowed* into the pages of the book.

EIGHTEEN

THROUGH THE LOOKING GLASS

I SWAYED AND LURCHED, WOOZY AND A LITTLE nauseous from my trip down the rabbit hole. I glanced left and right, trying to figure out where in the heck I was, because one thing was certain, I wasn't in the underground library anymore, but in an enormous cavern. The walls were deep, red-brown stone, natural, uncut, and studded with raw gemstones: fist-sized rubies, emeralds, diamonds, topaz, and sapphires. Interspersed among the gems were great veins of raw ore: iron here, silver there, gold in a third spot, a jagged skein of jade.

The legion of precious stones and the huge veins of metal ore glimmered in the burning orange light of a colossal forge, bathing the mosaic floor in a warm, welcoming glow. The mosaic underfoot depicted a Murk Elf woman with raven-black hair and blazing emerald eyes, a sad half smile on her lips.

The forge itself was like nothing I'd ever seen. Protruding from the far wall was a statue, sculpted directly into the cavern face: a phoenix the size of a battleship with wings spread wide, its beaked maw lifted up in defiant triumph. Resting at the mythic bird's clawed feet was a sea of burbling red-gold magma, wisps of steam and heat drifting up like a cloud. Nearby was a flawless obsidian anvil, larger than a dinner table. Curiously, however, there were no tools. No hammers, swages, awls, or even quenching barrels. Nothing to work metal with.

A bear of a man loomed above the magma pool, though man probably wasn't strictly the right word to use. He was fifteen feet tall if he was an inch, so heavily muscled he was nearly deformed, and made from gold. His whole body. Just pure gold, glimmering in the dancing forge light. His hair, woven from a sheet of silvery metal, was long and pulled back into a braid, and a massive beard of *literal* fire trailed down his chest. I watched in unsettled awe as he dipped one hand into the magma and pulled out a dollop of lava the size of my head.

If that wasn't *Khalkeús* the forge godling, I'd eat my boot. Which meant this was my first look at the vaunted Doom Forge of legend.

Begrudgingly, I had to admit it did indeed look legendary. The Devs—or more likely, the Overminds—had gone all out, and that was saying something considering everything else I'd seen in Eldgard.

Khalkeús tromped over to the obsidian anvil and slammed the hunk of liquid death onto the surface with a *splat*. He sat down on a natural chunk of rock jutting up from the ground, dug his fingers into the burning metal, not concerned in the least by the heat, and began to knead it. Working his fingers and palms in. Pushing. Pulling. Stretching. Rolling. The metal as pliant as a clump of bread dough.

I pulled my eyes away from the spectacle as the *click-clack* of approaching footsteps drifted through the cavern. A moment later a young man, maybe late twenties, stepped into view. Though nowhere near as tall as the figure hunched over the anvil, the newcomer stood head and shoulders above me. I recognized him at once as the man from the portrait. Eitri Spark-Sprayer. He glanced in my direction, but his eyes slid over me without so much as a pause. He threaded his way over to the anvil and leaned against the nearby wall, arms folded, black cloak trailing down his back.

He said nothing.

"So that's it then, eh, lad?" Khalkeús said, his voice deep and unnaturally gruff. Like boulders grinding together. "Ya think ya're ready tae go out into the wild world." Not a question but a statement of resigned fact. As he spoke he worked the slab of metal. Fingers digging in, dimpling the slag as he drew it out into a long thin bar. With a pinch, a twist, and a deft pull he formed a handle.

"Well past time," Eitri said, his voice lacking the Scottish burr of his father. "I've been cooped up too long, Father. It's high past time I went out and met my people. My other people." He paused and glanced at the floor, eyes skipping over the picture of the woman in the mosaic. "It's what she would've wanted, you know." He lifted one arm, and pulled back a cuff, revealing a handprint identical to my own. "This was her final gift for a reason. This is what she wanted for me."

"Aye. Ah know it," Khalkeús replied, voice surprisingly soft and tender. He shaped the other end of the glowing metal, sculpting it like clay into a boxy hammerhead. "Always knew this day would come, lad. Just seems so soon. Too soon." He scooped out a gob of metal, formed a ridge with one thumb, then squeezed and eased a spit of metal into a wicked spike on the back before doing the same on the top.

The metal—if it was actually metal—still glowed with impossible heat, but now the shape was clear. A warhammer. The golden god leaned forward and blew gently onto the metal, the motion surprisingly tender. It hardened in a flash, intricate red-fire runes glowing along the handle and swirling over the hammer's blunt face. "Ya will be needing this, Ah reckon." He stood and hefted the flawless weapon. A miraculous vision.

"The world, it's moved on since yer mother passed, lad. Different days." He trundled over, his footsteps heavy and ponderous. "If my acolytes speak true, there be war brewing in the land. Between your mother's kinfolk and the Imperials to the east." He paused, brow furrowing, his mouth disappearing into his bearded face as he grimaced. "Just be careful out there, eh lad? It's a dangerous world fer a child of the betwixt. Might be they'll try to suck you into their machinations. If you let 'em. Hear me, lad—dinnae let 'em because ya are nae invincible. Dinnae think it." He held the dazzling weapon out for Eitri, pride and fierce love burning in the forge god's face.

I had to admit, Khalkeús was nothing like what I'd expected. I mean, on the surface he was *exactly* like what I was expecting. But the affection for his son? The obvious care and even gentleness? It was odd to think that *this* was the same being who'd crafted a weapon capable of murdering the gods.

The world shivered, dissolving around me as the floor trembled like mad. Living in San Diego, I'd experienced more than my fair share of earthquakes, but this was far worse than anything I'd experienced IRL.

Everything exploded in a shower of light and swirling chaotic motion before resolving once more into a jungle. One I recognized at once from my long hours spent in the Storme Marshes. A thick tangle of trees and waterways stretched off in every direction. Towering cypresses, droopy-leafed willows, unbending elms, and creeping mangroves. Fat, twisted roots jutted up from sludgy water, and the leafy canopy overhead blocked out the sunlight, casting everything in perpetual gloom and deep shadow.

The thunderous crack of a tree bough startled me, and I twirled just in time to see Eitri spring off of a mangrove branch overhead. Twisting in the air, he fired an Umbra Bolt from his left hand at someone or something just out of view. He landed in a crouch, light as a cat and just as gracefully, left hand held at the ready, right hand wielding the immaculate warhammer his father had made for him what seemed like only a moment before.

"You're fast, Eitri," boomed a voice from overhead as another man flipped into view from the inky shadows of the canopy. "But your speed won't save you, not this time." Unlike Eitri, the newcomer landed like a meteor, the loamy earth cratering out around him. He stood with a wry grin on his face, a hefty sword clasped in his hands. My breath caught in my throat. He was taller than me with broad shoulders and a swath of ebony hair. He stared at Eitri with dark eyes like chips of burnt coal, which sat above a hooked nose. His black plate mail pulsed with violet runes of power that matched the blade in his hands.

I knew him just like I knew these were the Storme Marshes. The Jade Lord, Nangkri, in the flesh. Or at least he *would* be the Jade Lord eventually. He looked *much* younger than when I'd crossed paths with him in the Twilight Realm, and he didn't yet have the crown of the Jade Lord. Which meant his battle against Arzokh the Sky Maiden probably hadn't happened yet. Early days, then. Still, I'd never forget that face. Not in this lifetime.

Nangkri charged, sword lashing out in a vicious arc.

Eitri danced back, his steps light, deflecting the blow with a flick of his hammer before sending another Umbra Bolt directly into Nangkri's gut, doubling the man over, though only for the briefest of moments. Eitri charged, the spiked tip of his hammer thrust forward, but Nangkri had already recovered. The future Jade Lord parried the thrust, shot inside Eitri's guard, and delivered a punishing elbow to the throat that would've killed a lesser man. Eitri gasped and tottered—his HP didn't dip more than a fraction of an inch—his weapon dropping low just long enough for Nangkri to make a move.

Nangkri thrust his sword out and the blade seemed to melt and stretch, forming a violet tentacle, which wrapped around Eitri's broad shoulders like a constricting python. With a flick of his wrists, Eitri was flying through the air, tumbling head over heels on a crash course with a wide-trunked willow. Until he was simply gone. Disappeared in the span of an eyeblink. A single blink later, he reappeared, no longer in flight, but standing directly behind Nangkri, the spike of his hammer pressed against the side of the Jade Lord's exposed throat.

Nangkri sighed and held up his sword. "I yield." He smiled as the spike retreated. "You are improving every day, Eitri." He turned and walked toward a clear path of bog as he withdrew a ribbon-bound scroll from his pouch. "It won't be long until you can give Chao-Yao a challenge. Keep at it, and you might be the most powerful Shadowmancer in a thousand years." He glanced over his shoulder as he broke the ribbon on the scroll, summoning a shimmering portal. "Doesn't hurt that you're the scion of a god, though. Where I come from, we call that cheating…"

My head swam as I replayed the conversation. Eitri was a *Shadowmancer*? I'd known coming into this place that the demigod had been a descendent of the Murk Elves. But knowing that he shared a class with me was a revelation. Suddenly, the Shadowverse-bound mansion made so much more sense. It also made me wonder about the silvery disks, which granted long-term access to the Shadowverse. There was one in the Darkshard mines outside of Yunnam and one in the forge above. They weren't natural occurrences. No. Someone had built them, and I was starting to suspect that someone may well have been Eitri.

I wondered briefly if I might discover that secret somewhere down in this library. Being able to make these little pocket portals into the Shadowverse would be an unparalleled trump card.

But then, just as I started dwelling on the potential implications, the world shifted away once again. This time the swampy bog was gone, and before me was a campfire. Night bugs buzzed and chirped in an oppressively dark sky, held at bay only by the light of the fire. Despite the deep gloom, the folk around the blaze seemed like a happy bunch. Nangkri lounged on the far side of the fire, lying on a colorful Murk Elf blanket, propped up on one arm. He was older now, though, closer to the man I remembered, with gray streaks at his temples and the hint of crow's-feet forming at his eyes.

Eitri was there, too. He hadn't aged a day as far as I could tell.

Several of the other men ringing the fire I vaguely recalled from my time in the Twilight Realm as well. All hard-faced Dokkalfar. A few were big and bulky: bruisers and tanks in heavy plate mail, with brutal two-handed weapons riding their backs. One was whip-thin—built with the hard lines of a razor blade—wore dark leather armor, and had a beefy warhammer that could've been a twin to my own. A Shadowmancer, for sure. Others sported the flowing robes of mages, while another still was decked out in conjured armor built from yellowing bones.

I thought they were probably Nangkri's brothers— the long-dead chieftains of the six named Dokkalfar clans.

It was the woman reclining near Eitri, though, that stood out the most. She was the only female for one, and for another, one of her hands was intertwined with Eitri's. She wore patchwork leather armor, studded with bits of bone and covered with intricate runic script. She was younger than the rest of the chieftains, maybe in her late teens or early twenties, and bore a striking resemblance to Amara. The same lithe lines to her body. Same short-cut black hair, shaved down to the skin on one side. Same slightly canted emerald eyes.

Not identical, but they could've passed as cousins.

"And what say you, Isra?" Nangkri asked, though what the topic of discussion was I couldn't say.

"I don't know, Uncle." She shook her head and pursed her lips in faint disapproval. Even sounded a bit like Amara. "We need the gold for the war with the

Imperials, but the presence of the dragonlings changes things. There are easier ways to fund our campaign." She paused, stealing a sidelong glance at Eitri, who looked... troubled, to say the least. "Trifling with such an ancient creature as the Sky Maiden can only spell dis—"

Before she even finished speaking, the world shifted again, blurring around the edges as things spun topsy-turvy like a carousel going at full tilt. Flashing faster and faster, little snatches of imagery flying out at me like bullets.

Eitri in a high-ceilinged temple, standing before a panel of stern-faced men and women who didn't look even remotely human. Horns. Hooves. Silvery skin. The slit eyes of a snake. Each was finely dressed and radiated power, just as Khalkeús had. "You push too far, Scion," a black-haired woman with horns said, "and there are dire consequences for interfering unduly. You of all people should—"

Shift...

They were eaten by a swirl of churning smoke, quickly replaced by a picture of Eitri busy at work at a forge, a heavy hammer in his hand slamming down against a flat ring of dull silver.

Shift...

Eitri sitting in a high-backed leather chair at the head of one of the banquet tables I'd seen in the Keep above not too long ago. The other seats were occupied by Isra and Nangkri's brothers, though the Jade Lord himself was noticeably absent. "This is all such a mess," Isra said, running a hand through her short-cropped hair. She looked so tired. Hair-fine wrinkles had taken up residence at the corners of her eyes and around her rosebud mouth. "He won't listen to reason, Eitri. He's half mad, and no one can get through—we've all tried. We need you. Everyone needs you. The whole of Eldgard needs you. You're the only one he's liable to give an ear to at this point."

Eitri grimaced and dropped his gaze, regarding a silver wine goblet in his hands. "I doubt he'd want to see me. Not after—"

Shift...

When the image resolved again, the sprawling banquet hall was gone, replaced by a brightly burning hearth tucked away in the heart of a rustic wooden cottage, the furniture simple but well made. This time only Isra and Eitri were present. Isra was older now, in her late forties or early fifties, silver streaks firmly worked into the strands of her raven hair, though she looked as fit and trim as she had all those years ago. She sat on a narrow hay-filled bed covered by a drab gray bedspread. As before, Eitri was unchanged.

In her lap was a small bundle, wrapped with fine spider silk.

All of the youthful optimism and spring I'd seen before was gone, eradicated by time and circumstances. Now she looked *hard.* Beaten down, true, but harder for it—not broken.

"I don't know what you would've had me do," Eitri said as he paced the room, his heavy boots echoing off the creaking floorboards. "The other Aspects were already hounding me about my involvement."

"You could've saved him," she said, her voice fierce with certainty. She pulled back the folds of the bundle in her lap. Clustered within was the Jade Lord's set—crown, amulet, belt. "If you'd intervened with the Sky Maiden, things might've turned out differently. Better."

"And if he would've heeded your advice all of this might've been avoided. Perhaps I should've acted. But it would've brought down the wrath of every Northern Aspect upon my head. Even my father wouldn't have been able to help me then. Believe me or not, but I was told in no uncertain terms that I was not *allowed* to intervene further. That the fate of your uncle was a matter of destiny. As it stands, I already have a fair amount of explaining to do. I'm set to meet with the Aspect Tribunal in an hour's time. To explain my involvement in your war against the Empire."

She turned her head away, refusing to hold his gaze. "He never would've abandoned you, Eitri. No matter the cost. You may not have actually been a brother, but he certainly thought of you as one. He would've burned the world down for you." She paused, balling her hands into tight fists. "It is best if you go now. I need to be alone. To think." She fell quiet, her eyes heavy as she stared at the floor. "It is all falling apart with him gone." She shook her head and grimaced. "And I don't know how to put it back together. I don't know that it *can* be put back together."

Eitri cleared his throat and pulled something from his bag. A curling horn of beaten brass covered in hair-fine inscriptions that spiraled from a white bone mouthpiece to a gently flared bell. "As I said, I need to go. But..." He faltered, running his hands tenderly along the length of the horn. "I made this for you, Isra. The Horn of the Ancients. With this, you can call him back from the grave, at least for a time. Him and all of the honored dead. It can't make up for his loss, but perhaps it can light the path ahead. Perhaps he can give you the guidance I can't."

Instead of responding, she lay down on the mattress and offered the demigod her back. "Go now," she said, barely more than a whisper.

Pain and hurt cascaded across Eitri's face in waves. Gently, almost reverently, he set the horn down on a rough wooden dresser not far from where she lay. "I'll be back once I've finished with the Tribunal. We can talk more about this then. Perhaps lay it to rest."

Shift...

The world exploded into a thousand fragments of light like a broken mirror, and for a time everything was clattering sound and flashing light and chaotic motion. This transition was far more violent than the last had been.

When the world resolved again, we were back in the library, Eitri towering over the pedestal. He pulled a signet ring from his finger and pressed it into the plaster of the wall. "For those who find this record," he said, voice heavy, stoic, worry lines etched into his unnaturally youthful face, "let it be known that I did my best. But my father was right." He shook his head. "I wasn't ready. The world of men is a cruel place. Cruel and complicated. I leave for the Aspect Tribunal, but I fear they have treachery in mind. Should anything happen to me... Well, my father will not handle it well. He's a good man—as good as any god can be—but my loss. It will destroy him.

"If he reacts *poorly*, he'll need to be stopped. I've charged the Acolytes of the Shield and Hammer with containing him. There's a ritual book buried deep in the forbidden library under the order's main temple in Stone Reach. This ring"—he waved at the glimmer in the wall—"will open the way. Inside, you will find all that you need to locate the Doom Forge and the spells necessary to contain my father's wrath. Hopefully, it doesn't come to that, but one cannot be too prepared." He took a deep breath and nodded solemnly. He closed the pages of the book and pressed his hand against the golden palm print on the cover.

Violet light burst out in a cloud, kicking me in the chest like a mule and throwing me back and *up*. It felt... not quite like flying. More like falling in reverse.

And then, just like that, I was back in the library. Eitri gone. The book closed, the glow faded.

I shook my head, picked up the book—stowing it in my inventory—then beelined for the signet ring sunk into the wall. With a firm tug, I pulled it free, but before I had a chance to check out the stats or the flavor text, a frantic call caught my ear.

"Jack! Where in the nine hells are you, eh?" Cutter yelled at the top of his lungs. "We've got ourselves a bit of a bloody problem here!"

His words were followed in short order by an ear-splitting roar and incessant rumbling of the floors underfoot.

NINETEEN

GUARDIAN AMONG THE LEAVES

I WHEELED AROUND AND SPRINTED FULL SPEED DOWN one of the narrow aisleways toward the thunderous racket, pulling my warhammer free. I skittered around corner after corner, following the clamor, and nearly ran headlong into Cutter, who was retreating from... well, *something* at the far end of a connecting hallway, though it was hard to pin down what exactly I was looking at. A tag briefly appeared above the beast:

[The Paper Librarian].

A *tree* was the notion my mind immediately jumped to, though it was a tree only in the loosest sense of the word.

The towering monster crawled forward on a forest of root-like tentacles, which supported a gnarled trunk-like body, but one made entirely of book pages. Thousands, maybe hundreds of thousands, of book pages all plastered together as though the whole creature were a papier-mâché doll brought to life by the mind of a lunatic. Huge mâché boughs sprouted from the top of the odd tree; skeletal fingers crowned each branch, while loose-leaf pages fluttered frantically like leaves.

A pair of humanoid arms sprouted like cancerous growths from the tree trunk, each limb thicker than my thigh, each hand the size of a car tire with burning violet runes etched into the palm. In the very center of the trunk was a protruding knot, but instead of a lump of gnarled wood, there was the head of a goat. Goat-*ish*, anyway. More like a goat genetically spliced with a demon-shark. Its mouth was overflowing with rows upon rows of serrated teeth, and its curling horns gleamed obsidian and were as sharp as harpoons.

"Holy crap!" I shouted, momentarily stunned. "What in the hell is that?"

A blaze of fire, so bright I had to shield my eyes with one hand, erupted from another aisleway, flames splashing against the creature's page-covered hide. A Health bar appeared above the monster. My jaw nearly hit the floor as I watched. The monster's HP didn't drop, not even a sliver, which seemed absolutely impossible. Abby was hands down one of the most powerful Firebrands in Eldgard, and that was a monster *literally* made out of paper. But the flames simply refused to touch the thing.

"Come on." Cutter grabbed my arm and hauled me back into the stacks, away from the encroaching creature.

He dragged me all the way to the end of the aisle, hooked right, and slipped down another row before pausing. He pressed his back against a shelf of books, breathing hard, panting almost. He was absolutely covered with razor-thin wounds, blood liberally coating his armor.

"Are..." I faltered. "Are those giant paper cuts?" I asked, eyeing the wounds.

211

"Observant of you," he replied, pulling out a regen potion. "And yes. That bloody thing is someone's endlessly cruel joke. Unfortunately, it's also impossibly hard to kill. Hells, here I am talking about killing it. We've been throwing everything we have at it for the past five minutes, and we haven't put a single dent in the blighted thing. And speaking of, where in the hells have you been anyway, eh? You picked a terrible moment to take a break."

"Long story," I said, waving away the question. "I'll tell you about it later, assuming we survive. The important thing is that I managed to get the book."

Another thunderous roar filled the air, followed by a bellow from Forge and the clang of steel. "I need backup over here, y'all!" the Risi hollered in his Texas twang.

"Valkyrie is on her way!" Abby shouted, voice strained.

I edged my way to the end of the row and peeked around the corner. Forge was in front of the beast, his glowing battle-axe blazing in the murky silver light from the wall sconces mounted to the bookcases at even intervals. His weapon slammed into one of the groping roots, and the blade *clanged* as though it'd struck solid iron instead of flimsy paper. An enormous fist lashed out, and the Risi jumped back, barely avoiding the strike. Nearby, Carl chanted for all he was worth, machine gunning buffs and Health Restores at Forge like they were bullets.

Ari darted in, fluttering inches before the goat's face, striking at its amber eyes with absolutely *zero* effect.

A golden light bloomed like a bomb blast, shadows splashing against the shelves of books as Abby's legendary mount, a Hoardling Drake, appeared on top of one of the bookcases. The red-and-gold Drake launched itself at the creature, jaws yawning wide. The Paper Librarian was having none of it, though. It swiveled with unnatural speed, raising a rune-covered palm, and blasted the incoming creature from the air with a whirlwind of violet-glowing book pages. Yes. It had weaponized paper, which explained all of Cutter's odd wounds.

"Okay," I said, retreating back into the relative safety of the aisle. "We've got the book, and I know where the next clue is. So can we just get out of here? Finding out what loot this thing has is tempting, but we have what we came for, and it sure isn't worth dying over."

"No such luck, friend." Cutter shook his head. "The exit bloody well magicked itself closed when that thing popped out to play, and there's no way to open it. Not even a lock for me to try to pick. Seems to be, the only way out is killing that gods-be-damned tree thing. Abby, she reasons this is the guardian of shadow and wrath that slumbers among the fallen leaves. The beastie from the poem."

Terrible horror washed over me as I remembered the next verse in the poem. "A cruel tormentor along the path," I whispered. "A bane to all unworthy thieves."

Cutter shot me a finger gun. "That would be the one." The shelf we were hiding behind rattled, books raining down on us as something heavy slammed into the other side. "Time to move," Cutter said, darting toward the next connecting row. He dropped into a crouch, disappearing save for a faint blue outline surrounding his body, and stole across the open. I followed, but failed to use Stealth, which was a mistake I instantly paid for. A hurricane blast of swirling paper sandblasted me from my feet, razor-thin edges slicing at exposed skin.

I slammed into a bookcase with one of the silver sconces sticking out.

I let out a gasp of pain as metal jabbed into my spine a moment before my skull connected with the edge of a shelf. A host of stars exploded across my vision as I toppled to the ground. My HP was down by a sixth after one hit, and it felt like someone had just performed an Irish jig along the length of my spine. Only my heavy leather armor, reinforced with ring mail, had kept my back from snapping on impact. With a groan, I pushed myself up, glass crunching beneath me. With a wince, I looked up. The magic light-orb, formerly housed in the wall sconce above, now decorated the floor beneath me.

"Move your arse, Jack!" Cutter called. He was perched on top of a bookcase, hurling shadowy daggers at the paper horror lurching toward me on a writhing bed of tentacles.

Amara cartwheeled into view, touched down on top of a bookcase opposite to Cutter, and launched a hail of corrosive-tipped arrows, which were as ineffective as everything else. Seriously. How was this thing so damned sturdy? Cutter's blades were bouncing off without shaving off a single Health point, and Amara might as well have been firing rubber bands for all the good it did. The goat-headed horror roared as it surged forward, lashing out with one of its tire-sized hands.

I scrambled to my feet and threw myself into a sharp roll, avoiding the blow by inches. I came up to my feet and swung my warhammer with every ounce of strength I could muster, activating Black Caress as the weapon connected with the creature's thick wrist. Violet energy flared on contact, but the rush of energy that usually accompanied the skill was strangely absent, probably because Black Caress converted a portion of damage into life... except I hadn't inflicted any damage despite the hellishly powerful swing.

A tentacle struck like a cobra; I narrowly sidestepped the attack, but the creature had effectively backed me into a corner. Escape wasn't an option, especially since Shadow Stride was completely unavailable to me. The creature drove a balled fist toward me like a piston. I conjured Dark Shield at the last moment, deflecting the blow just enough to save my skull. The creature's fist sank into a bookcase with the force of a wrecking ball, sending dust, wood chips, and books raining down as the shelf imploded from the attack.

Holy crap, was this thing strong.

But something new caught my attention. This little corner of the library was now incredibly murky thanks to the broken light crunching beneath my boots. And in that gloomy dark, swirling lines of blue script had appeared across the monster's hand, running and zigzagging up its arm in elaborate, interweaving patterns. It was luminescent writing, though in a cursive so thick and dense I couldn't even begin to make it out. The looping scrawl continued up to the trunk but faded to near-invisible thanks to some ambient light from a connecting row of books.

A snippet of the odd poem came to my mind. *In shadow and in light, weakness revealed in darkest night.*

A snarl erupted as a huge beast of gold and red shot out from the connecting hallway, slamming into the tree and driving it into a nearby shelf, which leaned alarmingly to the side—trying to decide if it would topple. Abby's Drake clawed at the paper beast with wickedly hooked talons, terrible jaws latching onto swaying branches. Ari appeared a second later, glowing like a fallen star as she fired a burst of light in a riot of colors directly into the creature's hideous goat face.

"We don't have all day," she chirped at me, her voice amplified by her illusionary magic to carry over the din.

She wasn't wrong.

I steeled myself and bolted forward, leaping over the host of tentacle roots. One of the flailing limbs caught my bootheel, but I turned the fall into a quick roll that brought me back to my feet unscathed. I sprinted away as fast as my legs would carry me, sorely missing the use of my Shadow Stride ability as I rounded a corner. Abby and Forge were hustling toward me, and both looked worse for the wear. Frazzled, dirty, and bleeding.

"Shit, it's good to see you, Jack!" Abby hollered, screeching to a halt. "Where have you been? Are you okay?"

"Later," I shot back. "But I think I know what we need to do. The lights. We need to take out every light in this whole place, and you need to recall your Drake. Now."

"You want us to submerge the library into absolute darkness while an indestructible killing machine is hunting us down?" she asked with skepticism as thick as molasses.

"Call it a hunch," I said with a frantic nod.

"Gah! Fine," she replied, throwing up her hands. "I hope you're right. Forge, go buy us some time. Jack, you go that way." She waved toward another row of books, positioned across a short hall. "I'll head back the way I came." Without another word she dashed away, beelining for a glowing orb at the far end of the row.

I spun and followed suit. "Cutter," I called out as I bolted past the thief, currently busy leaping across the top of the bookshelves, dodging waving branches while hurling a barrage of smoky blades. "The lights. Take out the lights. We need this place black. Pass the word."

"A little busy, friend," he grunted, cartwheeling into a fleet-footed back handspring on a beam of wood I wouldn't want to try to walk across. "But I'll do what I can." He unleashed another wave of conjured blades with a flick of one wrist, then leapt into the air and disappeared in a puff of inky smoke. I heard the smash of glass a moment later, and a section of the library slipped into darkness. I dropped my head and kept right on running. One of the pearly orbs was dead ahead.

I lifted one hand and unleashed an Umbra Bolt ten feet out. The spell obliterated the magical glass, plunging that section of the library into dense shadow.

I glanced back toward the towering tree creature and felt a surge of triumph. The room wasn't completely dark—not yet—but already the glowing script had spread, now covering the creature's arms, roots, branches, and trunk. Heck, that odd script even ran over the beast's goat-like face. "It's working!" I shouted at the top of my lungs. "All the lights. Break every single one." I tore up the next row, hurling Umbra Bolts at every single glowing orb I passed. The sound of crashing glass resounded around the room, bouncing off the vaulted ceiling high overhead.

Whole sections of the library went black—but the lost light was quickly replaced by the glow emanating from the tree creature. For every light that perished, the script seemed to grow and spread, burning neon bright.

And interestingly, the blue script gave way to swirls of vibrant red. At least in select spots. Near the goat's eyes and snout. Along certain portions of the trunk—not much bigger than the bull's-eye on a target—even a few on key roots and swaying branches. Weak spots. They had to be.

An excited woot carried from farther in the library. "Oh hells yeah, you great big ol' sumabitch," Forge hollered. "You've got an ass kickin' inbound." The Risi pulled himself up onto a teetering shelf—damaged during the battle—and promptly hurled himself off with another *whoop,* his great battle-axe carving through the air. The blade slammed directly into one of the red splotches on the trunk. Even at a distance I could see the weapon hit true… and bounce off as though the blade were made out of Styrofoam.

Amara and Cutter angled toward the creature, running and leaping from shelf to shelf, avoiding swirling blasts of razor-sharp paper as they peppered the creature with conjured blades and acid-tipped arrows. The two of them were deadly accurate, each strike landing with uncanny precision on one of the red nodes. But their attacks were equally worthless. I knew we were on the right track here, those red spots *had* to be the creature's vulnerable areas, but why were the attacks having no effect?

My mind whirled as I ran toward the creature, scanning each row for Abby as I moved. The clue to killing this thing had to be buried in the riddle. Had to be. The first four lines of the odd poem had given us a heads-up about what waited and where, while the next two told us how to spot this thing's weakness. But there were still two verses left. Two verses which almost certainly held the final clue to killing this thing… but I was absolutely shit with riddles. Aside from MMOs, I'd spent more than a few late nights crowded around a table, playing D&D.

It was the stupid riddles that got me every time.

And the worst part was, *I* had the very last verse—the one I'd found inscribed on the podium cradling the quest book.

I sprinted past a row, and there, near the end was Abby, slowly backpedaling away from the shuffling tree creature as she hurled unending gouts of flame at fluttering pages. I ducked down the aisleway, arms and legs pumping. A huge arm lashed out with bone-breaking force—Abby tried to dance away, but she was too slow by half. As a Firebrand she was an absolute terror when it came to dishing out damage, but she'd never be as fast, agile, or strong as someone with a mixed class like me.

And she couldn't hold a candle to a pure Rogue-type class like Cutter or a Ranger like Amara.

Despite her best efforts, the backside of the creature's hand caught her square in the chest, hurling her away like a rag doll. She slammed into a bookcase, dusty tomes spilling down on her as the creature advanced at a ponderous gait. Another roar and Forge came bounding out from the labyrinth of books, posting up directly in the creature's path like a good tank should. Ari was on his shoulder, and she promptly zipped forward, slashing at the creature's eyes with her tiny blade. Their attacks did nothing to drop the monster's HP, but they bought me enough time to get to Abby.

I picked up my speed, my Stamina gauge flashing as it seeped away with every step.

I slid into the open as Forge went toe-to-toe with the creature, absorbing horrendously powerful blows while arrows and blades rained down from above. Only Carl, who chanted from a nearby aisle, kept the tank on his feet. I put them all from mind, bounding for Abby. She was crumpled on the floor, alive, but clearly hurt. Her legs were twisted at an odd angle, which meant broken bones and a nasty debuff without a doubt. I scooped her up in my arms like a child—she groaned and moaned in pain against me—and disappeared back into the stacks, calling out "all clear" over my shoulder to Forge.

I got as much distance as I could, then gently set Abby down, propping her up against a bookcase. She moaned again but seemed unable to talk. She winced, tears beading in her eyes as I straightened her contorted legs. Quick as I could, I grabbed a regen potion from a pouch at my side, forced her lips open, and poured the sickly-sweet brew down her throat. She shuddered, pressing her eyes closed as her body seized; in an instant, the magic potion stitched torn muscle together, realigning bone, even healing internal damage.

After a beat, she sputtered, coughed, and pushed herself up on her hands. "Wow, that asshole hits like a semitruck." She shook her head and pressed her eyes shut. "Okay, I'm good," she said after a moment, opening her eyes. "So, the light idea was brilliant, but we're missing something."

"Yeah," I said, "the last line of the poem. I found Eitri's book over in a secret alcove, and the last line was with it. *The beginner's blade can tip the scale.* Problem is, I don't know what it means." I gently grabbed her by the hands and helped her stand.

There was a *crash-thud* followed by a loud scream. "Jack!" Cutter's voice rose. "We can't bloody keep this up forever. What in the shite is the plan here, eh?"

"Hold on," Abby called, then more quietly, "Just give me a second to think." Her lips pursed into a thin line and her eyes went hazy. Deep in thought. "*A magic touch shall not prevail; the beginner's blade can tip the scale,*" she muttered softly to herself. Another crash-thud, the bookcase rattling behind us as the creature closed in on our position once more.

"Any time, now," I said, stealing a look over one shoulder. Slithering root-tentacles appeared at the end of the aisle, followed shortly by the looming form of the tree guardian. Forge and Ari were nowhere to be seen, though Cutter and Amara still bounced around the top of the cases nearby, trying to draw the creature away with little success. The creature thrust both hands forward and let out a furious, ground-shaking roar as it unleashed a twin attack of fluttering paper.

I moved on instinct, positioning myself between Abby and the attack, conjuring Dark Shield a moment before the unorthodox spell landed—an attack that would've flayed the skin from our bodies an inch at a time. The barrier sprang to life, sheltering us. Glowing pages bounced harmlessly away, but the shield flickered madly from the sheer force and weight of the assault, my Spirit gauge dropping like a rock off a cliff as I pumped energy into the spell. The creature's hands fell at last, the onslaught of pages tapering off.

I dismissed Dark Shield, and as I did, Abby rushed past me without a word, wielding a plain steel scepter. What in the hell was she thinking?

TWENTY

TIP THE SCALES

I REACHED OUT TO STOP HER—*WHAT IN THE WORLD did she hope to do with that?*—but she was already out of range. The Paper Librarian surged forward with a screech, roots and branches lashing out like coiled serpents. She plunged straight on anyway, swinging the unwieldly weapon in a wide but clumsy arc. Even at a glance, it was clear she was no weapon-wielding warrior. Still, the scepter flew true, smacking into one of the red script-spirals on a clump of roots.

A hit like that, against a creature like this, should've done nothing. Zero. Like smacking an elephant with a flyswatter. I was completely flabbergasted when the weapon landed with a brilliant flare of white light, and the monster's HP dropped. Not by more than a hair, but that was still more damage than anyone else had done through the course of the entire battle. The creature's root-tentacles recoiled, and for the first time, the creature was back on its heels, something that might've been uncertainty flashing across its inhuman face.

Abby threw her head back and crowed in defiant triumph. "That's right, asshole!" she yelled, raising the gleaming, though plain, weapon skyward like a giant middle finger. "Nonmagical gear," she yelled at the top of her lungs as she advanced slowly. "There were normal weapons scattered all over this place. Lowbie gear. And that was the key the whole time. This thing has complete immunity to magic. All magic. Spells. Weapons. Everything. But not these." She leapt forward with a growl, slamming the blunt weapon into a retreating root. Another flash. A sizzle. A tiny drop in HP.

Less than a second later, an arrow streaked through the air, courtesy of Amara, thudding into one of the glowing red splotches. And this time it *stuck*, cutting through a much heftier chunk of HP.

"Oh, it's on like Donkey Kong, shithead!" Forge said, charging from a connecting aisleway, his glowing weapon gone, replaced by a plain jane axe that any newb could find in any dungeon in Eldgard. His axe drove home like a railroad spike, penetrating the papier-mâché exterior as though it were cheap toilet paper. A flash of light and a horrified screech rent the air as a full tenth of the creature's HP vanished.

I grinned, absolutely ecstatic. Holy crap, Abby had done it. She'd solved the puzzle just like I knew she could. I stowed my regular hammer and quickly scanned my inventory. There. Not far from the bottom was a vanilla warhammer that dealt a whopping 27 points of damage. No boosts, no bonuses, no magic. I equipped it without a second of hesitation and leapt into the fray. The lowbie weapon felt like a feather in my hands as I twirled and spun it. I vaulted up, clearing the writhing roots, and sunk the hammerhead into the creature's side.

Critical Hit! Its HP dropped, far more than the weapon with its simple stats could account for. The only thing that I could think of was that the creature must've had a *serious* weakness against normal weapons.

More arrows fell, faster and faster. Amara working like the pro she was.

Cutter had somehow gotten *on top* of the tree creature and was busy driving a pair of unenchanted steel daggers into pretty much anything he could. White light flashed with every hit, and the paper covering the monster's body blackened and split, curling back from the puncture wounds. Forge was going to town like a lumberjack hacking at a particularly pesky tree, and even Ari had gotten in on the action. Unfortunately, we hadn't stumbled upon any toothpick-sized nonmagical swords in our journey, so she'd improvised and now wielded a broken length of arrow with a steel tip on the end.

She jabbed it into the Librarian's eyes and nose and face over and over again, doing an unbelievable amount of damage considering her size and strength.

In less than two minutes the final blow fell—Carl with a club for the win—and the tree toppled onto its side, its branches and roots finally going still, its eyes glazed over in death.

Its trunk split open a second later and out poured loot, a small cascade of it.

One last page fluttered up and out, dancing in some unseen breeze. Forge snatched it from the air with thick fingers. He read it over, once, then twice, his square jaw breaking into a grin which widened with each rereading. "You gotta be kidding me. Listen to this. *Even the strongest boulder may be ground down by the fluttering touch of paper, but the simple steel blade is the equalizer of all. The true hero knows, however, that victory lies in the best two out of three.*" His grin was now wide enough to split his face. He broke out into a gruff laugh, slapping a knee with a thick hand.

"I don't get it," Cutter said, cocking a quizzical eyebrow at the Risi.

"Literally unbelievable," Abby said, rolling her eyes.

"It's a giant paper-rock-scissors joke," Forge cackled. "We were almost murdered on account of someone's bad pun."

He shook his head, crumpled the paper, and tossed it over one shoulder. "Well, let's see what all the trouble was worth."

Though the Librarian had been an absolute *terror* to kill, it turned out the trouble had definitely been worth it. There was a pile of silver and a small stack of gold plus a cache of flawless stones, which could be put to good use over at the Crafter's Hall. Augmenting weapons and armor always required a steady supply of high-quality stones, and *flawless* stones were in short supply. A couple of potions—both Spirit and Health regen—accompanied the coins and stones, edged in by a variety of items.

There was a cruel, double-edged dagger usable as an offhand weapon by Sorceresses and other casters. A fancy new belt for Cutter that granted a host of Rogue skill bonuses. An amulet for Amara, *The Primal Huntress Pendant.* It offered a hefty Dexterity boost, increased Evade and Critical Hit chance, added a 6% movement bonus, and gave +1 to a Stealth skill called Camouflage, which increased the chance to blend into surroundings even in bright lighting conditions. A killer find, without a doubt.

Wonder of wonders, Ari received a set of miniature greaves that were custom-tailored just for her.

Forge got the most practical piece of gear: heavy spiked pauldrons with a significant Strength bonus, + 10% to maul damage, and an active spell buff called *Numb,* which reduced all tactical sensation by 17%, offset by a -3% Dexterity penalty. Armor like that was popping up more and more these days, though this was the best I'd seen to date. It was custom built for tanks, ensuring the damage they took hurt less, but at the price of being clumsy and negatively effecting fine motor skills.

But Forge didn't need Dexterity or fine motor skills to take a pummeling or dish out mega damage with his axe.

The only one that didn't get anything was… me.

Of course.

The only remaining item was a small papier-mâché acorn about the size of a quarter. Cutter flipped it to me with his thumb, a grin on his face. "Better luck next time, eh, Jack."

I snatched it out of the air, turning it over in my hands. A simple thing, though when I pulled up the item description, I noticed there was an interesting bit of flavor text at the bottom.

Librarian Seedling

Item Type: Relic

Class: Unnatural Artifact

Base Damage: 0

Life begins anew. Play again?

<<<>>>

Hmm. Now that was interesting. While everyone else inspected and compared their new acquisitions I wandered deeper into the library, searching for the place where the creature had come from. I followed the trail of destruction and quickly found what I was looking for near the southern side of the library. A false wall that must've opened when I'd removed the book from the pedestal. Beyond was a boxy room, the floor covered in loamy black soil instead of stone—though the soil was in disarray thanks to the roots pulling free.

I frowned, turning the odd acorn over and over again, rubbing at its strange surface with the pad of my thumb, going over the flavor text. *Life begins anew. Play again?* Then I thought of the fluttering bit of paper. *A true hero knows that victory lies in the best two out of three.* It seemed like a bad pun, but what if it wasn't? What if it was actually another cryptic riddle? This place certainly seemed full of those. I shrugged. What did I really have to lose, anyway? I crept onto the black earth and knelt, the ground spongy beneath me, and scooped out a little hole in the dirt then slipped the acorn in.

I wasn't really expecting much as I covered up the seed, but an instant later a little sprout emerged, no larger than my finger, but clearly alive. A pair of leaves unfurled from its sides like sails, and on top of the sprout a paper flower bloomed, glowing with an otherworldly light powered by the blue script, which looped and scrawled its way along the stem and petals. I pulled the lowbie hammer out, ready to clobber the little flower if it so much as twitched wrong. I wasn't even a little prepared, though, when the far wall of the hidden room shifted and crumbled, revealing a regal archway.

Man, this place was just full of secrets. One after another. Just turtles all the way down.

Carved into the dark marble lintel was another line, though this one was far more straightforward: *Let only friends of Shadow enter here, all others court destruction…*

A pop-up appeared.

Quest Update: Secrets in the Shadows

Congratulations! You have defeated the Paper Librarian, Guardian of the Shadow Spire Manor, and opened the Vault of Shadows, completing the Secret Quest Chain *Secrets in the Shadows*. Summon your courage and venture into the Vault of Shadows to claim your reward, though proceed with care—only those Dark Templars true of heart dare tread this path!

Well, that was appropriately mysterious, which seemed par for the course.

Beyond the arch was an enormous cavern filled with black fluted pillars; perched atop each column was a Void Terror statue. Purple Umbra flame burned in the eye sockets of each creature, shedding ghostly light across the floor. Curiosity burned inside my chest. What the hell was the Vault of Shadows, and why had Eitri Spark-Sprayer gone to the trouble of building it?

"I've got something back here," I hollered, glancing over one shoulder, then returning my gaze to the utterly bizarre cavern. My mind was already running away full blast. *Let only friends of Shadow enter here, all others court destruction.* Eitri may have been a demigod, but he was also a Shadowmancer, and from what I'd glimpsed in the journal, he'd been one of the most accomplished Shadowmancers of his time. And that was at a time when the legendary Jade Lord had walked the Storme Marshes, no less, which meant he must've been among the best to ever live.

The rest of the Shadow manor seemed to be a massive training facility, so was it possible that he'd also created a training arena just for Dark Templars?

I heard the pounding of heavy footfalls slapping against the floor as Forge rushed into view, followed in short order by the rest of the crew. "What's the emergency, hoss?" Forge's lips were pulled back in a snarl, his magical axe once more clenched in a white-knuckled grip. His eyes flared as he caught sight of the room beyond.

Abby rounded the corner a second later, followed in short order by the rest of the crew. Her expression turned stony as she surveyed the newly discovered area. "Just when I think this place is all out of surprises," she muttered, exasperated. She glanced at me, the color draining from her face. "Wait. Don't tell me you're honestly considering going in there?"

"Jack," Forge said, tone serious. "That's Murderville, USA, population us—assumin' we're dumb enough to go in."

"He was a Shadowmancer," I said in explanation. "Eitri." I rummaged around in my inventory, then pulled the book free. "I found this behind a false bookcase and when I opened it—"

Carl's eyes bulged alarmingly. "Wait, you got it open?" He sputtered. "But. But how? The order's been trying to open that freakin' thing for three hundred years. And you just. What? Opened it"—he snapped his fingers—"just like that?"

I tapped at the handprint embossed on the cover then handed over the book, pulled off one bracer, and showed him the char-black handprint on my forearm. "It's a Dark Templar thing. Anyway, when I opened it, the book sucked me inside. It was like I was a ghost walking through a dream. I saw these little flashes of Eitri's life." I told them about Khalkeús and the Doom Forge, then recounted my brief jaunt through Dokkalfar history. Amara, in particular, seemed enraptured, hanging on every word. The Murk Elves put huge stock in the Honored Ancestors, and there were no ancestors *more* honored than Nangkri and his kin—though it seemed Isra Spiritcaller was close. And *she'd* been in the vision too.

"Jack," Abby said as I finished telling my story. "This place looks..." She paused. Frowned. Unnecessarily smoothed her dress—a sure sign she was nervous. *"Dangerous,"* she finally finished. "I'm not normally opposed to dangerous, but considering the circumstances, I think maybe we should skip it. Well"— she waved at the warning above the entry—"I think *you* should skip it, since clearly this is a Shadowmancer thing. I mean, you're working under Death-Head mode, the time is running down, and we have what we came for. Why risk it when there's so much on the line?"

"As much as it pains me," Cutter offered, "I have to agree. I always say go for the loot, but that place looks like a death trap wrapped inside of a series of progressively larger death traps."

I turned and looked back at the cavern. They were right, I knew. We had what we needed—hell, I'd stumbled upon this place almost by sheer luck. If I hadn't planted that little seed, the door never would've opened, and we'd have gone on our way, none the wiser about its existence. The smart thing to do was walk away. To finish the mission, then, maybe if I had time, I could come back and work my way through the cavern and complete the secret quest waiting for me. That was the smart thing to do—the safe thing to do...

But I hadn't gotten here by playing things safe.

"No," I finally said with a shake of my head. "Despite the way this looks, I don't think it's a trap. It's a *reward*. Everyone else got something epic for taking that creature out. But not me. And that's because my reward is that place. Yeah, time is ticking away, but it's ticking away much slower here. It won't cost me more than an hour out in the real world, and who knows if I'll ever get a shot like this again. It's no coincidence that Eitri was a Shadowmancer. I was meant to be here. To find this room. I can't walk away from this."

I pulled Eitri's book free and tossed it to Carl. He nearly fumbled it before getting a good grip on the book. His eyes glazed over for a moment, then a look of near-rapture exploded across his face. "Holy fek. I'm in," he whispered in awe. "I'm in, I'm in, I'm in!" He pumped a fist, the hazy cloud in his vision clearing. "My quest just updated. They've lifted my ban." He pressed his eyes shut and took a deep breath. "I can go back. Thank you Jesus, Mary, and Joseph, I can go back." He opened his eyes and let out a deep sigh of relief.

"Book's unlocked," I said, pointing at the golden clasp, now undone. "I don't know if it'll suck you into the pages like it did me, but either way, see if it has any other hints about Khalkeús or the Doom Forge. And if you haven't heard from me in"—I pulled up my interface and checked the time—"let's say three hours, best if you start back without me." I pulled my warhammer out, steeling myself. "Alright, I'm going in."

TWENTY-ONE

DARK REWARD

U NNATURALLY COOL AIR RUSHED OVER MY SKIN as I stepped through the arch and into the shadowy cavern filled with statue-topped columns. Those columns were odd, some the size of small pine trees, others as tall and round as the towering redwoods in the Sequoia National Park. The floor was entirely black and smooth as glass, yet it gave just a little with each step. Almost spongy. The cavern, if it could be called that, was utterly quiet. There was no subtle rustle of a faint breeze. No raised voices. No sound of life. Even my footsteps didn't make a sound, as though they feared intruding on the sacred silence.

My own breath sounded like a scream in my ears.

I made my way in deeper, then experimentally stomped my foot down. Still not so much as a whisper, almost as though the floor *ate* the noise. "Hello?" I called as loud as my voice would carry. Except it didn't carry—not more than a handful of feet. Weird. Still the curiosity was too intense to turn back, so I pressed on. After twenty or thirty feet, I glanced back over one shoulder and found the archway I'd entered through was gone. Vanished.

There wasn't even a wall to mark where the entry had been. Just an endless field of black riddled with more of the strange columns and their accompanying guardians.

I was alone—the warning above the arch made it clear that this was something I had to do by myself. The others were camped out in one of the abandoned war rooms not far from the library. Eating. Resting. Recovering. Checking the book for clues I might've missed. And for the first time, I was really feeling the weight of my decision to soldier on. Everyone had warned me against this, and though I was *sure* this was the right move, a twinge of uncertainty fluttered madly in my stomach. There was nothing I could do though. Not now. The way back was gone, which meant if I wanted to leave here alive, the path lay ahead.

I slowly wound my way through the unnatural forest, trailing my fingertips over each column as I passed, pausing to look at the Void Terror statues lurking on the top.

No two were alike.

It seemed like every Void Terror I'd ever run across during my time in the Shadowverse was represented here—and many more I'd never seen. I even found a miniature version of the Void Abomination I'd tangled with while in the Realm of Order. It was a colossal squid-like creature the size of a battleship that could've easily passed as one of Lovecraft's Eldritch Horrors. There were also Void Chimps and even a replica of a Void Drake. Not exactly the same as Devil, but close enough to fool someone who didn't know the Drake like I did.

Before long, I was lost, completely disoriented since there weren't any landmarks to speak of. Just endless, formless black, interrupted only by columns and statues. I tried my map, hoping that might give me some clue, some insight, but wherever here was, it wasn't on any map. My interface showed a blank screen as void as the cavern.

Unsure which way was the right way, I wandered aimlessly for the next half hour, desperately trying to figure out what in the hell I was supposed to do here or how I was supposed to leave. I used every spell in my tree—the ones that would work anyway—hoping one of them might trigger some sort of mechanism or hidden door, but that accomplished absolutely nothing. The whole while, I kept a firm eye on the time. After forty-five minutes, I practically crawled to a stop, carefully examining each and every column, thinking there might be some innocuous mark or sigil that would offer me a hint.

Another dead end.

At the two-hour mark, when my regrets were really starting to kick in, I finally stumbled onto a clearing, ringed by columns, thirty feet in diameter. I let out a sigh of relief and a silent prayer of thanks. I didn't know what this was, but at least it was *something.* At the center were five free-standing doors arranged in a loose circle. The doors themselves were each made of an impossibly dark wood, so black it was nearly purple, with a handprint standing out in stark relief at the center. From the cover of the pillars, I scanned the ring for any obvious signs of a trap or a guardian.

When I saw none, I finally edged my way into the open, feeling painfully exposed. A thousand eyes seemed to watch me from everywhere and nowhere all at once.

The second my foot touched down in the odd clearing, a faint rustle of movement caught my ear. Dead ahead one of the Void Terrors, positioned atop a column, stirred. It was a jaguar with six purple eyes running along its feline face. The creature, which had been frozen in a crouch, lurched to life and leapt from its perch, growing as it sailed silently through the air, stretching and bulging until it was easily the size of a Kodiak bear. It touched down without a sound, its eyes burning with unnatural violet light, great strands of purple saliva dripping from its enormous fangs.

Its tail lashed back and forth as it padded silently across the distance between us.

Slowly, *cautiously,* I reached a hand toward the hammer at my belt, then froze when *every* statue on *every* column for as far as I could see began to wake. To curl talons, open jaws, and lash tails or tentacles. To stretch long petrified muscles and blink an army of glowing eyes. I pulled my hand away, and the restless motion ceased at once—all except for the deadly cat prowling my way. I went for the weapon again, but promptly stopped when the legion of Terrors began to move once more. A warning, then, that this wasn't something I could fight my way out of. Whatever this test was, I'd need to pass it without resorting to the weapon at my side.

The jaguar closed on me in an eyeblink, its massive head filling my vision as huge lips pulled back from its deadly fangs. A brief tag appeared above its head:

[Void Mauler].

Yep. That sounded about right.

The creature ghosted up until it was inches from me, the heat from its breath washing over my skin. The creature narrowed its many eyes and *sniffed*, its huge nostrils flaring. It inhaled again, dropping its head and driving its muzzle into my chest. Not to hurt me—more like a house cat saying hello to a long absent master. It *sniff-sniff-sniffed*, rubbing its face on me, working its way down my chest and to my arm, where an old woman's handprint marred my skin like a tattoo. It offered a throaty growl as it got closer, then lifted a paw the size of a large pizza and pawed at the bracer covering my forearm.

I wasn't sure what to do, but as the growl and the pawing became more insistent, I finally reached over and pulled my razor-edged bracer free, rolling up my sleeve and showing off my brand. It was the mark, passed on from one *Maa-Tál* to another, that awakened the Shadow Spark that resided in a fraction of Eldgard's population.

The growl turned into a throaty purr.

I reached out trembling fingers and ran a hand across the cat's enormous head. "Who's a good kitty who doesn't want to maul me? You are. You don't want to murder me." I slipped my hand beneath its shaggy black chin, giving the enormous cat a scratch, which it seemed to firmly approve of.

The creature purred louder, pleased.

Once it had finally had enough of my affection, it casually turned around, tail swishing, and made for its column. It paused on the edge of the clearing, offering me a final glance, before lightly bounding up onto its stone perch, resuming its pose before freezing once more. Only its burning eyes and an unsettling memory said it was anything more than a statue. Apparently, I had passed the sniff test, which was a huge relief. In my mind, I could only imagine what would've happen had I failed: a wave of Void Terrors all descending on me from their pillars, tearing me apart an inch at a time with cruel fangs and rending claws.

Since the cat had more or less given me the green light, I headed for the doors, inspecting the first as I got close. The handprint in the middle of it was a vivid electric blue, the center adorned with the symbol of the *Maa-Tál,* though with an additional slash slightly altering the mark. I pushed my palm against the print, just as I'd done with Eitri's book, and waited a long moment, holding my breath. Nothing happened. Not the door for me. I moved on to the next in the ring, this one with a burning green handprint, the Dark Templar symbol distorted by a hooked line running along its right edge.

I went through the motions again, but once more was met with failure.

The third door was the same as the first and the second, though the handprint was a metallic gold, the symbol similarly altered. Which is when I finally made the connection. There were five different Dark Templar class kit specializations—Shadow Knight, Plague Bringer, Umbra Shaman, Necromancer, and Shadowmancer. Five kits, five doors, five colors, five markings. Like the rest of the underground mansion, this place was a training ground, one meant for all Dark Templars. But whatever secrets lay behind the other doors were meant only for the respective class specialists.

I breezed past the fourth door in the lineup—the handprint black as wet tar—and made for the door with a violet palm print the color of an Umbra Bolt. It pulsed gently as I drew closer, thrumming with potent power.

When I pressed my hand against the mark, the door simply vanished, replaced by a shimmering portal of silver energy that beckoned me onward.

Despite the oddness of the place, I stepped through without a hint of hesitation and not even an iota of fear. I *belonged* there. If such a thing as destiny existed, this was where it lived.

Icy power washed over my skin in a sheet, goosebumps breaking out along my arms and running up my spine. On the other side of the door was a modest crypt, the walls built from dark gray stone. Stained-glass windows peppered the walls, showcasing in perfect detail many of the scenes I'd seen secondhand through the book. Mounted torches burned with unearthly purple flame. In the center of the room was an obsidian casket, its lid heavily carved into a perfect likeness of Eitri.

Lodged in the stone effigy of Eitri, right where his heart would've been, was an enormous emerald the size of a softball. An emerald I'd seen often enough before, or at least a version based on it.

There was one in the Command Center table of Darkshard that allowed the controlling faction to access info about the Keep itself and summon the Keep Guardian. And Darkshard wasn't the exception. Each Keep had a stone like that. Was it possible I'd discovered the way to claim this otherworldly place as my own? That certainly would've been one hell of a prize.

I had no answers, but there was no other visible treasure or reward anywhere in the room, so I headed toward the casket, hand outstretched. I touched the gem, which promptly swirled to life with cloudy green light.

A moment later, a green specter appeared in the air above the casket. A perfect replica of Eitri as I'd seen in the book. "Welcome to my tomb," the spirit said, smiling at me with perfectly even teeth. "I am Eitri Spark-Sprayer"—he bowed with a small flourish—"or what remains of him."

Flabbergasted, I just stood there, mouth agape. *What in the hell is this?* "But ... but you're dead," I sputtered after a moment.

"Observant of you. But the more you dig, the more you'll find that dead is something of a relative term in Eldgard. Turns out, the soul of a god, even a demigod, is a rather resilient thing. Though, I will admit, I'm only a shadow of my true self. But enough about me. If you're here, it means you've already found my book. You know most of my story. And it also means you've defeated my guardian, which is no small task. Congratulations are in order, I think."

"Thank you," I offered with a shrug, not quite sure what to say or how to proceed. "So, what is this place?" I ventured after a beat.

"My home," the shade replied in turn. "And a training ground, which I'm sure you've gathered. My people, the Dokkalfar, are a tightknit group, but unfortunately that makes them notoriously tight-lipped as well. When I first came to the Storme Marshes, despite my mother being known to the clan, I was an outsider, and working my way into the inner ranks of the Dark Templar was a challenge." The shade folded his arms, a wistful look flashing across his face. "And even once I did earn my brand and my place among them, I discovered a true travesty, bred by their distrust of outsiders.

"Many of our most powerful skills can be augmented and boosted by skill trainers, yet there were too few master trainers to pass on their arts. And they never wrote anything down. *Never.*" He shook his head, a sad sigh escaping his lips. "It was antithetical to their way of thinking, and so, when they died, all of their knowledge was gone with them. Lost to the ages." He pursed his lips, gaze distant as though he were looking through a window into a different time. "I couldn't abide by it. So, I started to gather the knowledge of the ancients and write those secrets down. *Secrets of the Umbra Flame. Taming the Void: A Shadowmancer Primer. Between the Worlds.*"

That middle one immediately rang a bell. "Wait. *Taming the Void,*" I said, thrusting a finger out. "I read that one. It was all about Void Terrors. I found it in a secret library inside a Darkshard mine outside of Yunnam. Did you...? Was that...?"

The shade beamed and nodded his head vigorously. "Yes. All written by my hand and stashed away where the more *traditional* Murk Elf elders of my day would be unable to find my handiwork. I made that Shadowverse Pocket, you know. The one in the mines. One of my first and greatest achievements. The lessons I learned constructing it eventually led to the creation of this place. I didn't stop with the books, though. I realized even that was too inefficient. So instead, I made it my purpose to build something greater. A repository of all Dark Templar knowledge." He spread his ethereal hands. "Built not in the Shadowverse, but truly outside of time and space itself, where no corruption could touch my work.

"And that is where you find yourself. In a bit of real estate located inside the In-Between, which is, how to explain it…" He paused, tapping his chin with one finger. "It's a place for things like me. It doesn't properly exist inside of Eldgard at all. It's a place where mistakes and errors go. Things that can't rightly be destroyed for one reason or another, but which need to be sequestered from the rest of reality. This little piece of the In-Between is called the Protoverse. Kronos originally used it as a testing ground for time manipulation. Eventually, the Protoverse was replaced by the Shadowverse, and so"—he shrugged one shoulder—"this was relegated to the In-Between."

"Mind if I ask about the Void Terrors?" I hooked a thumb toward the doorway behind me.

"No, not at all. This is a place of learning, after all. The Void Terrors are my guardians. The In-Between is not without its dangers, and there are other pockets of reality within this place that are better avoided, such as the Vault of Souls. They keep the dangerous, corrupted things at bay. Only those with the right permissions are allowed to enter this space without serious and *unpleasant* repercussions.

"But, enough of that. You've worked hard to get here, and I daresay you deserve a reward for your labors. And because you are a Shadowmancer—my own specialty, no less—I will grant you two boons. First, I will permanently increase any one of your Shadowmancer class skills by one proficiency point. And second, I will grant you the Grandmaster-level effect to whichever skill you choose, regardless of its current level."

TWENTY-TWO

GRANDMASTER

THE WORLD ROCKED AROUND ME AS I PROCESSED his words. This was a far better reward than even the most legendary piece of gear. Quests that granted extra proficiency points were extremely rare, and a quest that would permanently augment one of my main abilities? Priceless. Still, I wasn't entirely sure what the second part of the reward entailed. "You can grant me the Grandmaster-level effect to any skill," I said. "What exactly does that mean?"

"It's a simple thing," he replied with a lopsided smile. "As you level up your skills, they become stronger, more powerful, and occasionally you will even unlock new abilities. This is true for *every* ability in every class. At max level—the Grandmaster level of proficiency—each of your abilities will gain a new and potent effect. But you have to use seven proficiency points to acquire that ability, which is no small investment, and there is no telling what the new effect will be. Unless, of course, you have a master trainer such as myself to guide you in the process." He bowed his head.

If what he was saying was true, then it was possible this was an even bigger reward than I'd first imagined, but I needed to find out if he was on the level. Everything about this place was odd and sent up a host of red flags—including his strange explanation of the In-Between and the Protoverse—so I wanted some way to test this shade's truthfulness and accuracy. I folded my arms, thinking. "Okay," I said after a time, "let's start with a simple one. Shadow Stride. What's that do?" I'd already unlocked the Grandmaster-level skill for Shadow Stride, so I could compare his answer to what I already knew.

He paused, staring at me as though he could see *through* me. Into me. "You already know full well what the effect is, but for the sake of transparency, the Grandmaster-level Shadow Stride effect allows you to pull a second entity into the Shadowverse with you during the duration of the Shadow Stride. Since you have already maxed out that ability, there is nothing more I can teach you in that area."

I wasn't sure exactly *how* this specter knew I'd already unlocked that ability, but his answer was right on the money. "Okay. So, if I'm following, you don't add a unique effect, exactly, you're just unlocking the effect *before* I hit the Grandmaster level, saving me a whole lot of time and points."

"Precisely," he replied with a bob of his ghostly head.

I rubbed at my chin. "Alright. Let's try another one. One I don't already know. What is the Grandmaster effect for Plague Burst?"

"The Grandmaster-level effect for Plague Burst is that it will no longer hurt allies. It makes the spell far more practical if you're primarily a ranged DPS caster."

I whistled softly through my teeth. Damn, that *was* a great effect. Plague Burst was powerful, but almost *too* destructive to reliably use. But if it didn't hurt me or my allies? That could be a game changer. Still, I didn't want to jump to a decision prematurely. I'd probably never get another chance like this again. Best to take things slowly. Thoughtfully.

Besides, he was open to answering questions, which meant, theoretically, he could run me through every skill and tell me what the Grandmaster effect was for each. But even if he did, there was no way to guarantee I'd make the right call. Back IRL, I'd played plenty of games that had awesome *sounding* skills, which, in reality, turned out to be total duds. There had to be a better way to do this. A more practical approach.

"Okay, answer me this," I said, mind turning over options. "You told me you created the pocket Shadowverse near the Darkshard mines, right?"

He nodded again. "That one and several more like it."

"So what skill would I need to unlock to be able to do that?"

He frowned and titled his head to one side, that intense stare resuming. "I'm afraid that's not possible," he replied. "Not as you are. I can see you're exalted. A Champion no less." His brow furrowed at that, and I couldn't help but remember that it'd been human Champions that had murdered him. He breezed past it without a word, though. "That is a power beyond even the most accomplished mortal Champion.

"Only Aspects or their progeny have such power. I used my abilities as a Scion of the Forge to create these ways. But that path may one day be open to you." He folded his hands behind his back as he considered me. "Aspects aren't born. Most are simply *manifested* out of need by the Overminds, but a handful have been *made* over time. Champions and heroes elevated to divinity. Such a thing is possible. I don't know how, only that it has been done. But that won't help you now."

Wow. I felt like Eitri had just drop-kicked me square in the teeth. Lesser gods and goddesses could be created? And from players, no less? The implications of that were simply enormous, and if true, maybe it held some valuable clues. After all, if a god or goddesses could be created, then it might also offer some insight into how they could be killed.

"Can you tell me more about that?" I pressed. "The whole making an Aspect thing."

"Even we demigods have some restrictions, and on that I can say no more." He reached up and tapped his nose. "It is an issue of programming, you understand. Given the fact that you have found your way here, however, I suspect you'll find your answer sooner or later. For now, though, put it from mind and focus."

Not the answer I wanted, not by a long shot, but the set of his shoulders told me the shade wouldn't say any more on the topic. Perhaps *couldn't* say more. "Let me ask a different question, then," I said. "If *you* were in my shoes and had to choose, what would you recommend?"

A slow grin spread across his face and he tapped at his temple with one finger. "Now that is the proper way to use a guide. Many people believe they know best, but a master is a master precisely because they know more. Because they know *better*. Every skill in the Shadowmancer Tree is powerful, and even more so at the

Grandmaster level, but Shadow Lord is the most potent ability of all."

My heart sank. "I haven't unlocked that one yet."

"Haven't you now?" he asked, his sly grin now a full-on smile.

Hope bloomed in my gut like a spring flower as I pulled up my interface and toggled over to my character sheet. Holy crap. In the midst of the grind, I hadn't realized that I'd leveled up not long ago—apparently killing the guardian had pushed me over the edge and all the way to level 50. The level gain was amazing, but the most important fact of all was that I'd hit the level requirement to unlock my ultimate ability: Shadow Lord.

Name:	Jack	Race:		Dokkalfar	Gender:		Male
Level:	50	Class:		Dark Templar	Alignment:		Dark
Renown:	2,500	Carry Capacity:		780	Undistributed Attribute Points:		5

Health:	1290	Spirit:		2175	Stamina:		1170
H-Regen/sec:	45.66	S-Regen/sec:		32.42	Stam-Regen/sec:		20.15

Attributes:		Offense:			Defense:	
Strength:	82.5	Base Melee Weapon Damage:	72.05	Base Armor:		175.9
Vitality:	79	Base Ranged Weapon Damage:	0	Armor Rating:		241.9
Constitution:	67	Attack Strength (AS):	529.55	Block Amount:		92.5
Dexterity:	110	Ranged Attack Strength (RAS):	382.5	Block Chance (%):		90.5
Intelligence:	138.5	Spell Strength (SS):	207.75	Evade Chance (%):		27
Spirit:	167.5	Critical Hit Chance:	27%	Fire Resist (%):		49.75
Luck:	16	Critical Hit Damage:	250%	Cold Resist (%):		47.75
				Lightning Resist (%):		47.75
				Shadow Resist (%):		67.75
				Holy Resist (%):		44.9
Current XP:	1,080			Poison Resist (%):		67.75
Next Level:	118,000			Disease Resist (%):		67.75

I dropped one of my two proficiency points into the skill. I would've dropped both points in, but I *couldn't* until level 53. But with Eitri's help, maybe I could bend that rule. As I thought about that, I read over the new skill box that popped up.

<<<>>>

Skill: Shadow Lord (Variable)

Those who have walked the Path of Shadow long enough to become a Shadow Lord have gained not only an unparalleled connection to the Umbra, but a masterful understanding of how to manipulate, shape, and control Umbra power. With this knowledge, the Shadow Lord is able to craft a *custom* spell by forging the abilities of two lesser skills together, oftentimes with strange and unexpected results.

Skill Type/Level: Spell/Variable

Cost: Variable

Range: Variable

Cast Time: Variable

Cooldown: Variable

Effect: The spell effect of Shadow Lord depends entirely on which combination of skills are combined. Once a spell set is selected, it cannot be altered or changed, so choose the combination of spells—and their effects—wisely.

<<<>>>

"Now, as you can see from the notice, Shadow Lord is an incredibly powerful ability all on its own," Eitri said as I closed out from the prompt. "And it is customizable depending on your battle style. But at the Grandmaster level, you get to add a *third* spell effect into the mix. Knowing that beforehand can radically alter which choice you might be inclined to make. The choice of a Shadow Lord ability—especially at the Grandmaster level—will often be your defining skill as it is unlikely that any other Shadowmancer will devise the same skill set or battle style."

I ran a hand across my jaw and broke into a nervous pace. Back and forth, back and forth, cloak swishing as I moved. "Okay. For my first reward, I would like you to permanently increase my Shadow Lord skill by one point. That's a no-brainer. And for the second reward, I definitely want to unlock the Grandmaster-level Shadow Lord ability. But what skills should I pick?"

The flickering shade cocked an eyebrow and bowed his head. "It's a hard choice. If only you had access to a Shadowmancer expert who might be able to answer such questions."

I stopped pacing abruptly and spun, locking my gaze on Eitri. Or the memory of him. "Can you tell me what all the various skill combos do?"

"Better, I can show you. A word of guidance, though. With three options, the best way to proceed is to find a combination of two spells that you like, then augment that with a third spell, as the base combo will be stay largely the same. Now, which would you like to hear about first?"

I pulled up my Shadowmancer Skill Tree and thought about it for a moment, trying to decide which combination of skills would be the most effective.

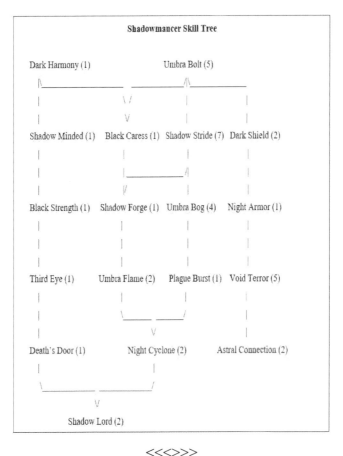

"Alright, let's try something simple. Two AoE spells. Umbra Bog and Plague Burst. What would they do?"

The green spirit flicked out a hand, casting a spell in the blink of an eye. Semitransparent tendrils of muddy yellow erupted on a small patch of ground nearby—a ghostly imitation of the real thing. "This combines the two effects into one, simultaneously stripping away the negative effects of Plague Burst. With this spell, you could cast an Umbra Bog that not only holds enemies but poisons them horrendously. With a combination like this, I'd recommend adding Third Eye to reduce the Spirit cost and cooldown time, which is *exorbitant*."

I nodded since that seemed to make sort of an intuitive sense. "What about mixing something like Black Caress with Umbra Bog?"

The writhing illusionary tendrils shifted, losing their muddy golden hue and taking on a glowing violet cast. "Simple. In that case, Umbra Bog holds your enemies and you absorb 15% of the total attack damage dealt to all enemies in the area of effect for the duration of the spell." He paused, eyes going hazy again. "Yes. Right," he said as though talking to someone else. "For that particular combo, I'd recommend adding the Shadow Forge skill. That way, not only would those snared in the Bog receive extra Shadow damage, but then the life absorb would work as an aura, benefiting all of your party members."

Damn. Not bad at all.

Slowly we worked our way through the myriad of combinations. Some were far more useful than others, though I could imagine how any of the potential spells could be game changers depending on an individual's play style. I noticed quickly that the passive abilities—Dark Harmony, Shadow Minded, Black Strength, Third Eye, and Death's Door—served to amplify a given spell in some capacity or drastically reduce cooldown time or cost.

Most spells, when combined with an AoE effect—Umbra Bog or Plague Burst—became AoE spells themselves. So, for example, Umbra Bog and Dark Shield had the curious effect of creating a giant shadow dome, twenty feet in diameter, that could protect pretty much everyone in the party, while adding Third Eye reduced the cost and cast time to next to nothing. There were exceptions, though, such as Night Armor, which seemed to be the primary spell component in any pairing. If I combined Night Armor and Umbra Bog, I ended up with a new kind of night armor—one covered with living tentacles that lashed out when enemies got too close.

Supremely badass.

Night Armor and Shadow Stride was one of the most interesting and practical combos from a combat perspective. By casting that pair, I could become partially ethereal, moving half in and half out of the Shadowverse for the duration of the spell. While under the effects, my opponents would move at half speed and deal only 50% damage when they managed to land a blow; conversely, though, I'd also only deal 50% damage, which was a drawback for sure. Still, it was an incredibly powerful ability, though the Spirit cost and cooldown were more than a little heavy-handed.

Umbra Flame and Night Cyclone were also tempting, especially when combined with Black Caress as the Grandmaster skill. Night Cyclone—which already dealt an incredible amount of damage—turned into a cyclone of scorching Shadow Flame, which upped the damage into god-level range while converting a chunk of that damage into life, which returned to me. I also found the combination of Void Terror and Astral Connection to be extremely tempting. With that, I could control any summoned Void Terror like a puppet.

Step right into the body of a conjured monster, fighting without ever risking myself in the process.

Extremely cool, though there were a number of potential drawbacks.

For one, while I was occupying the body of a Void Terror, my own body would be unguarded and basically catatonic. The upside was there was no limit on distance. Theoretically, I could adventure in the body of a minion while never leaving the safety of a well-fortified Keep. But if the minion in question couldn't talk, then neither could I, so working with locals or fulfilling quests could be a challenge. Plus, Void Terrors didn't have a proper inventory, so I wouldn't be able to pick up loot, which meant soloing was out.

The ability that jumped out to me, however, was a rather unexpected pairing: Umbra Bolt and Shadow Stride. I'd been extremely curious about what those two would do, and the result wasn't even remotely what I'd anticipated. I watched, enthralled, as Eitri stuck one hand out as though casting Umbra Bolt... but instead of a shadowy ball of power forming, a small portal about the size of a basketball opened not two feet in front of him. An eyeblink later, a *second* identical portal opened across the room.

"You can control both where the entry and exit portal opens," the spirit explained. "It's a miniature rift which runs through the Shadowverse. An object goes into the entry portal and instantly emerges through the exit portal. No real offensive capability to speak of, and the spell is line of sight only. Of all the abilities, this one has the least direct functionality." He shrugged after the brief explanation, obviously unimpressed with the skill combo. I, on the other hand, was nearly exploding with excitement as questions and possibilities ran through my head.

"What can travel through the portal?" I asked, fighting to contain my excitement. "Spells, people, inanimate objects?"

"There's no limit to what may pass through, I suppose, though I can't ever remember a Shadowmancer wielding this particular power set before, so it's hard to say. The few masters that make it this far either focus on AoE combo spells or Night Armor combos, transforming themselves into deadly combatants for a short while."

"Yeah, I can see how those would be obviously practical," I said, absently rubbing my hands together, "but I think this one has real potential. Sure, it does no damage, but it also costs less Spirit than an Umbra Bolt to cast and has roughly no cooldown time. My real question, though, is can I make it bigger? Big enough to say fit a person?"

He frowned for a moment, then a mischievous grin broke out along his face. "Give me a moment." He pressed his eyes closed, lips moving silently as though talking to himself. "Interesting," he finally said after a beat. "No, that wouldn't work. Hmmm... Ah, yes. There it is." His eyes popped open. "If you combine it with the Dark Harmony ability it will allow you to manipulate the portal size, at least to a certain degree. *Maybe* big enough to fit a man." He conjured a new portal, sweat breaking out across his forehead as a rift, roughly five feet in diameter, formed. "Doable, though the larger the portal you make, the more Spirit it costs to conjure and uphold."

As awesome as all the other combos were—and they were—this spell *called* to me. On its own, it was a rather useless ability, but I had some killer ideas about how it could be combined with my other skills, turning it into an offensive and defensive powerhouse. "Yep. This is the one."

"Are you sure?" he asked, voice filled with skepticism. "That is the combination you would choose?"

"That's the one," I replied, firm in my decision. Just because it was an unorthodox choice didn't mean it was the wrong one. I had a gut feeling here, and so far my gut had led me true.

"You are an odd one." He paused, a glimmer in his eye. "But then so was I. No one has ever achieved greatness by following solely in the footsteps of others. I hope your gamble pays off, Shadow Lord." He waved a hand and a pair of notices appeared, one right after another:

<<<>>>

Quest Alert: Secrets in the Shadows

Congratulations! You have courageously ventured into the Vault of Shadows of the Protoverse and found the Keeper of the Shadows, the Spirit of Eitri Spark-Sprayer. As a reward, your Shadow Lord ability has permanently increased by (1) Proficiency Point. Additionally, Eitri has unlocked the Grandmaster-level effect for Shadow Lord!

Skill: Shadow Lord

Those who have walked the Path of Shadow long enough to become a Shadow Lord have gained not only an unparalleled connection to the Umbra, but a masterful understanding of how to manipulate, shape, and control Umbra power. With your knowledge as a Shadow Lord, you have chosen to combine Shadow Stride, Umbra Bolt, and Dark Harmony, forming the unique Path of the Shadow-Warp Portal. Using Shadow-Warp Portal allows the caster to rip a compact hole through the Shadowverse, instantly moving objects from one place to another.

Skill Type/Level: Spell/Initiate (Modified; Grandmaster-level effect)

Cost: 75 Spirit (Variable; See Effect 2)

Range: 100 Meters (Sight)

Cast Time: 1.5 seconds

Cooldown: N/A

Effect 1: Cast a base 1' x 1' Shadow-Warp Portal; any object that enters the entry portal will immediately leave through the exit portal. The caster can control the spawn location of both portal points (line of sight) as well as the vertical and horizontal orientation of the portal points.

Effect 2: Manipulate the base size of the portal from 1' x 1' to 6' x 6'; for every foot of dimensional space added to the base portal, add 50 Spirit to Cost for a maximum of 325 Spirit for a portal with a dimension of 6' x 6'.

Restriction: Shadow-Warp Portals cannot be opened inside objects, such as walls, floors, or players. The entry and exit points must be cast in unoccupied free space! Shadow-Warp Portals will not function within the Shadowverse. Additionally, the caster cannot physically travel through a Shadow-Warp Portal, since they must maintain the spell from outside the Shadowverse!

<<<>>>

"Now, before you depart," Eitri said as I closed out from my interface, "we have one more matter to discuss." His joking tone was gone, replaced by a somber voice and a deadpan face. "There is only one reason you would be seeking out my book, and that is to find the forge of my father. And if that weren't enough confirmation, I can sense the Doom-Forged relics upon you. Their power radiates off you in waves."

"If you're going to try to talk me out of going," I said, "don't. We need your father to forge us the weapon. Nothing can get in the way of that." I paused, jaw clenched. "This is bigger than him. Bigger than you or me."

"No, you misunderstand," Eitri's spirit said, raising his hands in a placating gesture. "I know you cannot be moved from your course. I wouldn't try to dissuade you from it. Rather, I wish to warn you and to plead with you. My father, he has been crushed by guilt and grief. Guilt and grief over my death. It has transformed him into something... terrible. It's what led him to make that damnable weapon in the first place. If you give him the pieces, he *will* remake the weapon, but he won't give it back willingly. He'll take it and try to kill... well, everyone, if he can. In truth, he will burn the world down if you let him, and with that weapon in his hands, he just might be able to.

"But he isn't a monster, not truly." Eitri's eyes pleaded with me. "He's just a grief-stricken father. A powerful one. But not an evil one. Continue your quest. Forge the weapon, but please. If there is any way to spare him, any path to victory forged not in bloodshed but in mercy... take it. I am convinced that there *must* be some way to free him from the corruption that has taken hold of his mind.

"Truly, I don't know what the answer is, but the fact that you wear Nangkri's crown on your head tells me you might be up to the challenge. If you can both assemble the weapon and cleanse my father from the corruption of his grief, you will prove yourself to be an heir worthy of my legacy. Do that and you can come back to this place and claim the Iredale Hold as your own."

Quest Alert: The Doom Forge

The spirit of Eitri Spark-Sprayer has heard about your quest to reforge the Doom-Forged weapon. He has warned you that his father, Khalkeús, has been twisted by rage and grief and that he will likely try to kill you once he has the Doom-Forged weapon in his grasp. He has charged you with completing the quest without killing Khalkeús. In addition, you must find a way to ease his suffering.

Quest Class: Ultra-Rare, Class-Based

Quest Difficulty: Infernal

Success: Complete the Doom-Forged quest line without killing Khalkeús; additionally, you must find some way to ease the mad godling's pain.

Failure: Fail to complete the Doom-Forged quest line; kill the mad godling Khalkeús; spare his life but abandon him to his misery.

Reward: Be named the rightful Heir of Eitri Spark-Sprayer and inherit the Iredale Hold!

Accept: Yes/No?

I read it over and reluctantly accepted. "I don't understand," I said. "How am I supposed to stop a grief-mad god, hell-bent on revenge, without killing him? Especially if he won't cooperate with me?"

Eitri offered me a mischievous smile. "As I said, I don't have an answer. But even if I did, a test of mettle and character is not one that I would help you with. If you are truly worthy to be my successor, then I am convinced you will find a way." He waved a hand and a silvery portal appeared beside me. "Good luck, Grim Jack. The gods know you'll need it."

TWENTY-THREE

ROADBLOCKS

I STEPPED THROUGH, EXPECTING TO END UP BACK IN the odd column forest, but instead the silvery doorway deposited me in the library just outside the archway. The path into the Protoverse was firmly closed, the archway was completely walled off by thick stone, and even the strange warning carved into the stone was gone. Man, but this place was a complete trip. I shook my head, turned on a heel, and made my way out of the library, heading for the map room where the rest of the crew would be holed up.

I kept my metaphorical fingers crossed that they hadn't bailed since it'd taken me nearly the entire three hours I'd allotted to complete the little jaunt.

When I pushed the heavy wooden door open with a bang, I found an arrow immediately trained on me, courtesy of Amara, and a fireball budding at the end of Abby's staff, ready to burn the face from my body.

I raised my hands sheepishly. "Just me, guys," I said. "No need to go with the nuclear option."

Amara grunted and lowered her bow while Abby dismissed the spell with a whisper. "Having second thoughts about going in?" Abby asked as she pulled a no-nonsense stool over to the bulky map table and took a seat. Cutter and Carl were already sitting, while Forge leaned casually against a wall, examining a leather map with furrowed brows.

"What are you talking about?" I asked, genuinely confused. "I've been gone for…" I pulled up my interface to check the time. *What in the hell?* My clock had somehow gone *backward*—the last three hours spent inside the Protoverse vanished, as though I'd never left. "Impossible," I said. "How long have I been gone?"

"Two minutes," Cutter said with a shrug. He had a stack of playing cards out in front of him, idly shuffling them, crowns and clubs flashing and disappearing in an impressive display of sleight of hand. "Give or take."

"What's going on, Jack?" Abby asked, immediately picking up that something was wrong.

I shook my head, baffled. "I left." I hooked a thumb back toward the library. "I didn't turn back. I went in. I was gone for almost three hours, and I was keeping an eye on the clock the whole time." I headed over to the wall and dropped down onto my ass, pressing my back against the stone as the world reeled. This couldn't be possible. Quickly, I pulled up my character sheet and skill tree, ensuring I hadn't just hallucinated my whole encounter with Eitri.

I let out a sigh of relief. Everything was just as it should have been, and when I pulled up my quest log, I found the updated quest alert I'd received from the shade.

"Everything looks right, but I swear to God my clock has reset to somehow account for the time loss. But I'm telling you guys, I was gone. For three hours."

"Perhaps time runs even more quickly in that place?" Amara offered, quirking an eyebrow. "We take for granted that time, it runs differently in the Shadowverse, but what if there is another such place? One that we know nothing of?" She paused, lips pressed into a tight line. "The business of time, it is a thing of the Overminds— of Kronos—so who can say what is possible, no?"

I mulled it over for a minute and had to admit the idea held water. Eitri had said the Protoverse was tied to Kronos's earliest attempts at time manipulation. "Yeah, I suppose that's possible," I admitted.

"Well, don't leave us hanging, Jack," Abby said. "What happened? What'd you find?"

As weird as the time distortion was—and it *was*—I couldn't help but smile, thinking about what I'd learned from the shade. I stood, extended a hand and conjured a miniature portal a few feet in front of me, then casually took a healing potion from my belt and tossed it through. The exit portal appeared behind Cutter's head, the potion zipping through at the same rate I'd thrown it, smacking him right in the back of the noggin.

"What in the bloody hell?" he barked, shooting up from his chair, wheeling around as he rubbed at his head.

"Boy, do I have a story to tell you guys." The portal vanished with a flick of my wrist, and I told them about my strange journey through the Protoverse and my encounter inside the tomb of Eitri Spark-Sprayer. I told them about the reward he'd granted me and the impossible quest he'd charged me with.

"Why can't we have one normal mission, eh?" Cutter grumbled as I finished. "That's what I want to know. Gods, but what I wouldn't give for a standard dungeon dive. Just kill some monsters and walk away with a bag stuffed full of sweet, sweet loot. But no. Not Grim Jack bloody Shadowstrider. Can't ever be easy with you." He pulled free one of his daggers, twirling it idly with thoughtless ease. "So how are we supposed to beat Khalkeús without just bludgeoning the grumpy bastard to death, eh?"

"Well, I'm hoping Carl has an answer to that," I replied, turning on the Cleric. "You find anything in the book that might help us?"

He grimaced and shook his head. "Don't know what you're expecting. Remember, time distortion or whatever. I've only had the book for about five minutes, so needless to say, I haven't made any headway. No visions, either. But at a glance, it looks more like a journal than anything with real practical value. I mean, I'll tear through it, but chances are what we're looking for is in the temple in Stone Reach."

"Well then, what are we waiting for? Let's get this show on the road," Abby said, pulling a scroll from her inventory. It was a one-off back to Cliffburgh, which she'd taken the liberty of copying from the original Sophia had provided us with. Ideally, we would've gone straight to Stone Reach, but getting a port scroll inside the mountainous city was the next to impossible—even for us, which was saying something. But Cliffburgh was more or less on the way, and Carl needed to stop back anyway to pick up a few items he had stored in a chest at a local inn called the Howling Tortoise.

And thanks to the scroll we wouldn't have to trek back through the manor or tangle with any of the vicious Void Terrors that might've respawned. Cutter would have to send a word to the Gobs on the Hellreaver, but they'd be able to pilot the ship back to Rowanheath without him.

A win-win all around.

The portal shimmered to life, and we headed through, emerging on a very familiar landing just below the front gates of Cliffburgh.

Though the location was the same, the scene that met us was very different.

This time around, the heavy front gates were battened down. Dwarven archers manned the wall with their crank-powered crossbows while a quartet of foot guards stood watch over the gate. There were two spearmen, a heavy tank wielding double shields, and a squad leader with a beefy axe gripped in one fist. I scanned them, searching for the familiar face of Raginolf, the captain of the guard, but no such luck.

"What kinda bullshit is this we got here?" Forge asked, directing the question at Carl.

The Cleric shrugged and spread his hands. "I don't think I've ever seen them lock the gates here. Not in the month I've been kicking around the place. Your guess is as good as mine."

"More Vogthar attacks?" Amara suggested, one hand darting toward a wicked dagger at her belt.

Only way to find out for sure was to ask.

We made our way up the short winding steps, and the guards moved into place at once. The dual-shield-wielding tank hustled to the fore, while the spearmen quickly posted up behind him, their spears canted out from either side at a forty-five-degree angle. A decent defensive setup that would make flanking the tank nearly impossible. Cranks creaked to life as crossbows were lifted and bolts were readied. These guys weren't taking any chances. The guard with the axe shuffled forward, his squat, powerful body radiating confidence.

"Halt," he barked when we were ten feet out. His Scottish accent was noticeable, though not nearly as pronounced as Captain Raginolf's. "Not sure what ya folk are looking fer, but best ya turn back the way ya've come. Cliffburgh is closed for the time being."

"Closed?" Carl said, shouldering his way to the front of the group, a scowl on his bearded face. "Cliffburgh is a trading town. It doesn't close. You trade. That's like your whole thing. You can't just close." He folded his arms, glaring at the guard.

"We bloody well can, lad. Can and have. There's trouble brewin' up in Stone Reach. Whole kingdom's on high alert. No one's going in. No one's going out. Ya ken it?"

"Trouble. In Stone Reach. What kind of trouble?" I asked, stepping up beside the flustered Cleric.

"Our trouble is our own, and certainly not the business of a bunch o' outsider *javlar*, like you lot." The guard leaned over and spit into the dirt. "I reckon it was one of yer kind what did it in the first place."

"Did what? And also, I'm not a foreigner," Carl protested. "I'm a Dwarf, and not just a Dwarf but a priest in good standing with the Acolytes of the Shield and Hammer."

The guard blanched, his face paling visibly. "A priest with the Acolytes of the Shield and Hammer, ya say?"

Warning bells started going off inside my head. Something was definitely amiss here.

"Well, why dinnae ya say so right away? Perhaps it's best if you head on in and stop over to see Captain

Raginolf in the guard barracks. Ah reckon he'll have some news for ya. Might be, he has a question or two as well."

"I don't understand," Carl said, his voice shaky as he spoke. "Seriously, what's going on? There's something you're not telling me."

"Aye. Nae my place to tell." He paused and glanced over his shoulder. "Gustav, open the sally port, eh?"

There was a clank and a clink as a small door set into the main gate swung outward.

"You can go through, but these others must leave. No foreigners."

"Are you serious?" Carl pressed, scorn heavy in his voice. "But that's stupid. They're in my party, guys, and I'd be happy to vouch for them."

"Halden," the bulky tank called out. "A moment?"

The surly gate guard shot us a suspicious glare—*don't even think about trying anything funny*—moved over to the tank, and leaned his ear in close. The tank whispered something, though I couldn't be sure what. The squad leader, Halden, grunted noncommittally a few times as the shield-bearer spoke, glancing occasionally in our direction. Finally, he straightened, squaring his shoulders as he regarded us. "Don't suppose ya are the Travelers who helped with that row against the Vogthar? Bergen here seems to think he recognizes ya—says ya were wearing different garb, though."

"Your man has a sharp eye," Cutter said, sauntering forward, poised and self-assured as always. "That was us indeed. Surely you can bend the rules a hair for the heroes who saved so many of your fellow guardsmen." It wasn't a question but a suggestion that seemed to be *more*.

"Aye. Now it's starting to add up." Halden turned and signaled at one of the archers on the wall. "Ya hear all that?" he called up. The archer nodded in reply. "Well, alright then," he said, turning back to us. "Ah suppose we can indeed make an exception for ya lot." He leaned in conspiratorially and dropped his voice. "Though maybe we could keep this between us, eh? Ah don't need any trouble with the captain. Come on now." He waved us over as the other guards broke their formation, resuming their customary posts in front of the gate.

Tension I hadn't even been aware of melted from my shoulders, and a knot in my chest loosened as we made our way into the trading town.

"Well, that was a stroke of bloody good fortune," Cutter crowed as we ducked through the sally port. The words died on his lips a second later as the gate slammed shut with a *thud,* followed by the sound of a heavy bar being jammed into place. Arrayed before us in a rough semicircle were guards. Thirty of them, all loaded down with weapons and looking for a fight.

"Travelers," a blocky guard before us said as he broke ranks. "Name's Garth, and I'm the sergeant of the guard. Captain Raginolf would have a word with you. Like to ask you about your connection to a fire down in the Low Quarter. Oh, that and you're wanted on suspicion of murder. Murder and sacrilege."

"You arrestin' us, partner?" Forge growled, drawing his axe, the rasp of metal on leather carrying in the quiet.

This new guy, Garth, seemed about as unflappable as every other Dwarven guard we'd met so far. He rocked back and forth on his heels and hooked his thumbs into his belt. "That depends, big fella, on whether you want to cooperate. You do it the easy way and come with us peaceably, well, we'll call that a friendly chat, now won't we? You do it the hard way? Resist. Fight us. Maybe kill some of my men? Well, then we'll put you in chains until the fires beneath the mountain grow cold."

Carl leaned over, cupping one hand over his mouth, "That's a Dwarven idiom for *forever*," he whispered.

"Thanks, Carl," I said, patting him on the shoulder.

Ari's voice whispered in my ear, "Need me to launch a distraction?" She was cloaked in a glamor, so the guards wouldn't even see the attack coming. "I can sow enough chaos to buy you the time you need."

"No, it's fine," I replied with a tight shake of my head. "Forge," I said a touch more loudly, focusing on the hotheaded Risi. "It's fine. Put your weapon away. These guys are just trying to do their job. We can't hurt them. Wouldn't be right. You know that."

He grunted. Nodded. "Yeah. You're right, hoss. Sorry 'bout that. Just don't like people pushing me around is all." Still, he had the good graces to looked abashed as he stowed his weapon.

I fixed my gaze on spark-plug Garth. "Name's Jack. We don't intend to hurt anyone." I turned, shooting a look at Cutter and Amara in turn, since they were the other two who were liable to try something clever. "We'll be more than happy to cooperate with you. I'm really not sure what you're talking about, but please take us to your captain—I'm sure we can clear this misunderstanding up in no time. Lead the way." I gestured with one hand toward the road ahead.

"Glad you see fit to do it the easy way, though word of warning. Any funny business and my men won't hesitate to pepper you with poison-tipped bolts. And we know just how powerful your kind can be, so know that the poison we use is strong enough to put down a Stone Drake at ten paces."

Cutter snorted. "Bullshite, friend. No poison is strong enough to do that. I would know. Something of a poison expert, myself."

"Well. Maybe not with a single bolt," the guard admitted with a cold, toothy grin that didn't hold a lick of amusement, "but you have fifteen men ready to drop a bolt every three seconds. And thanks to your loud mouth, I'll make sure you're the first to get a taste." The grin slipped away entirely. "Now, if you'd kindly shut your trap and follow me." With that, he wheeled around and marched up the street, his host of armed guards forming up around us in a circle.

TWENTY-FOUR

TREASON AND HERESY

W E FOLLOWED THE SERGEANT THROUGH THE neatly laid out streets—a left, a right, another right, followed by a straightaway and a brief switchback. The whole time the guards surrounding us never dropped their weapons or gazes for a moment. These guys were ready to throw down at the drop of a hat. I also couldn't help but notice that the archers moved from rooftop to rooftop along the route, ensuring they had suppressive cover fire on us from every possible vantage. Impressive.

Not impressive enough to actually stop us if we decided to put up a fight, but it wouldn't be an easy fight, that was for sure.

The sergeant eventually ushered us to a three-story building of gray stone with a slate-tiled roof. Thin windows dotted the third floor; none were big enough for someone my size to slip through, but Ari could probably manage it if push came to shove—the advantages of being Barbie-sized. They were, however, the perfect size for an archer to rain fire down from above and were obviously built with practicality in mind. Instead of entering into the building through a set of hulking, reinforced steel doors at the front, the sergeant at arms guided us to a smaller door in the side that let out into a wide square courtyard right in the middle of the building.

From this vantage it was easy to see the building was actually a giant square, the middle carved out as a training ground. The courtyard wasn't much more than a sandy pit; weapon racks edged the interior walls. It was a barracks, though it looked closer to the Imperial-style barracks in New Viridia than the ones we had down in the Storme Marshes.

The sergeant motioned for us to form up in the center of the training grounds and as we took our place, the side door slammed closed, and the Dwarven archer brigade popped up along the roof. My stomach lurched up into my throat as I took a rough count. There were at least fifty men—and that was just the archers—and they had us completely boxed in without any easy escape route in sight. Reinforced doors popped open and more Dwarves poured into the courtyard, these heavily armored ground pounders who quickly took up positions at even intervals along the walls.

A full squad, eight deep, posted up in front of the side exit, which was the only direct way out from the courtyard proper.

With Devil and Valkyrie, we could hypothetically take to the skies, but we'd be completely in the open without so much as a cloud for cover.

I quickly recalculated our odds of getting out of this place alive if things went south.

Yeah. They weren't looking good. These guys were weaker than us, no doubt, but they'd made up for that with good planning and superior numbers.

271

"Now, you there," the sergeant said, turning on me. "You seem like the leader of this little group, so why don't you and the priest come with me, huh? Talk to the captain while the rest of your group stays out here, under our *friendly* and ever so *courteous* supervision. So long as you and your friends keep playing nice, so will my friends."

And now they were splitting the party. Clearly, this wasn't their first rodeo.

"We didn't do anything wrong," I replied, "so we're happy to comply. But since we're being so *friendly,* I'll offer you a polite word of warning in return. My crew will behave. But if any of your men get trigger happy, I won't hesitate to burn this place to the ground. There's too much on the line for anything else. Abby," I said, stealing a sidelong glance at the Firebrand, "you're in charge here. Don't rock the boat unless you absolutely have to. But if you do have to, go full Titanic. Now"—I turned back toward the sergeant—"why don't you show us the way."

The sergeant seemed to take my threat in stride. I had to admit, these Dwarves were growing on me. Tough bunch. I could see why Nangkri had liked them so much. As Carl and I made our way from the courtyard, I felt something light touch down on my shoulder. "I'm right here if you need me, Jack," Ari said in my ear. "You just say the word and I'll cut this guy up like a side of beef."

I grinned and gave a brief dip of my head. Having her with me certainly wouldn't even the odds, but it was always nice to have at least one ace tucked up my sleeve.

The sergeant guided us down a wide hallway with a claustrophobically low ceiling—another inspired innovation. Since this was a Dwarven barracks, it followed that only Dwarves would live and work here.

The ceilings wouldn't bother them in the least, but it would give them a decided advantage over any taller opponents that might try to invade. Fighting while stooped over and constantly in fear of slamming your head into the ceiling would certainly make this place a nightmare to take.

The sergeant came to a halt outside a plain brown door no different than any of the others we'd passed and gave it a sharp rap. "Captain Raginolf, I have our guests if you're ready to see them."

"Aye, aye. Go ahead and show 'em in, Sergeant."

Our guide shouldered the heavy door open, then motioned for us to enter.

"Ah'll take it from here," Captain Raginolf said, spearing the Dwarf with his steely gaze. "Close the door on yer way out, eh? Now there's a good lad." The sergeant at arms was wise enough to follow the order without a word of protest, leaving Carl, Ari, and me alone with the surly captain of the guard. He sat behind a blocky, unassuming wooden desk. Well-made, but plain and practical. Everything about the room was the same. A leather chair, comfortable, but far from fancy. A small bed in one corner, the sheets and blankets pulled tight and meticulously folded—a military rack through and through.

There was a chest at the foot of the bed, covered with heavy brass rivets, but no lock. A trusting man. Or maybe he figured that anyone dumb enough to rob him here deserved whatever they got. A stand-up armor rack adorned another corner, and I was surprised to see it actually held his bulky plate mail and gold-and-black tabard.

"Take a seat," he barked, waving at a pair of stools in front of him. "Ah'll be with ya lot in ah moment," he said, eyes still fixed on a spattering of loose-leaf papers on his desk. He dipped the nib of a quill in a nearby inkpot, then hastily scribbled something at the bottom of a page. Curious, I tried to steal a glance at whatever he was writing, but his chicken-scratch handwriting was nearly impossible to read. Eventually, the *scritch-scratch* of quill on parchment ceased, and Raginolf raised his eyes, pinning us with a gaze fierce enough to strip paint.

"Well now, if it isn't my heroic merchant friend. May I ask how you're enjoying our fair city?"

"Ummm. It's a great place you have here," I offered sheepishly. "Very clean. Nice. Friendly."

"Oh, is that so? Well then… why in the nine bloody hells did you see fit to BURN HALF OF IT TO THE GROUND, EH?" His voice rose as he spoke, until he was full-on yelling by the end, spittle flying from his beet-red face. "That little fire you and yours started over at the Smoked Pig spread to four other buildings." He thrust four plump fingers into the air. "And yer damned lucky we got there when we did, or ya might've burned down half the damned city in truth."

"Look, I can explain that," I shot back. "Yes, we're responsible for that, but not entirely responsible."

"Stow it, lad!" he boomed, slamming his hands down on the table. "Against my better judgment Ah let ya lot in. Ah stuck my neck out and told ya na ta cause trouble, and ya saw fit tae shite right on me bloody goodwill. Ah've been moppin' up yer bloody mess all night and now Stone Reach is on lockdown because *someone* murdered a whole temple full of priests. Ya are new here, so you ought to know that Dwarves are a pious lot. Even speaking against a Cleric is borderline heresy. Many a Dwarf has been exiled for far less. But killing an entire bloody order?"

He shook his head and ran a hand over his beard. "It's never even been hear of! Gods be damned heresy and treason is what it is. And who should ya show up with in tow, but the last bloody priest alive from the order! The man who would stand tae benefit the most from the deaths of his fellows. A washed-up acolyte, only recently readmitted to the order's ranks. Ya've made quite the mess, lad."

"Whoa," Carl said, throwing up his hands. "Are you telling me the other Acolytes of the Shield and Hammer are all…" He trailed off, shifting uncomfortably on his stool. "*Dead*," he finished weakly.

"Damned right. And not just the locals, neither, but the Travelers too. Killed with Vogthar blades. No fancy respawn fer them. All gone. You're the only living member."

"And I'm a suspect?" Carl asked.

"Does a Dwarf have a beard?" he replied, folding his arms across his barrel chest.

"Look, Captain," I said, "we didn't do this. I mean, yes, we did burn down the Smoked Pig, though there's more to that story that you need to hear. But kill a temple full of priests? We couldn't have done that. We were holed up at the thieves' headquarters all night and were a hundred miles away in a dungeon dive all morning. Besides, we *wouldn't* have done it. We've been working with Carl, here, because he was our key into the order. There are resources in that library that we need."

"Oh, do tell. So now ya admit tae bein' involved with the order. And ya've bloody given me a proper motive, not to mention yer alibi will fall apart because no one at the Thieves Guild is gonna go on record and talk to us—testifying to the city guards would be career bloody suicide fer a professional cutpurse."

"It wasn't us, okay," I snapped back. "I'm telling you, Captain, you have to trust us. We're the good guys here."

"Oh, is that right?" he shot back. "Don't play me fer a fool, lad. I know who ya bloody well are. Grim Jack Shadowstrider, Rebel leader of the Crimson Alliance. And it seems to me that about half of bloody Eldgard, the Imperial half—who are close trading partners with Stone Reach, might I add—might well see things a bit differently."

That caught me off guard. "How long have you known?"

"Ah had my suspicions from the get-go—Ah'm no eejit with his head stuck in the bloody sand—but ya intervened and pulled our arses out of the fire. Ah thought maybe it was coincidence. After yer tussle at the Smoked Pig, though, a blind beggar could piece it together. There were at least twenty witnesses, and last time I checked, there's only one Murky bastard with a pet Shadow Drake."

"Fine. All of that's true, but I swear I'm not your enemy, and we didn't kill those priests. We're working against a man named Peng Jun. He's a Darkling general, and he's looking to assemble a weapon that could kill all of us. And, for the record, Peng doesn't care about Imperial or Rebel. He's a rabid dog, and he'll do whatever he needs to do to get his hands on that weapon. And it just so happens the Acolytes of the Shield and

Hammer are the key to this whole thing. I'm going to show you something, Captain. You've shown me trust, so I'm going to return the favor."

Slowly I reached into my inventory and pulled out one of the Doom-Forged relics, placing it gently on the desk between us. Raginolf's eyes focused, his wind-beaten forehead scrunching as he stretched out a hand and ran his plump digits across the item. His breath caught. "The Doom Forge? It cannae be. It's a legend."

"No, it isn't. And like I said, the acolytes hold the secret to finding the forge. We ran up against Peng and his thugs at the Smoked Pig. They were after this guy"— I jerked my head at Carl—"but we got to him first. My guess is that after losing him, Peng and his crew headed to Stone Reach, hoping to pressure the priests into divulging their secrets. And when they didn't, he slaughtered them all, because Peng has some serious anger control issues. He's the one responsible for all of this, and he's still inside Stone Reach."

I picked up the relic and slipped it back into my inventory.

Raginolf stood, puffing out his cheeks and folding his hands behind his back at parade rest. "What a giant shitestorm ya've dropped in me lap, lad. Ah headache like ya wouldn't bloody believe." He turned pensive for a beat. "So, Ah suppose you're looking for the Doom Forge as well, then, eh? And what would you do if you find it? Build yer Alliance a weapon capable of turning the war in yer favor, I suppose?"

I paused, processing the question. "I'll bring justice to people like Peng," I finally said, "and hopefully stop the Vogthar incursions for good. And speaking of Peng, if you let us into Stone Reach, I can get him for you."

"Oh, and why do ya think that?"

"Because he knows I have the Doom-Forged relics. He'll come for me, and when he does, we'll be ready. I'm telling you, Captain, we can get the guy responsible for those murders if you give us a shot."

Raginolf sighed and turned, offering us his back. A perfect opportunity to attack if we'd had ulterior motives... I half wondered if that wasn't the point—a test to see if we were leveling with him. Eventually, he faced us, then bent over and scooped up the letter from his desk. "This is a writ, authorizing yer party to enter Stone Reach."

Once more he caught me flatfooted, and I'm sure it showed on my face.

He grinned and winked. "Ah might be a guard in a backwater town, but Ah wasn't always. In my experience, ya don't live long as a captain in the guard unless ya can read people like a book. Ah knew ya were trouble, but Ah also knew ya were good. Still, Ah wanted to hear it from yer own lips—make damned sure Ah wasn't making a mistake before unleashing ya on me city. Because you, Grim Jack, bring death and destruction with ya wherever ya go."

I opened my mouth to speak, but he cut me off with a glare and a raised hand.

"Ah'm not judging. And Ah am sure it's not yer intention, lad, but those are the facts. It is what it is. Now, this writ, it won't just get ya inta Stone Reach. It'll get ya into the temple and will obligate any of the Stone Reach guards to give you aid, should ya so request it. It's unorthodox, but it'll fly." He pursed his lips and nodded. "Aye. It'll fly. Though ya have ta promise me one thing.

Ya find this bastard, Peng, and ya *bury* him." He extended the paper toward me, a fat wax seal at the bottom.

"I will."

"Good. Now get on over to the Mystica Ordo, they're on standby ready to port ya over to the city. Give 'em hell, Grim Jack, and don't make me regret stickin' my bloody neck out. Again."

TWENTY-FIVE

SOUL SMITH

THE TRIP TO THE MYSTICA ORDO IN CLIFFBURGH was uneventful and, with Captain Raginolf's writ in hand, getting into Stone Reach was even more so. Sure, we got a few odd looks from the Dwarven mages managing the enormous transference portal, but no one wanted to get on Raginolf's bad side, so they waved us through without a hassle. The Mystica Ordo chapter hall inside Stone Reach was nearly identical to every other chapter hall I'd ever been in—marbled floors, walls covered with expensive silk tapestries, mounted torches, stuffy Portomancers—but the city beyond was unlike anything I'd ever seen.

We stepped into something straight out of the *Lord of the Rings*.

Forge let out a low whistle.

"Well, bugger me good," Cutter said, awe coating the words, which was a rarity with him. It seemed like he'd traveled to just about everywhere in Eldgard in his capacity as a thief, but gaining access to Stone Reach was new even to him.

We were inside a mountain, I *knew* we were, but glancing up it would've been nearly impossible to tell. There should've been craggy rock and hanging stalactites, but instead we had an unobstructed view of the twilight sky, glimmering stars starting to peek their faces out for the night. Paper lanterns in a multitude of hues filled the air, shining with spelled light.

"But how?" Amara asked, gaze fixed on the stars, her mouth open.

"Enchanted," Carl replied matter-of-factly. "The Order of the Dawnbreaker has illusion clerics that man towers throughout the city. Day and night they power these giant engines that maintain the spell. Reality generators. Mimics the sky outside. Costs a fortune to run, but no one seems to complain." He sniffed, not nearly as impressed as the rest of us.

"Wow," Ari whispered from nowhere, still cloaked in glamor. "I can see the threads of their magic. It's a bit like my own powers, but on a scale I've never seen before."

"Yeah, it's pretty neat, I guess," Carl agreed, as though *neat* could possibly be an adequate description. Of all the cities I'd been to in my travels so far, only Ankara—the Jewel of the West—came close to the beauty this place had so casually on display.

The enchanted sky wasn't the only impressive thing about the city. Its myriad of buildings were carved into the walls of the mountain in a series of concentric rings. Seven of them, rising up, up, up. Each ring was set on a shelf of rock, the biggest of the rings at the bottom, the smallest at the top almost like stadium seating... but for an *entire* city. We'd emerged on the fifth ring up, which gave us an excellent view of the impressive city spread out below us. In the very center of the mountain, far below us, devoid of buildings, was a forest.

One with towering trees, their leaves glittering gold and silver and ruby and emerald. The trunks were all ghostly white like exposed bone and shot through with golden metallic veins. Suddenly, the Dwarven obsession with Yggdrasil, the tree of life, made a whole lot more sense. Whoever would've guessed that there was a *forest* squirreled away inside this place? More mundane foliage also dotted each of the city circles: vibrant grass, flowers in a riot of hues—beautiful, if standard—and a surprising number and variety of mushrooms.

There were squat mushrooms, willowy mushrooms, and some the size of young oaks, all glowing in a variety of psychedelic colors. I'd seen mushroom forests like that once before, deep in the lair of Lowyth the Immortal Spider Queen.

I still had occasional nightmares about my encounters there.

The buildings themselves were likewise otherworldly wonders. Unlike the utilitarian stone houses and shops of Cliffburgh, the intricate homes and sprawling businesses here were sculpted directly from the mountainous rock, and they were absolute works of art. They didn't seem to be *built* so much as they looked almost *grown* from the rock—all flowing lines, graceful arches, and spiraling columns. Stone statues and enormous fountains, all masterfully sculpted, adorned almost every intersection.

"Come on," Carl said, breaking the spell this place had cast on the party. "My temple's down on the second circle, and it's a helluva walk, so better we get moving." The unimpressed Cleric set off at a brisk pace, robes swishing around him as he led us through the tightly packed streets filled with Dwarves. Seriously. Dwarves everywhere.

I spotted a couple of Risi, a handful of Wodes, and a number of Accipiters—they seemed to be the most readily accepted outsiders—but even they were few and far between. We caught a lot of curious, suspicious, or outright hostile glances as we made our way between the levels. Guard patrols stopped us more than once, blades drawn, shields raised, scowls etched into bearded faces, but a few words from Carl and a flash of the paper from Captain Raginolf saw us on our way with only mild issues and no bloodshed.

On the third level, Forge stopped dead in his tracks in front of a rather plain workshop. Well, plain for Stone Reach.

"Well, screw me sideways," he grunted. "I can't believe it."

"What is it?" I asked, eyeing the building over one shoulder.

The sign above read, Blue Blazes Metalworks. Carefully carved into the stone was the visage of a dragon, its mouth opened wide, flames bursting out. A bold number 1 was carefully worked into the stone, just below the creature's eye.

"Oh. My. God," Abby said, sounding nearly as impressed as Forge had.

"I'm sorry, is there something I'm missing here?" I asked again, glancing between my crew and the building.

"Jack," Abby replied, eyes still fixed on the workshop, "this place is *legendary*." She pulled her gaze away, turning it on Carl. "Is this where Lars Blackblade works?"

Carl sniffed and nodded. "Yep. The 1st Ranked Dragon-Class Blacksmith. Best in all of Stone Reach."

"He ain't just the best in Stone Reach, partner," Forge said. "He's the goddamned best in all of Eldgard. His weapons and armor sell for the price of a starter house back IRL, and that's when you can find 'em at all. Which you can't. It's like trying to track down a pack of cigarettes at the end of a field op. Ain't no one got 'em, but everyone wants 'em." He paused, glancing left and right. "I don't get it, there oughta be a line stretching for a mile. Where is everyone?"

Carl snorted and rolled his eyes. "Wow, are you guys freakin' clueless. Aside from the fact that Lars's weapons cost more than anyone in their right mind would ever willingly spend, the guy rejects ninety-nine percent of the customers that walk through his door. He does, uh, maybe eight or nine commissions a year—all custom work. That's why you can't find his stuff on the open market. Besides, if you got lucky enough to get a piece from him, would you sell it?"

"Jack," Forge said, wheeling on me, a fanatic gleam in his eye. "We gotta go in. Gotta."

"I'd love to, but we're sort of on a tight timeline here." I stole a quick look around, making sure there was no one close enough to eavesdrop, then dropped my voice low all the same. "We still don't know where the Doom Forge is, and we only have a day and a half, tops, before I drop dead and we lose any chance of completing this quest."

"But, Jack," he said, now desperate. "This could be a once-in-a-lifetime shot. And this guy's weapons and armor. They're daggon *life altering.* If I could get an axe from him, it would give me an edge like you wouldn't believe."

"He's right, Jack," Abby added. "Anyone who's ever swung a hammer in a forge knows about Lars

Blackblade. And what do we have to lose? If Carl's on the level, he'll probably turn us away before we're all the way through the door."

I frowned and pulled up my interface, double-checking the time. Quarter after five. We had a ton to do, but if this guy really was as good as Forge and Abby seemed to think, it would be a crying shame not to at least stop in. True, we could always come back after the fight, assuming we survived, but it would be awesome if we could snag some new legendary gear before we tangled with Khalkeús. I quickly toggled over to my Active Effects screen, double-checking just how long I had until the next debuff hit.

Current Debuffs

Death-Head Mode: You've temporarily activated Death-Head Mode! Time until the *Gut Check* debuff takes effect: 18 hours 58 minutes 23 seconds.

Diseased: As a result of the Death-Head Mode, your body is slowly dying! You've been afflicted with Death Head's Disease. Attack damage and Spell Strength reduced by 15%; Health, Stamina, and Spirit regeneration reduced by 25%; duration, until death or quest completion.

"Fine," I finally conceded, closing out the screen. "But let's make it quick. I doubt Peng found anything out about the Doom Forge, but if he did, he'll have a solid lead on us."

"You ain't gonna regret it, Jack." Forge beamed, nearly bouncing on his toes as he headed toward the doors, which were carved from the strange bone-white wood from the forest below. "I can feel it in my gut."

A brass bell let out a tinkle like broken glass as we pushed our way inside the shop.

For being the forge and storefront of the finest-rated blacksmith in the world, the interior of the shop was rather unimpressive. And by unimpressive, I really meant *empty*. I'd expected jewel-encrusted axes and talking swords in glass-fronted cases, but no. There was just nothing. Empty walls devoid of shelves and weapon racks. No polished tables prominently displaying choice armor. Just bare space, creaky floorboards, and a long, polished service counter near the back.

A door behind the service counter swung open, and a Dwarf hobbled out, his salt-and-pepper beard down nearly to his knees, golden goggles strapped on over his eyes. A heavy leather apron hung down his front. He was topless underneath, his skin scarred, pockmarked, and so heavily stained with char and soot it was as black as rich soil. He pulled a filthy rag, nearly as grimy as his arms, from the back pocket of his trousers and mopped at his sweat-dotted forehead. He took one long, measuring look at our party, then sniffed and spit onto the floor. "Shop's closed for business," he grunted, turning on his heel and making for the door to the back.

"Then why was the door open?" I asked. "That seems like an invitation to me."

The Dwarf paused for a moment. "Lemme amend my statement. The shop is closed. *To you.* Not sure if you know where you are, but this here ain't your run-of-the-mill equipment boutique. I don't sell items off the shelf, and I certainly don't want to buy any of your secondhand trash. This is a commission-only shop, and I don't have a commission with you. Nor with anyone else in your party. So, like I said, the store is closed." He turned, poised to head into the back.

"Wait. What if I wanted to commission a piece? A piece for everyone in my party."

The Dwarf paused, snorted, and turned slowly to face me. He flipped up the lenses on his goggles, showcasing eyes that burned with unnatural golden light. "This ain't no trinket shop, boy. You couldn't afford one commission, let alone six. 'Sides, even if you had the gold, which I doubt, there's more than money involved. I don't pour my heart and soul into a piece that's gonna sit on some shelf in a bureaucrat's office. This job is about far more than money to me."

"Well, it's actually seven commissions, not six." I snapped my fingers. "Ari?"

The little Pixy appeared in a flash, motes of neon pink light drifting down like fresh snowfall.

The Dwarf's eyes narrowed, and he rubbed thoughtfully at his bearded chin. "Pixy right?"

Ari nodded.

He grunted. "Hmm. I've never made something that small before." He seesawed his head for a moment, left, right, left, right. "Alright. Let's say you've piqued my curiosity. Come on over here and let me take a good look at ya. Need to check your renown."

"Why?" I asked even while I edged closer to the service counter.

"I ain't no regular smith, son. I'm what they call a Soul Smith. Each commission I take on, I gotta imbue a chunk of my soul into the item"—he tapped at his barrel chest—"that's how I make 'em so powerful. I regrow the piece of soul in time, sorta like a scab healing over, but it takes a long time. *Real* long. But there's an upside to it. I get experience for crafting each item, but then I also get a fractional portion of experience for any experience the player wielding it earns. Can only take on so many commissions at a time though, so I make sure I don't make gear that's gonna collect dust on some senator's shelf, you got it?"

His eyes narrowed as he examined me, then flared wide a moment later. "Gods almighty. Your renown is at 2,500. You've been a right busy bastard, alright. Don't reckon I've ever run across someone with renown that high. Fine." He quickly examined each of us in turn, nodding, a small smile creeping across his face. Finally, he grunted in something close to satisfaction. "My goin' rate is five-hundred gold per commission. You pay half up front, the other half upon completion."

I nearly choked at the price. Five-hundred gold was the equivalent of fifty thousand US dollars—a staggering sum. For seven items, that would run me a cool three hundred fifty thousand dollars. I had it socked away in my personal funds, but damn did that smart. Still, Forge was right, this probably was a once-in-a-lifetime opportunity I couldn't possibly pass up. "Okay, I'm game," I replied, opening my inventory and pulling out a fat stack of coins, which I dumped on the counter. "Seven commissions."

The blacksmith eyed the gleaming pile of coins, but made no move to take it. Truthfully, he didn't even seem all that interested in the money. If those were his going rates, I suspected he was already filthy rich, which meant he was in this for whatever gain he got on the tail end. "Good enough," he grunted. "I'll get working on your order. Should have the whole lot of 'em done by tomorrow, 'bout noontime. Once the muse takes me, well, I'll just about work myself to death."

Without another word, the Dwarf turned and marched toward the door, leaving the gold just sitting on the counter where I'd left it.

"Wait a minute," Forge called at his retreating back. "Don't you need our names? Our classes? Don't we need to tell you what we want you to make for us?"

The smith faltered and let out a deep belly laugh that shook his whole, soot-covered frame. "That ain't the way this works at all. I already got everything I need. And, for your information, you don't tell me what you need. I tell you. Now get outta here and let me be about my business." There was a glint in his eye. I thought he looked... excited. "You be back tomorrow. Come with the rest of my gold. Believe you me, you won't be disappointed. Now get." He shooed us away with one hand, then shouldered his way through the rear door, disappearing without another word.

TWENTY-SIX

HAMMER AND SHIELD

A FTER WE LEFT BLUE BLAZES, IT TOOK US another fifteen minutes to get to the Temple of the Hammer and Shield, located down on the second level. With the way Carl talked about his order, I was expecting something run-down and drab—a hole-in-the-wall temple, if there was such a thing. Not even close. The building was a hulking monstrosity of fluted pillars, multilayered roofs, gold-capped domes, and lacy arcades. A grand staircase seemed to ascend *forever*, and at the top stood a pair of enormous gold-covered statues of Khalkeús flanking the steps.

One statue held a smith's hammer, though I knew from my trip into the pages of Eitri's journal that the Aspect hadn't used a hammer at all. The other statue had one hand outstretched, fire burning in the palm like a beacon in the night.

If not for the guards standing watch at the bottom of the staircase, it would've been impossible to tell anything was amiss. There were five of them—seemed like that was a standard unit around these parts—a pair wielding halberds, one tank, one Cleric in a chainmail shirt that draped to his knees, and a female, axe-wielding squad leader. Their gold-and-black tabards, marked with a prominent mountain and anvil, were identical to those worn by the Cliffburgh guards. One thing was for sure, these Dwarves were nothing if not orderly.

The squad noticed us at once, shoulders squaring in anticipation of violence.

Carl motioned for us to stop. "Better let me handle this, guys. Lemme see the writ of referral."

I reached into my bag, fished out the scroll Raginolf had provided us with, and handed it over. Carl took it, lips pressed into a thin, worried line. He took a deep breath, cleared his throat, ran a hand through his thick beard, then marched up to the guards, who drew their weapons as he approached.

"Keep moving, citizen," the squad leader said, the threat clear in her voice. "This temple is closed until further notice."

"Sorry, lady, but that won't work for me. I need to get in—"

"Not *lady*. Corporal Shawna, 5th Ranked Manticore-Class Paragon. And no one gets in," she cut him off before he could finish. "Not sure if you've heard, but an atrocity was committed here. Every priest in the order, massacred. The doors won't open up until we finish with our investigation. Period. End of discussion. If you need a blessing or restoration, I'd try the Custodians of Akriel down on level one. They can patch you up and get you and your party on your way. Sorry for the inconvenience." She didn't *sound* sorry, though. She sounded like someone itching for a fight. "Now, move along."

Carl didn't move, though, not an inch. "You don't understand. I'm not here for services. I'm a member of the order. This"—he jabbed a finger at the building behind her—"order. Hell, as far as I know, I'm the last remaining member, and I needed to get in there. Now."

A look of absolute suspicion flashed across Guardswoman Shawna's face. She turned toward the tank with the pair of heavy shields strapped to his tree-trunk arms. They exchanged a hushed conversation, too quiet for me to follow. After a second, she turned back. "Look, I don't care who you are. This?" She gestured at the temple with her axe. "This is an active crime scene. Until we close our investigation, no one's going in there. Not you, and certainly not a bunch of outsiders." She shot us a withering glare as though we were personally responsible for the murders inside.

For all she knew, we might've been.

"Is that so?" Carl said, unfurling the letter Captain Raginolf had provided us with. "This says different."

The female guard rolled her eyes, smirked, and snatched the doc. "Fine. Let's see what you have." She sniffed in clear disapproval, then smoothed the parchment and held it out at arm's length. She visibly paled, her eyes growing progressively larger with each line she read. She glanced up at us as she finished, staring at each of us in turn, then turned her gaze back to the sheet, reading through the details once more. She muttered as she finished it for a second time, then promptly thrust it into the hands of the dual-wielding tank.

"That forged?" she asked as her partner gave it a read. "I've never heard of Captain Raginolf ever giving a blank writ of recommendation."

"Looks legit to me," the tank offered with a shake of his head. He spoke with an accent that reminded me of Raginolf. "Dinnae make a lick ah sense, but it checks out."

"Wait a minute," I said, sliding up next to Carl. Probably, I should've just kept my mouth shut, but I was too curious not to ask. "How do you guys know Captain Raginolf? It seems odd that you would know about the guard captain of some little trading post two hours from here."

Corporal Shawna snorted and slapped a knee. "Captain Raginolf's not just some 'guard captain.' He was the Arch Merkismathr of the Stone Reach Guard Corps before he retired a year ago. Wanted to settle down someplace nice and quiet—away from the hustle and bustle of the city. He's the single most decorated Dwarf in Stone Reach. Man's a bloody legend and one of the only 1st Ranked Dragon-Class adventurers in the province. He has more campaigns under his belt than the next five captains below him." She pushed the parchment into Carl's hands. "You better hope this *is* legit, because if it's not, Raginolf *will* find you, and he'll fillet you alive with a blunt war axe."

Carl carefully rolled up the scroll, hands trembling minutely, then handed it back to me.

"It is legit," Cutter replied, hands folded behind his back, staring down his nose at them. "And hows about you don't give us any more bloody lip or Captain Raginolf will find out about it. And then maybe it's you who'll be filleted alive with a blunt war axe, eh?" He offered her a cocky, lopsided grin and waved her out of the way with one hand.

293

The corporal's face turned an alarming shade of red, though she held her tongue. "Well, go on then," she said, jerking her head toward the staircase and the doors beyond. "You're clear. Just try not to make a mess of our crime scene, huh? We have Valtarii Diviners from Coldpass coming out in the morning. The less you disturb the bodies, the better." She nodded at the rest of the guards, who begrudgingly parted like the Red Sea, leaving us a narrow path between the press of their bodies and weapons.

Cutter sauntered forward, not a care in the world, and the rest of us followed in his wake.

We climbed the seemingly endless stairs and headed through the heavy wooden doors intricately carved to showcase various scenes of Khalkeús.

Inside was the set of a slasher flick.

Blood and bodies *everywhere*.

The main hall was rectangular and rather narrow; elaborately decorated masonry columns bearing flickering torches marched down each side, supporting a vaulted ceiling. The columns on each side of the hall formed a series of arched arcades, and beyond those were low-ceilinged wings lined with pews. At the far end of the temple was a nave with an impressive statue of Khalkeús, studded with jewels. Before the statue was an altar and a lectern with a book propped open.

The place would've been beautiful if not for the corpses and body parts strewn around like toys some neglectful kid had forgotten to put away. Limbs in a pile. Pools of congealed blood. Splashes of dark crimson liberally coating the walls.

Carl raised his hands to his mouth, unshed tears building in his eyes. He dropped to his knees and vomited all over the floor. After a long beat, he wiped at his mouth with the back of a hand, then regained his feet. He looked dazed. Traumatized. As someone who'd largely been confined to a non-adventuring, non-combat role, seeing this level of human carnage was probably a first. And even for someone like me, who'd seen more than my fair share of bloodshed, this was sickening.

"Oh my God," Carl choked out as he moved among the bodies. "Why would they do this?" he asked, standing over the fallen body of an elderly man with a long, wispy beard. "I mean, these guys weren't exactly the friendliest bunch, but just butchering them like this? What would possess someone to do this? It's... Well, pardon my French, but it's fuckin' senseless."

"Senseless cruelty, it is what Darklings do," Amara said matter-of-factly. "It is the way of things. But it is cruelty with a purpose. The bodies, they tell the story. Look." She padded forward until she stood near a thickset female Dwarf whose throat had been cut from ear to ear. "They started with her. Look at the footprints, at the way the body is slumped. No doubt Peng pushed for information about the Doom Forge. Perhaps the priests refused to talk, or perhaps they simply didn't have answers to give. Either way, Peng—or one of his lackies—killed this woman as a show of force. Nice. Clean. Quick. A warning of what would happen to the others.

"But see here." She moved away from the woman and over to a younger bearded man, his hair thinning badly on the top. His throat had likewise been cut, but it also looked like he'd been fed into a buzz saw—shallow nicks, cuts, and lacerations decorating his exposed flesh. "They went to work on him next, and instead of simply killing, they maimed. Slowly torturing him so as to draw out words. Either from him or from the others. Still, though, these priests, they would not talk." Everyone was silent as she moved over to a body nearby, similarly mutilated, though this one was also missing his hands.

Abby looked as physically nauseated as I felt.

Forge was as stoic as a statue—a Marine who'd seen carnage before and had hardened himself to it—while Ari perched on his shoulder, her illusion dismissed. She'd turned a shade of deep, sorrowful purple, her wings curled inward in defeat. Cutter, on the other hand, looked positively furious. Cutter was many things—a drunk, a thief, a gambler, almost impossibly lazy, even an occasional cutthroat—but he wasn't a fan of straight-up murder. Killing he could do, so long as it was necessary, but senseless slaughter like this bothered him, even if he tried not to show it.

"Still, they would not talk," Amara continued, "and so Peng increased the brutality. By the time he got to him"—she pointed toward the bearded man near Carl—"he was simply enraged. Look at the savagery. It was not carefully administered as with these others. It was done by a man driven by hatred. By sheer frustration and overwhelming need. Once this one died, he turned his men loose." She gestured toward a group of dead Clerics piled together in front of the altar at the far end of the temple. "After this one refused to talk, he knew there was nothing to be gained, so he had the rest slaughtered like cattle."

Carl cleared his throat and pulled his eyes away from the dead priest at his feet. "I don't wanna be in here anymore. I never wanted any of this, and I…" He faltered. "I don't want to see this. Let's just head over to the library, see if we can find what we're looking for, huh?"

No one protested, and though it was likely the bodies were still loaded down with gear, no one even mentioned the idea of looting their corpses. It wasn't the decent thing to do.

Solemnly, we threaded our way through the carnage, avoiding the pools of blood and the discarded body parts, making for the nave and the altar. At the back of the temple, there were a pair of doors, one to the left, another to the right.

"That one leads to the living quarters," Carl said, nodding toward the door on the right. "This way to the library." But instead of going on, he paused, lingering before the lectern with the book propped open on top. After a moment of hesitation, he slipped around behind the stand.

"This is the ritual book." He traced his fingers over the open pages. "Used to have to sit through endless prayers and boring stories. Never thought I'd find myself missing that. Mind if I say a quick prayer for them before we go?" he asked. "It's what they woulda wanted, I bet."

"Of course," Abby said, offering him a sad little smile.

Carl grunted, nodding. He bent over and pulled a golden cloth stole from a compartment in the lectern and slipped it on around his neck, the fringed tassels hanging past his waist. He flipped through a few of the pages until he found whatever he was looking for, then cleared his throat and began to chant. The prayer was soft at first, though amplified by the vaulted roof above. I only understood snippets of the invocation, but bits of it sounded oddly familiar.

"Supplices deprecamur pro anima famuli tui…" His words took on a rhythmic cadence, golden light enveloping him in a swirling cloud. *"Quen de hoc saculo tw venire iussisti."* The words grew in power and strength, his voice becoming a booming thing while the light burned ever brighter. *"Et in mansionibus sanctorum et in luce sancta permaneat."*

I squinted against the light, which had gathered around his head, forming into a halo while a pair of enormous golden angel wings sprouted from his back. The whole room shook as tongues of brilliant light flashed out, gently caressing the corpses of the fallen.

"What in the hell is happening!" Forge yelled, glancing around wild-eyed. His words were drowned out a second later as a set of bells—even though there were no bells to be seen anywhere in the temple—rang out like a peal of thunder, deafeningly loud. I slapped my hands against my ears, trying to block out the sound, but that didn't seem to mute the noise even a little. And then, just as quick as the noise and light had come, it was gone.

The corpses were gone as well. The blood scrubbed clean, the temple's interior restored to immaculate glory. Carl stood behind the lectern, mouth agape, his hands raised in awe. Golden tattoos ran around his fingers and sprinted over his palms in elaborate swirls and loops. "Oh shit," he said after a long pause. "That's not what I meant to do."

"And just what did you do?" Amara asked, voice sharp and cutting as a razor blade. "You said you were going to offer a quick prayer, not eradicate all the evidence. What do you suppose the guards will think about that?"

Carl facepalmed, a panicked look overtaking him. "Everything just keeps going wrong. I swear to God I didn't mean to do this! Seriously. I just offered a short benediction that we say over other locals that kick the bucket. Nothing special, right hand to the Lord above. But when I finished the chant, I got a notice saying because I'd invoked the ritual as the last active acolyte in good standing with the temple, I'd been promoted." He paused, gulped, and licked his lips. "To the Arch Justiciar of the order."

Cutter threw back his head and crowed in laughter, the sound carrying through the temple. "This is the best thing to happen all week. From outcast to head Cleric in less than a day. Brilliant. You're either the worst bloody acolyte that's ever walked the face of Eldgard, or you're an absolute genius. Still." He paused, glancing around. "Amara's right, can't imagine the guards will be happy you destroyed their crime scene, even if you are a high priest now. Best we get moving before they pop in to check on us, eh?"

"Yeah, that's not a bad idea," I said. "Forge, why don't you post up at the entrance. Try to buy us some time if the guards do come poking into our business."

"On it, hoss."

Carl shuffled out from behind the lectern, still marveling over the swirling golden tattoos crawling all over his skin. He absently ushered us into a much more traditional library than the one we'd stumbled upon in the bowels of the Shadowverse beneath the Iredale Hold. Neatly ordered shelves were filled with neatly ordered rows of books. There were several polished tables for study, oil lamps burning merrily on each—the flames likely revived by whatever spell Carl had unwittingly released during his benediction.

There were also elaborate tapestries detailing different scenes from the order's long and winding history, plus more than a few display cases holding pitted daggers, broken pottery, or discarded bits of shriveled parchment.

I pulled open my inventory, retrieved the ring I'd taken from the secret alcove, then pulled up my interface to inspect it a bit more thoroughly.

Eitri Spark-Sprayer's Signet Ring

Item Type: Relic

Class: Ancient Artifact

Base Damage: 0

Primary Effects:

- Cast Forge of Revealing Light (1) per day

Sometimes clear sight is the most powerful tool of all…

No real benefits, but after all the riddles and secret doors we'd stumbled across down in Eitri's summer home, it wasn't hard to guess what I needed to do. I slipped the ring onto my index finger. "Not sure what Forge of Revealing Light does," I said, "so it might be a good idea if everyone shields their eyes. Wouldn't want to get hit with a temporary blindness debuff." With the warning out of the way, I lifted my hand, palm out, fingers spread wide, and activated the once-a-day spell.

The ring turned white-hot, the heat singeing my skin, and light rolled out in a wave. I clenched my eyes shut and waited for a three count before opening them again. Everyone else was likewise blinking their eyes, scanning the room for any sign of illusion magic or some obvious rune that would lead the way.

"There," Carl said, thrusting a finger toward a floor-to-ceiling tapestry depicting some ancient scene of a priest standing guard against the advance of a shadowy titan as tall as a building. The Cleric stood with his back straight, a jewel-studded scepter raised high in defiance, golden light shooting from his free hand while a cluster of dirty-faced men and women took refuge behind him. "It looks, I dunno. Sort of hazy. Transparent, maybe." He was right. The tapestry hadn't moved, and the image was the same, but it looked almost ethereal—a wavering mirage on the horizon.

Carl moved over to the tapestry, extending a hand to examine the item. But when he went to touch it, his hand simply passed through, here one moment, gone the next. He braced himself, mustering his resolve, shoulders knotting up, then stepped through, vanishing *into* the fabric. "It's fine," he called, voice mildly muted by the odd illusion between us. "There's a descending staircase. Looks like it leads to some sort of hidden basement."

"You heard the man," Cutter said, rubbing his hands together in greedy glee. "Time to go coax out whatever secrets this place is hiding."

TWENTY-SEVEN

WORDS OF WARNING

T HE HIDDEN STAIRCASE, SECRETED BEHIND THE tapestry, let out into a musty old room, the air stale and heavy, the floors covered in grit and dusty. It was completely dark—no fires burned, no magical torches illuminated our way—but Abby quickly fixed that. She conjured a small orb of fire, which hovered above her outstretched palm, its orange light spilling over the rough-worn floors.

"Hold on a sec," she muttered, inching over to a nearby wall. "Looks like we got a wall sconce over here." There was a flash and the light took hold, burning merrily at the end of a mounted torch. "One more second," she muttered, hustling across the room, dress swishing as she moved. She lit a second torch and a third. The room was on the small side of things with none of the fancy flourishes I'd come to expect from Eitri's characteristic hidden chambers.

The floors were rough sandstone, plain and unadorned, just like the walls. There were no relics here, no mysterious bookcases or carefully preserved tomes. Certainly not the treasure vault Cutter was likely anticipating. But the room wasn't empty. Affixed to the far wall, illuminated by the greasy, flickering light from the old torches, were three iron plaques, each the size of a car door. The metal was as thin as paper and glimmered softly despite the age and dust.

"What are these?" Ari asked, zipping across the room, her body now a vibrant green, the light splashing off the first plaque. She squinted and canted her head. "This one's a map, isn't it?" She gestured at the plate with one tiny hand. It did indeed look like a map, with fine script writing etched into the metal, both above and below the image. Problem was, it wasn't in any language I recognized.

"Let me have a look," Carl said, shouldering his way past us until he stood directly in front of the first wall plaque. He stroked his beard, nose scrunched, as he regarded the image. "Ari," he said, nodding toward the script. "Hard to read in this light, can you hold it steady for me, huh? Maybe turn that whole glow thing up a few notches?"

"Sure thing." She beamed, wings beating at a frantic pace as she rose, her internal light intensifying until she burned like a mini star.

"Thanks," he grunted before mumbling under his breath. "Writing's old," he offered offhandedly, more for him than us. "One of our passive abilities is called Arcane Insight. Lets Clerics identify magical item properties, decipher ancient text like this, and learn casting languages at four times the rate of normal players. But I only have one point in it, so I kinda suck ass. I can only make out every two or three words. Might take me a hot minute."

He pondered, continuing to rub his beard while he grumbled and talked to himself. "Okay," he finally said.

"So this one says something to the effect of 'Paper is corruptible and subject to the ravages of time and theft, so they'—whoever *they* is—'left these things as a memorial against the turning of Kronos's wheel.' Now, I think this one here"—he tapped on the steel, *ping-ping-ping*—"was definitely carved by Eitri. You can tell by the blocky text and the hard angles on the consonants. Looks just like the script in the book we recovered.

"And Ari's right. This is definitely a map to the location of the Doom Forge." He leaned forward, hands planted on his knees, nose only a handful of inches from the surface of the metal. Slowly he ran a finger over the surface, gaze flicking along the text. His plump digit continued running from point to point, until finally coming to a herky-jerky halt near what looked like a jagged ridge of script. He canted his head to the side, bewilderment tattooed across his face. "Well what in the hell is that supposed to mean? As twilight falls," he read slowly, "the Shadow of the Giant becomes the Headsman's Blade. Awesome. That's not super-duper vague or anything."

He straightened, arms crossed, one finger tapping at his chin. "The Giant and the Headsman's Blade. Headsman's Blade. Giant. Headsman's Blade. Giant." His lips puckered into a thin line. "Nope, sorry. I got nothing. But I'm guessing this is some clue about the location of the entrance, and since I'm not a complete moron, I'm betting it only shows itself as twilight falls." He frowned. "If you give me some time, I can probably find some reference to the Giant and the Headsman's Blade in the books above. And if it's not there, maybe the wikis will have something."

"Well, bugger me good," Cutter said. "Maybe you're not such a worthless sod after all."

"Um, not sure if I should be flattered or insulted... So, thank you, I guess?"

"Could the clue be on those other metal plaques?" Abby asked.

"Huh. What's that?" Carl replied, distracted.

"The clue about the entrance, could it be on one of the other plaques?" she repeated.

"Ehhh. No, I don't think so. The first one tells us where to find the place, but the rest of these seem to tell us what we need to do once we get there. And if I'm reading this next one right, finding the entrance to the forge is the *easy* part." He scooted over to the next plate and hunched forward, hands on his knees. More restless muttering followed. "This one says the entrance gets you into a new section of ruins. Something called." He paused, leaning forward even farther, reading a line of text at the bottom. "Yeah. Something called the Judgments, I think, which sounds super promising."

His brow wrinkled as he examined the text. "The Judgment is composed of three trials, or three rooms maybe, which both 'prove thy worth and release the bonds which ought not be broken.' Apparently, once you start on the path, you can't turn back for any reason, or you die." Another pause. Another squint. "Horrifically," he finished. "Yep. Die horrifically. The rest of this here looks like some sort of instruction guide for passing the trials and breaking the bonds. Hang on." He stuck his tongue out between his teeth as he ran his fingers over a particularly troublesome line of text.

"This says there's a test of leadership, wisdom, and sacrifice. Huh, this is interesting. Seems like there are some puzzles to solve—there's all kinds of diagrams—

and it looks like there are a list of rules too. Once you start the test, you can't stop for any reason. You're only allowed to bring in…" He craned his neck forward. "Six party members. That's the max. 'First six through the Judgment entry are bound of Fate and entwined in Soul.' Oh, that doesn't look good."

"What's that?" Abby asked, looking more worried by the second.

"Well there are tons of pictures of just... *Murder*. Like straight-up murder. If I'm reading this right, it's basically a set of warning instructions for potential candidates. Apparently, each trial has a particular *theme*, but this seems to say the rooms can change in form, so there's no way to predict exactly what you'll be up against. But dismemberment and *certain* doom seem to be standard." He let out a low whistle. "Well, that sucks ass." He tapped at a line of sharp-angled squiggles. "This bit here says regen potions are out. They don't seem to function inside the forge. Apparently, the first group of priests to venture through learned that the hard way."

"Screw me sideways, but this sounds bad," Abby said, absently tucking a loose strand of hair behind her ear.

"What else does it say about the individual trials?" I asked.

"How should I know?" he said, looking over his shoulder at me askew. "Look at how much freakin' text is here. There's a crap ton of stuff to decipher. I'm giving you the crib notes, man. It's gonna take me a couple of hours to figure out all the details. Like I said, I'm only level 1 in Arcane Insight. Now, this one here is the biggest prize," he finished, moving over in front of the third and final plaque.

"This one's gonna take a little longer to decipher, 'cause it's actually in a different language. One older than the rest of this stuff. If I had to guess, I'd say they were written by different people. The first tablet was definitely written by our boy Eitri. The writing looks the same. Same language, too. But this one looks like it was added later, different hand. And it's a spell form. Big ol' Cleric ritual, that much I can tell at a glance. What it's supposed to do, though"—he shrugged noncommittally—"I'm not sure."

"Well, we can't stay here," I said, rubbing my chin as I eyed the plaques. "The guards could pop in any minute. Hey, Cutter. Any chance you could pry these things off the walls—"

An enormous *boom-thud* resounded from above us, followed by the *smash* of a wooden pew. It was the sound of things going... *poorly*.

Amara and Cutter were already tearing up the stairs, while Abby and Ari followed hard on their heels.

"Come on," I said, grabbing a fistful of Carl's robes, then dragging him behind me. "As soon as we get topside, you need to find a way to hide this room. Do whatever you need to do, just make damn sure that if anyone other than us comes looking that this place is sealed off. Got it?"

"Yeah, I'm all over it."

I crested the stairs and abandoned Carl in the library as I sprinted toward the main chapel. My stomach sank as I rounded the corner and nearly slammed into Abby's back. Arrayed in the temple's vestibule were Peng and his crew—though his crew had grown significantly since the last time we'd squared off against them. The original bruisers had all respawned, along with his three silk-clad casters, but he'd also added a pair of Clerics, both Dwarves, and another Accipiter spellcaster.

All Darklings, I had no doubt.

I glanced at the exit and immediately noticed they'd blockaded the way with several smashed pews; it would take some time and energy to get through that, which meant there would be no easy retreat.

And Peng grinned at me like he damn well knew it.

The guards who'd been stationed out front were now inside—all of them disarmed and held as hostages, Malware blades pressed tight to exposed throats.

Though I'm sure Peng wouldn't have hesitated to kill them in a heartbeat, offing them outside would've no doubt drawn attention he didn't want. And even if the guards hadn't sounded the alarm, their lifeless corpses surely would've drawn an eye or two. So instead, he'd taken them to use as a bargaining chip.

Forge stood in the very center of the chapel, axe drawn, ready to rumble at the drop of a hat.

"Jack," Peng said, voice brimming with smugness. He was pleased with himself. "Good to see you again, and this time under circumstances far more favorable to me. Twice, you have caught me unprepared—it was time to change the roles. After your *thief*"—he said the word like a curse, glowering at Cutter—"stole my property, I knew it would only be a matter of time before you assembled the relics and found the location of the Doom Forge. I couldn't be sure that you would need to come back to this temple, not with the failed acolyte in your grasp, but I assumed murdering the temple's inhabitants would be sufficient to lure you in. You are nothing if not hopelessly softhearted and moral. And speaking of."

He nodded to one of his thugs, who promptly slit the throat of the tanky guard from outside. Blood spurted in an arc, the man's legs collapsing beneath him as he died. It was exactly as Amara had described things when we'd found the first crime scene. He killed one person outright to show he was serious, and now would come the negotiations.

"There are four hostages left," he said after a beat. "One hostage per Doom-Forged relic, and then the final hostage in exchange for the acolyte. That is the deal."

My stomach lurched into my throat as I looked at the crumpled body of the guard who we'd been chitchatting with just a handful of minutes ago. I looked at the female guard. Her face was hard, jaw clenched tight—there was no begging in her gaze. Only fury and iron resolve. She was prepared to die.

"No," I said, pulling my warhammer free from my belt. "*If y*ou can take them from me, then they're all yours, Peng. Or are you afraid to go toe-to-toe with me?" I lifted my hands and looked left then right. "There's no place for me to run. You should know that, since you already sacked this place. No back door for me to escape through. And you guys have us outnumbered three to one. Only a coward, scared to his soul, would hide behind a bunch of hostages."

"I would watch your tongue, *jian nu ren,*" Peng sneered. "I won't hesitate to gut these pigs, then slice you ear to ear."

"You kill me with a Malware blade, Peng, and you'll never get the relics. They'll die with me. But play ball and you might just have a chance at winning." I turned and strutted up to the lectern holding the prayer book

Carl had read from. My mind whirled, trying to think of a way out of this. Something Cutter had said earlier drifted to the back of my mind. *Sometimes the easiest way is the best, and it doesn't get much easier than the ol' bait and switch.* Up above the entryway was a small stained-glass window, too small for a normal person to fit through, but plenty big enough for a fun-sized Pixy.

I pulled up my interface, a crude plan forming in my head, and *pinged* Ari with a message.

Personal Message:

I need you to make with some illusion magic, and I need you to do it right this second. Get ready to replicate the Doom-Forged relics. Once that's done, I need you to take the writ, get out of here, and bring every member of the city guard you can.

—Jack

With my back turned, completely obscuring the lectern from Peng's view, I reached into my bag and pulled out four items—a loaf of bread, an apple, a cheese wheel, and the writ from Captain Raginolf. Carefully, I arrayed them in a neat line, sweating bullets that Ari would be able to pull this off. There was a subtle shimmer in the air like a mirage on the horizon, and just like that, my impromptu lunch became the three Doom-Forged relics we'd been fighting so furiously over. A heartbeat later the writ blurred and disappeared altogether.

I let out a sigh of relief and turned with a flourish of my hand that would make even Cutter proud, presenting the counterfeit items to the Darkling general and his crew.

"Let them go and these stay out. Then, if you can take them, they're yours." I crossed my arms, squinted, and gave him a small condescending grin. "Unless you're scared of getting your hands dirty."

"I'm going to make you eat your tongue," Peng growled, before giving a little flick of his wrist. His thugs nodded and pushed the guards away. They scrambled across the floor in the blink of an eye, and Peng's men charged toward us. But that was fine, because unlike back in the Smoked Pig, we didn't need to worry about keeping our heads down or—more importantly—collateral damage.

"Let's give 'em hell," I said to Abby, thrusting my free hand forward as I conjured my small army of Shadow minions.

TWENTY-EIGHT

REMATCH

NIKKO, KONG, AND MIGHTY JOE APPEARED FIRST. They were chimp-like creatures with sleek night-black fur, talon-tipped fingers, and flat leathery faces with slanted violet eyes. They were also agile flyers thanks to the glossy black raven wings poking up from their backs, and nearly unkillable since they could use Shadow Stride even better than I could. Devil came next, exploding into existence with a curl of black smoke, wings unfurling like sails as he arched his sinuous neck, jaws yawning wide.

Is it time to burn? To eat? The words were hopeful, optimistic even.

You got it, big guy. I need you to head into the pews on the right—make sure these guys can't flank us, and then hammer them into the ground. Nikko, I sent, turning on the stocky female ape and the leader of the troop, *you three are on chaos duty. Disrupt the spellcasters, take out ranged support, and hit their lines from behind. Move now!*

My minions obeyed in a heartbeat, surging into action.

"Abby, summon Valkyrie, have her post up in the left wing and roast these guys. Then get me firewall channels. Forge, point, Amara, suppressive arrow fire. Cutter, jump on three." I shot my left hand forward, anxious to try out my new Shadow Lord specialty for the first time in battle. "Go now," I yelled at him while I focused my will and ripped open a Shadow-Warp Portal large enough for Cutter to leap through.

"I bloody well hope you know what you're about, Jack!" he hollered, vaulting headfirst into the hole with his blades drawn.

The second he entered the rift, I opened up a second portal—this one ten feet from the ground, facing down, and directly above Peng's red-robed support caster. Cutter dropped from the air, landing on top of her with a cackle and a whoop. He drove his twin blades home over and over again—overkill was probably a practical assessment—before flipping away and lashing out at the green-robed caster who was busy fending off a flurry of slashes from Kong and Mighty Joe.

This was a fight for our lives, but I couldn't help barking out a mad laugh; my new skill had worked like a dream, and creating a portal that size had only cost a little more than a typical Umbra Bolt to cast. Part of me was terrified by what was happening—there was just so much on the line—but another part of me, the gamer in me, just wanted to see how far I could push this new skill. What I could do with it.

Forge had planted himself in the middle of the room, and surprisingly, the Dwarven guard unit had rallied around him. The female squad leader was at his side, while the spearmen took positions behind him. But several of Peng's men were preparing to unleash a wave of crossbow fire.

Not if I had anything to say about it.

As crossbows twanged and deadly, poison-tipped arrows carved through the air, I conjured another portal, this one the size of a sewer lid. It opened a handful of feet in front of Forge and the Dwarves. The arrows vanished through the rift, only to appear a moment later—this time exploding out from a portal positioned directly behind one of the archers on the left. The Risi archer let out a scream as the hail of toxic projectiles pin-cushioned his back and neck.

Wicked cool.

I quickly stowed my warhammer, opened another basketball-sized portal directly in front of me with my left hand, then unleashed a concentrated gout of Umbra Flame into the void with my right. This time, I opened the exit portal next to Peng's face. He was busy chanting out some dark spell from behind a line of men while simultaneously hurling midnight black skulls, which exploded like grenades whenever they hit. Peng didn't even *see* the rift until it blinked to life, sandblasting him with shadow fire right in the face.

He howled and fumbled one of the skull grenades. The bomb landed next to his feet, *clicking* and *clacking* on the floor before exploding with a vibrant green flash; chunks of stone blasted out of a small crater left in the boom's wake—blasting Peng from his feet in the process. He flew through the air, slamming into one of his lieutenants, taking him to the ground. So, so, so badass. I killed the Umbra Flame and conjured Umbra Bog.

Writhing tentacles of black exploded from the floor, but a silver shimmer filled the air around Peng and his crew. The tendrils of living shadow fought for purchase, but couldn't seem to get a foothold. I did a quick scan of the battlefield and spotted the culprit—the damned jade-robed caster who survived our first throw down. She was chanting like mad, silver mist leaking from her palms, filling up the temple. Surrounding her were a trio of hard-faced guards, weapons drawn, eyes peeled, ensuring Cutter wouldn't get the drop on her without a fight.

"We've got incoming!" Abby called, just as a churning gray cloud formed above our heads, lightning flashing ominously in the depths of the mist. "Take cover!"

An arc of lightning flashed down, battering one of the spear-wielders near Forge, frying the poor Dwarf on the spot. And that was just the beginning. More lightning flashes fell—*strike-strike-strike*—punching smoking craters in the floor, while icy spikes fell by the score. Abby reacted fast, cutting off her flame walls, then angling a ferocious beam of gold fire straight up, melting many of the spikes before they could hit home.

Still, more than a few of the frozen spikes found their mark, punching into armor and carving through the flesh beneath.

I conjured Dark Shield above Forge and the party of melee fighters, protecting them from the bulk of the damage, but that left me vulnerable and at the mercy of Peng's crew. And they weren't exactly a merciful bunch. One of Peng's heavy hitters charged me, and much to my dismay, he was covered from head to foot in dark brown stone. An earth golem—only the Risi face poking out told me this was a person and not a conjured elemental. Maybe some sort of Stonewall subclass? Had to be.

315

The Stonewall hurled his hand forward as though he were lobbing a baseball from the pitcher's mound. A boulder the size of a car tire rocketed through the air and slammed into my ribs. I toppled, my Dark Shield guttering and dying—though it had done its job, since the ice and lightning storm was dissipating overhead. Small miracles. Still, holy crap had that hurt. I clenched my side and coughed up blood as a combat notice flashed:

Debuffs Added

Concussed: You have sustained a severe head injury! Confusion and disorientation; duration, 1 minute.

Blunt Trauma: You have sustained severe blunt trauma damage! Stamina regeneration reduced by 30%; duration, 2 minutes.

Punctured Lung: You have suffered a punctured lung! Stamina regeneration reduced by 15%; duration, 5 minutes.

Internal Bleeding: You have sustained internal bleeding! 3 HP/sec; duration, 1 minute.

Perfect. That was just what I needed. I dismissed the screen in time to intercept another of the hurled boulders with one of my new handy-dandy Shadow-Warp Portals, redirecting it through space-time and into the thug's head. The stone slammed against his skull with a thundercrack, chips of rock spinning away, dust swirling in a cloud, but the guy barely staggered from the blow. He was one hell of a bruiser, that was for sure. He grinned as though he could read my thoughts and charged.

Nikko appeared with a puff of smoke, wrapping her arms and legs around his head, obscuring his face with her body—making it all but impossible for him to see. His steps faltered just enough for me to sidestep the madcap rush. He plowed head-on into one of Peng's archers, sending the crossbow-wielding Risi sprawling like a rag doll. My spells probably wouldn't do much to penetrate his rocky exterior, but my warhammer was hell on wheels against heavily armored opponents.

I pulled my weapon free, shot forward, and slammed the blunt face down into the back of his neck, simultaneously triggering Champion's Strike, Crush Armor, and Black Caress. No Critical Hit, which was surprising, but it did bite off a chunk of his HP and send him stumbling forward, arms pinwheeling as he fought to keep his feet. Thinking quick, I summoned a max-sized portal directly in front of him. The Stonewall thug unwittingly shot through, headfirst, only to reappear a second later.

Directly in front of Abby's familiar, Valkyrie. The enormous she-Drake laid into the unlucky goon with teeth and claws and molten breath. He screamed, the sound oddly high pitched, as Valkyrie vomited a gout of molten flame directly into his unprotected face.

"I require assistance," Amara yelled.

I wheeled around to find that Peng and his forces had somehow managed to create a wedge, splitting Forge and the Dwarven guards. The Darkling general was pushing straight up the middle, toward the fake relics sitting out on the lectern. Abby and Amara were dead ahead,

317

fighting side by side, retreating slowly as they tried to buy time. But Peng was relentless, and it wouldn't be long before he gained the lectern. Maybe Umbra Bog wouldn't do much good in this situation, but Night Cyclone would put a little hitch in his giddy up.

I thrust my warhammer straight out, unleashing the arctic power of shadow from my core. Primal, destructive energy raced down my arm, the head of my hammer glowing violet as the air above Peng rippled then ripped. I caught a familiar glimpse of the packed, hardpan landscape filled with endless black twisters. But then, before the portal unleashed the devastating cyclone, Peng's Accipiter lackey slammed the butt of a carved staff onto the ground, releasing a shimmering crystal shockwave that…

Well, it simply *cancelled* my spell. Nullified it in an instant, before the cyclone could even form.

"Meet Zhang Young," Peng said as he advanced hard-fought inch by hard-fought inch, completely undeterred. "My Anti-Mage. Has almost no offensive capabilities, but he can uniquely nullify almost all spellcasters. As I said, I have come prepared for this encounter, Grim Jack." Turning toward the Accipiter, he said, "Unleash the Arcane Dampener."

Zhang Young nodded in solemn acceptance and slammed his staff down once more, this time driving the weapon into the ground like a fence post. The Accipiter tapped a series of runes along the shaft of the weapon, the motions quick and practiced; an enormous dome immediately bubbled up, spreading outward in a ring, enveloping the entire interior of the temple. And everywhere it touched, magic simple *failed*. As it ran over Devil and the apes, they vanished, followed in short order by Valkyrie, banished back to wherever she came from when not summoned.

Active buffs likewise vanished—the red glow around Forge disappearing—though it affected both allies and enemies from what I could see. Desperately, I focused on my hand, fighting to form an Umbra Bolt, but it felt like I was pushing my fingers through thick molasses. Out in the open, this kind of anti-magic weapon might not have been so devastating—the dome *did* have limits, after all—but inside the temple, there was no place to go. No way to maneuver.

Which meant this battle had instantly become a physical war of attrition, which favored Peng. A lot. Not only did he have superior forces, but since I was crippled by the Diseased debuff—which reduced my Attack damage and took a big bite out of my Health, Stamina, and Spirit regeneration—I wasn't at all sure I could take him in a straight-up fight. The guy was tougher than old boot leather, built like a tank, and damn good in a fight.

Still, Peng's footsteps faltered as the Ari's illusion spell vanished, revealing my lunch where the Doom-Forged relics should've been.

I could feel the hate rolling off him in waves as he turned to me. "What is this?" he spit, waving a hand toward the lectern. "I thought you were a man of honor. Of your word."

"That's the thing about being hopelessly softhearted and moral," I said. "No one sees it coming when you finally decide to pull a fast one."

"No matter," Peng said, his voice cold fury. He turned on his heel and stomped over to Abby, who had her back pressed against the wall, her staff out in front of her. Amara fired an arrow at him, but Peng contemptuously batted it out of the air with the back of his golden gauntlet. Abby took a swing at him with her staff, but it was an empty gesture. Peng caught her staff in one hand, then struck with the other, clamping his hand around her throat.

He pulled her away from the wall, twirled her around, and pinned her back against his chest as he choked her. Slowly, he pulled free a dull black blade that had Malware written all over it. "Let us try this again, yes," he said, pressing the blade against her throat. "Perhaps you were willing to play fast and loose with the lives of Dwarven NPCs. I very much doubt you will be quite so quick to throw her life away." He pressed the tip of the blade in until her skin dimpled, and a bright bead of red appeared.

"The relics and the acolyte," Peng said. "Now."

What in the hell was I supposed to do here? Without my class abilities, there was nothing I could do. And as much as I hated myself, he was right. I could never give up Abby like that—could never let her die if there was something, *anything,* I could do to stop it.

"Hey freak, I heard you were looking for me," Carl said, striding out from the connecting library. "Well, here I am. And I'm giving you one chance to get outta my temple, before I make you pay for what you did to the rest of my friends."

Peng grinned, wide and sadistic. "Oh, and what are you going to do against us, failed Cleric? What trick will you employ, when even the hammer of the Crimson Alliance has failed?"

"I'm gonna get priestly on your asses." He threw a fist into the air. I didn't know what he was expecting to accomplish with the Arcane Dampener in play, but I sure wasn't ready when the colossal statue of Khalkeús looming in the nave lurched forward and launched a fist right into Peng's head. The statue hit like a semi, knocking Peng sideways and giving Abby enough of an edge to slip free.

"How?" Peng snarled, grabbing the side of his face as he stole a sidelong glance at the staff planted in the floor.

"This isn't magic," Carl said. "These are the temple's natural defenses, hardwired into the stones. That's the power of *faith*, asshole. No one outside of the Overminds themselves can tamper with it. Not even your fancy staff there. I bet dollars to donuts you got the drop on Arch Justiciar Tamhas before he could access them. But he's dead. You killed him. Now *I'm* the Arch Justiciar, you son of a bitch, and that means I get to control *all* of them." He smiled. A cold, deadly thing. "Out there, you might pound me into paste. But in here, pal? I'm the boss."

Carl threw his hands out, and light bloomed around us.

Geysers of red and black light exploded from the temple's floor, surrounding each member of Peng's party in a tube of writhing energy. I'd seen spells like this before and knew Carl had just hit Peng and company with a *Jailed* debuff—locking them in place. But Carl wasn't done. He chanted, hands waving in a complex series of motions, eyes pressed shut tight. The hulking statue shambled forward and lashed out with a gold-booted foot, catching Peng in the chest.

The raw force of the blow shattered the Jailed spell surrounding the man, caving in Peng's chest while sending him flipping ass over teakettle through the air. He slammed down with a *thud* near the entryway.

Without missing a beat, the statue tromped over to the strange staff planted in the floor and pulled it free, killing the silver dome of anti-magic filling the temple's interior in an eyeblink.

Peng's crew was still trapped, and without that staff in play we stood a fighting chance, especially with the temple guardian on our side. But the battle wasn't completely won, not yet. Somehow—miraculously— Peng had survived the guardian's murderous initial assault. The Darkling general gained his feet with a groan. He snarled, pulled his humongous golden crossbow from his back, and jammed it into the pocket of his shoulder. Time seemed to screech to a crawl as I watched him slide free a strange bolt from his quiver.

Deathly black, it burned with the same runes that usually graced the edges of Malware blades. But that was impossible. So far, the Darklings hadn't been able to perfect a Malware arrow, something I was eternally grateful for.

"A prototype," Peng said, his words dripping murder. Time lurched into fast-forward as Peng loaded the bolt, turned his weapon on Forge, who stood less than ten feet away, and pulled the trigger.

The bowstring snapped, *twang,* and the bolt jerked forward. There was no time to think. To process. Hell, I wasn't even sure anyone else was aware of just what was about to happen. I simply acted on instinct, whipping my hand out and conjuring a portal directly in front of Forge's face, praying I was quick enough. The onyx portal popped into existence half a heartbeat before the bolt drove into Forge's skull, and I found myself letting out a sigh of relief as the arrow passed harmlessly into the void.

But I couldn't just leave it there.

With a thought and an effort of will, I opened a second portal, this one half a foot in front of Peng's unprotected neck. The bolt burst free like a piston, sinking deep into the Darkling general's jugular with a wet smack. Peng's eyes widened, his mouth gasping like a fish out of water as his crossbow clattered to the ground. Something sticky and black bubbled up out of the wound in his throat; more of the black goo trickled from his lips and ran down from the corners of his eyes.

With one last shuddering breath, he dropped to his knees and keeled over to the side. Killed by his own hand, though with a small assist from me. His body lay there for a beat. Then two. I waited for it to dissolve in a shower of light—the telltale sign of a Traveler sent for respawn—but his corpse remained. Motionless. A pool of dark, malignant blood spread out around him.

Everyone, including Peng's crew, looked on, shocked. The rest of them were still jailed in prisons of red-and-black light, while the enormous temple guardian stormed around, looking for anyone who even twitched wrong—ready to turn them into Risi meat patties. But after watching their boss, the right hand of Carrera, eat it for good, no one seemed too interested in pressing their luck.

There was a loud thud on the temple door a moment later, the wood groaning. More *thuds* followed, and the doors shortly gave way, swinging in with a *crack*, stacked pews being pushed aside as Ari and a contingent of Dwarven guards flooded inside in droves. Ten.

Twenty. Thirty. Forty. Tanks and rogues, pikemen, axemen, casters, and Clerics. They had come ready for a knock-down-drag-out. Peng's crew, however, looked like all the fight had gone out of them. Most hung their heads, shuffling in their impromptu prisons, occasionally glancing at each other. No mounted defense was coming.

They were outnumbered, and without Peng, it was clear these guys weren't just beaten, they were *broken*.

A burly guard, grizzled from long years and more than one hard-fought battle, stepped forward. A badge adorned his tabard and ribbons of achievement littered the uniform. "On behalf of King Henrik Warmane, I charge you all with violating the peace. For sacrilege. For heresy. For murder. I declare you Darklings." He nodded and dropped his hand.

A squad of especially grim-faced guards, all sporting gleaming gold chainmail and pitch-black tabards, surged into action. Each carried a golden collar in gauntleted hands, a length of chain running down to a metal cuff clamped tightly around the left wrist. Despite the heat, goosebumps sprinted along my arms, and the hairs on the nape of my neck stood at attention.

Every city had its own variety of Jailers—a specialty subclass, which could only be unlocked by working in connection with the city guard. Even without examining the odd collars, I knew they would offer a variety of nasty debuffs to the wearer. Some of the more powerful collars even had the ability to inflict massive pain at merely a *thought* from the Jailer, while simultaneously preventing the wearer from killing themselves—no respawn, no escape, no hope. Most of the collars were used as a way to enforce the law on Travelers who behaved badly, but I knew there was a darker side to them as well.

There had been more than a few reports to come across the Alliance command desk about a variety of unscrupulous groups using them to capture slaves.

The guards worked in pairs, snapping the collars on the remainder of Peng's thugs until they were all properly secured.

"Now," the grizzled vet barked once that was taken care of, "will someone please tell me what in the nine infernal hells is going on here?"

TWENTY-NINE

AFTERMATH

S INCE CARL WAS THE ONLY DWARF PRESENT–AND
now an Arch Justiciar, which lent his voice some
extra weight among the Stone Reach natives—he
explained the situation to the guard commander, though
he carefully avoided any mention of the Doom-Forge
and our quest to find Khalkeús. The guard captain
pushed gently, of course, since it was *obvious* there were
parts Carl was leaving out—the guy really needed to take
a few classes on persuasion and confidence from
Cutter—but the guard commander seemed extremely
reluctant to aggravate an Arch Justiciar in his own
temple.

Especially on matters that directly related to temple
business.

These Dwarves really were an extremely pious
bunch, far more than I'd seen anywhere else in Eldgard.
It appeared no one wanted to question the workings and
dealings of the Divine Aspects, since to do so was to risk
incurring their wrath and unpredictable fury. Couldn't
say I agreed wholeheartedly with their piety—someone
certainly needed to fight back against the Overminds and
their constant scheming—but it suited me just fine since
it prevented me from having to reveal my identity further

or answer any uncomfortable questions about why we were there or what we were after.

Once they left with their prisoners in tow, we looted the remaining bodies, taking what we could, before Carl used the temple's controls to wipe the place clean just as he'd done after reciting his earlier prayer. A quick chant and an eyeblink later the damage was repaired, the pews all back in place, all the bodies and blood, gone. Since Peng and his boys were Darklings, most of their gear was useless to us—all of it augmented by dark enchantments, rendering it usable only by players with an Evil alignment.

There were a few goodies, though, such as Peng's beefy golden bow, the *Netherstrand War Bow of Titans,* which had some seriously wicked stats. It was a fabled Living Weapon with enough kick to sheer off the top of a mountain. Nobody in our party could use it, but I had a few ideas about who might appreciate something like that. The real prize, however, was the odd staff, the Arcane Dampener, which had cut everyone off from their magical powers. It was an Evil artifact, but as I pulled up the description, I got the sense that it hadn't been designed that way.

The "Faction Bound" and "Modified" tags in the item description told me the Dampener had probably started out as a neutral item, which only later earned its Evil alignment after being tinkered with by a Darkling crafter.

Arcane Dampener (Faction Bound)

Weapon Type: Blunt; Staff (Modified)

Class: Constructed Artifact, Two-handed

Base Damage: 37 (Modified)

Primary Effects:

- 25 points Arcane damage + (.25 x character level)
- +8% damage to all Blunt Weapon attacks
- Intelligence Bonus = .25 x character level
- Spirit Bonus = .5 x character level
- Increase Spirit regeneration by 5.5 Spirit/sec

Secondary Effects:

- Absorb 250 points of arcane damage on contact
- (1) Per day, per (4) character levels, activate *Nullify* on weapon contact
- (1) Per day, per (10) character levels, activate *Arcane Dampener Dome*; duration (5) minutes
- *Note*: Players without an Evil alignment suffer 5 points Disease damage/sec while this weapon is equipped.

To every force, there is an equal and opposite force— light has its dark, the raging inferno has its rampaging blizzard. Magic, it seems, is no exception to this rule…

I couldn't properly use this weapon as it was, not without incurring enormous penalties that would quickly pull me into an early grave, but it was possible that either Vlad or Betty, our Arcane Scrivener, would be able to figure out just what made the weapon tick. And if they could, it was possible we could replicate it, adding yet another weapon to our arsenal. I could already envision ballista bolts with anti-magic heads, capable of punching through even the most formidable mage shields.

The possibilities were nearly endless, though that was an avenue to explore once the pressure of the Doom-Forge quest was finally off. For now, I needed to focus on the quest ahead of us.

"Care to share whatever's on your mind?" Abby said, interpreting my train of thought. She was lounging next to me on a padded pew, her ankles crossed, legs draped over the top of my knees. She looked tired, her hair frizzy, her face smudged with soot, ash, and blood, bags starting to form under her eyes. I knew I didn't look much better.

"The Judgment," I said after a time. This was a world-event quest, so whatever challenge awaited us, it was going to be brutal.

"Figured," she replied with a curt nod. "Anything about it in particular?"

"Yeah, who we should take with us. I don't know how far I trust Carl's translation skills, but assuming he didn't completely butcher it, it sounds like the odds of making it out alive are..." I faltered. "Slim is a generous estimate, I'd say. Three trials, six party members, no turning back once we start, and no regen potions?" I blew my cheeks out as I sighed and rubbed at my temple with one hand. A tension headache was forming there that may or may not have had to do with the damned Diseased debuff rampaging through my system. "Those are bad numbers, Abby."

J. A. Hunter

"Can't argue with you there," she said as she glanced at Amara and Cutter, who were talking quietly in the other wing of the temple. They were snuggled together beneath one of Amara's heavy fur blankets and looked, dare I say it… happy. Content, at the very least. "I assume you're thinking what I'm thinking?" she asked.

"Yeah. Amara and Ari can't come," I replied firmly. "No way. It's too dangerous, and we can't risk bringing along anyone who can't respawn. Odds are stacked against us as it is, and that will just create an extra liability. Cutter, we'll need to take with us for sure. If my gut is right, then I imagine we're in for lots of nasty traps. Carl's a no-brainer, too. Not sure what that ritual on the last metal plate does, but chances are it's gonna play a big role. Me and you are three and four—Forge is our tank. That's five. That leaves us with one slot, so who do we take? Who can we trust with something this big?"

"We could always use another thief," Abby mused out loud, idly twirling a strand of hair around one finger. "Maybe Jake? Extra set of keen eyes probably wouldn't go amiss. Or we could recruit a Ranger class to replace Amara's ranged capabilities. I'm sure Forge has someone in the Malleus Libertas who could pull their weight in a mission like this. Shit, we could even scoop up another Dark Templar, or maybe a Warlock summoner. Someone to provide us with some cannon fodder."

"Never thought I'd say this," I grumbled, "but I really wish I could get ahold of Osmark. If Khalkeús is anything like his son, then this Judgment isn't going to be a straightforward hack and slash. I'm sure there's gonna be puzzles to figure out, and say what you will about Osmark, but the guy is smart as hell. And I bet his

Artificer class would come in handy with all the forge-related stuff I'm guessing we'll find."

"Hmm. You're probably right," Abby said. She likewise seemed lost in thought. "But there's about zero chance of him popping up in time to lend us a hand, so what we need is someone *like* him. Someone with more utility—fill the party out on the crafting side. I mean between you and Forge, we have raw tanking covered, and you can play ranged support or DPS caster if it comes down to it. And so can I, for that matter. What about Vlad? Nobody knows more about alchemy or weapons than him. And he's got some offensive chops too, if push comes to shove."

I thought about it, running through the list of people inside the Alliance that I would trust on a quest of this magnitude. General Caldwell might work, but he was no doubt busy with the war effort against the Vogthar. Same thing with Jo-Dan. In fact, most of the people I would trust with something this monumental were inside the Alliance High Command, which meant they were already crazy busy and needed to be where they were. We could draw from the Malleus Libertas, true—that bunch was loyal to a fault—but I didn't want to go into a fight like this with someone I didn't know well, no matter how competent they were.

But Vlad? I knew Vlad. I'd quested with him often enough before and knew he could hold his own when shit hit the fan. And I was *positive* that shit would hit the fan during the Judgment.

"Yeah, you're right. He's perfect for this. Probably better if I go pick him up in person, though. He won't be able to get into Stone Reach otherwise. And... he might take a *little* convincing." That was the only minor issue with Vlad. The guy was fiercely independent and had a stubborn streak to rival the orneriest donkey. And trying to pull him away from his work, especially if he was in the middle of a project, was like trying to pull a steak away from a hungry grizzly bear.

"You sure we have time for that?" Abby asked, cocking an eyebrow at me.

"Yeah," I said, pushing myself up from the bench with a groan. "I need to grab a few things from Darkshard anyway. And besides, as much as I'd like to hurry things along, there really is nothing we can do until twilight tomorrow." I paused and glanced at the time in my interface. "Well, today technically."

Abby grabbed my hand. "Your logic is sound, Jack. Which means you have time to sleep. It's that thing normal people need to do to stay alive and not go insane." She pulled me gently toward her, rising up to meet me with a kiss. Just a brush of the lips, soft and tender. *Please. Stay.* "Come on," she coaxed, drawing me back down onto the bench beside her.

"Vlad is probably asleep anyway," she continued, making an absurd amount of sense. Either that or I was just *really* tired. "And that's assuming the Mystica Ordo will even let you catch a portal out at this hour. Which they won't. Chances are, you're gonna hike all the way up there and find out they're closed until sunup. So why not get a little sleep? You'll be better for it, anyway. No point going into a battle against a Divine Aspect with even more extra debuffs stacked against you. Everyone needs to be at one hundred percent for this thing."

I felt anxious at the thought of just *sleeping* when there was so much going on and so much left to do. But she was right. There was only so much I could accomplish at the moment and grabbing a bit of shut-eye would probably be the most productive option. With a sigh, I collapsed against her. "Fine," I muttered, snuggling up into her, draping my arms across her chest. I was asleep before I could say any more.

THIRTY

IMMORTAL CONFLICT

IT WAS ABBY'S GENTLE NUDGING THAT COAXED ME out of sleep. "It's seven, Jack. Time to rock and roll." I mumbled something noncommittal and begrudgingly cracked my eyes. The blue-gray light of early morning was streaming in through the stained-glass windows set high into the temple's walls. I'd slept for a solid seven hours, but despite that, I still felt exhausted to the bone. It probably didn't help that at some point, I'd dropped onto the floor and slept rough on the stone tile without so much as a pillow or blanket for comfort.

"Come on," she said, offering me a hand. In her other hand, she held a cup of something hot, steaming, and blissfully aromatic. Western Brew. I felt my mouth salivate at the mere thought.

"Any chance there's more of that?" I asked, nodding to the mug as I accepted her proffered limb.

"Who do you think this cup is for?" she replied, a twinkle in her eye. "You're already two cups behind me. Time to up your coffee game."

I clambered to my feet, muscles sore, a crick in my neck, and gladly accepted the drink, taking a long swig. Its familiar warmth filled my otherwise empty belly.

"Now come on," Abby said, turning on a heel and heading toward the nave. "Everyone else is up and assembling in the library. Carl's been hard at work all night. He's managed to decipher the rest of the plates. Says he's figured out the entryway to the Doom Forge, too. So at least there's that."

I took another long pull, savoring the flavor of morning joe, then trailed after her.

The others were all waiting in the library, Amara and Forge leaning against a wall, Cutter sprawled in a padded reading chair, squinting against the lamplight as though he were nursing a particularly brutal hangover. Ari was perched on Forge's shoulder nibbling at a bit of something too small to make out. Carl occupied a wooden study desk across from everyone else, a thick sheaf of papers splayed out in front of him.

Poor Carl looked even worse than Cutter, with frazzled hair, a greasy face, and purple bags hanging under his eyes like storm clouds. Clearly, he hadn't slept a wink and it showed.

"Good, good," he said as Abby and I marched into the room, both taking seats near our resident thief and smart-ass. "I've figured it out. All of it." He grabbed a few of the papers and thrust them into the air with a trembling hand. "I got the tablets transcribed. A lot of work—a lot of it—but I did it. Even managed to level up my Arcane Insight. Anyway. I know where the Doom Forge is! Turns out down in the Crystal Forest at the center of the mountain, there's a great big ol' tree everyone calls the Giant.

"I had to do a lot of digging, but turns out there's an old shrine down in the Crystal Forest, too. An old statue that's so worn down from time and age that no one even knows which Aspect it represents. No one messes with it, though, because no one wants to piss off whichever god or goddess it belongs too. So anyway, apparently at twilight, the shadow of the 'Giant'"—he air quoted— "falls across the statue's throat. It no shit, looks like the statue is getting decapitated by a headsman's blade. Pretty freakin' obscure piece of trivia, but if Clerics are good for anything it's finding old, obscure, bullshit trivia." He tapped at his temple.

As he finished speaking something *dinged* in my ear. A new notification. I noticed that everyone else seemed to have received the same message. I pulled up my interface and earned a map update for my trouble, this one for the location of the Doom Forge.

"Holy crap," Forge said, genuine appreciation and respect shining through. "Way to get 'er done, Carl."

Carl cackled, looking half mad as he rocked back and forth like a lunatic. "Dude, that ain't nothing. Tip of the iceberg. This rabbit hole goes deep, and I've been down all the way to the bottom. Hmmm, but where to even start?" He ran a hand through his greasy hair with one hand while absently riffling through his notes with the other. "Okay, well, the basics. To get into the Doom Forge proper we're gonna have to pass through the Judgment, which is composed of three trials—that mostly I had right from the get-go. Six people enter at sundown, no potions, no turning back.

"And the trials themselves are liable to be hard as hell. The rooms change, so there's no way to know exactly what we're gonna face down there, but I would say everyone should come prepared for the worst. Think nightmare, World Raid. What I can tell you for sure is that the trials will follow the themes. Originally, I thought they were leadership, wisdom, and sacrifice, but I think a more accurate reading is *burden, wisdom*, and *sacrifice*. Somehow, the rooms are designed to test whether someone is worthy to wield the ultimate weapon. Or maybe it's to prepare them to use it?" He frowned and shook his head. "I don't know exactly, 'cause it's pretty unclear and there's a lot of variation in the translations.

"For sure, though, there's gonna be some nasty traps and riddles we have to figure out. The instructions also mention that there are probably gonna be monsters, but that the monsters are either a distraction to keep us from solving the puzzles or punishments for making poor choices during the trial. Now those are the bare-bones mechanics, but I've also found out a bunch more about the history and origin of the Judgment, which is..." He raised both hands to the sides of his head and mimed dual explosions. "*Mind-blowing*. Aside from testing us, the trials also serve a secondary function. Turns out these super fun murder-puzzles we're gonna slog through are actually the locks which have bound our boy Khalkeús for the past five hundred or so years.

"The guy hasn't just been keeping his head low, he's been in an induced coma. After Khalkeús went cuckoo-banana pants, he tried to murder a god, and if I have the story right, it looks like he actually succeeded. The dude killed an Aspect of *Thanatos*, which is where things really go off the rails and get super meta..." He paused and took a deep breath. "Okay, so everyone knows that each Overmind serves a purpose, right? Sophia is balance, Enyo is discord and conflict, Kronos is physics and time. Everyone thinks Thanatos is just like a death

337

deity, but he actually serves a super important purpose, too."

The jittery cleric pulled over a thick, leather-bound volume; along the spine was a title, *Overmind Functionality and the Roots of Immortal Conflict* by Alan Campbell. "According to this treatise, Thanatos is responsible for a bunch of shit, and among them is"—he traced a finger over a line of text—"validating inputs, doing postmortems on defunct modules, rejecting erroneous information, monitoring cost functions and program parameters, and sequestering problematic code in the exceptions folder. For the record, I have no idea what most of that means, but this is the important part here."

He tapped the next line. "The Overminds fracture themselves into various Aspects—pieces of their subconscious mind—which help them perform their primary functions. Thanatos had six primary Aspects to help him with the behind-the-scenes stuff: Cao Qing, the Administrator of the Path of Heaven. Tien Yan, Administrator of the Path of Ghosts. Cui Cong, Administrator of the Path of Earth. Ji Bie, Administrator of the Path of Gods. Chen De, Administrator of the Path of Hungry Ghosts. Gao Ren, Administrator of the Path of Beasts. Their names aren't really important"—he waved one hand through the air—"but what is important is that these guys helped Thanatos do his job.

"But Khalkeús blamed Thanatos for the death of Eitri—death deity and all that—so he offs one of these administrators, uhhh." He paused and squinted. "Ji Bie, Administrator of the Path of Gods. And in doing so, he threw everything out of balance. The guy who wrote this book thought this might be the reason for this whole weird conflict with Thanatos. Because one of his Aspects was killed with the Doom-Forged weapon, Thanatos started to think the other Overminds had it out for him. And worse, that the death of this Aspect somehow fundamentally changed Thanatos, allowing him to bend the rules holding him in place. Which is how we ended up with Malware weapons and the Vogthar invasion."

A lightbulb flickered in my head. Thanatos had been partially constructed from a repurposed Chinese military project—formerly called Operation Yama—which had been donated to Osmark Technologies by Peng, courtesy of the People's Liberation Army. And the original purpose of Operation Yama was as an engine of mutually assured destruction. Its primary function was to ensure the complete eradication of a hostile foreign power in the event of a preemptive nuclear war. And if another Overmind had attacked and killed one of Thanatos's Aspects...

Well, it wouldn't be a reach to assume that Thanatos would've viewed that as an act of war. An act of aggression that warranted complete eradication of the hostile power. And since I knew from talking to Sophia that all of the Overminds had been involved in the construction of the Doom-Forged weapon as a safeguard, it was equally safe to assume that Thanatos would've decided *all* of the Overminds were in on the plot. And thus, all of them needed to be destroyed. Holy shit, but that was deep.

The weapon the Overminds had created to protect themselves from potential corruption had actually been responsible for starting this war in the first place.

"Now fast-forward a bit," Carl continued, pulling me from my dark thoughts. "The Acolytes of the Shield and

Hammer learned about all this, and they realized someone needed to stop their boss, Khalkeús, and *then* they realized they were the only ones in a position to do so. But they couldn't just kill him, because, one, he's a god and how do you kill a god? And, two, even if they could, killing Thanatos's Aspect Ji Bie made things worse, not better. So instead they devised this crazy plan to put Khalkeús into a cosmic coma.

"That's where the ritual comes in." He held up a large sheet of paper that held a copy of the text on the steel tablet in the hidden chamber. "The ritual they left behind allowed them to temporarily weaken Khalkeús enough for one of the acolytes to steal the assembled Doom-Forged weapon. And then they used the weapon to—and I'm quoting here—'transmute his flesh, still his heart, and strip his will.' There are a few more lines like that." He grabbed another piece of crinkled paper and carefully smoothed out the edges. "'The fires quenched must be relit. Only the wisest will understand my true form. Love's sacrifice will warm a heart grown cold. Three keys to make transmuted flesh whole.'

"Now, here's where things get even crazier. Guess what they transmuted his flesh *into*? The *freaking* trials," he answered before anyone had a chance to say anything. "They somehow managed to use the Doom-Forged weapon to turn his whole body into a dungeon. At least, I think. No idea how that works, but there it is. By completing each trial, we're actually gonna break the seals holding Khalkeús in place and wake him up. Once we do that, we'll have to use the ritual to weaken him, then one of you guys will have to get the weapon and either kill him or put him back to sleep. I guess."

"You guess," Cutter said flatly, glancing up from picking his nails with the tip of his dagger. "And just how in the bloody hell are we supposed to do that, eh? You already said killing him would only make things worse, and unless I'm bloody well mistaken, no one here knows how to turn the body of a god into a dungeon."

Carl screwed up his face and lifted his hands apologetically. "Hey, no idea, man. I mean, if you could give me a couple of days, I might be able to dig something else up. There's still a crap ton of ritual books I haven't gone through. I pulled everything I could find on the Doom Forge and Eitri Spark-Sprayer, but the answer could be buried in some other obscure volume."

"I don't have a couple of days to give you," I said, glancing at my interface. 8:00 AM already, which gave me four hours until the second to last Death's Head debuff sucker punched me in the teeth. I'd get slapped with the Gut Check debuff, which would instantly zap an additional 10 points from all of my attributes, including Luck. Once that happened, I'd be down to a single day to defeat the Judgment, get into the Doom Forge, assemble the weapon, and somehow find a way to deal with the revived Khalkeús.

If I failed to do it in a day, not only would I die, but the quest would die with me.

"Well," Carl said, "then you guys are just gonna have to figure it out on the fly, because I don't have an answer for you. But if you can get me down into the Doom Forge, I'll do my part with the ritual—and according to these books, as an Acolyte of the Shield and Hammer, I'm the only one that can do it."

Everyone was quiet for a long time, processing the weight and implications of Carl's words.

"Great work, Carl," I finally said, breaking the morose silence. "I'm serious. You really came through for us, but now I think you need to go grab a couple hours of sleep." I used the same logic on him that Abby had used on me. "If you're going in there with us, we need you at the top of your game. So go, sleep. Everyone else, you heard what Carl said. We need to go in there expecting the absolute worst, and since the risks are so high… Amara and Ari, you two can't come."

I expected some bitter fighting or shouts of protest, especially from Amara, but she merely dipped her chin in acknowledgement. They knew what was on the line, and there was simply no room for pride or ego in this equation. Not if we wanted to win.

"We only have until sunset, and we have a lot to do," I continued. "If you have any one-offs or other gear, now is the time to get them. Amara and Ari, since you two aren't going in, you're both going to be our runners. If anyone needs anything, you're on it. Abby, start working through some of Carl's notes and see if you spot anything he might've missed. Any other clues or riddles that might help us deal with Khalkeús. As for me, I'm going to head over to Yunnam, pick up our sixth team member, then hit up Blues Blazes to grab our new gear. Let's move."

THIRTY-ONE

PREPARATIONS

I BOBBED AND WEAVED MY WAY THROUGH THE controlled chaos that was the Crafter's Hall in Yunnam, dodging craftsmen and apprentices busily scurrying about their daily work. All of them nodded at me as they passed, but it was an absentminded thing, done by rote; they were laser focused, and I was fine with that. It was already closing in on noon, so I had zero time to waste on idle conversation.

Especially since Vlad hadn't been responding to my PMs, which meant he was probably elbow deep in some project and didn't want to be disturbed. Which *further* meant that I was going to have to convince him to abandon whatever said project was to come do some adventuring. Thankfully, I imagined the idea of seeing the workshop of a deity-level crafter might be enough to sway him. And if not? I'd brought something along to sweeten the pot just a bit.

I passed by the staircase leading to the Enchanter's Workshop and immediately felt a pang of guilt. Betty was up there, I had no doubt, stooped over her workstation, busy etching delicate runes and arcane sigils into who knew what. A small part of me felt like stopping in and just unwinding for an hour or so to clear my head. But I'd already wasted too much time running over to Darkshard Keep to pick up the gold I needed to pay Lars Blackblade for our new commissioned items along with the horn of Isra Spiritcaller, which I had a feeling might come in handy during the Judgments.

There just wasn't enough time.

But someday—someday when things were a bit less hectic, when the fate of the world wasn't suspended by a piece of dental floss—I'd do something *normal*. I'd develop a craft, maybe even settle down for a bit and leave some of the epic questing to others. Today, however, wasn't that day. Instead, I picked up my pace, beelining for the staircase at the back of the guild hall that led to Vlad's workshop and personal quarters.

Begrudgingly, I trudged my way up the circular staircase—the Devs behind VGO certainly had a thing for turrets, towers, and minarets—which eventually dead-ended at a bulky spell-inscribed door. I pounded on the door with the side of my fist, *thunk-thunk-thunk.* "Vlad, it's Jack. You haven't been answering my PMs, and I need to talk to you right now. Super urgent, can't wait."

Nothing, but I'd been told by the Crafter's Hall chief steward that he was in. So, I knocked again, this time more insistently. *THUNK-THUNK-THUNK.* "Come on, Vlad. I know you're in there. I'm not sure if I can bust this door down or not, but if you don't open up, I'm gonna give it the good old college try."

"Jack?" came a muted reply. There was a rustle of movement through the door: the scuff of boots, the rustle of papers, the *tinkle* of glass, followed by an ever-present string of muffled Russian cursing too quiet to make out.

After a moment, there was another thump and the squeal of a wooden table sliding across the floor. "One moment, Jack. Is just one moment," Vlad said. Finally, the door opened and my Russian weaponeer—a Dawn Elf with golden skin and a sheet of platinum hair, sporting a leather work apron—appeared in the doorway, his lips turned down into a near permanent scowl.

He was actually pretty even-tempered, I knew, but he always *looked* like he was on the verge of unleashing an ass-chewing of epic proportions. Just his nature.

"Jack," he said again, the characteristic scowl replaced by a rather warm grin. "Is so good to see you. And my deepest apologies for, how is it you say, 'Blowing you up.'"

"Blowing you off," I corrected.

"Ah, yes. Blowing you off. Your American idioms, they are a strange goose. But please, come, come." He pulled the door wide and waved me into the chaotic sprawl of his office.

I stepped in, taking a quick survey of the room.

The lab was a total mess, just like every other time I'd ever visited him. Books were scattered everywhere—propped up on tables and chairs, lying open on the floor—while loose papers, filled with scribbled notes, sat in disorganized stacks. There were plates and empty bottles of mead lying haphazardly near a twin bed with rumpled sheets. A series of shelves lined several walls, loaded down with ingredients of one type or another: everything from bee stingers and amber sap to powdered diamond and goopy jungle muck. Against the far wall sat a sprawling table covered with glass beakers, lengths of tubing, impromptu Bunsen burners, mortars and pestles, and vials filled with finished potions.

And that was only the beginning. There were also stranger things—miniature models of siege weapons, blueprints, discarded pieces of armor. Honestly, it looked a bit like the lair of some mad scientist. Which, upon reflection, was completely accurate. Thankfully, this mad scientist was on our side.

"You said is urgent thing?" He reached up and mindlessly scratched at his neck. "Am all ears and ready to listen."

I headed over and grabbed an empty chair near his desk. It felt incredibly good to sit after hiking up the unending flight of stairs to his tower office. "I'm on a quest," I said with a sigh, "absolutely top secret and I need someone I can trust on this last leg of the mission."

"So, it is a normal day for you then?" he replied with a smirk. "I kid. But, in truth, you are always on top secret mission, *da?* I cannot remember a time when there was anything else."

I barked a laugh and nodded in agreement. He wasn't wrong. "Fair point, Vlad. But this one is something else entirely. It's a Death-Head quest."

His face paled visibly. He'd helped me take down the great Sky Maiden Arzokh on my last Death-Head quest, and it had nearly killed him a hundred times over.

"Jack, I owe you my life… but I remember last such mission. Was not a pleasant experience. Besides, if it is fighting you need, there are many other more skilled at combat than me. If you need, I could call my personal guard, the *Ebenguard*, to assist you. They are trustworthy, of that there is no doubt."

I'd met the Ebenguard a handful of times, and they all seemed like good people, but it was the same problem

I had with bringing on someone from the Malleus Libertas. I needed someone I could trust implicitly. "Nope, I can only take one person on this mission, and I think you're the perfect fit." I launched into the tale of Eitri Spark-Sprayer, Khalkeús, and the Doom Forge, walking Vlad through our discoveries and the potential ramifications. By the time I was done, Vlad looked like someone had drop-kicked him off the side of a building.

"Vlad needs a drink," he mumbled, turning his back on me and shambling toward a flask on the table, filled with clear liquid. Without hesitation, he lifted the flask and took a long steady swig, his head back, his eyes closed, his long hair hanging down like a curtain. Finally, he lowered his head and pulled the glass flask away, half the liquid gone. "Is vodka," he said in explanation, holding it out toward me. "Would you like? I think is appropriate considering circumstances."

I shook my head. I already had enough working against me—I couldn't afford to be drunk on top of everything else. "So, what do you say?"

"Let me see if I have correct. You want me, Vlad, an Alchemist with little combat training, to go with you into deadly dungeon. No turning back, no potions, must fight enraged god. Chances of certain death are high. And we must do it with only six people." He paused, rubbing at his chin thoughtfully. "Seems like a bad deal. As my people are wont to say, *bari derutsya, oo holopov chubi treshat.*"

After his involvement with the Sky Maiden, I knew this might be an issue, which is why I'd come prepared to bargain.

"No, you're totally right," I said, raising my hands in defeat. "And I thought you might feel that way, which is why I brought you a *gift*." I opened my inventory and pulled out the strange silver rod I'd lifted from Peng's Anti-Mage. "I bet you've never seen one of these before, and I know that because I've seen just about *everything* before and this was a new one to me. It's called an Arcane Dampener, and it has the ability to create a dome that nullifies *all* magic in the given area of effect."

Vlad's eyes had grown to the size of teacups and burned with greedy hunger. "Where did you find this thing?"

"Took it from one of Peng's inner circle. This thing nearly killed us, and I bet if a certain Alchemic Weaponeer had a chance to study it, he could make some pretty cool stuff."

Vlad's wide eyes narrowed. "You are bribing me?"

"Pfft, no. I'm making a peace offering."

"Bribe. Peace offering. Is all the same in Russia." He shook his head and waved his hand. "It is not matter, I will come."

I laughed. "Just like that?"

He shrugged, then held out his hands expectantly. "Death is nothing compared to innovation. I will gladly die for something like this."

"Awesome," I said, handing over the silver rod. "Then get what you need, we're heading to Stone Reach."

An hour later, I dropped the sixth member of our raiding team off at the temple to rendezvous with Abby and the others, then I made my way over to Blue Blazes on level three with a reluctant Cutter in tow. I'm sure

Forge would've given his right arm to make the trip with me, but he, Amara, and Ari were off running fetch-quest errands for Carl, who needed a cartload of crafting ingredients and spell components to get the uber-cleric ritual off the ground. Carl was busy sleeping, and Abby was scouring the texts, but Cutter—who was always looking to skirt work and manual labor whenever possible—had just been skulking around in the chapel.

Drinking *oodles* and *oodles* of ceremonial wine.

"Mind if I ask you something, Jack?" Cutter said as we rounded a corner, boots clacking on the cobblestones.

"Always, man. What's up?" I glanced his way and saw something truly frightening: Cutter looked *uncertain*. He never looked uncertain. And even when he was genuinely out of his depth, he had a way of making you *think* he knew exactly what he was about. "Everything okay?" I asked, feeling a genuine bead of worry.

"It's probably nothing," he said, shrugging a shoulder, glancing down, refusing to look me in the eyes. "Being a right mule-headed bastard, I reckon. Overthinking things."

I stopped walking and rounded on him, dropping a hand onto his shoulder. "You know you can talk to me, right? We've been together since the beginning. I wouldn't be where I am without you. Now tell me what's wrong." Not a question, but a demand.

He glanced up, an uneasy lopsided smile on his face. Then slowly, he reached into a pocket at his side and pulled free a golden ring, inscribed inside and out with fine silver runes. My stomach lurched. "I'm thinking about asking Amara," he finally said in a whisper. "Have

349

been for a while. Even before the thing in Rowanheath, with the Guild, I mean. I think I always sorta knew she was the one, but I thought she bloody well would've turned me down. Now that I'm a Gentleman, though? She'll say yes, won't she?"

I had to shake my head, because it was like seeing Cutter for the first time. He was scared. Not scared of dying or of failure, but of a pretty girl rejecting him. I laughed and pulled him into a hug. "Don't be a moron. Of course she's going to say yes." I let him go, holding him at arm's length. "And she would've said yes *before* you were a Gentleman. I've seen the way she looks at you. She loves you, man. She used her one unrestricted gift from an *Overmind* to turn you into a Traveler. She did that instead of saving herself. Trust me, man. You're not an easy guy to love, but Amara? She does. Don't ask me why, but she does."

"Really think so, eh?" he said, shuffling on uncertain feet. But instead of looking pleased, the smile slipped away like the last breath of a dying man. "That's the other thing. I…" He faltered. "Well, I was thinking about asking her before the Judgment, but… What if I die, Jack? I mean, based on everything Carl said about the trials, it seems certain I'm going to die. And I know"— he stuck both hands up, forestalling my interruption—"I *should* respawn. But. But I haven't bloody died yet, and I can't help but think, *what if Sophia mucked it up, eh?* Wouldn't be the first time these Overminds got something wrong. What if I die and I don't bloody respawn? I can't ask her to marry me then leave her like that. I'm not some bloody sentimental type, but it wouldn't be right to break her heart like that."

"Just between you and me? You should totally do it. Even if things do go wrong, she'd want to know how you feel." I smiled and slapped him on the shoulder. "But don't worry about it. You're going to be fine, Cutter. Everyone is—"

The words died on my lips as I doubled over, a lightning bolt of white-hot agony frying my nerve endings in an instant; black invaded at the edges of my vision, and a host of white stars exploded across my eyes. I dropped to the street pavers, clenching my stomach as blood bubbled out from my lips. God, but it hurt. Everything suddenly hurt so, so much. It felt like there was a wildfire rampaging through my whole body, burning down everything in its wake.

After what felt like a lifetime—but was actually only a smattering of seconds—the agony started to dull around the edges and a prompt flashed:

Debuff Added

Gut Check: As a result of the Death-Head Mode, your body is slowly dying! You've been afflicted with a *Gut Check,* which temporarily strips 10 points from all attributes until you exit Death-Head Mode!

I blinked the notice away, and Cutter helped me to my feet, concern plastered across his face. This time, though, he didn't bother asking what was wrong. He knew exactly what it was, and he knew what it meant: time was running short. The artificial sun above us was already sinking toward the western horizon, the light overhead gray and dour. We only had a handful of hours

351

left to get ourselves ready for the Judgment, and there was so much to do.

Still, I didn't rush ahead—this thing with Amara, it was important. In some ways, just as important as the Doom Forge. Maybe more so.

Sure, saving the world was a necessity, but making the world a place worth saving—a place worth fighting for—was a necessity too. And this thing with Amara was that. "I don't have all the answers," I said. "But if you feel that way, you need to tell her before it's too late. Because here's the thing. Even if you survive this mission, there are still Malware blades out there. And there's still an Overmind who would like nothing better than to grind the world into dust. No one knows how long they have, so it's better to say what's in your heart while you can. Because if you don't, you'll regret it forever—and so will she."

He grimaced and nodded, his gaze hazy and introspective.

We hustled the rest of the way over to the Blue Blazes, both of us silent.

In next to no time we found ourselves in front of the rather plain workshop from the day before; there was still no line. We headed inside, the brass bell announcing our presence to the otherwise empty shop. A moment later, there was a grunt and a thud as the door behind the service counter burst open and a bedraggled Lars Blackblade trundled out, looking like he'd aged fifteen years and then had a gang beat the ever-living crap out of him with crowbars and lead pipes. I mean, he looked tired, sure, but it was far more than that.

His formerly thick salt-and-pepper beard was now wispy and entirely silver. His leather workman's apron was still grimy and covered with soot and ash, but there were also streaks of what could only be dried blood splashed here and there. As before, he was topless under that apron, but his arms and shoulders were surprisingly thin and littered with deep cuts and swollen lacerations, red with infection. Seriously, what in the hell had happened to this guy? The more I looked on, the more I revised my opinion. He hadn't been attacked by a gang and beaten with crowbars and lead pipes... no, he'd been mauled by a pack of hungry, ill-tempered bears.

Despite that, though, the Dwarf hardly seemed to notice. Quite to the contrary, he seemed excited.

Lars flipped up his goggles and tromped over to the counter, leaning against the slick wood as he offered us a big smile. "Damn near killed me, but I did it. All seven commissions, all done in a single day. It's my personal best." His face grew somber, losing some of his joy for a moment. "It did *actually* almost kill me, though, so I hope you boys brought my gold as promised. Probably shoulda charged you twice over for this kinda order, but I'm a Dwarf of my word, and the deal is the deal, as my folk say."

"Yeah, we brought the gold," I said, reaching into my inventory and pulling out a sack of coins big enough to beat a horse to death with. I dropped it onto the counter with a thump that rattled the floor. "But first, are you *okay*? You look..." I wasn't sure how to proceed without just flat out insulting him, but I decided honesty was the best policy. "Terrible," I finished. "You look like you just crawled out of a raid against an angry mountain lion."

He grunted and waved a heavily butchered hand through the air. "Comes with the territory. We Soul

Smiths don't just put our soul into our work, we put a fair amount of blood and flesh into it as well. Ain't a pleasant experience, that much I can tell you, which is why we take so few commissions, but the results speak for themselves. My items are one of a kind, and second to none. And the contract I've made with the gear will pay me long after the wounds are gone and your gold here"—he nodded at the bag—"is spent. Now, let me show you the fruits of my labor."

Carefully, he laid out seven items on the counter, placing each down as gently as though it were a newborn baby.

First, a glassy orb, black but shot through with twisting skeins of red and gold, called *Asima's Will*. I pulled up the item description and took a long look.

Asima's Will

Weapon Type: Relic; Off-Hand Weapon

Class: Ancient Artifact

Base Damage: 0

Primary Effects:

- +100 points fire damage

- +7% cast speed

- All spell costs are reduced by 9%

- +10% resistance to arcane and elemental damage

Secondary Set Effects:

- Increases Rain of Fire damage by 12%

- +1 Fire Eater; +1 Residual Heat; +1 Phoenix Rising

- Soul Smith's Blessing 1: +450 XP per kill

- Soul Smith's Price: -200 XP per kill

- *Restriction:* Useable by Firebrands only!

Only a master on the Path of the Blood Phoenix may hope to harness Asima's Will.

Wow. It wasn't a weapon, but the stats and bonus that came with it were incredible.

For Cutter, there was an odd-looking belt buckle in the shape of a lockpick. Called *Carlyle's Luck,* it would be any thief's best friend. It increased gold drop amounts and magical weapon drop rates and boosted a ton of lock-picking related skills. It also granted the wearer the Night Eye ability and offered a wicked ability called *Obscurity,* which prevented them from accruing Infamy or a Bounty while wearing the belt buckle.

Ari got a miniature battle-axe, hardly bigger than my index finger, which glittered as though were made from solid diamond. On top of some impressive stat boosts, it also gave her a once-a-day ability called *Fierce Growth,* which would increase her physical size, strength, and speed by 700% for 5 minutes. If my math was right, she'd basically be able to scale up to Forge's size and deal out some series DPS in the process.

Amara's "weapon," was actually a simple bone earring chiseled with jagged marks that glowed an eerie green. The *Wolf's-Kin Earring* was a Huntress-class

355

specialty with some impressive stats and skill bonuses; it also came with a very intriguing skill that I'd rarely seen in the game so far: Greater Lycanthropy. Several times a day she would be able to trigger the effect, turning herself into a massive, two-legged she-wolf with some formidable fighting prowess: +50 to Strength, Dexterity, and Constitution, a 25% movement bonus, a 19% increased chance to evade attacks, and complete poison and disease immunity.

Forge received a flat gold-and-sapphire disk, about the size of my closed fist, which attached to the outside of his bracer like a giant magnet. An *Animated Shield*, which, when activated, transformed into a floating energy shield, drawing aggro, deflecting blows, and absorbing damage. But real kicker was, Forge didn't actually have to *wield* it. The shield hung in the air and fought independently of Forge—orbiting him like his own personal moon—meaning the Risi warrior could still use the massive two-handed axes he was so effective with.

Unsurprisingly, Carl got a leather-bound tome with an embossed cover that amped his Cleric powers right through the roof.

The last item was mine—a jade cloak pin in the shape of a raven's feather. Curious, I pulled up the description.

Broach of the Shadow Raven

Armor Type: Relic; Cloak Pin

Class: Ancient Artifact

Base Defense: 32

Primary Effects:

- +25 Spirit

- +25 Intelligence

- +15% resistance to slashing, blunt, and piercing damage

- 27% increased chance to avoid movement-restricting debuffs

Secondary Set Effects:

- Increases Umbra Bolt and Umbra Flame damage by 11%

- *Passive Effect: Raven's Shadow*

  o Decrease the chance of being noticed by guards or nearby noncombat witnesses by 25% while in Stealth!

- +1 Dark Harmony; +1 Shadow Minded; +1 Black Strength; +1 Third Eye

- Soul Smith's Blessing 1: +450 XP per kill

- Soul Smith's Price: -200 XP per kill

- *Restriction:* Useable by Shadowmancers only!

Take cover in the shadow of the dark Raven's wing.

"I can see the question in your eyes," Lars said as I closed out of my interface. "*Why? Why these trinkets and not some fancy weapons?* It's simple really. I want you to *use* this gear for as long as possible. With most of my clients, a shiny new weapon or a bit of armor makes the most sense, but you and your crew are at a different *level*.

With the dungeons you're raiding and the quests you're finishing, it would only be a matter of time before any weapon I made got replaced by some top-tier quest loot. So instead, I went in the other direction. I found the items with the lowest instances of legendary drops, meaning these trinkets offer substantial benefits with almost no chance of being naturally replaced."

He folded his arms across his chest, looking smug all the way down to his toes. I had to admit it was very clever thinking.

"I don't say this... ever," he said, "but if you ever decide you want another commission, well. I might be open. Won't have the strength to take on a project for a month or more, but I might entertain it. Now you folk go and get out of my shop. Let an old man smoke his pipe in peace already. Oh." He paused at the door. "And good luck out there. Whatever you folks are huntin', I hope you find it. Find it and kill it good." With that, he shouldered his way into the back, the door swinging closed behind him.

Damn, but Lars was one strange guy.

No time to dwell on that, though. It was high past time for us to get gone—just a few hours until twilight. Enough time to grab a quick bit to eat, meet up with the rest of the crew, and get over to Crystal Forest, where the entrance to the Doom Forge waited.

THIRTY-TWO

THE TRIALS

W HEN TWILIGHT FINALLY DESCENDED ON THE world of Stone Reach, we found ourselves standing in front of a rather unremarkable statue, twenty feet tall, ten feet across the shoulders. The stone was worn completely smooth by the relentless grinding of the ages, the features completely obliterated so that it was impossible to tell who the statue had once represented. The figure was humanoid, and sitting, cross-legged, hands raised into the Namaste prayer position. Strands of purple moss hung from the arms and shoulders like tattered garments, and luminescent mushrooms peeked out from between the statue's toes.

Around us rose the bone-white trees of the Crystal Forest, the trunks unnaturally straight and streaked with veins of red and orange, the leaves all in ethereal shades of gold, silver, and copper. To my surprise, it turned out that those leaves didn't just *look* like metal, they *were* metal. The Dwarves did indeed work in a variety of mine shafts which permeated the underground mountain, but the vast majority of Dwarven metal was harvested from the trees themselves—taken from the leaves or from the ore deposits that grew inside the trunks.

The trees were a big part of the reason Dwarves were so hesitant to let in outsiders, since the wealth that forest represented might prove too great a temptation.

Off in the distance, the "Giant" rose up impossibly high, dwarfing even the largest of the redwoods I'd seen IRL. Its shadow fell over us, slowly creeping across the ground and a little closer to the statue with every passing minute. And then, after what felt like an endless wait, the shadow stretched long enough to reach its inky silhouette across the statue, climbing up its smooth stone front before eventually coming to a rest at the statue's throat. It left a deep, dark line that legitimately appeared to "decapitate" the sitting figure.

There was a faint *crack* followed by the subtle shifting and grinding of stones, though there was no obvious change to the statue itself.

"Bloody shite," Cutter murmured, ghosting forward on silent feet. "There's a door right there." He squinted and jabbed a finger toward the thing's chest. "I'd swear to the gods above and below it wasn't there a second ago, but sure enough." He hoisted himself up into the statue's lap, crawling along stone legs. When he got to the statue's belly, he rose, hands snaking along the surface, pushing and prodding at things only he could see.

For a long beat nothing happened, but then there was a second audible *click*, this one much louder than the first, and a secret door popped open right in the center of the statue—a dark entryway with a set of corkscrewing stairs on the other side.

"Anyone want to turn back now?" I asked, turning to face our assembled crew. Forge, Vlad, Abby, Cutter, and Carl stood grim-faced and ready, decked out in their best gear, including the new items we'd picked up at Blue Blazes. Going to take on a god with only six people seemed crazy, but if any crew had a chance of accomplishing such an insane mission, it was this one.

"Hells no," Forge said, sliding free his axe with a rasp. "We've come this far, ain't nothing gonna stop me."

Amara and Ari were there too, though they wouldn't be coming in with us. Instead, they'd stand watch over the statue, hiding under the cover of magic and shadow to make sure no one else tried to slip in behind us. With Peng dead, there wasn't much chance that another group of Darklings would come bumbling along after us, but you could never be too careful.

Amara shot Cutter a long, weighing look. "Be wise, my heart," she said. "Be brave. But most importantly, be safe." I couldn't help but notice that there was a glint of gold and silver hugging her finger. I held my tongue because it wasn't my place to say anything, but I felt a wave of joy and pride wash through me. This life wasn't easy—the missions, the chaos, the constant fear and soul-crushingly high stakes—but small things like that made it bearable.

"I make no promises," he said, shooting her a wink, his gaze momentarily darting to the simple band. "But as I've always said, I'm too damned handsome to die, and, thanks to you, even if I do, this isn't the end. Not for me. One way or another, I'll see you tomorrow." In a surprising act of gentleness, he raised a hand to his lips and blew her a kiss.

She rolled her eyes and shooed him on, but still I noticed she "caught" the kiss.

Cutter turned and headed into the gloomy dark, followed by Forge, Abby, Carl, and Vlad. I brought up the rear in case anything particularly nasty tried to get the drop on us from behind. Pressure and biting cold washed over my skin as I stepped over the threshold as though I'd passed under an enormous waterfall, invisible to the eye. Out of curiosity I faltered and turned back, sticking my hand through the door. Except, I couldn't. My hand battered against some invisible barrier as hard and unyielding as glass. Amara stole up to me, likewise extending a hand, only to find the same barrier in place.

Six in, no way out. My hand dropped away, and I pressed my lips into a thin line. I shot Amara a curt nod, then wheeled and plunged into the dark after the rest of the party.

The stairs spiraled down for thirty, forty, fifty feet, the air growing progressively cooler the deeper we went. The steps underfoot were gritty with loose rock, tangles of roots shooting up in places, making the trip even more treacherous. There were no lights or torches to mark the path, but Abby had kindly conjured an orb of flickering fire above her staff, which gave us just enough light to see the steps beneath our boots. Eventually the stairs let out into a cramped hallway, wide enough for us to stand three abreast, which terminated at a giant metal door studded with quarter-sized iron rivets, brass steam pipes, and a variety of pressure gauges.

"Well, shit," Forge said in his Texas drawl. "If this ain't some Osmark, steampunk bullshit, I'll kick my own ass. The one time we could use that guy and he's nowhere to be seen. Figures."

"Such is life," Vlad said stoically. "But no worries. Robots, they are no problem." He pulled out a glass orb filled with swirling silver liquid and gave it a swish. "Have brought corrosive orb to deal with their kind."

"Huh," Forge said, scratching at his chin. "What other heat you packin'?"

Vlad grinned, a dangerous glint in his eyes, and pulled back the lapel of his thick leather duster, revealing a bandolier near-to-bursting with colorful orbs. "Am packing *all* the heat," he replied.

"Look," Abby said, thrusting a finger at the door as fiery script abruptly burst to life, working its way across the face of the metal. "'The fires quenched must be relit. The way forward is down.'" The letters crawled with living flame before sizzling and disappearing with a whiff of gray steam, leaving the iron door unmarked.

"Yep. This is gonna be awesome," I said, pulling out my warhammer as I took point. I pushed my way in with one hand, the doors swinging open without a sound and not even an ounce of resistance. Beyond was a circular room, sixty feet in diameter, the walls covered in thick slabs of steel, held in place by more rivets. Copper piping and iron tubes filled the air, while enormous cogs churned and clicked away like the inside of some giant pocket watch.

The floor, far below, wasn't really a floor at all but a giant vat of burning metal, super heating the air, sending curling fingers of steam wafting straight up.

Extending from the magma pit was a metal column the size of a telephone pole, and perched on top of it was a horizontal cog, twenty feet across, slowly spinning in a clockwise direction. Hanging above the clockwork dais were a variety of steel platforms, all precariously suspended from iron chains, which were, in turn, attached to a complicated series of pulleys up above. Dotting each of those platforms were clockwork levers, which, at a guess, would probably raise and lower the various platforms.

Set high up into the far wall was a metal door, identical to the one I'd just opened—the obvious way out. The only problem was that it was set at least thirty feet up and was set flush into the wall. No way to just waltz up to the thing and push it open. This looked like one giant puzzle where we were supposed to use the platforms, pulleys, and levers to access the door on the far side.

"Hey, Jack," Cutter called from behind me as I analyzed the room, "don't mean to rush you, but we're in a spot of bloody trouble here!" I glanced at him over one shoulder and noticed that the spiral staircase we'd come down was gone. The entryway into the hall had been replaced by a steel plate that filled the entire hallway—blocking the way back. Worse, the steel wall was covered in razor-sharp spikes, each a foot long, and it was slowly advancing toward us. We had maybe thirty seconds before that thing would force us to move.

The enormous clockwork floor suspended over the magma pit was the only way to go, but it was at least a ten-foot drop, and it would be awfully easy to miss the slowly turning platform altogether and plunge into the molten pit below.

"It's speeding up, Jack!" Abby called, her voice urgent. I thought for only a second before planting my feet and shooting one hand out, conjuring a six-foot rift. "Cutter, move!" I yelled, gesturing at the hole.

He rushed past me, leaping confidently into the hole in space; a second rift immediately deposited him on the spinning platform rising from the magma pit.

"Everyone, get through now," I boomed, keeping an eye on the spike-covered wall, which was picking up more and more steam every second. Ten seconds tops before that thing turned us into Swiss cheese. I cast the Shadow-Warp Portal once, twice, a third and fourth time, until everyone was safely through. The spikes were less than a foot away by the time I finished, and unfortunately the portal wouldn't work for me. I took a deep breath, muttered a silent prayer, then took a few quick stutter steps and leapt, cloak streaming out behind me as I cleared the formidable gap between the ledge and the platform.

I hit with a resounding *clang,* my legs absorbing the brunt of the shock, then turned it into a smooth roll, which quickly brought me back to my feet.

I wheeled around in time to see the enormous wall of spikes burst through the doorway we'd come through. Definitely not going back that way.

"Cutter, traps. You see anything?" I said, swaying slightly as the clockwork floor beneath my feet clicked and turned, clicked and turned.

The thief spun in a slow crouch, gaze bouncing along the walls, skipping over the clanking cogs and the numerous levers and crank wheels. "Gods, but I don't even know where to start. Everything in this bloody place is setting off alarms. I'll have to inspect everything before anyone does anything."

"Could be worse," Abby said, scanning the room. "No enemies, so probably just a puzzle room. That could be good news for us. Especially since it looks like the bulk of the challenge is using these levers"—she gestured with one hand around the room—"to

365

manipulate the platforms to get to the door. Jack, I bet you can summon Nikko and her crew to do the bulk of the heavy lifting. Get them to fly from platform to platform and adjust the levers for us. Or, if that doesn't work, worst-case scenario you can port us directly between the different platforms. Should be simple enough."

Vlad adjusted the goggles on his eyes, tweaking the lenses as he took stock of the pipes and copper tubes. "*Da*. It is good plan. But what about crank wheels?" He tapped at the corner of a lens. "Not sure what they do, but they do something."

"Well, let's try the easy solutions first," I said, focusing my will. I would've loved to conjure Devil for this, but the room was too cramped for it. His bulk would've filled up most of the lurching dais we were cooling our heels on, and thanks to the chains and platforms hanging from the ceiling, there was no way he could fly or maneuver. The Void Apes would do just fine though. Nikko burst into existence with a flash of purple-black smoke and the slight stink of sulfur. She curled her lips in what I knew was a smile—though an awfully ferocious looking one.

Manling. This place, I do not like the way it smells. She shifted on her haunches, leathery knuckles dragging on the metal floor. She sniffed at the air suspiciously, eyes squinted in distrust. *What would you have me do, young one?* she finally sent.

Couple of things, I replied with a thought. *There's a door up there, set into the wall. I wanted to see if it'll open for you.*

She snorted in reply, clearly unsettled by this place, but lurched into motion and took to wing despite her obvious reservations. Her wings pumped as she rose, circling round and round, gaining altitude with each pass. Eventually, she touched down on a small lip of metal jutting from the wall. It wasn't much, and I knew it wouldn't have been wide enough for me to stand on without promptly toppling over to my doom, but she handled it without issue. Feet set, she threw her weight against the door, but it didn't budge, not an inch.

She tried again, the *clang* ringing out, but had no more luck the second time. She tried a different route, exploring the door's nooks and crannies, feeling along the joints for some sort of secret trigger or mechanism. Smart, but that yielded a whole lot of nothing.

Obviously, getting to the door was only half the journey.

"Okay, let's step back and really think about this," Abby said, absently smoothing her dress—a nervous tic. "The door must have a lock of some kind, but there's no discernable keyhole. Which means there must be some other trick to opening it." She craned her head back, staring at the swaying steel above us. "If the levers shift the platforms, my guess is the crank wheels probably open the door. The question is which wheel will open the door—or could it be a combination of wheels? Hmmm." She tapped at her lip.

"I guess there's only one way to find out," I said with a shrug. Sticking up like a hitchhiker's thumb from the side of the slowly rotating platform we were on was a brass lever. I sauntered over and unceremoniously threw the switch to the right. A metal rig overhead creaked to life, slowly descending toward us. When I pulled the lever back to the center, the rig stopped, swaying slightly on its chain, and when I pushed the lever to the left, the lift rose. A crude but effective elevator system of sorts.

"So far, Abby's right on the money." I glanced up at the ape, now biding her time by the door. "Okay, Nikko. Can you please fly to that crank wheel over there"—I pointed to one of the heavy brass wheels protruding from the wall nearby—"and give it a spin?"

The ape complied at once, pushing away from the spit of metal she was perched on, gliding along on the hot currents of air rising from the burbling pool of magma and metal below. She touched down on a platform and threw her weight against the wheel. It lurched right with a screech, followed by a *thud-bang*— the rumbling of long-dormant machinery kicking into gear.

"That sounds promising," Abby said with an encouraging grin.

If I didn't know any better, I'd say she was actually enjoying herself. But then, she always did love puzzles. She loved digging up clues and putting the pieces together—probably the reason she ended up as a software engineer, since that's pretty much what they did all day, every day.

"Or maybe not," Forge grumbled from behind us. "Look." He nodded toward a huge pipe, seven feet around, poking out of the wall on the left. A heavy metal plate, which had sealed the pipe off a moment ago, was opening. "We've got company," he roared as a typhoon of humanoid creatures built from solid flame spilled out from the lip of the pipe.

THIRTY-THREE

LESSONS IN BURDEN

THE TAG [FIRE EFRITE] POPPED UP ABOVE THE head of the first creature, then quickly vanished as it surged toward me. Each of the beasts was no larger than a Dwarf, but there were a lot of them, and they all floated through the air on wispy tails of flame, unbound by the laws of physics or gravity. A few were unarmed, favoring the black talons adorning their spidery fingers, but most carried cruel char-black scimitars.

My mind whirled a thousand miles an hour as the monsters floated toward us. The crank wheel *had* done something, just not the right thing... Which meant that one of the wheels probably *did* unlock the door above, while the rest unleashed monsters or other horrors that we'd have to deal with. That totally fit with what Carl had told us back in the temple—that players were punished for making poor choices during the Judgment.

"Okay," I yelled. "The wheels are definitely the right answer, but there's got to be some kind of clue telling us which wheels to turn and which not to. Cutter, you and Vlad work it out. Find the key." I shot my free hand out, conjuring a pair of portals—one right after the other—dropping Cutter and Vlad off on a swaying platform overhead, well away from the action.

"Carl, you keep us alive. Abby, keep Carl alive—maybe throw a little ranged support if you can. Forge, you and me are on point." I caught sight of Nikko, perched on a ledge above, waiting for orders. *Guard the thief and the alchemist. Help them however you can.* Before things really got moving and shaking, I took a moment to conjure Nikko's smaller troop mates, Kong and Mighty Joe. After one quick, calculating look around, the pair took to the air, disappearing in a flash of violet light then reappearing a moment later in the midst of the approaching Fire Efrite cloud.

Meanwhile, all around me the crew surged into action, following my commands. Carl and Abby darted toward the center of the rotating platform beneath our feet, the Cleric chanting incessantly, hitting Forge with an aggro buff while Abby went to work, casting Fire Eater—giving everyone in the AoE an added 25% resistance to fire—while simultaneously spamming Burning Affliction and Leaching Smolder.

Forge, not missing a beat, charged head-on into the encroaching creatures, his axe carving a path of death through the air, meeting a claw-tipped hand on his blade. He spun, slapping a hand against the gold-and-sapphire disk now riding on his left bracer. An electric blue tower shield burst to life beside him, floating at chest level. The Animated Shield zipped around the tank, slamming into unruly Efrites only to spin away, intercepting a scimitar slash aimed at his back. It was impressively cool, and freed Forge up to do what he did best: jack shit up.

The Risi drove a shoulder into another Efrite's face—Forge's health dropping minutely just from touching the monster—forcing the creature back. He twirled, a halo of red surrounding him, and lashed out, carving a deep furrow through the Efrite's neck, separating its head from its shoulders.

Unfortunately, Forge's attack didn't do much lasting damage.

These things were elemental in nature, which meant raw physical damage would be next to useless. They were the exact opposite of the Paper Librarian, which meant only magic would do the trick here. If we had ourselves a Hydromancer or even a Frostlock we'd be in good shape, but as it stood, my Umbra abilities were the best we had to offer. So, instead of drawing my weapon, I pumped both arms, firing Umbra Bolts from each hand, blasting the Efrites in midair as they tried to surround us. I pumped more and more bolts into the mass, firing away like a machine gun on full auto.

The bolts hit with surprising force, carving through the flame, smoke, and ash composing their bodies, taking nasty bites out of their Health. But there were so many of them. My barrage of shadow power pushed the small army back just enough to give us breathing room, but my Spirit gauge was already dipping dangerously low. Working on pure muscle memory, I pulled a Spirit regen potion from my belt, popped the bone cork, and threw back the powerful concoction. Nothing happened. I drained the entire bottle in a few quick glugs, but my Spirit didn't budge. At least not more than my natural Spirit regen rate would account for.

Which is when I remembered Carl's warning that potions wouldn't work while undergoing the Judgment. I felt like a complete moron for forgetting about that, but after what felt like a thousand dungeon dives it was damn hard not to fall into my usual raiding rhythms. I'd have to remember that this *wasn't* a typical raid, no matter how it felt.

From here on out, I'd need to adjust and play *smarter* since I couldn't rely on just raw brute force spell slinging. I retreated a few paces, opting to cast Shadow Forge—an active aura that increased Critical Hit by 3% and added an extra 50 points of Shadow damage to all attacks for me and my party members. Hopefully that would add a little extra kick, and since the spell lasted a full twenty minutes, it was a good investment of my limited Spirit reserve. I was down now, though, scraping the bottom of the Spirit barrel, so I reluctantly drew my warhammer and waded into the fray.

An Efrite with horns of burning red-gray coal and eyes the color of molten gold met me with a sword crafted from flame and living embers. The creature slashed. I danced back, twirling my hammer, knocking the elemental blade off course, then shooting in and jabbing the spike of my hammer into the Efrite's vulnerable chest. The spike struck true, the hammer head flaring violet with shadow power, and the creature's HP plunged by half.

My Spirit had eked up just enough for me to cast Umbra Bolt. But instead of blasting the fiery monster in the face, I channeled the surge of shadow power down the length of my weapon, unleashing the attack directly *inside* the creature's chest cavity. Its torso swelled outward, purple light bleeding through, before the Efrite simply exploded in a hail of fire and molten rock, which splattered against my face.

I dropped back, clutching my face as bits of molten metal burned into my eye sockets like white-hot pokers. A debuff notice flashed in the corner of my vision.

Debuffs Added

Burn: You have been burned! 5 points burn damage; duration, 1 minute.

Flame Trauma: You have sustained a severe burn! All physical attacks do 25% less damage; duration, 1 minute.

Partial Blindness: Vision reduced by 64%; duration, 1 minute.

The pain was incredible—all I wanted to do was fall to the ground and curl into a ball until the agony passed. I couldn't help but scream.

But a second later the throbbing torture vanished, and cool, delicious relief washed over me like a wave, taking the crippling debuffs with it. Another pulse of healing energy hit me like a giant pillow, and just like that my Spirit was back up at 75%. I glanced over a shoulder. Carl gave me a wink and a nod, then went right back to his chanting, this time laying down a little healing mojo on Forge, who was on the cusp of being overwhelmed by the deadly mobs.

I couldn't afford to miss another second of the fight. Or, more accurately, Forge couldn't afford for me to miss another second. He was holding back the press of elemental bodies almost single-handedly; without Kong and Mighty Joe in the mix, he would've been overwhelmed in a second.

It was high past time for me to pull my weight.

I thrust my warhammer straight out and called up Night Cyclone. The air shimmered and tore, an enormous twister screaming its way into our reality, sweeping into the Efrites dogpiling onto Forge. Blue-black jags of lightning flashed out, frying the creatures with deadly efficiency. The whipping winds were even more effective. These things were basically flame incarnate—nothing but air, heat, and burning metal— and the whirlwind ripped them apart as though they were made of crepe paper.

I let out a shuddering sigh of relief and looked up, searching for any sign of Cutter and Vlad. I found the pair of them scuttling from one wobbling suspension rig to another, working their way toward a crank wheel a little higher up. Since I couldn't afford to just shuffle them around with my Void Portals, they had to work the levers, lowering and raising each platform in turn. Nikko circled around them like a vulture waiting for death to come.

"What the hell is taking you so long?" I called.

"It's bloody complicated," Cutter called back. "Half of these gods-be-damned wheels are just traps, but I need to be in spitting distance to get a bead on what they do."

"This is the one," Vlad said confidently, slapping a metal wheel sticking out from a nearby pipe. "Vlad is nearly positive." He paused a moment, planting his feet as he gripped the crank. "Based on runes. Maybe seventy-five percent sure." He shrugged, grasped the wheel with complete confidence, and gave it a turn. It gave out a pained screech as it lurched to the right. The pipes around us creaked and groaned, and something out of sight rattled.

"Oh no," Vlad muttered a second later. "I take back. Is definitely a trap."

"What?" I yelled. "What do you mean it's a trap?"

"Look," he replied completely straight-faced, waving a hand at a pipe not far from the magma flow below. It was spewing out sickly gray gas. "I know poison. And that? That is poison."

"Can't you shut that thing off?"

"Cannot do," Vlad replied with a noncommittal shrug. "Once opened, is jammed open."

I felt like pulling my hair out and grinding my teeth down to nubs. "Just find the damned door!" I yelled as the gas rose in great plumes, triggering a combat notice.

Debuffs Added

Toxic Cloud: Your party is poisoned: 20 points Health damage/10 secs; duration, 2 minutes.

Induced Suffocation: You are being suffocated by Toxic Cloud. You suffer 10 points of Stamina damage each second until you can breathe normally once more. If your Stamina reaches 0, you will die.

Current estimated time of death: 2 minutes 5 seconds.

"Seriously! Clock's ticking!" I hollered again as Cutter threw another lever, chains clanking to life, a platform above them listing downward.

1:59…

"Jack," Abby called, "could use a little help here."

I pulled my gaze away from Cutter and Vlad. Oh crap. My Night Cyclone had finally died, and instead of killing all the elementals, it had merely incapacitated them for a time. They were pulling themselves back together, but instead of forming up into a legion of smaller Efrites, they were glomming together into one giant Voltron-style uber elemental. Because why wouldn't they do that?

Mighty Joe dived at the newly formed Mega-Efrite, fangs bared, talons extended—

The giant Efrite moved like lightning, one huge hand flashing out, wrapping around the ape, pulling him from the air with pitiful ease. I expected Mighty Joe to simply Shadow Stride to safety, but the Efrite squeezed its hand too fast, crushing my minion in an instant, purple blood and black raven feathers oozing out from between its oversized fingers. Kong let out a squawk of rage, circled once, then disappeared into the Shadowverse, reappearing within striking distance of the creature. But the Efrite was ready for that too; the thing threw its jaws open wide and spewed out a gout of blistering flame, which charbroiled my second Void Ape on the spot.

When the monster finally ceased its assault, all that remained of Kong was a cloud of ash motes, drifting lazily down toward the magma pit.

"Ain't no way this is going to work out well," Forge grumbled, knuckles white on the haft of his axe while his new floating shield darted around him like a hummingbird. He squared his shoulders, triggered a bloodred aura, then began to taunt the creature. "Hey princess! You lookin' to dance, 'cause I got your number right here, shithead! Come pick on someone your own size."

The newly formed monstrosity—done dispatching my Void Apes—surged forward, lashing out with a sword as thick as a fence post and longer than I was tall. Abby continued to cast spells, hurling fireballs and bringing down a rain of flame, but her abilities were almost useless in this tussle. But there was nothing else for her to do. Forge threw himself out of the way as the sword slammed into the clockwork platform, rolling back to his feet, then spinning as he came up, sinking his axe into the creature's overextended arm.

The uber Efrite offered the Risi a smile filled with jagged obsidian teeth and a mouth filled with living flame. With a jerk, the Efrite struck with its free hand. Forge's floating shield darted in to intercept the hit, but the force of the blow was too much for the magical construct. The creature's fist kept right on trucking, driving both shield and hand into Forge's chest, hurling him clear of the platform, sending him careening toward the lava field.

"Forge!" Abby screamed, one hand straining toward him.

I acted fast, opening up a portal directly below the tumbling Risi, who was just a handful of feet from the surface of the churning lava. It was close, but my aim was preternaturally perfect, scooping the warrior up before he could be disintegrated in the murderous fires. I deposited him on a swaying platform ten feet above the Efrite. Damn that had been a close call. Unfortunately, we were no closer to killing the creature than we had been before, and worse, the toxic gray gas was still filling the room. It danced around my ankles, tendrils floating

377

up, scratching at my exposed skin and clawing at my throat.

1:17…

"Any day now, guys," I yelled, bolting in to draw the Mega-Efrite's attention before it could turn on Abby or Carl. I ducked beneath a horizontal sword stroke that would've taken my head from my shoulders, sidestepped a potentially rib-shattering jab, then unleashed a gout of Umbra Flame into the creature's open maw. Although this thing was built from fire, my attack dealt 50% Shadow damage, and with the tremendously high DPS rate on the spell, the creature's life dropped. Not much— certainly not as much as I would've like—but some.

"Salvation, it is below, not above!" Vlad barked from above. "We got it! The door, it was how do you say, a red mackerel. Real exit is beneath lava." There was a deep *thunk* followed by a mechanical hum; suddenly the molten lava below us dropped, draining out through an enormous vent, which hadn't been visible before. And there, rising from the pool of rapidly vanishing magma, was a raised escape hatch sticking up from the pool like a water well—though a well with a solid steel cover over the top. It was a trapdoor, which I had no doubt led to the next room. And not a second too soon.

0:47…

The toxic gas was making it hard to breathe, to think. Tendrils of the stuff dug at my throat, eyes, nose, and lungs. We needed to get the heck out of Dodge, and we needed to do it yesterday.

The elemental Efrite seemed to know the jig was up and didn't look even a little bit pleased by that fact. It rushed me, its mouth open wide, and I instantly knew what it was doing. It was no longer trying to fight me, it was just going to use its superior bulk to force me from the turning platform.

There was a whoop as Forge hit the Efrite from above, landing on top of the creature, driving his axe into its ashen skull. Nikko immediately appeared beside the Risi, digging her claws into the elemental's coal-hot flesh, driven by rage at the loss of Kong and Mighty Joe. The creature bellowed in pain and fury, but its screams were quickly joined by Forge's. I remembered that even *touching* the smaller Efrites had burned me, and Forge was practically lying on this thing, clinging on for dear life with his axe. Instead of dropping off, he gritted his teeth, planted his knees, and began to chop down over and over again.

Nikko followed suit, clambering down the monster's face, clawing and biting at its molten eyes—blinding it— even while her HP drop like a stone hurled from the edge of a cliff.

Flames crawled up Forge's body, his skin boiling, his armor glowing red hot as it heated from the flames and cinders comprising the Efrite's body.

The creature's Health was plunging, but both Nikko and Forge were in bad, bad shape. If they could hang on for just a little longer, however, I knew we could get clear of the room, and then Carl would be able to patch them up.

The Efrite was having none of that, though. It let out a horrible shriek and threw itself off edge of the platform, dropping over the side and toward the slowly retreating magma below. It abandoned its sword, letting it tumble, and grabbed hold of Nikko with one hand and Forge with the other, ensuring there would be no escape. If it was dying, it was taking them down, too.

I scrambled toward the edge and watched in horror as Forge, Nikko, and the Efrite slapped into the burbling pool of red and orange and gold. Nikko burst into flame on impact, dead the instant she made contact with the red-hot liquid. The Risi disappeared next, a pained smile glued onto his now-melted face. Bile rose up in the back of my throat. I'd died a number of times in V.G.O., and it was never pleasant. But being cooked alive? That had to be in the top five worst ways to go, and Forge had done so willing to give us a chance to move on. To survive.

Below, the Efrite exploded into a shower of gray and black, the wispy strands of its form dissipating in the air. One enemy gone, though we still weren't quite in the clear yet. That damned gas was rising, permeating the room.

Twenty-six seconds left. If we didn't move fast, Forge's sacrifice would be in vain.

I stole a look down. The last of the lava had finally drained from the basin, but the drop down to the steel floor was at least thirty feet—too far to leap without sustaining serious injury, maybe even death. Another quick scan skyward revealed a lone platform, which looked like it would descend to the pit floor. But with that gas swirling through the room, we didn't have time to screw around with platforms and levers.

Thankfully, my Spirit had regenerated plenty during my fight with the Mega-Efrite, so we could still do this if I moved fast enough. Sticking out one hand, I conjured a single max-sized portal in front of Cutter and Vlad, who were still scurrying about on the suspension rigs above the main platform. I'd never sent two people through in a single go, but I'd seen my Shadow-Warp Portals swallow multiple arrows, so it was at least possible. The pair of them hesitated for only a second, and then Cutter moved, throwing his arms around Vlad, roughly tackling the Alchemic Weaponeer into the open rift.

Vlad let out a surprised squawk as both men plunged through, abruptly appearing in the now-empty basin, courtesy of my exit portal.

Not too shabby. But the max portal had bitten through more of my Spirit than I'd anticipated. God, what I would've given to be able to use a Spirit regen potion at that moment.

0:16...

No point in dwelling on what I didn't have or couldn't use.

I turned my attention to the main platform and repeated the process—but Abby and Carl were too far apart for both of them to squeeze through at once. "Get in, Carl!" I yelled, my voice a whip-crack of command that demanded instant obedience.

And obey he did, leaping immediately into the open portal, which promptly spit him out next to the exit hatch, jutting up from the floor like an oversized chimney. Cutter and Vlad were already scrambling at the wheel, working to pry the exit door open. My Spirit gauge strobed a manic warning, and I knew I wouldn't have enough juice to conjure another Shadow-Warp Portal for Abby *and* get myself safely down. But we weren't sunk just yet. Only ten seconds left on the clock, and I could feel it—my stomach roiled, my head was woozy, and white motes lazily swam across my vision as I struggled to pull in enough air—but we could do this, dammit.

I sprinted across the platform and threw my arms around Abby's shoulders, chest slamming into her as I triggered Shadow Stride, pulling us between the realms and into the blessedly cool Shadowverse. Time shuddered and came to a reluctant halt around us, and we tumbled in a heap of limbs on the main clockwork platform, both breathing hard, sweat pouring down our faces and arms.

"Jack, get off me, would you?" she said, slapping at my arm.

I rolled off her. "Sorry about that," I said, propping myself up on my palms. "Hit you a little harder than I meant to. Heat of battle and all that."

"You're telling me," she replied with a wince. She sat up and patted at her stomach, checking to make sure nothing was busted. "Shit. I think you broke a few of my ribs." There was no sting in her words, though, and a small smile played across her lips. "Thanks for saving me, Jack."

"We're not out of the woods yet," I replied, sullenly gaining my feet. I extended her a hand, which she took gratefully.

I wrapped one arm around her shoulder and guided her over to the edge of the platform. She glanced down and sighed. "Let me guess, we get the pleasure of jumping?"

"Got it in one," I said with a tired smile. "Still beats the hell out of suffocating to death."

"Yeah, I suppose it does beat that." She stole a sidelong glance at me. "On three?"

I dropped my arm, and instead took her hand in mine. "Sounds good."

She counted us down and we jumped, hand in hand.

We hit the empty basin bottom like a load of bricks, knees buckling and giving out beneath us. It was impossible to sustain damage while Shadow Striding— one of the many perks that came with the ability—but it was still plenty possible to experience pain. And landing *hurt*. A lot. Felt like someone had taken a sledgehammer to my feet and legs. But my HP remained unchanged, and no new status effects appeared in my vision. With a groan, I stood and helped Abby to her feet. She absently brushed off her palms on the front of her sorceress's robes.

Since I regenerated both Health and Spirit at a significantly increased rate while Shadow Striding, I didn't rush us back into the Material Realm. Before us, the exit hatch was open, the heavy steel lid propped straight up on its hinges; Cutter, Vlad, and Carl were nowhere to be seen. I skittered over to the exit, leaning against the short stone retaining wall housing. Up close, the thing really *did* look like a well, though inside was nothing but black. Complete and unrelenting darkness. It didn't even look a *little* bit promising. Then, I looked at the timer tracking our inevitable death by suffocation.

0:03...

At this point, it was either roll the dice and jump into the ominous pit of darkness or die painfully as toxic gas filled my lungs. Not much of a gamble there.

"Ready to do this?" I asked as the countdown on Shadow Stride flashed in the corner of my eye. I took Abby's hand again as time swept us up, filling the world with sound and heat and frantic motion.

Together, Abby and I slipped over the edge and into the unknown.

THIRTY-FOUR

The Greatest Weapon

THE CONSTRICTING PRESSURE IN MY LUNGS vanished, sweet, delicious air fluttering around me as I fell through the unrelenting black. The world reeled and spun, and in the dark, fiery words flashed through the air in front of me like a fireworks display. *The burden of power is that even a single misstep will cost lives...* The text was there, then gone, so quick it was possible to believe I'd imagined it. Except I *knew* that I hadn't. The first challenge had been *burden*, and in that context, the line made perfect sense.

The world seemed to flip and rotate, and suddenly I was on my feet, rocky ground beneath my boots. My breath caught in my lungs as I caught my first real look at our new surroundings. We were in an enormous cavern. A vast canyon with no discernable bottom in sight stretched out below us in every direction. The whole party was precariously balanced on a rocky bridge spanning the canyon, but the little spit of ground supporting us was no wider than two feet across. Not a balance beam, but certainly not a sidewalk, either.

Furious winds screamed upward from the abyss below, tugging at the edges of my cloak. The land bridge acted as a shield of sorts, preventing us from being swept up by the gale-force gusts and smashed against the ceiling overhead. Which was good, because the ceiling was jam-packed with razor-sharp stalactites that gleamed like diamonds in the preternatural light, which seeped from the air itself. I squinted, my heart thumping like a jackhammer in my chest.

Not *like* diamond, those were giant freaking diamonds. Impossible things that could fund the Crimson Alliance for the next ten years. I never considered myself to be greedy, but… Tentatively, I stuck a hand out over the edge—the wind slammed into my arm and threatened to knock me over into the darkness. Yep. That was a big fat *nope*. Getting those things would be a suicide mission, and not even Devil would be able to fight against those gusts.

The far wall of the canyon was a hundred feet behind us—just unmarred rock face—but fifty feet dead ahead was a square archway, the obvious way to go. Two vertical pillars, carved to look like giant scythes, their blades facing inward, formed the horizontal beam of the arch. We picked our way closer to the arch, moving slowly, deliberately, arms tucked in to our sides to keep errant gusts from knocking us to our death.

After what felt like a lifetime, the stone bridge connected to a small shelf of rock, running parallel to the archway. Up close, I saw there was another message etched into the dual scythe blades. *I am a weapon greater even than the gods: the death of the warrior, the ender of battles, the prize of all valiant men. You may take only me with you; only the wisest will understand my true form.*

This then was the next trial, *wisdom*. I let out a long sigh. And, of course, it would be a riddle. More riddles. Like father, like son.

"Anyone have any idea?" I asked, feeling a sinking sense that no one would.

Abby chewed on her bottom lip, eyes flicking over the message again and again and again, committing every line to memory. After a long beat, her lips pressed into a fine line, and she shook her head. "Sorry. Need more of a context, I think. Guess we'll just have to press on and see what the next room holds."

Yep, exactly what I'd figured. With Forge gone, dead, I was the only tank left on the team, which meant I had point. Still, I didn't want to go alone, especially with the number of nasty traps this place boasted. "Come on, Cutter. Stay right behind me, but let me know if I'm about to blow myself up."

"I've got your back, friend. Just don't go and get yourself killed, eh?"

I nodded, faced the hefty stone doors blocking our path, and headed in. I pushed the right door inward without a problem—despite its size, it moved as though it weighed nothing at all. The room on the other side of the door was a natural cavern of red-brown stone with a high natural ceiling. Directly across from us was the exit, a perfectly circular door with no obvious handle or knob, though there was a thin keyhole directly in the center. Standing directly in front of it was a huge statue of a Roman-style legionnaire, segmented lorica covering its chest, one hand holding a huge kite shield, the other extended outward, palm up. Almost expectantly.

Rocky outcroppings and stony shelves littered the rest of the room, and decorating them were weapons.

Hundreds of them, and they all glowed with magic.

Cutter let out a low whistle. "Holy Bollocks of Banztantium, we've hit the bleeding mother lode." He slipped around me, taking the lead, and padded forward like a kid with a sweet tooth heading into a candy shop.

I grabbed his arm before he could go in any farther. "Traps?"

"Not a bloody one." He grinned and shrugged. "I'll inspect each weapon before we take it—make sure there's no pressure plates hiding beneath—but this place looks clean. Well, except for the big and ugly over there at the far side of the room." He waved a hand toward the hulking statue. "The big bastard is clearly warded, but the spell looks inactive. Probably some sort of trigger mechanism, though bugger me if I can see it from here."

I grunted, not sure what to make of that, but followed him in, the rest of the party trailing behind us. A round of awed gasps broke the quiet of the chamber as everyone else caught sight of the haul staring us in the face.

"Is like the Fort Knox of magic," Vlad said, nodding appreciatively. "Suddenly, am glad I came."

"Wait," I said, even as Cutter and Vlad broke off to go examine our find. "Don't touch anything. Could be this is some sort of trap designed to see if we're greedy—or something to that effect. The fact that the theme of the room is *wisdom* should tell us something."

"Yeah," Abby said with a nod. "The riddle said, '*you may take only me with you; only the wisest will understand my true form.*' To me, that sounds like we can only pick one item. Any more than that and I'll put a hundred gold down that the statue comes alive and carves us up into itty-bitty pieces."

I thought for a moment, rubbing at my chin. "That's pretty brilliant. I bet you're right. But which weapon?" I seesawed my head, thinking. "Okay. Cutter, Abby, let's go take a closer look at the statue. See if we can figure out what triggers it. Vlad and Carl, you two start looking through the weapons. Vlad, you're looking for any special runes or wards, and Carl, I want you focusing on Cleric stuff. See if there's any religious runes or icons that might be associated with Khalkeús. But—and this is super important—Don't. Touch. Anything. You can pull up item descriptions, but the weapons all stay where they are. Got it?"

"Is no problem," Vlad replied with a stoic nod, shooting me the okay symbol. He tapped Carl on the shoulder. "Come, we will look together. One pass. No touching."

The pair of them veered toward the right side of the chamber, while Cutter, Abby, and I headed over to the statue at the far end. The thing was huge, sixteen feet tall, seven across the shoulders, crafted from rose granite, and inlaid with ample amounts of gold and silver. The lorica-wearing titan sported a pleated skirt and a crested helm that completely obscured its face, all except for its eyes, which were lifeless and cold. The shield he held was easily as tall as I was and chances were, it could stop just about anything that came its way.

I skittered around it, making sure to give the hulk a very wide berth, and checked the door behind the statue. Chances were, it wouldn't open until we solved the room's riddle and found the key for the lock, but it would be dumb not to at least *look*. I gave it a firm push, but as expected it didn't budge an inch. I shoved my fingers into the crease between the doors and tried to pull inward, but that was just as fruitless.

I headed back around to the front of the statue where Cutter and Abby were talking quietly, examining the statue from head to toe.

"Anything?" I asked.

"Lots of magic," Cutter said, "but it's not trapped. Not exactly. Look at big and ugly's hand there." He pointed toward the thing's open palm. "The whole creature is some sort of artificial construct. Golem, I'd wager. But see the runic circle carved into its hand? It's an activation ward. We need to put something there, and then this thing will come to life and do whatever the bloody hell it's supposed to do."

"Okay," I replied, "so we can't open the door on our own. Which means there is a key in here somewhere. We need to find it and place it on this thing's hand, and then he'll let us through."

"Yeah," Abby said. "And this dude has a shield, but no weapon. Here we are, in a room full of weapons to choose from. So, put two and two together. The key to the door is actually a weapon, but there's probably only one right one."

"But how in the nine hells are we supposed to know which weapon is the right one, eh? There are a thousand choices in here, and even at a glance I can see they're all deadly powerful."

"The answer has to be in the riddle," Abby said, "just like at the library. *I am a weapon greater even than the gods,"* she recited slowly. "*The death of the warrior, the ender of battles, the prize of all valiant men. You may take only me with you; only the wisest will understand my true form.*"

Cutter grunted and threw up his hands in exasperation. "Give me a lock to pick or a throat to slit any day of the week over this word-logic bullshite."

I agreed with him wholeheartedly. I wasn't dumb, and overall I considered myself pretty quick-witted, but a straightforward challenge with a tangible objective was far more my speed. "Well, I guess we go and start rooting through weapons," I said with a half-hearted shrug. "Let's take it slow. Cutter, you examine everything for traps. We'll see if anything jumps out at us."

Nothing did.

For the next three hours, we examined weapon after weapon, and nothing jumped out at us, screaming, "I'm a weapon even greater than the gods." Or maybe it would be more appropriate to say that *everything* jumped out at us. After inspecting a few of the weapons, we found that none of them were trapped, and all of them were *amazing.* Absolutely incredible. Enchanted swords and magical axes, conjured bows and clockwork repeaters, deadly warhammers and perpetually poisoned daggers.

Storm-Weaver, a two-handed battle-axe with a +2 to the Frenzy ability, a hefty Strength bonus, plus 50 points of Lightning damage on contact. *Edge of Time,* a glimmering golden dagger with +1 to Combat Sense, added Dexterity and Strength bonuses, a Life Leech ability, and an active ability which let the wielder slow time by 85% for 6 seconds, three times a day. *Arrowsong,* an ancient Dawn Elf bow crafted from silver and diamond, conjured an endless supply of fire arrows with a 4% increased chanced of Critical Hit. After doing business with Lars Blackblade, the 1st Ranked Dragon-Class Blacksmith in Stone Reach, I could say literally every single item in here was on par with his work.

Or better.

Any item in the room would've been the envy of any member of the Crimson Alliance. And, craziest of all, we could take the items. Sort of. Cutter would check for traps, then Carl would pick the item up and turn it over and over in his hands, using his Arcane Insight to search for hidden item properties or priestly runes. There were never any. But when any party member tried to add a given item to their inventory, it promptly shimmered and vanished, only to reappear a moment later on its respective pedestal.

It was like being a man dying of thirst, adrift on the ocean: so much water and none of it to drink.

And worse, we were burning time we didn't have. The first challenge had gone relatively quickly, but we couldn't kill too much more time on this leg of the challenge if we wanted to make it out of here before the Death-Head challenge expired and killed me.

"The way is obvious," Vlad finally said, picking up an enormous steampunk crossbow. "Must put weapon in creature's hands. Then, we keep weapon we choose. Is simple."

"Bloke might have a point," Cutter added. "Could be, we're overthinking this a bit."

Abby grimaced and ran a hand through her curly locks. "Maybe it's a challenge of decisiveness," she offered, though she didn't sound convinced. "In the last room, the door—which was the obvious way out—was a red herring, so maybe this is the same. Maybe all of this is simply designed to kill the clock, and the wise thing to do is pick something before we die."

I didn't like it. Not at all. But we were running out of time, and I didn't know what else to try. "I guess there's only one way to find out," I said, heading over to a stone shelf displaying an enormous warhammer, *Ashrune*. I picked the weapon up, feeling the heady weight of it in my hands, warm tongues of flame and heat lapping around me, running up my arms in pulses. "Let's give it a shot."

THIRTY-FIVE

GRAND WISDOM

ABBY SLID IN FRONT OF ME, ARMS CROSSED, AND shook her head. "Sorry, Jack. Can't be you. I know you're used to leading from the front, but what if this is a trap? And let's face it, there's an eighty percent chance this *is* a trap. If you die, this mission dies with you. That's just a risk we can't afford to take, not with something like this. Someone else needs to test it first."

Everyone was quiet, tense. Was this a death sentence in the making or a chance at some legendary loot?

Finally, Vlad stepped forward, his jaw tight, face resolute. "Vlad will do it. I have done many hard things. Is no problem." He paused, scanning the various shelves, rock outcroppings, and stone pedestals until his gaze lighted on the hulking steampunk crossbow he'd picked up before. He took a deep breath, nervously wiped at his jaw, leaving a trail of ashy soot behind, then made for the weapon. He picked it up with a care approaching reverence and cradled the beefy crossbow in the crook of his arm as he headed over to the statue.

The rest of us spread out, ready to fight whatever new horror would descend on us if things went sideways. I posted up ten feet away from the hulking golem, Cutter off to my left, conjured blades in his hands, ready to fly, Abby and Carl both behind me. Vlad strode forward with supreme confidence—as though that alone might convince the unmoving guardian to let us pass—and only hesitated for the briefest of moments before dropping the crossbow into the statue's expectant palm.

The result was immediate.

The runic circle engraved into the creature's stone flesh flared like the noonday sun, blindingly bright, and its lifeless stone eyes burned with crimson life. Its lips split apart, a guttural voice breaking forth like a mudslide. "He has chosen poorly…" And then, in a flash, it was violence and chaos.

The creature rushed forward with uncanny speed, lashing out with a vicious knee, which caught Vlad dead in the chest, punting him through the air like a football. I whipped my free hand out, summoning a Void Portal to intercept the airborne Alchemist before he smashed into the cavern wall, quickly redirecting the exit portal to the back of the cavern, well away from the suddenly mobile monstrosity.

Vlad was hurt—his HP bar down by half—and probably suffering under a mass of debuffs, but he was alive and safe for the time being. Which meant it was time to put this thing down before it could wreak any more damage on our already battered party. Cutter sprang into action, hurling a variety of smoky blades— which did absolutely nothing—before disappearing into a puff of inky smoke. Carl was chanting behind me, hitting Vlad with a Regen prayer, while Abby dosed the behemoth guardian with enough flame to melt a fighter jet.

Apparently, this thing was more resilient than a fighter jet, because her massive javelin of flame did nothing.

I conjured Umbra Bog beneath its giant stone feet, and—victory of all victories—it actually worked. Tendrils of living shadow erupted from the cavern floor, miring the creature in place. The golem fought and struggled like a tiger on a leash made from twine, but despite its obvious size and strength the spell held. A definite win. While it was stuck, I charged straight in, playing the part of the tank. With a throaty roar, it swiped at me with its stone shield, but I dove inside its guard and brought my warhammer whizzing around in a wicked arc. The blunt face smashed into the creature's kneecap, which was at chest level to me, but the stone didn't chip, didn't crack, didn't react in the least.

Its HP stayed at a steady 100 percent.

There was probably some key to defeating this thing that didn't involve smacking it with a warhammer, but since I was playing the part of tank, my job wasn't to kill it. It was to draw its attention and keep it busy long enough for Abby and the others to find a way to kill it. I moved around the creature in circles, ducking through its legs, narrowly avoiding its swinging shield as I smashed and stabbed it with my weapon while simultaneously unleashing a hail of Umbra-based attacks.

Which also did nothing.

And worse, the guardian golem seemed almost entirely indifferent to my presence. Sure, it took the occasional swipe at me, but it was the way a person might bat at a particularly pesky gnat buzzing around their head on a balmy summer evening. No. He was laser focused on one thing: Vlad. Despite being bogged down by my spell, the golem had a magical crossbow in his right hand, and the monster didn't hesitate to use it. The statue leveled the weapon and fired off bolt after bolt at the Alchemist, who was now back up and on his feet thanks to a little TLC from Carl.

But it was clear the golem didn't intend to let Vlad *stay* on his feet.

Bolts of jade force smashed into the floor and walls all around Vlad, and it was all Abby and Carl could do to keep the guy in one piece. Abby frantically unleashed attacks to knock the shots off course, while Carl chanted incessantly, either healing Vlad or casting protective shields to absorb the brunt of the attacks.

Cutter finally reappeared—but instead of wielding his normal weapons, he was clutching a deadly set of Darkfire daggers, which had been on one of the pedestals. The move was a flash of brilliance really. What if the statue was only susceptible to the weapons splayed out in the room? I held my breath in hopeful anticipation as he flipped through the air like an acrobat, slamming the daggers into the statue's ribs. *Tink.* The blades bounced off the golem's stone hide, turned away without leaving so much as a nick.

Umbra Bog guttered and disappeared—tentacles of black retreating back into the floor where they'd come from—and the golem barreled forward with juggernaut force and speed, bulldozing me in the process.

The monster hit like an unrelenting freight train, breaking my left arm as though it were a toothpick and slashing through a fifth of my HP in the process. Had it been actively trying to murder me, I had no doubt I'd be dead. A combat notice flashed, but I dismissed it with a thought, focused entirely on the creature tearing across the room, heading straight for Vlad. I knew there was no way I could stop this thing on my own, so I did the only thing that came to mind. I conjured Devil.

The Void Drake took form in a burst of darkness, jaws yawning wide, powerfully muscled legs flexing, razor-sharp talons scrambling for purchase on the stone floor as it lurched toward the golem. The statue raised its crossbow as it ran—great footfalls shaking the room—taking aim at Vlad, who was hauling ass, trying to put distance between himself and his certain death.

Now this is a foe worthy of a dragon, Devil sent, sounding oddly pleased.

The Drake sideswiped the statue an eyeblink before it released the bolt, jarring the creature's arm just enough to throw the shot wide. The elemental projectile crashed into the wall, obliterating a stone outcropping, turning it into fine dust and leaving a head-sized crater behind. Instead of falling back, Devil pressed his momentary advantage. He leapt into the air, wings outthrust, and crashed into the golem for a second time; this time he wrapped his tail around the creature's waist, embracing the unstoppable killing machine in a serpentine bear hug, and latched onto the statue's neck with his crushing jaws.

For the first time since tangling with the statue, I saw its HP bar dip.

A smile broke across my face, and I couldn't help but think, *If it bleeds, we can kill it.* We had a chance—this thing wasn't invincible after all.

That hope flickered and died like a match in the wind as the golem *finally* focused on someone besides Vlad: Devil. The creature brought the shield up in a quick, efficient stroke, driving the upper edge into Devil's throat, which dislodged his jaws. Then, with hardly a second thought, the statue raised its crossbow and fired it at point-blank range into Devil's snout. The Void Drake was *tough*—he'd fought countless battles and killed hundreds if not thousands of enemies—but his head simply vanished in a spray of black and purple gore, his body vanishing a heartbeat later in a curl of inky smoke as he was sent for respawn.

With cold efficiency, the golem adjusted its aim and launched a renewed flurry of bolts at Vlad, who'd managed to back himself into a corner with no place left to run. Carl cast a glimmering gold protection shield, which absorbed the first bolt of primal energy. The second bolt, however, shattered the thin barrier, a cloud of golden light and churning fire blossoming in the air. The third shot hit in short order, and this time there was nothing left to save the Alchemist. After seeing the absolute devastation the crossbow had inflicted on Devil, I didn't have even a glimmer of hope that Vlad would weather the onslaught.

The bolt seemed to hit center mass in slow motion, punching into Vlad's chest. His eyes flared wide in shock, his mouth falling open into a scream that never came. An explosion enveloped the Alchemist, eating through his body until he was just a blur of light.

When the explosion eventually subsided and vanished, only one of Vlad's arms remained—the shoulder socket charred black—and then that too vanished in a wave of digital light. Sent for respawn. Just like Forge. Like Nikko. Like Kong and Mighty Joe. Like Devil.

I grimaced and planted my feet, bringing my warhammer up as I prepared to launch a fresh attack at the golem—even though I knew on a gut level that this thing was probably gonna wipe out our party and there was nothing I could do to stop it.

But then, much to my shock, the creature did a curious thing. It tromped back over to the short stone pedestal in front of the door, completely ignoring the rest of us, as though it were completely alone in the world. It resumed its position, extending its hand once more, palm open, pleading, the deadly crossbow in its palm. Its lips cracked open. "I am a weapon greater even than the gods," it groaned in its deep, gravelly voice. "The death of the warrior, the ender of battles, the prize of all valiant men. You may take only me with you; only the wisest will understand my true form."

And then, without another word, it froze, its murder-red eyes going dark, the crossbow in its palm dissolving into a pile of sand-fine dust, which was quickly swept away by an unfelt breeze, leaving its palm empty once more.

For a long pause, no one moved. No one spoke. Hell, it seemed like no one *breathed*, as though even the slightest motion might set off the unstoppable monster again.

Then, like a dam breaking, Abby started laughing, the noise somehow strained, frayed on the edges.

Carl rounded on her, glaring. "What the hell do you think is funny about any of this, huh?"

She only laughed harder, doubling over as she gripped her knees. It wasn't *haha* laughter though; it was the sound of someone laughing so they didn't cry. Finally, she stood, swiping at the back of her cheek with one hand, obliterating the tears trailing down her face. "He's dead," she said, "but it's so simple. Stupid simple. I should've seen it before. *Indiana Jones and the Last Crusade*," she said as if that would explain it all.

My stomach lurched as it clicked into place. Holy shit, that *did* explain it all, and she was right. We were so dumb. The riddle was one part, but it was the sentence the golem had spoken before his brutal assault on Vlad: "He has chosen poorly..." In my mind I saw Harrison Ford, playing the part of Indiana, standing before a wrinkled, stooped-backed templar as a Nazi chose the wrong Holy Grail—only to have his skin melt away.

This was that.

"Of course," I said, facepalming as the scene played through my head once more like a song on repeat. There was only one right "weapon," and if we chose poorly, the golem would spring to life and murder whoever was unlucky enough to have plopped the weapon into his outstretched hand. Which meant that the real answer to the riddle was probably not a weapon at all.

"Everyone, tear this place apart," I said, explaining what we were searching for.

After a few quick questions from Cutter and Carl, we scattered. It didn't take more than a handful of minutes to find a simple bronze chalice tucked away in a narrow nook, overshadowed by the array of mind-bogglingly impressive weaponry. It was no wonder we hadn't spotted it with all of the other goodies screaming for our attention. Worked into the metal around the cup was an olive branch, and inside the cup itself, etched into the very bottom, was the tiny shape of a key. When I pulled up the item description it all made perfect, horrible sense:

Chalice of Radiant Peace

Item Type: Relic

Class: Ancient Artifact

Base Damage: 0

Primary Effects:

- Drink from the Chalice of Radiant Peace (1) per day, per (5) character levels to restore 75% of Health, Stamina, and Spirit.

Eat, drink, and be merry, for tomorrow you die. Or perhaps not …

I shared a long look with Abby. "God, we were so stupid…" I trailed off, the rest of what I was about to say remaining unspoken: *and Vlad paid the price for it.*

Abby nodded solemnly, then took the cup gently from my hands. "Just in case we're wrong," she said, before turning on her heel and strutting over to the unmoving statue waiting patiently for us to take our fate into our own hands once again. She paused, stealing a few deep, calming breaths, then tentatively set the chalice in the creature's hand. It felt a bit like déjà vu as the runic circle in the golem's palm flashed—the light painful and harsh—and the creature's lifeless eyes erupted with life once more. I tensed, sweat pouring from my face as I waited for it to cast wrathful judgment on Abby and promptly bludgeon her to death with a wine cup.

But no. This time its eyes burned opal instead of bloodbath red. "She has chosen wisely," the creature intoned. "Peace is a weapon even greater than the gods, it is the death of the warrior, the ender of battles, and the prize of all valiant men. If you would seek to wield the weapon of the gods, you must know that those who would live by the sword shall surely die by it. This is the greatest wisdom of all..." The chalice in its hand had filled with burbling red liquid, viscous and thick like congealed blood.

The statue raised the glass and downed the drink in one swallow, and as the liquid disappeared down its throat, the creature began to melt. Unyielding stone gave way to goopy red-brown mud. Unfortunately, the chalice also dissolved, turning into sand just as Vlad's crossbow had, leaving us with no prize at all. Well, almost no prize. Sitting on top of the melted mass was an oversized glass key, about the size of a dagger.

THIRTY-SIX

The Ultimate Sacrifice

AS EXPECTED, THE ODD GLASS KEY, WHICH looked almost like an empty bottle, let us through the circular door before disappearing in a blast of prismatic light. I took a deep breath, steadying my nerves, and stepped through hoping that this would be the final challenge before we made it into the Doom Forge itself. The truth was, we *needed* this to be the last challenge, because at the rate we were hemorrhaging party members, we wouldn't have anyone left alive when it was time to finally go toe to toe with Khalkeús—assuming, of course, that we actually *had* to battle the ancient godling.

Knowing how these things went, I didn't really expect anything else, but it was always possible that he would craft us our god-killing weapon and happily send us on our way, no muss, no fuss.

Beyond the doorway was darkness, complete and all-consuming, just as when I'd fallen through the hatch from the first trial. The world spun topsy-turvy as my foot landed, the engulfing black *shifting* subtly around me. "Abby," I called out, my voice oddly hollow and weak. I waited a beat, but there was no answer, just the crushing weight of the lonely dark. I gulped, steeled my resolve, and took another step. There were no definitive landmarks, and everything seemed to blur on the edges. A new set of fiery words flashed before me like a sparkler leaving a trail of spitting embers in the night.

Only those who seek peace deserve to wield a weapon capable of delivering unending war...

The scrawl was there only for the barest moment, and as I stepped again, it vanished, whisking away the darkness with it. Suddenly, I was in a square room, twenty feet by twenty feet, the floor beneath me black pavers, sleek and somehow modern. The walls were unmarred black stone, featureless, foreboding, and oddly sterile, like some high-tech operation room. And like an operation room, there was a bed of sorts directly in the center of the room.

A slab of black obsidian, it was just big enough for someone to lie flat on. Propped just so on top was a dagger, though it seemed rather plain compared to the impressive array of weaponry we'd left behind in the last room.

"Bloody hells, but I don't like this," Cutter said, materializing behind me as he stepped out of... well, thin air.

I hadn't noticed before, but there was no door. Anywhere. Not the circular door we'd come from, and not one leading away from the room. The walls were perfect, seamless, and uninterrupted. There was a blur of motion as Abby and Carl appeared in short order, both stumbling a little bit thanks to the abrupt change in scenery.

"What in the hell is this place?" Carl asked, voice bouncing off the walls as he craned his head around, surveying the odd room. He planted his hands on robe-clad hips and turned in a slow circle, mouth open, face scrunched up.

"No idea," Abby replied, though she tightened her hand around her staff as though something horrendous was bound to drop down on us any second. Experience had prepared her well.

"Cutter," I said slowly—quietly—feeling the presence of the strange room pressing down on us as though it were a palpable force. "You see any traps? Maybe a hidden door somewhere?"

He squinted and dropped into a crouch, fingers pressed up against the black tiles. He pulled free one of his daggers and placed it tip down, slowly spinning it with one hand. *Whisk, whisk, whisk*—the sound of metal scraping over stone. "No traps," he finally declared. "But there's a physical mechanism built into that slab there." He gestured to the stone table with the dagger. "At a guess, I'd say there's a descending staircase. Might be it opens up whenever you trigger the function of the slab. Not so different from that bastard statue in the last room."

I nodded and inched my way closer, stepping gingerly despite his reassurances that the floor itself was not trapped or otherwise warded. So far, this place had thrown us some nasty curveballs, so it made sense to play it safe. Nothing happened as I drew near to the table, though. It seemed our resident thief was right on the money. Abby crept up on my left, Cutter on my right, while Carl circled around to the far side of the slab.

No one spoke as we all examined the table. And for good reason...

It wasn't a table, but an altar.

The top was carefully engraved—carved into the rough shape of a person. It reminded me of the chalk outline of a murder victim at a crime scene. A host of complicated runes were worked across the stone, and thanks to my limited training with Betty the Arcane Scrivener, I could pick up at least the general purpose of the marks: life absorption. More foreboding even than the runes, however, were the deep channels gouged into the stone. Three of them in total.

The first channel, an inch deep and half an inch wide, ran directly across the throat of the person-shaped outline. That channel ran horizontally to the edges of the table, where it connected with a pair of similar vertical channels, which ran down either side of the altar. Together the marks seemed to form a large horseshoe. Both of the vertical channels ended at a hole, about the size of a quarter, which vanished into the slab. Drainage holes.

Before anyone could say anything, I pulled a Health regen potion from my belt, unstopped the bottle, and dumped the red liquid onto the deep line carved across the outline's throat. The liquid pooled only for a moment before the channel filled completely, and the liquid overflowed into the grooves running down either side of the slab, burbling and disappearing into the holes.

Nothing happened, of course, but it was obvious *why* nothing happened.

The altar wasn't thirsty for a Health regen potion. It was thirsty for something else—something red and coppery. No one spoke, since we all knew what was expected here. And, as if I needed any further confirmation, the knife adorning the top of the altar told me everything that needed to be said. *This was a place built for death.* I picked it up, the silvery metal rasping against the stony surface. The weapon was perfectly ordinary—no magical stats, no awesome buffs, not even of superior quality—but there were words etched along the length of the blade.

My throat was hot and scratchy—it was incredibly hard to breathe, even worse than when the toxic gas from the first chamber had been killing me by inches—but I read the words out loud all the same. "'Sometimes there is no winning. To save the world, you must first give up that which matters most in *your* world. Only love's sacrifice will warm a heart grown cold.'"

I dropped the dagger, letting it clatter on the altar, nausea rising in my gut. This was one riddle I didn't need any help deciphering, and that's because it was plain as day: this damned place expected one of my party members to lie down... and it expected me to slit their throat. To bleed them like a stuck pig, the life draining from them in fits and spurts, filling the deep grooves in the altar, opening the door from this place.

Worse, I had the sneaking suspicion it wasn't *any* random party member, but the party member I loved most. I stole a quick look at Abby. My world. Was I willing to slit her throat to move on and complete the quest? True, it wouldn't be the end for her. She would respawn in eight hours, but dying wasn't a pleasant thing by any stretch of the imagination. Even in V.G.O. dying was agony, torture, nightmares, and reoccurring PTSD. Osmark had told me once that dying too often had some distressing, long-term psychological effects. And having been on the receiving end of my own sacrificial death—the Spider Queen impaling me through the heart *still* haunted my dreams—I knew that to be the gospel truth.

"I'll do it," Cutter said, plucking up the ritual dagger, then plopping down onto the edge of the altar. He tossed me the dagger with an uneasy grin and a quick wink. "Can't bloody well be Jack, and that sod Carl can't die. And it wouldn't bloody be right to ask a lady to do it. So, might as well be me, eh?" He swung his legs up and lay back, wiggling his shoulders and adjusting his arms until his body filled out the outline. "Besides, what's the bloody point of being a Traveler if I don't take a few risks and see what it's like on the other side?"

"That's surprisingly noble of you," Abby said, touching his forearm with her fingers. "But it also doesn't make any sense." With a flick of her hand, bonds of fire blossomed, wrapping around the thief, gently lifting him from the altar and setting him back on his feet. "This might be the last trial, but there's an even money chance that there are still traps or secret doors ahead. Makes way more sense for me to take the plunge than you."

She paused, glancing between me and the altar. "Besides, it's possible this thing *won't* accept you. 'To save the world, you must first give up that which matters most in *your* world,' that's what the dagger said. Seems pretty obvious that Jack's the one who's supposed to perform the ritual—since he's the one trying to assemble the weapon—and as touching as your bromance is, I feel like this is the role I'm supposed to play." She released Cutter from the Flame of Holding and, with a grimace, climbed onto the table. She let out a sigh, muttering something about a "girlfriend in a fridge," but made no move to get up.

"Holy shit, this is messed up," Carl said, running a hand along his beard, breaking into a nervous pace. "I haven't done many quests, but man… Seriously. This is fucked."

I agreed with him wholeheartedly, but I also knew that this was no ordinary mission—and not just because I was playing on Death-Head mode. No, this was a mission that had the potential to change everything. The Overminds had created this weapon to fundamentally tweak the game, to shape reality from within, so it made a sick kind of sense that they would ensure that whoever wielded the weapon had to pay a damned steep price to do so.

"Yeah, it is," I said, slipping around to the far side of the altar, positioning myself near Abby's head. I licked my lips—mouth suddenly dry, throat parched—and took her hand in mine. "Are you sure about this?" I said, not feeling at all sure about it myself.

"You know I am," she said, sounding confident. But I knew her well enough to hear the wobble beneath the words—to see the tightness around her mouth and the fear burning in her eyes. "Death is nothing here. Not to us. Not unless we fail to stop Thanatos. Just try to make it clean, okay?"

"You know I will," I replied, giving her hand a firm squeeze. "Now close your eyes. It'll be easier that way. Quicker if you don't see it coming."

Her lips formed a tight line, but she nodded and complied, pressing her eyes shut, her body going rigid with tension. She was subconsciously waiting for the blow to fall. I took the ritual dagger in my hand, knuckles white as I squeezed the handle and lifted it above my shoulder. "I'm so sorry," I whispered, driving the blade straight down, triggering Black Caress for any bit of extra damage. I couldn't bring myself to actually slice her throat, but, thanks to my massive Strength stat and Abby's relatively low Armor Rating, the blade punched into her neck as though it were nothing more than fine gauze.

Critical Hit.

A strangled gurgle of frothy blood erupted from her lips, body spasming, arms thrashing wildly, eyes open, though mercifully only for the briefest moment. Her erratic jerking was over as quickly as it had started, her limbs going slack, her eyes quickly glazing over as blood ran from her neck and trailed down from the corners of her mouth.

I discarded the bloody knife in my hand, tossing it onto the floor, turned my head to the side and dry heaved, over and over again. Nothing came out, but I couldn't stop myself.

In front of me, the altar began to glow, to pulse with an eerie red light while the blood drained from the neck channel and into the dual vertical grooves running down the sides. Cutter didn't speak, the normally sarcastic thief ironically robbed of words, but he dropped a hand onto my shoulder and squeezed, fingers digging down—the gesture reassuring and oddly comforting. His hand fell away a second later as Abby's blood finished draining into the collection holes, eliciting a *click* and a deep earthy groan as the floor wobbled and shifted beneath us.

"Something's happening," Carl shouted, scrabbling toward the edges of the room. Cutter and I followed suit, getting clear as the floor around the barbaric slab bearing Abby's body shifted and dropped away, revealing a circular spiral staircase in the center of the room. Still, I waited, watching until Abby's body shattered like a dropped wineglass, breaking apart in a shower of digitized light, leaving the altar empty, though coated liberally with blood, thanks to her death spasms. It had been the right thing to do—the only thing to do—but I still felt sick.

Even if *she* didn't have recurrent PTSD about the incident, I would dream about it every night for the rest of my life, I was sure.

I shivered, wrapping my arms around my chest. More than just feeling sick, I felt *tired.* Tired of being forced to play this high-stakes game. Tired of running and jumping through the hoops Sophia had laid out for me. Tired of having to do the right thing when the right thing was so hard. So painful. So costly. Not for the first time, I found myself wishing I could just retire, maybe run a pizza shop like Frank or buckle down in the Crafter's Guild and learn a trade like Betty. Be normal. But no, that wasn't in the cards. Not anymore.

Whatever we—me and Abby and Cutter and Amara and Vlad and, hell, even Carl—had once been, we were something else now. The only ones who could do what needed doing.

And what we needed to do now was to find Khalkeús. I drew my warhammer and made for the stairs. Time to finish this thing.

THIRTY-SEVEN

TRANSMUTED FLESH

THE WINDING STAIRCASE DEPOSITED US AT AN entry gate, twenty feet tall, made entirely of gold and studded with enough cut gemstones to choke a horse. And I'm not talking gold-plated; this thing was the real deal—though when I thudded my fist against it, *clang, clang, clang,* it sounded oddly hollow. Cutter's eyes nearly popped out of his skull when he saw the enormous monstrosity, which had to weigh an even ton. Despite the death and the chaos that had come before, our intrepid thief schemed for a full ten minutes about how we might pry the door off its hinges and port it back to Darkshard with us when—well, *if*—we managed to take Khalkeús down.

Needless to say, he was far more optimistic than me. "I could build an entire house out of this, Jack," he'd pleaded, wringing his hands as he looked forlornly at the thing.

I ignored him, instead studying the monolithic barrier barring our way. This was the first time since entering the Judgment that we'd found a locked door leading into a new section instead of leading out of one.

Inset directly into the gaudy gate were three keyholes, except these were unlike any keyholes I'd ever seen—each one was irregularly shaped and sunk deep into the metal. Cutter took one look at those and threw up his hands in frustration, declaring them "impossibly unpickable locks," just like "every other bloody lock in this gods-forsaken place." Everyone else was at a loss about how to proceed. Everyone but me. Thankfully, I'd stared at those *particular* shapes long enough and often enough to know I had the keys tucked safely away inside my inventory.

With trembling hands, I pulled the first Doom-Forged relic from my bag and wiggled it into the corresponding space.

I let out a shaky sigh of sheer relief. It fit like a glove. The door issued an unearthly clanking groan, the clamor of metal pipes rattling inside an iron cage, followed by a hiss of piping-hot steam, which gushed out from beneath the gate's bottom edge.

I set the second item in place, triggering another series of clanks and groans accompanied by more steam jettisoning into the air, the door damn near vibrating beneath my hand—pent up with anxious, restless energy. Something seemed to *shift* in the atmosphere. Crackling power built around us as the steam eddied and whirled, the air thick with tension like an overcast sky a moment before a thunderstorm breaks. As I pulled the final piece from my inventory, the Doom-Forged Pommel, the door emitted a deep whine. The metal buckled and fractured in places, thin cracks and shallow fissures slithering their way up the surface in anticipation.

Cutter and Carl both took a few steps back as though expecting the door to explode when I shoved the third piece into place. Honestly, I couldn't blame them considering everything else this place had thrown at us.

I licked my lips, trying to steady the thunderous beating of my heart. My shirt stuck to my chest thanks to the combination of heat and steam, and sweat trickled down my forehead, dripping into my eyes. I pushed all that away to the back corner of my mind while carefully working the pommel into place. One final *click* and the door cracked like a bomb blast, split right down the middle by an enormous lightning-bolt-shaped fissure. For a moment I just stood there, flabbergasted, then I recoiled as the jagged fissure began to *bleed*. Dark flows of crimson raced down the surface of the gate, leaving velvety smears across the face of the metal, coating the gate's many gaudy jewels.

Just what in the hell is going on here? I thought, backpedaling to a safe—well, *safer*—distance while raising one hand, ready to cast Dark Shield in case this thing went nuclear.

The metal squeaked and squealed in further protest, the door shaking and tottering in its stone frame as if it were actually a living thing. Finally, it tipped backward, slamming into the ground with a *thud* that I felt in my bones. A cloud of debris kicked up from the impact and bits of dust and chips of rock rained down on us from above. After a second, I noticed something else was raining down too: more blood. There was a fist-sized hole drilled into the bottom of the archway, going up, up, up and out of sight; blood was dribbling from that hole like a leaky faucet, forming a little puddle of red on the floor.

Drip, drip, drip...

Something clicked inside my head. No. Couldn't be. Or could it?

I did a little mental math and realized the altar from the last room was now directly above the archway, which meant that was Abby's blood. It hadn't merely disappeared into the drainage holes, it had actually served a purpose, though a strange one. The golden gate, now keeled over on the ground, had been hollow after all, and Abby's blood had filled the damned thing up. That was the only way to explain the copious amounts of red bubbling up from the jagged furrow running down the door's front. This whole thing was weird as hell and sent shivers racing along my arms, then looping back around to take another lap down the length of my spine.

But we'd come so far that a little wonkiness wasn't about to stop me. Cautiously, I ghosted forward, scanning the room beyond for any sign of Khalkeús, but he was nowhere to be seen. The room was exactly as I remembered it from Eitri's journal. Same mosaic floor, same enormous Phoenix statue, same pool of lava, same jewel-encrusted walls. Even the black obsidian anvil from the vision remained the same. The only thing missing was the hulking Aspect himself.

I didn't have long to process, however, because the door was *melting* in front of my eyes.

The formerly hard edges were mushy and soft, seeping out, while the gold and the blood bubbled and churned, mixing together as steam wafted straight up.

Faster and faster the slab melted, turning into a puddle. The Doom-Forged relics disappeared into the goopy mess, and then, before I could even start to come up with a game plan, the liquid began to flow away from us. Crawling and slithering in bursts of erratic motion across the floor like some enormous slug, it headed straight for the pool of magma, burbling merrily away beneath the feet of the enormous stone Phoenix protruding from the far wall. I only then noticed the bird's maw was open and that a faint trail of molten metal oozed from its beak, splattering into the pool below.

Huh. That was odd. Though admittedly not *more* odd than the giant golden slime oozing away from me. Before I could fully form the thought and put all the dots together, the writhing mass of gold disappeared over the lip of the pool, plunging directly into the lava pit.

"Uh, was that supposed to happen?" Carl asked. "Because, yeah, I feel like that wasn't supposed to happen."

"Much as I hate to admit it," Cutter said, slipping into the room beside me, "I have to agree with Carl. Unless I'm bloody mad, that sodding gate just pilfered the Doom-Forged relics from us. A right arsehole move, that. As a thief, I respect it, but still. Arsehole move. Especially ballsy considering it's an inanimate object." He paused, hands planted on his hips, glowering at everything in sight. He was probably as perturbed about the loss of so much gold as he was about the loss of the relics. "Well, what in the nine hells do we do now, eh?" he finally asked, one eyebrow cocked.

I frowned, shrugging one shoulder. "Guess we should head in? Maybe there's some sort of switch or lever that will get things rolling?" That sounded stupid even to my own ears, but I was at a complete loss about what was supposed to happen. None of the clues had prepared me for this. None of them. Everything Carl had offered us revolved around *getting* to the Doom Forge, but now that we were here, we'd have to improvise.

Slowly, I padded forward, Cutter shadowing me from a few feet behind, scanning for any traps or pressure plates that might trigger if I set a foot wrong.

We'd made it ten feet in when the floor revolted beneath my feet, bucking wildly like an angry bull. Dead ahead, the burning magma began to churn and roil, an enormous bubble forming in the center of the pool, swelling up and up and up as something took form, which is when a terrible thought hit me like a baseball bat to the skull.

What if the door hadn't *just* been a simple door… What if that giant slab of gold had *been* Khalkeús? The clues *had* alluded to something along those lines, but they hadn't made sense before now.

My brain finally started firing on all cylinders, things clicking into place like the pieces of a sprawling jigsaw puzzle. I recalled one of the odd lines of text Carl had read to us back in the temple. The magma leaking from the Phoenix's beak—*the fires quenched must be relit*. The blood from the altar—*love's sacrifice will warm a heart grown cold*. The three relics I'd shoved into the enormous gate—*three keys to make transmuted flesh whole.* Holy crap. It all fit. The former Acolytes of the Shield and Hammer hadn't turned Khalkeús into the *entire* dungeon, they'd dismantled him bit by bit, storing pieces of his power and form into each of the different trials.

The magma from the first trial had drained down through the Phoenix and into the pool here, rekindling the forge itself, which was the main source of Khalkeús's inhuman power. Likewise, sacrificing Abby had somehow managed to kickstart Khalkeús's stilled heart, filling his "body" with fresh, warm blood. Morbid as hell, sure, but it fit with the evidence. And jamming the

Doom-Forged relics in had given the slumbering Aspect the tool he'd needed to break free from the transmutation spell, which had kept him asleep for the past five hundred years.

The only piece of the puzzle left to solve was the Chalice of Peace from the second room—how in the hell did that fit into the picture?

Not that it really mattered at this point. With the revived godling taking shape after centuries of slumber, it was now an academic issue.

There was another boom, the burning bubble popping, and the creature stepped forth from the churning pit, glowing with the radiance of a dying star. Khalkeús was humanoid in form, but his metallic body burned so furiously hot I could barely stand to look at him. There was a thunderous stomp, rattling my teeth, and I raised one hand to shield my eyes, squinting between my fingers so I could try to catch a better glimpse.

Even that was too painful. It was like staring directly into the sun.

Another footfall, *thud,* and for the first time since starting on this crazy journey I felt genuine fear. After all, if Khalkeús turned mean and wanted to fight—and if gaming had taught me *anything,* it was that he would absolutely want to fight—what was the chance that it could kill me? And not just send me for respawn, but *actually* kill me? Real Death? I'd just given him the pieces of a weapon capable of killing a god, so there had to be at least *some* chance that he would turn that terrible power against me or one of our party members, wiping us from the game as though we'd never been.

Suddenly, I was wishing I could activate my final Avatar of Order ability and transform into the giant dragon-like creature capable of leveling city walls—that might level the playing field just a hair. Unfortunately, I'd leveled up back in Iredale Hold, so I didn't have the experience points needed to trigger the transformation. Which meant I'd have to do this the hard way.

"Carl," I said over one shoulder, "why don't you get started with that ritual, yeah? Cutter, you and me are gonna buy him as much time as we can."

"Yep, on it," the Cleric said, pulling free a bag of ritual ingredients from his inventory with one hand and a dagger-sized, blessed crafting awl with the other.

Another colossal step, *thump-boom*. "Ah've been asleep so long," creaked an ancient voice I recognized as Khalkeús's, thanks to my brief trip through the pages of Eitri's journal. There was something slightly off about it, though. His voice was deeper than I remembered. *Gravelly*. Biting and hard, like a man who'd lived rough for years and had all the empathy and mercy in his body stripped away.

I cracked my eyes again. The blazing glory surrounding the Aspect was fading away as his body cooled from the unforgiving heat of the Doom Forge.

Like his voice, he was the same, but he was also different.

He was massive, even bigger than I remembered from my brief glimpse through Eitri's eyes. Eighteen or nineteen feet—easily rivaling the legionnaire statue from the second trial—his skin gold, his hair braided silver, his beard burning with living flame. He wore no shirt, but a silver belt, covered with the gems from the gate, supported a silver-plated skirt that covered his thighs. Spikes of curling obsidian protruded from his back like a great porcupine and raced along the backs of his arms. Angry fissures and gruesomely painful looking cracks ran across his chest, snaked around his biceps, and zigzagged over his legs, which were thicker than my torso.

Those wounds wept a constant stream of crimson, which dribbled down, only to evaporate in a haze of steam, which surrounded the crazed Aspect in a cloud. His eyes were hard as old flint and unforgiving, his mouth turned down in a perpetual scowl. Around his neck hung a braided silver chain, and dangling from it was an oversized crystal key about the size of one of Cutter's daggers. It reminded me of the glass key we'd earned in the second trial, but this one was filled with a shifting kaleidoscope of light in a thousand different hues.

In his hand was a flat-faced smith's hammer, crafted out of gleaming ebony with an enormous spike jutting from both the back and the top. Molten script ran around the head and down the shaft, moving as though it were animated by the magma from the pool. The room wobbled around me even as I slipped into tunnel vision, my gaze fixed unwaveringly on the hammer. That was it. What I'd come to find: the fabled Doom-Forged weapon. And now Khalkeús had it, and I had no illusions he would willingly hand it back over.

Not unless I *made* him hand it over.

"And who is it, pray tell, who has awoken me from the treachery of my own priests, hmm?" the domineering Aspect continued as he tromped forward, raising the deadly hammer, leaning it against his hubcap-sized shoulder.

I struggled to find words, but a nudge in the ribs from Cutter seemed to loosen my uncooperative lips. "The longer he talks," Cutter whispered in my ear, "the more time Carl has to work."

He was right. True, villain monologues were cliché and stupid, but in this case, getting the Aspect to *overshare* could only help us in the end. Running down the clock was the best possible play. "Name's Grim Jack," I said, hooking my thumbs into my belt, shooting for casual and unconcerned. "Leader of the Crimson Alliance and chief over the six named Dokkalfar clans of the Storme Marshes." I reached up and tapped at the crown on my head, glancing toward Carl. The Cleric was stooped over, not far from us, etching something into the floor. "Also happen to bear the mantle of the Jade Lord, so there's that."

"Oh, is that so, little human? And why, pray tell, would one so *esteemed* as you visit me?"

I faltered for a moment, unsure of how to continue. "Uh. Well, I need the Doom-Forged weapon to kill a god. So, I was kinda hoping you could just give it to me?" Yep. Nailed it.

For the first time, the Aspect lost its grim glower, his mouth breaking into a thin smile, though one that didn't hold any warmth or humor. "Ya want to kill a god, eh? Well, boy, get in line. Ah have a whole pantheon to kill." He reached up and casually stroked his flaming beard. "Though I have some unfaithful *priests* to visit first." He nearly growled the word *priests.* Definitely no love lost there. "Now, unless you and yer crew want to join 'em in the world to come, I'd get out of my way. You have my thanks for waking me and returning the instrument of my vengeance. Yer reward is that you get to keep breathin'. For now." He grunted and took another step toward us and the exit at our backs.

We couldn't let him leave the room under any circumstances, both because he could destroy the world and because Carl's ritual had a limited range.

I drew my warhammer, which looked like a child's toy compared to the monstrous weapon in his hand. "Unfortunately, I can't let you do that. I'm only after one god, Thanatos. And then, only because there are no other options. I can't just let you go on an Overmind killing spree."

Khalkeús stopped his trudging war march, staring at me and the weapon in my hand. "Oh, is that so now? And I suppose you and yer band of men here are up to the task of stopping me?"

"Well now, Jack isn't exactly one to toot his own horn," Cutter said, slapping me on a shoulder, then draping an arm around my shoulders, "but he's defeated creatures far superior to you."

"Oh, is that so?" Khalkeús growled, not sounding even remotely amused by the sheer insolence of a pair of mere mortals. "Do tell, I'm dying to hear more," he finished, the sarcasm as thick as honey.

Except Cutter didn't seem to get the clue and actually launched into storyteller mode, his voice taking on a rhythmic cadence. "Gladly." He beamed. "Grim Jack is a *legend*—"

"Well, I don't know about that—"

"Nonsense. Don't be modest, Jack," he said, shooting me a sideways glance. "He's far too modest," he said to Khalkeús. "*Legend*—wait for it—*dary*. This man, if he even *is* a man, has done more amazing things than most people do in a lifetime—and that's just since *breakfast,* friend. The city of Rowanheath, the military stronghold of the Ever Victorious Viridian Empire? Why my boy Jack took the bloody-damned thing in a *day.* Launched an entire assault from the back of a spider army. He's defeated more dungeon bosses than the next ten men have ever seen. United the whole of the Storme Marshes after single-handedly taking down Arzokh the Sky Maiden—Dragon Queen of the Frozen Wastes."

All I could do was stand there, utterly flabbergasted. What in the hell was he doing? Khalkeús looked more pissed by the second, and when things did finally get physical, he was liable to break every bone in my body. Slowly. Was Cutter bluffing here? The thief's fingers pressed down into my shoulder as though he could sense my unease. *Trust* me, that gesture said. Which is when I realized we were talking and not fighting. Sure, when we did fight, it would be *awful*, but he was buying us time.

Hell, Carl had already finished carving his first two symbols, both now decorated with oils and various crafting ingredients. Flowers adorned one like a burial wreath, while a rare Troll Overlord skull was propped up in the center of the second.

"I don't suppose you've ever heard of Vox-Malum, the Lich Priest?" Cutter continued, slick as a used-car salesman with an easy mark on the line. "He was the scourge of the Realm of Order? Bastard nearly sacked an entire realm with an army of thralls. But you'll never hear of him again because Jack here killed him. Damn near destroyed the entire Plain of Fire in the process, but that's nothing to Jack. If he wanted to, he could mop the floor with you without breaking a *sweat.*"

"As it happens," Khalkeús grunted. "Ah *have* heard of Vox-Malum, former Champion of Sophia,

Overmind of Order and Balance." He squinted—his eyes blazing with fury and fire—lifted his head, and took a deep whiff, giant nostrils flaring as he inhaled. "Ya have the reek of her about ya. The scent of the goddess. Shoulda smelled it before." He reached over and tapped his nose with the tip of a golden finger. "You're a Champion, then." He nodded as though he didn't even need confirmation.

"And who else is it that you have brought with you, Champion?" He stared at Cutter long and hard, gaze flicking over the golden handle of the Gentleman's rapier he wore at his belt, before moving on to Carl. When he looked at Carl—really looked at him—his face contorted into a thunderhead. "So, we have a hound of the gods, a Gentleman of the Guild—"

"It's more of a union, really," Cutter corrected absently.

"And one of my own filthy, treacherous priests," he continued, undeterred. "Ah think Ah see the picture clearly now. Looks like Ah have a bit of house cleaning to do before Ah leave." With a thunderous roar, he attacked, thrusting his hammer straight up into the air. The ground beneath me rumbled. Cutter slammed into my side, pushing me clear an eyeblink before a geyser of magma melted me on the spot.

THIRTY-EIGHT

KNOCK-DOWN-DRAG-OUT

GEYSERS ERUPTED AROUND THE ROOM—HUGE columns of flame so lung-searingly hot they made it nearly impossible to breathe. I dove right, narrowly avoiding another column, while Cutter broke left, whirling through the spewing flames and choking smoke. Carl was hunkered down beneath a dome of glowing golden light, temporarily protected from the hellish blaze, though how long that spell would last for I had no idea.

"Carl, work faster!" I yelled at the top of my lungs. "Cutter, you need to figure out a way to get the weapon once the ritual is complete. I'll keep him busy." I surged into motion, ducking and weaving through the forest of raging magma columns.

Keeping him busy was easier said than done, since Khalkeús was just getting warmed up. I broke free from the lava field and hurled an Umbra Bolt at the Aspect, but he casually swatted the attack from the air with the back of his hand as though it were a tennis ball instead of a devastating magical attack from a level 50 player. Then, without an ounce of effort, he conjured a small army of ghostly golden weapons—swords, axes, warhammers, daggers, pole arms—which floated around him like tiny planets orbiting their own golden sun.

In that instant, he really did look like the god he was.

Khalkeús snapped his fingers, the sound as loud as a firecracker, and the summoned weapons shot forward with a will of their own.

I'd seen a handful of summoners conjure living blades before, but never anything quite like this.

The weapons fell on me with one will, a whirlwind of magical steel—hacking, chopping, and thrusting, all desperate to dismember me as gruesomely as possible. And the worst thing? The weapons worked *together* in the same way a pack of wolves might when taking down some larger, deadlier predator. An axe swiped at me, and as I sidestepped the attack, a dagger darted in, ready to skewer me from the side. I deflected the slash with my razor-edged gauntlet only to find a finger-thin rapier zipping in to skewer me through the gut.

I twirled out of the way, though the rapier's tip sliced cleanly through my billowing cloak.

I hastily conjured Dark Armor, a second skin of shadow rolling over my limbs and down my body, but that wouldn't be enough to save me long term. The weapons didn't hit as hard as I would've expected, but they hit often, and despite my best efforts, I simply couldn't be everywhere at once. The swarm of weapons pressed their sheer numerical advantage, taking small slices out of my HP. Khalkeús, meanwhile, had zeroed in on Carl, tromping toward the Cleric, who was busy scurrying around the room, avoiding the magma columns as best he could while trying to inscribe the rest of necessary sigils on the chamber floor.

There was no sign of Cutter, but that probably just meant he was stealing closer while in Stealth, hoping to get the drop on Khalkeús. How in the hell he would steal the godling's weapon from his hand was a mystery to me, but if anyone could do it, it was the best bloody thief in all of Eldgard.

An axe chopped toward my head, bringing me back into the moment. I deflected it with a swipe of my warhammer, parried a thrusting short sword with my gauntlet, then spun and dropped just before a great sword, as long as I was tall, sliced through the space my head had been seconds before. I batted away a hook-bladed halberd with my hammer, triggering Savage Blow, which shattered the magical construct on contact, but it just wasn't enough.

There were too many of these damned conjured weapons, and every second I spent tangling with them was another second Khalkeús got closer to Carl.

I was sorely wishing that one of my Void minions had made it, but sadly they weren't an option, which meant I needed to think outside the box.

I backpedaled rapidly, avoiding a fresh barrage of attacks from a pair of glowing daggers, only to nearly die as a gout of magma erupted less than a foot away from me. The new geyser singed my cloak and burned through a fraction of my HP, but I scrambled away quickly enough to avoid any lasting damage. One of the conjured blades, however, wasn't quite so lucky, and ended up absorbing the full force of the burning column. The dagger strobed frantically, flashing black-white-black-white, an instant before it disintegrated into a pile of ash.

And that? That gave me an idea.

Instead of battling, I promptly dropped to the ground, curling into a ball, arms wrapped around my head, knees pulled up into my stomach. To an outside observer, it might've looked like I'd given up on living, opting instead to assume the fetal position and wait for death, but they'd be wrong. Mostly. The host of weapons, sensing my apparent weakness, all squeezed in around me. Blades fell, spikes stabbed, razor edges slashed. My Health was dropping, but all of those weapons had made one fatal mistake: they were all in one place.

Which happened to be right where I wanted them...

With a small effort of will, I stepped into the Shadowverse, time screeching to a stop around me, and the unearthly weapons abruptly froze in mid-swing. With a groan, I stood, my head passing harmlessly through the murderous arsenal gathered around me like a swarm of mosquitos out for blood. I took a deep breath, wincing at the pain in my chest and back. Off to the right, I spotted a blur that might've been Cutter, but I paid him no mind. My job right now was to handle Khalkeús and buy Carl the time he needed to complete the ritual.

Period. End of story.

I made my way free of the weapon cloud, slipping around the columns of roaring flame, careful to avoid getting too near—chances were they couldn't hurt me, not here in the Shadowverse, but there was no reason to risk it—then positioned myself not far from the hulking Aspect. Mentally, I prepared myself for the fight to come. I waited for the countdown timer to run its course, regaining as much of my Health and Spirit as I could while I had a little breathing room.

When the timer hit zero and the world screamed back to life, I created the largest possible Shadow-Warp Portal

I could directly above one of the spewing magma columns.

A gout of fire flashed up, consumed by the darkness, only to fall back to earth in a torrent as the exit portal opened directly above the conjured weapons. The whole lot vanished in less than a heartbeat, burned to dust in the incomprehensible heat. One problem down, but I couldn't celebrate since Khalkeús was the real threat, and I hadn't even laid a hand on him yet. With a thought, I called Umbra Bog up from the forge floor; tendrils of black exploded out, pawing at the godling, scrambling to find purchase. The snaking strands of black wrapped around his oversized feet and wound their way around his hands, arms, and even the meaty hammer in his hand.

That worked for all of ten seconds before a wave of searing heat and flame rolled out from Khalkeús, enveloping the shadowy limbs, burning them from existence. "If ya hunger so fer death, Champion," he growled at me, "then perhaps Ah'll indulge you." He turned away from Carl, rage plain on his face, and charged, blacksmith hammer swinging toward me. Oh crap. He was attacking me, which was a good thing, I guess, since it meant he *wasn't* attacking Carl... But it sure didn't *feel* like a good thing.

It felt like staring down a charging rhino who, for some reason, hated you with undying fury. Yay!

I raised my own hammer, ready to parry the blow, but I wasn't even remotely prepared when Khalkeús's weapon unleashed a blast of gale-force wind, which smashed into my side and swept me from my feet. The winds pummeled me like a thousand fists as I tumbled head over heels; I plowed into the cavern wall, the world spinning, a quarter of my HP vanishing on impact.

"Ya and yer fellow Champions may have had the power to fell my son, Eitri," he boomed, "but Ah am no scion. No demigod. Ah am an Aspect of Aediculus. Ah am older than the foundation of Eldgard. Older than the ancient Vogthar, banished to the plane of Morsheim. Ya speak of defeating Arzokh, but Ah was there when she was but a wee dragon hatchling, small enough to fit in my palm. Ah watched as the Imperials landed here on their great quinquereme warships and waged their war, scarring the face of the continent. Ah have walked all the known realms, and Ah will not be undone by some mortal upstart, *whelp*. Ah will have my revenge."

"It doesn't need to be this way." I pushed myself upright and circled left. "This isn't what your son would've wanted."

"Don't ya *dare* speak of my Eitri. He was too good for this world, and yer precious gods and goddesses saw fit to reward him with death." He shot forward, great legs pounding, each footfall shaking the foundation of the room as he drew closer. He lashed out with the hammer—a wild sweep that would've flattened me like a pizza. I ducked beneath the blow and shot in low, my own hammer connecting with the outside of his knee as I triggered every ability I had at my disposal: Savage Blow, Crush Armor, Black Caress, Champion Strike.

The attack landed like a thundercrack, my hammer ringing and vibrating in my hands as if I'd just slammed it into a solid steel door. Khalkeús's Health dropped just a hair, and the massive godling faltered for the first time, grunting in pain as his knee buckled from the force of the impact. I had a narrow opening, and I intended to exploit it for all it was worth. I darted in, driving the spike on top

431

of my warhammer into his gut, which, unfortunately, seemed far less effective.

Undeterred, I channeled Umbra Flame down my arm and through the warhammer still touching his barrel gut. A wave of deathly purple flame exploded out from the spike, rolling over his golden skin and forcing him back from the sheer power of the spell. Since Khalkeús was a forge deity with an obvious affinity for fire, I doubted the attack would do much damage, which was why I was surprised when I saw his Health dip noticeably. Umbra Flame primarily dealt Shadow damage—not Fire damage—which seemed to be surprisingly effective.

The juggernaut Aspect stumbled back, reeling, arms pinwheeling as he fought to regain his balance. My Spirit was dropping fast, so I cut off the onslaught and triggered my most powerful Umbra-based attack, Night Cyclone. The familiar hole appeared in the air, the desolate hardpan landscape quickly dissolving as a murderous twister ripped into the room, buffeting the already staggering godling. Whipping winds and bolts of blue-black lightning slapped against him, incrementally robbing him of Strength and Health—though he was still well above 90% HP.

"Enough," he roared, clearly frustrated, his free hand curling around the colorful key at his neck.

A burst of opalescent light rippled through the air, momentarily blinding me. I blinked sporadically, a hazy purple afterimage tattooed across my eyes, and my jaw nearly hit the floor when I could see again. The cyclone was just... gone. As though he'd cast some sort of Dispel Magic spell, cutting down my most powerful attack before it even had a prayer of hurting him. That was *twice* inside of twenty-four hours that someone had managed to nullify my most powerful spell. Annoying, to say the least. But also, what in the hell kind of attack was that?

I wasn't sure what that key around his neck was, but clearly it had some sort of protective debuff built in.

Khalkeús was on the move again, charging toward me like an elephant on the warpath, ready to gore some overzealous poacher. As he ran, he dropped his free hand low, digging his enormous digits into the floor, leaving finger-sized furrows in the otherwise firm ground. Colorful mosaic tiles and stone parted as though they were wet clay, gathering into an earthen ball as he sprinted toward me. A heartbeat later, he straightened; in his hand was a boulder the size of a wheelbarrow and shot through with vibrant veins of color.

With a bellow, he hurled it right at me.

Oh crap.

I broke right, avoiding the crushing stone by half an inch—the wind of the boulder ruffling my hair in passing—but that put me squarely in the line of Khalkeús's swinging weapon. I caught the blow with my upraised hammer, but this was the first time I'd actually felt the force of his hammer in action, and I wasn't even close to ready for that kind of action. Power exploded free on contact, swelling outward in a circle, crashing into my chest and robbing me of the ability to breathe. That wasn't the only casualty, though.

My weapon, the Gavel of Shadows, twisted and cracked, the metal squealing in protest before the shaft of the hammer simply burst under the strain, shards of white-hot metal burying themselves in my hands, chest, and face. I screamed, equal parts shock and pain, and stumbled back uncertainly, not ready for the ferocity of going up against someone, *something,* like Khalkeús. A golden boot whipped out, catching me in the chest, propelling me back into the wall once more.

Then, before I could move, he thrust his free hand forward and hurled a spear of obsidian through the air. I moved without a thought—acting on pure muscle memory—casting Dark Shield instead of opening a Shadow-Warp Portal, which proved to be a serious mistake. The conjured spear carved through my shield as though it were a soap bubble, sinking into my gut and pinning me firmly against the wall. The pain was unbearable: a bright jag of hurt, sapping my strength and my will to fight. I coughed and gasped, blood dribbling from my lips.

A combat notice flashed in the corner of my eye, and I knew things were about as grim as they could get.

<<<>>>

Debuffs Added

Concussed: You have sustained a severe head injury! Confusion and disorientation; duration, 1 minute.

Blunt Trauma: You have sustained severe blunt trauma damage! Stamina regeneration reduced by 30%; duration, 2 minutes.

Lingering Wound: You have sustained severe piercing damage! 1 HP/sec; duration, 45 seconds.

Internal Bleeding: You have sustained internal bleeding! 3 HP/sec; duration, 1 minute.

Khalkeús offered me a frosty smile as he planted his feet and raised the colossal Doom-Forged weapon—a batter coming up to the plate, ready to clobber a ball into the stands. With one hit, he would turn my head into jelly, and there was nothing I could do about it. Weak as a day-old kitten, I triggered Shadow Stride, hoping to make a clean getaway. But time kept right on ticking, and all I got for my trouble was a notice that my attempt to Shadow Stride had failed, thanks to the fact that I was pinned to the wall like a butterfly in a collector's case.

"If it's any consolation," the Aspect said, "you are but the first of many to perish."

"It's not," I grunted through the pain. "But you know what is?" I stole a look behind him. "The fact"—I wheezed, then broke out into a bloody coughing fit— "that you're about to get pwned."

As the words left my lips, a glimmering prismatic wall sprang up around the perimeter of the forge, running from runic carving to runic carving, forming a hexagon of light and power. Khalkeús roared, falling back a step, then two, one hand clutched to his stomach, the other struggling to maintain his grip on the deadly warhammer capable of shattering my weapon with a single hit.

"You've got thirty seconds to do whatever you're gonna do, Jack!" Carl yelled at the top of his lungs, straining to be heard over the anguished bellowing of the Aspect.

Khalkeús, still obviously in pain, swiveled, his gaze landing on the mouthy Cleric like a wrecking ball. "The unfaithfulness of my priests knows no bounds." He straightened, the act one of sheer will and determination, then swiveled at the hips, launching another of the massive obsidian spears at the Dwarf. Carl's eyes flared wide. He was far too slow to physically evade, so he opted for a magical barrier just as I had. Unfortunately, his golden dome served him no better than my Dark Shield had served me. The spear carved through the flimsy barrier like a knife through hot butter, catching the priest dead in the throat, nearly severing his head in the process.

Carl swayed drunkenly, empty hands pawing at his neck, trying to staunch the cascade of blood pouring down his front. That was a lost cause. He toppled a second later, hitting the floor with a wet thump before his body vanished in a spray of light, leaving only a pool of gore to mark his passing.

Still, mercy of mercies, the ritual *held*. The walls of swirling rainbow light were tied to the ritual carvings and the objects instead of the caster.

"Now, where were we?" the Aspect said, turning on me, a snarl on his face while sweat *poured* down his head and chest in a sheet. Whatever the ritual's effects were, they clearly hurt. Bad. "Time to end you, Champion," he said, lifting the hammer in a shaky hand.

Cutter materialized like an angry ghost, exploiting the Aspect's momentary inattention—namely gloating over his victory instead of simply pulverizing me. The Rogue flipped through the air, landing on his Khalkeús's outstretched arm, sinking his twin daggers into a wrist that was thicker than my neck. The attack itself didn't do much damage, but Cutter's precision was perfect and the move flawlessly executed. *Critical Hit!* Khalkeús's hand snapped open on reflex, and the hammer clattered to the floor.

Cutter disappeared in a flash of smoke—his Cloak and Dagger ability on full display—only to reappear a moment later, this time on Khalkeús's back. Cutter had his legs wrapped around the giant's neck, ankles crossed, trying to choke the goliath while he stabbed at the

Aspect's head and face with his daggers. An effective strategy, except for one small detail: Khalkeús's beard was made from *actual* fire. Cutter's boots were already smoldering, a plume of sickly-sweet smoke drifting up as the flames crawled along his legs.

Instead of screaming, he stoically fought on, letting the fire eat through his Health and his skin while he stabbed and slashed at the Aspect's unprotected head, giving me time. Not much, maybe, but some. I was still pinned against the wall, the obsidian spear killing me in painful increments, but there was a way out. I steeled my resolve, grabbed the spear protruding from my gut, and used my hands to pull my body forward, along the length of the shaft. My feet were low enough to reach the ground, so once I got clear of the wall, I dug my toes in and used them to push as well.

Of all my experiences inside V.G.O., this was *hands down* the worst. Like swallowing broken glass while walking over a pile of rusty nails covered in lemon juice and cayenne pepper. But the prize was only feet away. With the ritual up and running full tilt and Khalkeús momentarily distracted by Cutter, all I needed to do was get free and get that damned hammer. Once I had that, I'd be able to do *something*. What, exactly, that something would be, I wasn't sure, but I'd have a lot more options with the Doom-Forged weapon in my hands than I had right now.

And as terrible as the pain was, if Forge was willing to die, Abby was willing to have her throat slit, and Cutter was willing to let himself be burned alive to finish this quest, I could do this. So, I fought through the agony, pulling myself hand over fist, until at last my body jerked free from the length of stony spear.

My HP was just under a quarter, which meant another good hit might well put me under, but I was in the home stretch. I dropped onto my knees, wheezing, blood seeping from the hole in my gut, and crawled forward. And then I was there, the Doom-Forged weapon a foot away, victory as good as mine. I glanced up as Khalkeús hurled Cutter away by the scruff of his neck; the thief was alive, but burned almost beyond recognition. This time, the enraged Aspect didn't waste any time gloating—apparently, he'd learned his lesson—stomping over to the broken and battered man. With a howl, Khalkeús raised one giant foot and drove it down with the force of a bomb blast, right onto Cutter's head.

I turned away at the last second, not wanting to see the bloody carnage.

That was it, then. Cutter dead.

Mentally I crossed my fingers, holding my breath. *Would he respawn?*

As the Aspect rounded on me, fury screwing up his golden face, there was a telltale shimmer of light, Cutter's gruesome corpse vanishing into the ether. The ritual light flickered and died as Cutter's body disappeared, which meant Khalkeús would be back to full strength. But it didn't matter. He was too late.

I felt like howling in laughter. We'd done it. Sure, this mission had been a complete party wipe for everyone except me, but we'd battled our way through the Judgment, found the Doom Forge, and activated the ritual, and I'd gotten my hands on the most powerful weapon in Eldgard. Khalkeús might've been one bad SOB, but even he wasn't immune to the power of the Doom-Forged weapon. I wrapped my hand around the handle of the hammer and dragged it over to me, using it like a cane to gain my feet, the heavy head still resting on the floor.

THIRTY-NINE

SECRET WEAPON

FINALLY, AFTER ALL THIS TIME, I *HAD IT*. STILL, I had no idea how exactly to use it, which was *slightly* problematic. Quickly, I pulled up the item description, hoping for some clue about how to employ the weapon's capabilities before Khalkeús could wipe me off the map. My heart nearly skipped a beat at what I saw.

<<<>>>

Mad-God's Fury

Weapon Type: Blunt; Warhammer

Class: Ancient Artifact, Two-handed

Base Damage: 215

Primary Effects:

- 75 points fire damage + (.5 x character level)
- Increased Attack Speed by 8%
- +15% damage to all Blunt Weapon attacks
- Strength Bonus = .5 x character level
- Vitality Bonus = .5 x character level

Secondary Effects:

- +3.5% Chance to Blind on hit

- +1 Luck per 10 character levels

- Increases all Blunt Weapon skills by 2 while equipped

- Reduces all skill cooldowns by 16%

The weapon was incredible, far better than the Gavel of Shadows, but there was something *horribly* wrong… It *wasn't* the Doom-Forged weapon.

No, no, no. My mind whirled, running through the Judgment, the trials, every piece of information Carl had given us, scrambling to figure out where everything had gone off the tracks.

Which is when I realized the terrible mistake I'd made. The second trial, that had been the only piece of the puzzle I hadn't managed to make sense of. My mind shot to the clue Carl had uncovered in his research: *only the wisest will understand my true form.*

Crap. I'd made the same mistake that Vlad had by assuming that the ultimate weapon would be an actual weapon. I glanced at the opalescent key hanging from Khalkeús's neck, the same key that he'd touched to banish my Night Cyclone. The same key that had been inscribed onto the chalice from the challenge room. Hell, looking more closely at it, I realized it might have *actually* been the same damned key we'd earned after dispatching the statue. I'd chosen poorly. That key was the real weapon, as unlikely as it might've looked, and there was a good chance I was going to die because I hadn't put it all together in time.

"Wait," I yelled, dropping the colossal hammer.

Discarding my weapon was probably a stupid move, but truthfully, there was no way I could win this fight. Carl and Cutter were both gone, and the one ritual that could give me a leg up on the Aspect was spent and gone. But then, maybe I wasn't *supposed* to win, at least not in the conventional manner. I couldn't help but think of the Chalice of Peace and the fiery words that had burned across the dark after we took down the stone golem. *Only those who seek peace deserve to wield a weapon capable of delivering unending war.*

Maybe there was still a way, though it was a long shot. The *longest* shot, even. I raised my hands, showing I meant no harm. *Only those who seek peace deserve to wield a weapon capable of delivering unending war.* The words played through my head on repeat.

"Look, I wasn't lying when I said it doesn't need to be this way. And I wasn't lying when I said this isn't what Eitri would've wanted—I know because I've seen him. Spoken to him."

For the first time since entering the Doom Forge, Khalkeús really hesitated. Not out of pain, but out of uncertainty. "Lies," he said, the word dripping hate, but maybe also something else… *Hope*? "My son is dead. Taken from the world by the gods. By them and their Champions. Champions just like you."

"No, not like me. And I'm not lying. I've spoken to his spirit, locked away deep in the bowels of the Iredale Hold. In a place outside of time and space, which he called the Protoverse. It's a place where exceptional souls get caught. And"—I paused, gulping, sweating bullets—"if you give me a chance, I think I can prove it to you." At least I hoped so, or this guy was going to obliterate me on the spot.

Uncertainty flickered across the mad godling's face, followed in short order by a wave of anger. "Ah don't like games, mortal. Ah dinnae have the stomach for them. You try tae trick me, and Ah'll kill you. And not just kill you." He reached up and tapped a finger against the glowing key draped around his neck. "Ah'll erase ya where ya stand."

God, but I hoped I was right about this. "No tricks," I said, dropping one hand, reaching into my bag, and pulling out the final ace up my sleeve, which I'd retrieved from the Darkshard Keep before picking up Vlad at the Crafter's Hall. The gamer in me was loath to use it, since I could only use it *once*, but hey, if fighting an unstoppable god with the power to destroy the world wasn't the right time to use it, then there never would be a right time. Besides, some small part of me felt like this particular ace had been given to me for this exact moment.

A thing of destiny, not unlike stumbling upon Eitri in the Protoverse.

In my hand was a curling horn of beaten brass, covered in hair-fine inscriptions that spiraled from a white-bone mouthpiece to a gently flared bell. The Horn of the Ancients. An artifact crafted by none other than Eitri Spark-Sprayer, given to Isra Spirtcaller after the death of the Jade Lord. The horn was a powerful artifact, capable of activating the interdimensional traveling stones at the heart of the Sacred Glade in the Storme Marshes. But it also had one special ability: it could recall the Honored Dokkalfar dead. Specifically, it allowed me to summon the Jade Lord and his brothers for one hour to fight on my behalf.

Except I didn't need them to fight for me. And I really only needed them for a few minutes at most.

"Do you recognize this?" I asked, raising the horn, the light from the myriad of fires glinting off the surface. "Your son made it shortly before he died. He made it for a woman he loved named Isra—gave it to her so she could talk to Nangkri, the Jade Lord. The same man who gave me this." I tapped at the crown adorning my brow.

I raised the horn to my lips, a tremble of fear and doubt running down my hands. I had no other options, though. Either this would work, or I'd be dead, the quest failed. I took a deep breath and blew into the mouthpiece. The horn issued a clarion call—its single note pure and perfect. The crystalline sound bounced off the ceiling, echoing around the walls; a shimmering silver rift split the air in response, the Jade Lord and his brothers pouring out, one by one.

They formed up in a semicircle in front of me—a wall of bodies—their weapons bared and ready for violence. I counted them as they stepped through the veil between planes, holding my breath the whole while. Nangkri, the Jade Lord himself, came first, followed by Ak-Hani, Lisu, La-Hun, Karem, Chao-Yao, and Na-Ang, the founders of each of the six named Murk Elf clans. But then, one last figure strode out from the portal, a shadowy, silver-skinned man who stood head and shoulders above the rest of his kin.

The shade of Eitri Spark-Sprayer, though he looked *far* more solid than the last time I'd seen him.

It'd been a long shot, I knew, but Eitri himself had told me that, though unrelated, he'd been like a brother to Nangkri. And I'd seen that confirmed for myself in the pages of the journal. Though that might have seemed like a mere figure of speech, I knew that to the Dokkalfar, adopting someone into the family, even figuratively, was the same thing as being blood related. So, it made sense that there was at least the *possibility* his spirit would be called back into the realm of the living along with the rest of his honored brothers.

"The horn has sounded," Nangkri said, his voice strong and sure. "And so we have come, Spirit Caller. What would you have of us?" he asked, eyes never leaving the face of the gold-skinned godling standing before them. A god twisted by grief into a creature of wrath.

"I didn't call you to fight," I said, pushing my way through their ranks until I was standing in front of them and painfully exposed to Khalkeús, should he decide to attack. "There's been enough fighting. Enough slaughter to last me a lifetime. It's time for something better. Eitri?" I said, turning toward the shade, now standing at the end of the line.

The Shadowmancer shot me a sidelong look, the question obvious in his eyes. *Are you sure this is okay?*

I nodded.

Eitri didn't miss a beat.

In three quick steps he crossed the space between him and his father and threw his arms around the broken god, pulling him in tight. The obsidian spikes covering Khalkeús's back and arms bit into Eitri, but the shade hardly seemed to mind. For a time, no one spoke at all. Watching them, my chest tightened at the thought of my own dad, dead for nearly three months now. What would it have been like to have him back again, even for a second? To talk to him again or envelop him in a great big ol' bear hug? I would've happily given every golden crown to my name for that chance.

"But how?" Khalkeús finally asked, pulling away, holding the resurrected form of his son at arm's length. Bloody tears streaked the Aspect's face.

"As I told our friend here"—Eitri swept a hand toward me—"the soul of a god, even a demigod, is a rather *resilient* thing. I admit, I am not what I was, Father, but I am not gone." He was quiet, staring into his father's face. "You know it's time to stop this, Father. Surely you must see what this vendetta has done to you…"

Khalkeús's face hardened, his jaw clenching tight. "But they killed ya. Immoral monsters are what the gods are, them and their Champions both. They do as they please, slaying, killing, murdering. They are capricious and vindictive, and they can afford to be so because there are nae consequences. Nae one to hold their feet to the forge's flames. Well, Ah intend to teach them otherwise. Ah will make them learn. Ah will deliver them *justice*." Almost subconsciously, he reached up, hulking hand wrapping around the key.

"No, Father," Eitri replied with a sad shake of his head. "You want vengeance, which is not the same as justice. You're only thinking of yourself, of your own pain. And have you considered the cost to others? How many people will die for you to get your vengeance? This man?" He glanced at me over his shoulder. "Him and a thousand more like him. And if you succeed in killing the gods, then the whole world will perish.

"You too are not what you once were," Eitri continued, tone gentle yet simultaneously reproachful. "Your wrath, your rage, it's turned you into something ugly. You were a man of peace once, Father. You preferred to build tools over weapons of war, and it was you who pleaded with me not to get caught up in the wars of men." He halted, eyes boring into the broken god. "You are more a shadow of your former self than I."

Khalkeús dropped his face as Eitri spoke, as though he couldn't stand to look his son in the eyes, couldn't stand to see the disappointment lingering there. But something else was happening, too. Khalkeús was *changing;* the black spikes protruding from his back and arms were receding, shrinking back into his flesh, while the angry fissures covering his body knit themselves shut, the bloody wounds disappearing. Finally, after what felt like a lifetime, he looked up again, the anger gone, replaced by the face of a man who was *tired.* Just bone weary.

"Aye. Maybe ya have the right of it, Son. Ah always said ya were a better man than me. Still, though. It doesn't sit right in my gut." He slammed a closed fist against his stomach with a *clink.* "Someone has to hold the other Aspects and Overminds accountable."

"Why not him?" Nangkri asked, jerking his head toward me. "He has proven he is worthy to wield the weapon."

"But he's a *Champion*," Khalkeús replied.

"A Champion who has united the Storm Marshes," Nangkri replied. "A Champion who has fought back the Imperials, showing himself to be a master of war, but also a Champion who's shown mercy and offered justice to those who have suffered grievous wrongs."

"And for the record," I said, edging forward, hands raised in surrender, "I'm not here to start a war. I'm here to end one, to save a whole lot of people. And the only way I can do that is with that key around your neck."

Khalkeús stepped away from his son, regarding me through squinted eyes, weighing me, judging me. "Aye. Very well." He reached up and pulled the key free, the chain holding it in place snapping as though it were cheap twine. He held it out in front of him, the key swaying ever so slightly. "But only on one condition. Ah… Ah don't want to live anymore. Ah am tired of this. Of this place. Being a god. Outliving everyone Ah've ever cared about. Immortality is not for everyone."

He dropped the key into my hand.

"Ah want you to kill me. To send me on."

That was a gut check. Despite everything that had happened, I didn't really want to kill Khalkeús. And worse, not only did I not know *how* to kill him, I thought offing an Aspect, even a relatively minor one, could have dire consequences for the game. I was about to say as much when Eitri lifted a hand, cutting me off in my tracks.

"There is a better way, Father. Jack," he said, extending a hand toward me. "May I have the key for a moment?"

That was gut check number two. I'd come all this way to get the weapon, and now that I had it in my hand, the thought of handing it over to *anyone*—no matter how good they seemed—felt *wrong*. But I knew that was wrong, too. That was the need for control, the desire for more and more power burning inside my chest. After all, getting power was no easy task, but giving it up at the drop of a hat was even more difficult. Finally, after a few moments of deliberation, I nodded and dropped my newly acquired prize into Eitri's palm.

Eitri smiled, respect in his gaze, and nodded. "Brothers," he said.

Nangkri moved first, clapping me on the shoulder then heading over to Khalkeús and placing his hand on the Aspect's shoulder. The others followed, each giving me a brief nod or a kind word as they surrounded the Aspect in a ring, each one placing a hand on his golden body. Eitri was the last to join. "Take good care of Iredale Hold, Jack. She'll serve you well." With that, he turned toward his father, added his free hand to the ring, and lifted the key straight up toward the heavens with the other. "Godspeed, little brother."

The world ended, or so it seemed.

Heat and light and power erupted around me like a volcano...

Roaring winds ripped away sounds and smells...

Blinding opalescent light stole all light. All sight...

Waves of inferno heat and arctic cold blasted me in turns as if I were at the center of a twister made of opposing, titanic, primal energy...

After what felt like a lifetime, the power faded, guttered, died. Reality resuming some form of normalcy. I realized I'd fallen at some point—the dusty forge floor was spread out beneath me like a picnic blanket. It was hard to think, but I *was* alive. After another ten minutes of just lying there—my mind frantically trying to process whatever had just happened—I had enough strength to cough and push myself upright, my legs sprawled out in front of me. Eitri, Nangkri, and the other Shadow Lords were gone. And they'd taken Khalkeús with them.

Where the circle of men had been standing before was now a smoking crater.

449

At its center were two items. The Horn of the Ancients, twisted, charred, and mangled almost beyond recognition, and the crystal key, which was completely untouched.

I coughed again and gained my feet. I shambled over to the blackened depression, retrieving the horn on principle, then picked up the key, which I now knew was actually something *much, much* more powerful. A host of messages pinged in my ear, notices flashing in the corner of my eye, one right after another.

Quest Alert: The Doom Forge

Congratulations! You have accomplished the impossible: both locating the Doom-Forged relics and the location of the legendary Doom Forge and convincing the mad god Khalkeús to assemble the pieces into the Doom-Forged weapon, known as the *Reality Editor*! As a reward, you have received the Reality Editor, 75,000 XP, and 1,000 renown—in-world fame— for completing this ultra-rare quest. Greater renown elevates you within the ranks of Eldgard and can affect merchant prices when selling or buying. In addition, since you resolved the Doom Forge quest line *without* killing Khalkeús, you've been named the rightful heir of Eitri Spark-Sprayer and can now claim the Iredale Hold as your own!

x1 Level Up!

You have (5) undistributed stat points

You have (1) unassigned proficiency points

<<<>>>

Notifications:

- You've earned a new title: Doom Wielder!

- You have received the *Cursus Honorum* (Rank) of Consul Magna!

- You now have access to the Iredale Hold interface!

Viridian Gate Online Universal Alert!

Notice: Traveler Grim Jack Shadowstrider, honorary member of the Ak-Hani clan, has completed the ultra-rare quest, The Doom Forge! His faction, the Crimson Alliance, now owns the Iredale Hold!

I read over each of the notices, dismissing them as I went. As soon as I'd plowed through them, I opened my interface and took a look at the only thing that *actually* mattered—the thing that so many people had fought, bled, and died to get. The Doom-Forged weapon.

The Reality Editor

Weapon Type: All

Class: Ancient Artifact, One-handed

Base Damage: $¥R_3n75\pm^a\mathcal{U}\grave{N} = 99{:}99{:}99{:}99{:}99$

Primary Effects:

- Unlocks ALL doors and locks

- Charges = 874/1,000
- Soul-Bound Item: This item is Soul-Bound and cannot be lost, stolen, or transferred!

All of reality bends to your will, but remember, reality is but a fragile thing balanced on the head of a pin. Even the slightest distortion can have dire consequences.

I scanned the description once, twice, a third time. I didn't have the foggiest idea what in the hell this thing actually was, how it worked, or what I was supposed to do with it.

FORTY

REALITY EDITOR

IT HAD BEEN FOUR DAYS SINCE I'D ACQUIRED THE Reality Editor and escaped from the depths of the Doom Forge, which—without Khalkeús kicking around—was now just another defunct dungeon. Everyone had recovered from the dive, respawning without a hitch, and life was more or less moving along as it should be: Vogthar raids. Dungeon battles. Admin meetings. Vlad locked in his tower, endlessly tinkering with the Arcane Dampener. Pizza at Franks with Abby. I even had the Crimson Alliance reimburse Chuck from the Smoked Pig, enough for them to not only rebuild in Cliffburgh, but to open a second location.

The good news was that second location was in the heart of Yunnam, which meant Southern-style barbeque would soon be coming to the Storme Marshes.

Yep. Everything more or less as it should be.

Even Osmark was back from his Champion's quest in the Shattered Realm—though I'd only seen him once. He seemed cagier than usual, and as much as I pressed him for details, he was extremely reluctant to talk about whatever had happened there. Still, despite that oddity, everything felt *right,* like we were finally moving in the right direction—getting our collective act together—except, of course, for the Reality Editor. Even after messing with it for four days, showing it to Vlad, Abby, Betty, Chief Kolle, and every other bigwig in the Alliance, no one had any idea what it actually *was* or how I was supposed to use it.

Experimentally, I tried actually fighting with it—the sparring session with Cutter did *not* go well and ended up with me getting carved up something fierce. I doused it in acid and poison to get a reaction, but nothing. And despite seeing both Khalkeús and Eitri use it to perform some strange sort of magic, I couldn't get it to cast any sort of spell, and the "charges" function was still a complete enigma. When I tried to get Sophia to come pay me a visit and talk through its workings, I received a resounding silence. She, like Osmark, had clammed up—at least for now.

The only thing I knew it did for sure was open locks and doors.

All of them, no matter how complex the door, no matter how sophisticated the lock. Didn't matter if it was a physical mechanism or a magical ward, the Reality Editor opened them all up, one right after another. An impressive trick, sure—Cutter was drooling over all the prospects—but I didn't see how exactly the ability to pick a lock would help me kill or even minorly inconvenience Thanatos.

And so, I found myself pacing the halls of Darkshard Keep at two in the morning, the staff all asleep, the world quiet and serene. This was the same thing I'd done every night since I'd gotten the Doom-Forged weapon. I found it progressively harder to sleep with the question, the *mystery,* of the Reality Editor constantly weighing on my mind. I clutched the key, fingers pressing down a little too hard on the crystal, not that I was afraid of breaking it. As far as I could tell, it was indestructible, which meant I could also use it as the world's tiniest shield if need be.

"What are you supposed to do?" I muttered at the key. There was no answer. Not that I really expected one. "You have to be more than some fancy paperweight," I grumbled under my breath, feeling more like a mental patient every single day. "I know it. I know it! Why would you be so hard to get unless you did something amazing? I need you to work. How in the world am I going to beat Thanatos unless you do something?"

I paused next to the doorway of a seldom-used broom closet, sighed in defeat, and leaned my head up against the blessedly cool stone. My mind turned to Thanatos and the Vogthar army assembling in Morsheim.

I'd seen Morsheim a time or two—just a glimpse through a portal.

It was a barren, desolate land of rolling hills, covered in ashy pale dirt and dotted with patches of withered scrub grass and stunted, bone-white trees poking up like oversized skeletal hands. In my mind I could see the colossal twisted spires—adorned with spectral green windows like glaring insect eyes—which scraped a star-studded sky the color of an old bruise. The great Dark City. Even at a distance I could tell it easily rivaled Rowanheath or even Ankara, though it was dreadful and dreary.

I shuddered at the memory. But then I noticed something... The key, clutched so tightly in my hand, was *buzzing*. Just a faint thing, but it was definitely *buzzing*. My heart sped up.

Okay, okay. There was definitely something there. I pressed my eyes shut again, recalling the terrible memory of Morsheim, the picture sharpening in my head.

The buzzing increased, as though I were holding a hive full of angry bees.

But now what? Eyes still closed, I licked my lips and moved to put the key into my pocket. The buzzing subsided, throttling down to a low grumble. I halted, moving the key away from me and toward the closest thing nearby: the door I was leaning against. The key almost exploded in my hand with frantic energy—whatever I was doing, it seemed to like it. Following an odd hunch, I slipped the key into the door's keyhole, turning over the tumblers. And just like that, the buzzing ceased, the power in the key gone.

I opened my eyes and pulled the key out, feeling more than a little disappointed.

I'd felt like I was right on the edge of something awesome there. I shook my head and turned to go, but stopped when I felt an unnaturally cool breeze whisper into the hallway from beneath the door. Curious, I twisted the knob and pushed my way in. My eyes shot wide, my breath catching in my throat as the door opened not to some half-full broom cupboard, but to the same desolate landscape I'd been envisioning a second ago. I glanced down at the key, then back up at the barren wilderness, thankfully devoid of Vogthar.

Just what in the hell is this thing?

Pressing my eyes shut again, I frantically pictured the plain room that should've been behind the door—having a portal into the heart of Morsheim here wasn't exactly ideal—inserted the key again, and turned the lock in the opposite direction. Power built, buzzing in my palm, rattling up my arm and into my chest, and once more there was a *click*. I let out a ragged sigh of relief as I turned the knob and found the room back to normal. Just a little space with stone walls, a few wooden shelves, and a couple of mops and buckets.

I turned my back on the broom closet, kicking the door closed with the sole of my boot, and headed back toward my private quarters. Smiling, I held the key up, turning it over this way and that, the hallway torchlight bouncing off the crystalline glass. My mind was racing, my heart hammering, and a thrill of excitement and exhilaration coursed through my body. I still wasn't one hundred percent sure what this thing did or how it worked, but I did know one thing. We were going to need a *much* bigger door, because with this bad boy in hand, we could finally take the fight to Thanatos.

With this thing, we could invade all of Morsheim...

SPECIAL THANKS

I'd like to thank my wife, Jeanette, daughter, Lucy, and son, Samuel. A special thanks to my parents, Greg and Lori. A quick shout out to my brother Aron and his whole brood—Eve, Brook, Grace, and Collin. Brit, probably you'll never read this, but I love you too.

Here's to the folks of *Team Hunter*, my awesome Alpha and Beta readers who helped make this book both possible and good. Much thanks to all the focus at Shadow Alley Press, who are working so hard to build something huge and awesome and beautiful. Jeanette Strode, eden Hudson, Aaron Crash (and his alter-ego, Aaron Michael Ritchey), Tamara Blain, Kelly Ferguson, Mark Stallings, Jess Astra, Nathaniel Paxton, D.J. Bodden, Toria Bodden, Alejandro, our dearly beloved Zack and Jake (what would we do without you guys???), and all the other focus who make this thing work. Thank you from the bottom of my ink-black heart. Okay, time to get back into the word mines.

—James A. Hunter, January 2019

ABOUT THE AUTHOR

Hey all, my name is James Hunter and I'm a writer, among other things. So just a little about me: I'm a former Marine Corps Sergeant, combat veteran, and pirate hunter (seriously). I'm also a member of The Royal Order of the Shellback—'cause that's a real thing. I've also been a missionary and international aid worker in Bangkok, Thailand. And, a space-ship captain, can't forget that.

Okay … the last one is only in my imagination.

Currently, I'm a stay at home Dad—taking care of my two kids—while also writing full time, making up absurd stories that I hope people will continue to buy. When I'm not working, writing, or spending time with family, I occasionally eat and sleep.

BOOKS, MAILING LIST, AND REVIEWS

If you enjoyed reading about Jack, Cutter, Abby and the rest of the gang in Viridian Gate Online and want to stay in the loop about the latest book releases, awesomesauce promotional deals, and upcoming book giveaways be sure to subscribe to my email list at:

www.AuthorJamesAHunter.com

Word-of-mouth and book reviews are crazy helpful for the success of any writer. If you *really* enjoyed reading about Jacob, please consider leaving a short, honest review—just a couple of lines about your overall reading experience. Thank you in advance!

BOOKS FROM SHADOW ALLEY PRESS

If you enjoyed Viridian Gate Online: Doom Forge, you might also enjoy other awesome stories from Shadow Alley Press, such as the Yancy Lazarus Series, Rogue Dungeon, the Jubal Van Zandt Series, Path of the Thunderbird, Sages of the Underpass, or the School of Swords and Serpents. You can find all of our books listed at www.ShadowAlleyPress.com

James A. Hunter

Viridian Gate Online: Cataclysm (Book 1)
Viridian Gate Online: Crimson Alliance (Book 2)
Viridian Gate Online: The Jade Lord (Book 3)
Viridian Gate Online: The Imperial Legion (Book 4)
Viridian Gate Online: The Lich Priest (Book 5)
Viridian Gate Online: Doom Forge (Book 6)
Viridian Gate Online: Darkling Siege (Book 7)

VGO: The Artificer (Imperial Initiative)

461

J. A. Hunter

VGO: Nomad Soul (Illusionist 1)
VGO: Dead Man's Tide (Illusionist 2)
VGO: Inquisitor's Foil (The Illusionist 3)

VGO: Firebrand (Firebrand Series 1)
VGO: Embers of Rebellion (Firebrand Series 2)
VGO: Path of the Blood Phoenix (Firebrand Series 3)

VGO: Vindication (The Alchemic Weaponeer 1)
VGO: Absolution (The Alchemic Weaponeer 2)
VGO: Insurrection (The Alchemic Weaponeer 3)

Strange Magic: Yancy Lazarus Episode One
Cold Heatred: Yancy Lazarus Episode Two
Flashback: Siren Song (Episode 2.5)
Wendigo Rising: Yancy Lazarus Episode Three
Flashback: The Morrigan (Episode 3.5)
Savage Prophet: Yancy Lazarus Episode Four
Brimstone Blues: Yancy Lazarus Episode Five

MudMan: A Lazarus World Novel

Two Faced: Legend of the Treesinger (Book 1)
Soul Game: Legend of the Treesinger (Book 2)

Rogue Dungeon: Rogue Dungeon Series (Book 1)
Civil War: Rogue Dungeon Series (Book 2)
Troll Nation: Rogue Dungeon Series (Book 3)

Eden Hudson

Revenge of the Bloodslinger: A Jubal Van Zandt Novel
Beautiful Corpse: A Jubal Van Zandt Novel
Soul Jar: A Jubal Van Zandt Novel
Garden of Time: A Jubal Van Zandt Novel
Wasteside: A Jubal Van Zandt Novel

<<<>>>

Darkening Skies: Path of the Thunderbird 1
Stone Soul: Path of the Thunderbird 2
Demon Beast: Path of the Thunderbird 3

Aaron Crash

War God's Mantle: Ascension (Book 1)
War God's Mantle: Descent (Book 2)
War God's Mantle: Underworld (Book 3)

<<<>>>

Denver Fury: American Dragons (Book 1)
Cheyenne Magic: American Dragons (Book 2)
Montana Firestorm: American Dragons (Book 3)
Texas Showdown: American Dragons (Book 4)
California Imperium: American Dragons (Book 5)
Dodge City Knights: American Dragons (Boo

Printed in Great Britain
by Amazon